CON LAW

Mark Gimenez

sphere

SPHERE

First published in Great Britain in 2013 by Sphere

A CIP catalogue record for this book is available from the British Library.

ISBN HB 978-1-84744-379-3
ISBN CF 978-1-84744-380-9

Typeset in Bembo by Hewer Text UK Ltd, Edinburgh
Printed and bound in Great Britain by Clays Ltd, St Ives plc

Papers used by Sphere are from well-managed forests
and other responsible sources.

MIX
Paper from
responsible sources
FSC® C104740

Sphere
An imprint of
Little, Brown Book Group
100 Victoria Embankment
London EC4Y 0DY

An Hachette UK Company
www.hachette.co.uk

www.littlebrown.co.uk

CON LAW

To Laurence J. ("Larry") Rice Jr. (1954–2009), devoted husband, father, son, brother, friend, and lawyer.

Acknowledgments

My sincere thanks and appreciation to David Shelley, Jade Chandler, Iain Hunt, and everyone else at Sphere/Little, Brown Book Group in London; Professor Emeritus of Law Charles E. Rice at the Notre Dame Law School, a scholar and a gentleman, for teaching me constitutional law (again); Barbara Hautanen for the Spanish translations; Joel Tarver at T Squared Design in Houston for my website and email blasts to my readers; and all of you who have emailed me. I hope to hear from you again.

The layman's constitutional view is that what he likes is constitutional and that which he doesn't like is unconstitutional.
—Supreme Court Justice Hugo L. Black, 1971

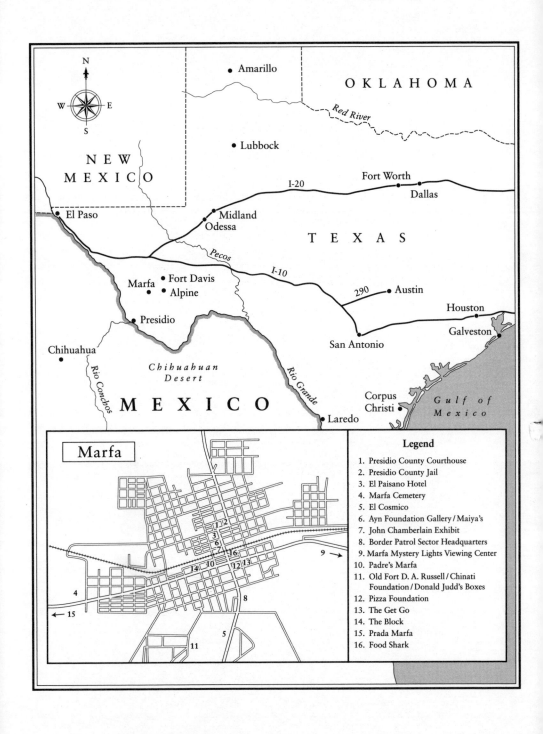

Prologue

'Professor—he's got a gun!'

'Get down, Renée.'

His young intern ducked down behind Book.

'Goddamn outsider,' the man holding the gun said, 'coming to our town and stirring up trouble.'

The three young men reeked of beer and sweat and testosterone. They sat on the tailgate of an old pickup truck; crushed beer cans littered the bed behind them. The gunman sat in the middle; he was unshaven and wore a cap on backwards and overalls over a bare chest that revealed a KKK tattoo on his right biceps. He held the gun with his right hand; that would be his strong side. The second man held a three-foot length of pipe with his left hand, slapping it into his right palm like a principal about to render corporal punishment to the class bully; he was a southpaw. He sat to the gunman's right and wore a camo cap and a wife-beater muscle shirt. The third man was empty-handed; he sat to the gunman's left. He wore a straw cowboy hat and a *Don't Mess with Texas* T-shirt. He shuffled his boots in the dirt of the parking lot.

Book took a small step to his left.

He and Renée had just eaten lunch with Ronald and his sister at a café situated hard against the railroad tracks on the black side of town. It was all laughs and good times as they walked out back to say their goodbyes and to ride home on the Harley. But they found these three hillbillies waiting for them; their truck blocked access to the motorcycle. A Confederate flag adorned the back window. Some folks simply refused to evolve. The Klan lived on in East Texas; these young men were the progeny of the three Klansmen who had made East Texas infamous by dragging a black man to his death behind their pickup in 1998. Book could imagine the same fate for Ronald. The man waved the gun at Book.

'You and your gal there, get on that motorbike and get the hell out of our town. Me and the boys, we're gonna take Ronnie for a ride out to the piney woods, remind him about the facts of life: black boys don't mess with white women.'

'I take it you boys aren't NBA fans.'

'You a funny goddamned Injun, ain't you?'

Book's coloring and coarse black hair often made people think he was at least part Native American; perhaps he was. As a boy, he would paint his face and pretend to be a great Comanche war chief. The moment did have a cowboys-and-Indians feel to it. But Book did not wear war paint that day; he did wear his hair too long for someone in his profession, jeans, boots, and a black Tommy Bahama T-shirt. These boys' fuses were already lit and fueled by alcohol and inbred racism, but he still tried to defuse the situation.

'Well, it's possible I have some Comanche blood in me, but—'

'You fixin' to have blood on you, you don't get on that bike, you goddamned skinny-ass Injun.'

Book stood six-one but weighed only one-seventy-five, so he was a bit on the lean side, especially compared to these three sides of beef. They were big and muscular twenty-somethings, and they had too much alcohol on board to

2

succumb to reason or mild physical persuasion. He was thirty-five and skinny. But he did have skills.

'Ronald,' Book said without breaking eye contact with the gunman, 'you and Darlene take off.'

Ronald stepped in front of his sister.

'No way, Professor.'

'You just got out of prison. You don't need this.'

'I survived seventeen years in that prison. I know how to fight. You're a law professor.'

Ronald Westbrook had been incarcerated for the last seventeen years for a crime he did not commit: aggravated rape. Of a white woman. In East Texas. No DNA or other physical evidence of any kind had been collected or introduced at trial. But he was convicted nonetheless, guilty only of being a black man in his late twenties with tattoos covering his upper body, the same as the perpetrator. In his youth, Ronald had been a high school football star whose dream of a pro career ended with a knee injury; he had always lived on the right side of the law, but the law said he would live the rest of his life as an inmate in the state penitentiary.

He was not alone.

In the last decade, fifty innocent black men had been released from prison in Texas after being exonerated by DNA evidence. Ronald was not one of them. DNA testing was not standard police procedure seventeen years before in that small East Texas county. Ronald was convicted solely on the victim's testimony; she pointed him out in the courtroom before the jury, as certain as a witness could be. Studies have shown that eyewitness testimony is almost always unreliable; a terrified person with a gun stuck in her face remembers almost nothing with evidentiary clarity. Fear blinds a human being. But the local district attorney sent another black man to prison and earned another term in office. Ronald Westbrook resigned himself to dying in prison.

Until his sister wrote a letter to Professor John Bookman.

Book and Renée rode the Harley to East Texas. They

discovered that Ronald had in fact had sex with a white woman that night, but not with the victim; at the time of the alleged rape, he was in bed with Louise Parker, a respected widow in town who had met Ronald at the church where she worked. She was lonely; he was the janitor. They shared a love of the Bible and each other. But Louise could not face the social stigma she would have to endure in her small hometown if she testified to having sex with a black man. So she watched in silence as Ronald was convicted and sentenced to life.

Now it was her life that was ending.

She had terminal breast cancer. For seventeen years, she had kept her secret; and Ronald had never betrayed her. 'Professor, I grew up in this town. I know how it is. I would've been sentencing her to a place worse than prison,' he said when Book had asked, 'Why?' His sister knew there had been a woman, but not her color or her name; so Book and Renée played detective. They tracked Ronald's life from the football field to the church; they learned of Louise. They went to her home, but her son, now a respected lawyer in town, refused to talk to them or allow them to talk to his mother.

They found her in the hospital.

She too refused to talk. The nurse called her son, and he called the sheriff. Book's mind raced, trying to think of something that would get Louise to tell the truth. But the sheriff arrived and handcuffed them. Just as he pulled them to the door, Renée broke into tears and cried out to Louise.

'My mother died without saying she was sorry!'

Louise turned her eyes to Renée and held up a weak hand to the sheriff.

'What did she do?'

'She cheated on my father! She cheated on us!'

Tears came to Louise. She gestured the sheriff away and Renée close.

'I'm sorry,' she said. 'For what I did to Ronald.'

Louise Parker made amends before meeting her Maker. She revealed her secret on videotape. Two weeks later, Ronald Westbrook came home. His hair had turned gray, and his body had aged, but his handshake remained firm. He thanked Book, payment in full. His sister hugged Book and cried until his shirt was wet. Ronald forgave Louise before she died. They were the only witnesses to her burial; her son did not attend. There was no celebration in town upon Ronald's return. Book had learned that most people, even good people and especially people in small towns, preferred that their past acts of injustice remain in the past. And others were just one generation removed from white hoods. Like these three men. Book addressed the gunman.

'Ronald and Darlene are going home now.'

The gunman spat tobacco juice then stood; he was at least six-four.

'The hell you say. See, I don't figure you making any decisions, Injun. I believe this three-fifty-seven Magnum's making the decisions today.'

A .357 Magnum is one of the most powerful handguns manufactured in America, which is to say, in the world. One possible future played out in Book's mind: the gunman firing point-blank into Book's chest, the massive piece of lead piercing his sternum, exploding through his heart, blowing a fist-sized hole in his back, then striking and killing Renée; the man then turning the gun on Ronald and Darlene ducked behind her brother. Two shots and the four of them would be dead. One shot from a .357 Magnum twenty-one years before, and Book's father was dead.

'Ronnie, he's coming with us,' the gunman said. 'We got some unfinished business with him. And his pretty little sister.'

Darlene emerged from behind Ronald and gazed up at the gunman with a look of recognition.

'Wait. I know you. You're Dewey Randle. We went to school together. You were always looking at me. You didn't do that Klan stuff back then.'

Dewey glared down at her.

'Nig—'

He dropped his eyes. His expression softened slightly, almost as if embarrassed. His voice came out soft.

'Black man rapes your mama, you change.'

'It was your mama who pointed Ronald out in court, said he raped her.'

Dewey's face and voice turned hard again. His anger spilled out.

'It was my mama he raped. Now folks are sayin' she's a liar. I figure Ronnie and that dead woman, they're the liars. Maybe we take Ronnie out to the woods, he'll confess—or he'll watch us do to you what he did to my mama.'

Ronald took a step toward Dewey, but Book blocked him with an outstretched arm. He locked eyes with Dewey Randle, and in his eyes Book saw the same emptiness he had seen only once before, in the eyes of a convicted killer about to be executed.

'That's not going to happen.'

'I got nothin' to lose, Injun. I'm ready to die. Are you?'

'I am.'

Dewey gave Book a bemused look. 'You ain't afraid of dying?'

'I'm afraid of not living.'

'What's the difference?'

'Not living is worse than dying.'

'Good. 'Cause you fixin' to die, Crazy Horse.'

'Son . . . you don't know crazy.'

Dewey raised the gun to Book's head, all the opening he needed. His mind had already played out the three moves he would execute to disable Dewey; it all happened in less than two seconds, but the world seemed to move in slow motion as he swung his open right hand up and against Dewey's wrist, moving the gun away from his face . . . the gun discharged . . . Renée screamed . . . Book swung his left arm up from the inside and grasped Dewey's wrist . . . the tenets of martial

6

arts dictated that Book's next move would be to pull the gun hand down to the outside of his left hip, bringing Dewey's head down and close enough to strike, but that move would also bring the gun closer to Renée . . . so instead, Book jerked the gun hand hard and up past his own head . . . which brought Dewey's head close enough for a temple strike . . . Book tucked his right fist and launched himself into the taller man, slamming his right elbow into Dewey's left temple, knocking him unconscious. The gun fell to the ground, followed by Dewey Randle. Book kicked the gun away then spun to a knife-hand-guard position to face the man with the pipe; but he addressed his intern behind him.

'You okay, Renée?'

A timid voice from below: 'Unh-huh.'

'Ronald? Darlene?'

'We're good, Professor. But how did you . . .?'

The other two men's faces told him that either the alcohol or their egos would not allow a retreat. Book blamed it on the Alamo. No self-respecting Texan—or should he say, no self-respecting drunk Texan—would surrender without a fight. The wife-beater came at Book with the length of pipe; he stepped forward with his left foot and swung as if trying to hit a home run off a high fastball . . . Book ducked under the pipe swinging past his head and executed a spinning sweep, whipping his left leg against the back of the man's leg and knocking his feet out from under him, then a ridge hand strike to the bridge of his nose as the man fell over back- wards. He collapsed to the ground, writhing in pain and cupping his broken nose as blood gushed forth. Book spun to face the third man. 'Don't Mess with Texas' stood frozen over his buddies. He considered his options.

'Don't,' Book said.

He didn't.

The gunfire had brought a crowd out of the café and the sound of a distant siren. Ronald and Darlene would be safe, for now. Book turned to his intern; she was crouched on the ground as if saying a final prayer. He bent down and took her shoulders and lifted her up. She seemed to be in a state of shock.

'Renée, it's okay. You're safe now. I told you I would always protect you.'

He helped her onto the back seat of the big Harley. He swung a leg over and stood the bike upright. Renée leaned into him from behind and wrapped her arms tightly around his torso; he felt her body trembling.

'Thought you're a law professor?' Ronald said.

'I am.'

'Never seen no professor fight like that.'

'It's the Comanche blood.'

Book shook hands with Ronald then fired up the engine, shifted into gear, and gunned the motorcycle west on the highway to Austin. He let out a war cry that would have made Crazy Horse proud.

ONE MONTH LATER

Chapter 1

'Professor Bookman—'

'Answer the question.'

'But, Professor—'

'Ms. Edwards, do you or do you not have a constitutional right to take the pill?'

'I don't care.'

'You don't care if you have a right to use contraceptives?'

'No.' She shrugged. 'I'm a lesbian.'

Book sighed. His mind offered up a list of biting retorts—not to her lesbianism, but to her lack of interest—but he decided against uttering a word. Even a tenured law professor had to be careful with class lectures these days, when every cell phone and laptop doubled as a video camera; this morning's lecture might be that night's viral YouTube video. So he turned from Ms. Edwards and searched the sea of faces for another female student who might care or at least be willing to answer his question in front of the other hundred students. Most had their heads ducked behind their laptops, assured that Professor Bookman would not use his classroom authority to humiliate them in front of their peers. The days

11

of law professors wearing bowties and suits—Book wore boots, jeans, and another Tommy Bahama T-shirt (*Nothing but Net* stenciled under a hammock strung between two palm trees)—and employing the Socratic method to browbeat their students were over. Students paying $30,000 a year (twice that at private schools) demanded a kinder, gentler law school experience. Consequently, Book prodded them to participate in the class debates, but he did not force it upon them. Although it seemed counter-intuitive for prospective lawyers, he knew it was not everyone's nature to seek attention.

It was, however, Ms. Garza's nature.

She sought attention. She demanded attention. She sat directly in front of Book on the front row to ensure his attention. She stuck her hand in the air and puffed her chest out proudly, not to show off her feminine attributes to her handsome professor but to display the message-of-the-day printed in big black letters on her white T-shirt: IF I WANTED THE GOVERNMENT IN MY WOMB, I'D FUCK A SENATOR. No doubt she had chosen her attire in honor of that day's constitutional law topic as stated on the class syllabus: 'The Right of Privacy and Women's Reproductive Rights.' Book admired Ms. Garza's commitment to social justice, but after facing her (and her T-shirts) on the front row for fifty minutes four mornings each week for eight months, her hand always waving frantically, desperate for another opportunity to espouse her political views to the class, the new had worn off. But she remained his go-to student to ignite a class debate.

'Ms. Garza, do you have a constitutional right to take the pill?'

'You're damn right I do.'

'Why?'

'Because in *Griswold v. Connecticut*, the Supreme Court found a right of privacy in the Bill of Rights—'

Book held up an open hand. 'Does the Bill of Rights—the first ten amendments to the Constitution—expressly mention a right of privacy?'

'No. But the Court found a right of privacy in the penumbras of the Bill of Rights—'

'*Penumbras?* What, Ms. Garza, is a penumbra?'

'Uh . . . I'm not really sure.'

'Look it up.'

While she typed on her laptop, Book sat on the front edge of his desk and surveyed the one hundred freshman students— '1Ls' in the vernacular, the first year of their transition from human being to lawyer almost complete—rising before him in the fan-shaped, theater-style seating in Classroom 2.138 at the University of Texas School of Law. They attended his constitutional law class, 'Con Law' as it was known in the curriculum catalog, only because it was a required course; they needed the class credit to earn a law degree. These students much preferred studying the nine million words of the tax code and regulations, for their lives would be lived among those words. Those legal dos and don'ts, rules and regulations borne of generous lobbying and conveniently painted in gray rather than black and white, allowed for a lawyer's creativity.

Many a legal career had been forged in the gray margins of the law.

But not his career. He had never been attracted to the words defining capital gains. After one reading of the Constitution—4,543 words; 7,591 including the twenty-seven amendments—back when he was a 1L, he knew his legal life would be lived among the words of James Madison. He had fallen in love with the Constitution at age twenty-two and the affair continued to this day. 'We the People of the United States, in Order to form a more perfect Union, establish Justice, insure domestic Tranquility, provide for the common defence, promote the general Welfare, and secure the Blessings of

13

Liberty to ourselves and our Posterity, do ordain and establish this Constitution for the United States of America.'

How could you not love those words?

But try though he did—and he did try Monday through Thursday from 9:10 A.M. until 10:00 A.M.—he could not instill the same love for the Constitution in these profit-minded students. If the Constitution had a Facebook page, few of these students would 'like' it. Few would follow it on Twitter. Few seemed to even entertain such lofty legal ideals as liberty and justice these days. Those were concepts you read about in the casebooks, not rights you fought for in the real world. They were not the children of the civil rights era; they were the grandchildren. Twenty-two, twenty-three, twenty-four years old, they had grown up in an era of affluence and entitlement, beneficiaries of the fights fought before they were born. Consequently, they cared more about their job prospects upon graduation, most hoping to become well-paid corporate servants.

Who else could pay $1,000 an hour?

And that was the role law schools now played: farm teams for the major league law firms. 'A' students were valuable commodities in the law business. They were currency. The schools funneled the best and the brightest to the plush offices on the fiftieth floors of skyscrapers across the nation. In return, the law firms endowed chairs at the law schools, ensuring the curriculum would be shaped to further corporate interests, offering such classes as: Corporations; Corporate Finance; Corporate Governance; Taxation of Corporations and Share-holders; Federal Income Taxation of Corporations; Corporate and Securities Law and Transactions; Corporation Law, Finance, Securities, and Regulation; Mergers and Acquisitions; and, of course, White Collar Crime.

Even for this millennial generation, a law degree was viewed as their ticket in life. Most, those sons and daughters of the working class, chose law school because their parents had not.

14

They borrowed a hundred thousand dollars to finance a legal education at UT law school (twice that at Harvard law school) because a law degree still constituted a viable vehicle for social mobility in America, a way to get ahead. To be successful. To have a better life. Perhaps even to get rich.

Others, those sons and daughters of the one percent, simply needed a station in life, a place to be when they weren't at the country club.

Only a few still came to law school with a desire to change the world. Like Ms. Garza here. She burned hot with political desire. She read off her laptop.

'*Webster's* defines penumbra as "the partial or imperfect shadow outside the complete shadow of an opaque body, such as a planet, where the light from the source of illumination is only partly cut off."'

'A shadow?' Book said. 'Let me get this straight: the Supreme Court found a right of privacy in the shadows of the Bill of Rights, where it had been lurking for almost a hundred and eighty years?'

'That's what they said.'

'But I thought the Bill of Rights lists all the rights of the people guaranteed by the Constitution?'

'That's not correct.'

'Please explain.'

'The Framers figured right-wing Republicans—'

'In seventeen eighty-nine?'

'—would read the Bill of Rights as an exclusive list of the people's rights, so James Madison added the Ninth Amendment specifically to negate that interpretation.'

'And the Ninth Amendment states what?'

She read: '"The enumeration in the Constitution, of certain rights, shall not be construed to deny or disparage others retained by the people."'

'To translate, the Framers wanted to make clear that there were other rights retained by the people, even if not specifically mentioned in the Bill of Rights?'

'Yes.'

'And in *Griswold*, the Court determined that one such unmentioned right was the right of privacy. The Court struck down a state law that banned the use of contraceptives, holding that that decision—whether or not to get pregnant—is within a woman's zone of privacy. That the government has no say in such a personal decision.'

Mr. Brennan, also seated on the first row, raised his hand. He tried to transcribe every word Book uttered in each class on his laptop, more court reporter than law student. Book nodded at him.

'Professor, after "whether or not to get pregnant," did you say—'

'Mr. Brennan, you don't need to record my lectures *verbatim*. Just listen. Or better yet, participate.'

Mr. Brennan's hands hovered over his keyboard. Book surrendered, as he had each class.

'I said, "that decision—whether or not to get pregnant—is within a woman's zone of privacy. That the government has no say in such a personal decision."'

Mr. Brennan typed furiously.

'Got it. So the rule of *Griswold* is—'

'Mr. Brennan, this is Con Law not Civ Proc. You're not trying to learn discrete rules of the Court. You're trying to learn to think for yourself, which, unfortunately, few of you will ever do in the private practice of law.'

Mr. Brennan held his gaze. Book again surrendered.

'The rule of *Griswold* is that there is an unwritten but fundamental right of privacy in the Bill of Rights, and a state ban on the use of contraceptives by a married couple violates that right. Which the Court extended to unmarried couples in *Eisenstadt v. Baird* in nineteen seventy-two.'

Mr. Brennan typed. He wore a Boston Red Sox jersey and cap on backwards. He was one of those working-class sons, intent on graduating in the top ten percent of his class, hiring on with a large Boston law firm, paying off his student loans, and living a better life than his father, a Boston cop. Mr. Brennan couldn't get into Harvard, so he had come south for law school. He kept his head down, his fingers moving across the keyboard, and his mind focused on final exams. Book addressed the class.

'*Griswold* was decided in nineteen sixty-five. Eight years later, the justices handed down perhaps the most controversial decision in the history of the Court: *Roe v. Wade*. In *Griswold*, the Court said a woman has a fundamental right not to get pregnant. In *Roe*, the Court said a woman has a fundamental right to end a pregnancy. Mr. Stanton, who was the appellee in *Roe*?'

Mr. Stanton occupied the top row, leaned back in his chair against the wall and dressed like the frat boy he was, his hands buried in his lap and his fingers tapping against his cell phone. Texting in Con Law class. Again, Book held his tongue. Mr. Stanton was smart and rich, and he acted the part. His father was a senior partner in a large Houston firm that had endowed two chairs at the law school. Consequently, Mr. Stanton acted more like a shareholder of the school than a student. The transition from the UT law school to the River Oaks Country Club would be smooth and seamless for E. Roger Stanton Jr.

'Mr. Stanton, if you have a moment, would you please answer the question?'

Mr. Stanton still did not look up from his phone.

'Sorry, Professor, I'm dumping my Facebook stock I got in the IPO. Henry Wade, the Dallas County district attorney, he was the appellee.'

'Who was the appellant?'

Still texting.

'Norma McCorvey, aka "Jane Roe, a pregnant single woman."'

'Who was her lawyer?'

'Uh . . . I don't know.'

17

'Read the opinion.'

Mr. Stanton's eyes lifted to his laptop.

'Sarah Weddington.'

'From what law school did she graduate?'

'Doesn't say.'

'Anyone?'

No one.

'Not even you, Ms. Garza?'

She turned her palms up. 'I wasn't born until nineteen ninety.'

Mr. Stanton, texting again: 'Didn't your mother know that abortion was legal in nineteen ninety, even in Del Rio?'

'Not funny, Mr. Stanton.'

But the class thought he was; they too had grown weary of Ms. Garza. She had been born poor on the border, at the opposite end of the socioeconomic spectrum from Mr. Stanton. She had entered UT an underprivileged female; she had graduated an in-your-face feminist. Book often saw her manning the pro-abortion booth on the West Mall, the free-speech zone on campus. He finally answered his own question, something law professors often had to do.

'Sarah attended this very law school. She graduated in nineteen sixty-seven. Only four years later, she argued *Roe v. Wade* and became the youngest lawyer ever to win a Supreme Court case.'

The students smiled, as if they could put her victory on their own resumés. Ms. Garza seemed especially proud. Perhaps Sarah the law student had burned hot with the same desire to change the world. She had certainly changed the world; some would argue for the better, some would argue for the worse, but no one could argue that she didn't change the world. Book had won two search-and-seizure cases at the Supreme Court. Both were groundbreaking—every Supreme Court case is groundbreaking—but neither had changed the world.

'Mr. Stanton, what law did the appellant challenge?'

Still texting. He did not look up.

'The Texas law that made all abortions criminal acts unless necessary to save the mother's life.'

'And what did the Court decide?'

'That the law violated Roe's right of privacy and was thus unconstitutional.'

'Mr. Stanton, in which article of the Bill of Rights is abortion mentioned?'

'It's not.'

'Why is that?'

Ms. Garza couldn't restrain herself.

'Because racist, misogynistic white men who owned slaves and didn't allow women to vote wrote the Constitution!'

Mr. Stanton coughed words that sounded like 'affirmative action.' His posse of fellow frat boys on the back row laughed. Book did not defend Ms. Garza. She needed no help. She turned in her chair and aimed a finger (not her middle one this time) at Mr. Stanton.

'Your days are numbered, Stanton. Apartheid in America is coming to an end. Enjoy it while you can.'

'I will. In a month, I'll be lying by the pool at the country club surrounded by white girls.'

'And if you get one of those girls pregnant, your rich daddy will pay for her abortion. A poor black or Latino girl gets pregnant, your daddy wants to force her to have the baby. Fifty million abortions since *Roe*—does your daddy want to pay more taxes to support all those babies?'

The senior Stanton was a prominent and very rich Republican in Texas.

'No, but I'll get him to endow a lifetime abortion pass for you. God knows we don't need any more Irma Garzas in this world.'

The junior Stanton shared a high-five with his posse. Book kicked the front panel of the desk as if the heel of his boot was a gavel, and order was soon restored. Book had warned the students that his classroom was an intellectual free-fire zone, like the Supreme Court but more civil.

'Mr. Stanton, if the Constitution says nothing about abortion, how did the Supreme Court determine that a woman has a constitutional right to have an abortion?'

'They discovered it.'

'Where?'

'In the right of privacy.'

'The same right of privacy they discovered in *Griswold*?'

'Yep.'

'Another unmentioned right lurking in the shadows?'

'Who knew?'

'But, as Ms. Garza correctly stated, the intent of the Ninth Amendment was to make clear that there are other rights not mentioned in the Bill of Rights that are nonetheless protected by the Constitution. The Court ruled in *Griswold* that one such unmentioned right is the right of privacy. Mr. Stanton, isn't abortion another such right?'

'No. Abortion was not an unmentioned right of the people at the time the Bill of Rights was ratified. In fact, it was a crime at common law in every state of the Union.'

Ms. Garza stood and faced Mr. Stanton. The debate was on.

'That's bullshit, Stanton. The Court said abortion was *not* a crime at common law.'

'They lied. The only authority the Court cited were two law review articles written by the general counsel of a pro-abortion group, which articles have been roundly discredited as distortions of the common law. In order to justify their hijacking of the Constitution to push their political agenda, the liberal justices misstated history by adopting one biased author's point of view.'

'History is just a point of view,' Ms. Garza said. 'Usually written by white men biased against women and minorities. The right to have an abortion was another right not mentioned

20

in the Constitution because women did not serve on the Constitutional Convention. Women's voices were not heard at the time, Mr. Stanton.'

'Thank God.'

Which elicited a round of boos from the women in the classroom. Book kicked his desk again and gestured Ms. Garza into her chair.

'Mr. Stanton, what was the key ruling of *Roe*?'

'That the right of privacy includes the right to have an abortion.'

'No.'

Mr. Stanton frowned.

'Ms. Garza?'

'That before viability of the unborn child, the state has no legitimate interest in the unborn.'

'The Court so held, but was that really the key ruling of the case?'

No takers.

'Come on, people, you've read the case. Think.'

Heads ducked behind the façade of laptops.

'I know you're back there. You can hide but you can't run, at least not for'—he checked the clock on the back wall—'fifteen more minutes. Was viability the key ruling of *Roe*?'

'No.'

A small anonymous voice.

'Who said that?'

Book searched the laptops for a face.

'Come on, fess up.'

A hand slowly rose above a laptop.

'*Ms. Roberts?* Was that you?'

'Unh-huh.'

Ms. Roberts peeked over her laptop on the sixth row. She had never before spoken in class.

'Ms. Roberts, welcome to the debate. So what was the key ruling in *Roe*?'

21

She looked like the shy girl in high school who had never been on a date being asked to the prom by the football star. She took a handful of her hair hanging in her face and wrapped it around her left ear. With her index finger she pushed her black-framed glasses up on her nose. She took a deep breath then spoke in the softest of voices to the hushed classroom.

'That under the Constitution, an unborn child is not a living human being at any time prior to birth. As Justice Stevens said, it is only a, quote, "developing organism." Thus, the Constitution offers no protection whatsoever to an unborn child.'

'Correct. Please elaborate.'

'The Fourteenth Amendment states that, quote, "nor shall any state deprive any *person* of life, liberty, or property, without due process of law; nor deny to any *person* within its jurisdiction the equal protection of the laws." Thus, if an unborn child were a "person," Roe's case would fail because the Fourteenth Amendment would expressly protect the unborn child's right to life. So, in order to find a right to an abortion, the Court had to first rule that an unborn child is not a "person" under the Constitution. Which is exactly how they ruled: an unborn child is not a living human being and thus abortion is not the termination of a human life.'

Ms. Roberts had found her voice after eight months of Con Law classes. Another small victory for Professor John Bookman.

'So?'

'So, if the unborn child is not a living human being, what's growing inside the mother—a vegetable? Dogs and cats aren't persons under the Constitution either, but we have laws that prevent us from killing them for sport. And this ruling seems especially cruel given that the Court had previously ruled that corporations do qualify as persons under the Fourteenth Amendment and are thus entitled to the full protection of the Constitution.'

Mr. Stanton, from the back row: 'As my man Mitt said, "Corporations are people, too."'

Which evoked a round of laughter. Book kicked his desk again.

'People, this is important. Ms. Roberts is on to something. Listen up.' Back to Ms. Roberts. 'So corporations have more rights under the Constitution than an unborn child?'

'Yes. In fact, a rock has the same constitutional rights as an unborn child.'

'You're almost to the finish line, Ms. Roberts. Now tell us why that particular ruling matters.'

'Because it makes us question whether we matter. It makes us question our place in the grand scheme of things. Do human beings occupy a special place in the universe or are we just a species that has evolved to a higher state of cognitive ability than, say, chimpanzees? When our highest court of law says human beings have absolutely no rights until we're born, that delegates an unborn child to the same constitutional status as an earthworm or a tomato or a—'

'Rock?'

'Yes.'

'And you think you're more important in the universe than a rock?'

'I hope so.'

'So what are the possible legal consequences of this ruling?'

'What if the unborn child has a genetic defect? Can the government force the woman to abort in order to avoid costly future treatment for that child? What if the government decides to solve poverty by instituting mandatory abortions, like in China? New York City public schools are giving the abortion pill to eighth-grade girls without their parents' permission. When our highest court says that unborn humans are not "persons" under the Constitution and may be killed without constraint but corporations that manufacture weapons of war that kill millions of born humans are "persons" with constitutional rights, I say, Who are those guys? Why do they get to decide what is or isn't human? Who elected them God? How do we know they're right? If they're right, who are we and what are we and what is our place in the universe? Is human life nothing more than a biological coincidence? Are our lives no more important in the universe than road kill on I-Thirty-five? Do we matter? Or are we just matter?'

'And if they're wrong?'

'We're all in deep shit, so to speak.'

The students stared at her with stunned expressions. Except Ms. Garza. She glared at Ms. Roberts.

'What, now you're Sarah Palin? You want women to go back to coat hangers and poison?'

Ms. Roberts did not wither under Ms. Garza's hot glare.

'I had an abortion, Ms. Garza. I was ra—'

She ducked her head, and an awkward silence fell upon the room, until Mr. Stanton said from the back row, 'Ms. Garza, you are the poster child for abortion on demand.' Which evoked a round of supportive hoots.

'Unacceptable, Mr. Stanton,' Book said. 'In this classroom we are civil lawyers, able to disagree without being disagreeable. What is my absolute rule of conduct?'

'We shall remain civil at all times.'

'You have violated that rule. An apology, please.'

Mr. Stanton seemed contrite.

'My sincere apology for my incivility, Ms. Garza.'

She faced him.

'Fuck off, Stanton.'

He threw up his hands.

The first time a student had blurted out the F-word in his class, Book had sent him packing. Eight years later, he didn't blink an eye. He was beyond being shocked by profanity—in class, in the corridors, anywhere in public for that matter. Profanity was as much a part of speech for this generation as 'howdy' was for Book's. The F-word had made its way from the locker room to the law school. Athletes, actors, CEOs, and even vice presidents employed the F-word. It's a noun, verb, adverb, adjective, and interjection. It's mainstream speech. It's freedom of speech. The Supreme Court had in fact ruled that the government could not fine a broadcast company for the singer Bono blurting out the F-word during an award show. Book often wondered if the Framers had anticipated that the First Amendment would one day give constitutional protection to 'fuck off.'

'Not gracious, Ms. Garza,' Book said. 'People, I know this is an emotional issue. But as lawyers we must keep our heads while others around us are losing theirs. In this classroom, we are lawyers, not protestors.'

'But we're one Supreme Court justice away from abortion being banned in America!' Ms. Garza said.

'Who told you that?'

'Biden. He said so on TV.'

'He's wrong.'

'He's the vice president.'

'He's still wrong.'

'But Justice Scalia wants to ban abortions!'

'No, he doesn't. Scalia said that as far as he's concerned, the states may permit abortion on demand. The conservative justices don't think there's a constitutional right to have an abortion, but they've never said that the Constitution bans abortion or that an unborn child is a "person" under the Constitution. They've never disagreed with the key ruling of *Roe*, that abortion is not the taking of human life under the Constitution.'

'You sure about that?'

'I'm teaching Con Law, Ms. Garza.'

'Professor,' Mr. Brennan said, taking a respite from his furious typing, 'do you think the Court correctly decided *Roe*?'

'Mr. Brennan, in this classroom what I think is irrelevant. What you think is relevant. And that you think. I don't care whether you agree or disagree with the *Roe* case, only that you think about the case. As students of the Constitution, we are more concerned with the Supreme Court's reasoning than with its decisions, its thought process rather than who wins or loses the case.'

'Bullshit.'

'Ah, a dissenting opinion from Ms. Garza. In any event, we may disagree with the Court's decisions, but so long as the justices *interpret* the Constitution, they are acting within their authority. If, however, they *amend* the Constitution, they are usurping we the people's authority.'

Mr. Stanton: 'And that's exactly what they did in *Roe*. The Court can't *interpret* words that don't even exist.'

'Ms. Garza, doesn't Mr. Stanton make a good point? If the Framers of the Constitution—'

'White men.'

'Yes, we know that, Ms. Garza. If the Framers wanted to give a woman the right to have an abortion, wouldn't they have just written it into the Bill of Rights?'

'Their misogynistic belief system prevented them from considering the plight of women, just as their racist attitudes prevented them from freeing the slaves.'

'All right. Let's assume that to be true, that our Founding Fathers were unable, due to their upbringing, their religious beliefs, their views about women's place in society . . . for whatever reason, they were incapable of including a right to an abortion in the Constitution. Now, fast forward to nineteen seventy-three. Women may vote, use contraceptives, attend law school. States are liberalizing abortion laws. Why didn't the Court just say to Roe, "We're sorry, but the Constitution does not address abortion. Therefore, you must take your complaint to your state legislature to change the law." Isn't that the correct action for the Court to take, to defer to the democratic process?'

'Changing the law through fifty state legislatures would have taken decades, and without a national abortion right poor

26

women like Roe might have to travel to another state to obtain an abortion. A Supreme Court opinion is the law of the land. It changes the law in all fifty states in a single moment. Like that.'

She snapped her fingers.

'But, Ms. Garza, isn't the appropriate avenue to a national abortion right a constitutional amendment? The Constitution has been amended twenty-seven times to add the Bill of Rights, end slavery, guarantee the right to vote to women and persons of all races, create an income tax, begin and end prohibition . . . Why not abortion?'

'Because the justices knew right-wing religious nuts would block a constitutional amendment granting women the right to an abortion.'

'But isn't that the nature of democracy? We the people determining our own rights?'

'Not when they the Republicans deny me my rights.'

'But what do you do in a democracy when you can't convince a majority that you should in fact possess a particular right?'

'I do what Roe did—I get the Supreme Court to give me the right I want.'

'So, in a nation of three hundred twenty million people, nine unelected lawyers sitting as the Supreme Court should circumvent democracy by removing certain issues from the democratic process and declaring those issues constitutional in nature?'

'Yes. And it only takes five justices to win.'

'But by removing abortion from the democratic process, didn't the Court poison political discourse in America? Abortion wasn't even part of the political conversation before *Roe*. Now it's a litmus test for judges and politicians, and it has polarized the nation. *Roe* didn't settle a political fight; it started one.'

'It gave women control over their reproductive decisions. Just like men enjoy.'

'Oh, yeah,' Mr. Stanton said from the back row. 'We've got it real good. A girl lies about being on the pill, and we're paying child support for the next eighteen years. Try telling that to your dad.'

Another awkward silence captured the classroom.

'Uh, okay, let's move on. In nineteen ninety-two, after two decades of protests, political fights, and contentious judicial nominations, the Court again took up a major abortion case, *Planned Parenthood v. Casey*. The Court's stated intent was to put an end to the abortion wars in the country. In a five-to-four decision, the Court reaffirmed *Roe* but allowed the states more leeway in regulating abortions. Justice Kennedy's lead opinion appealed to the American people to respect their decision and accept a woman's right to an abortion as the law of the land, a lawyer's way of saying, "Trust us. We know what we're doing."'

Ms. Roberts jumped back into the fray.

'How are we supposed to trust those guys when Kennedy can write that nonsense in *Casey*?' She read off her laptop: 'Quote, "At the heart of liberty is the right to define one's own concept of existence, of meaning, of the universe, and of the mystery of human life." Really? Maybe it's just me, but it's hard to imagine Jefferson or Madison saying goofy stuff like that.'

Mr. Stanton, from the back row: 'I said goofy stuff like that back in college, but I was stoned at the time. I made a video and posted it on YouTube, got a hundred thousand hits.'

'And you still got into this law school?'

'Rich daddy,' Ms. Garza said.

Mr. Stanton shared a fist-bump with his buddies.

'Was Kennedy like that when you clerked for him?' Mr. Brennan asked.

Book's clerkship for Justice Kennedy had made him a hot commodity among constitutional lawyers because Kennedy was often the swing vote in crucial five–four decisions.

'I came on board ten years after *Casey*. Kennedy was just trying to broker a peace in the abortion war. He respects the Court, and he wants the people to respect it as well.'

'Too late for that,' Ms. Garza said. 'We're not stupid. We know the Court's just another political branch.'

'The Constitution is just politics?'

'Professor, everything is just politics.'

Book felt as if he had just been told that the love of his life had cheated on him. The Constitution is just politics? The Court no less partisan than the Congress? Ms. Garza read his mind.

'The only difference between Congress and the Court is that we can vote those Republican bastards out of Congress.'

'Mr. Stanton—'

He looked up from his texting.

'Ms. Garza is mistaken, isn't she?'

'In so many ways, Professor.'

'Make your case.'

'First, her T-shirts are getting old. Second, she—'

'About the Court being a political branch.'

'Oh. The Court is perceived as being political because the justices subverted democracy in *Roe*. In America, we don't stage violent protests and burn down cities when our side loses an election. We organize for the next election. But we want to vote. The people didn't get to vote on abortion.'

Ms. Roberts again: 'As Scalia said in his *Casey* dissent, quote, "value judgments should be voted on, not dictated." And quote, "the people know that their value judgments are quite as good as those taught in any law school—maybe better." I like that.'

Ms. Garza again glared at her classmate.

'Now you're quoting Scalia? Jesus, Liz, you wouldn't talk for eight months, now you won't shut up. Quote this.'

Ms. Garza jabbed her middle finger at Ms. Roberts.

'Unacceptable, Ms. Garza. An apology, please.'

'Oh, I'm really fucking sorry, Ms. Roberts.'

That constituted sincere for Ms. Garza.

'Civility, people. This is a classroom, not the Supreme Court conference room on decision day. Ms. Garza, your rebuttal to Mr. Stanton's case—the rebuttal that does not include your middle finger.'

'Two generations of women have grown up with total control over their reproductive decisions, both contraceptives and abortion. If men get to vote on our right to abortion, they'll take that right away from us. Then they'll take the right to use contraceptives. Because men want desperately to control women—our lives, our liberties, our work, our pay, our sexual activity, our bodies, and most of all, our wombs.'

Mr. Stanton: 'Trust me, I don't want anywhere near your womb.'

The class laughed. Ms. Garza did not.

'Stanton, you're just mad because women won a right to an abortion.'

'I'm mad because the liberal justices hijacked the Constitution—they made it up!'

'You don't know that.'

Mr. Stanton pointed down at Book. 'He said so in his last book.'

Another round of laughter.

'How do you know I'm right?' Book said.

'Because you're down there lecturing, and we're up here taking notes.'

More laughter.

'How do you know I'm not just another tenured professor pushing my personal political beliefs on his captive audience of impressionable students?'

'Because you're not teaching over in the English department.'

The entire class laughed and let out a collective sigh of relief when the bell rang. They rose as one and gathered their belongings. Book yelled over the noise.

'Read *National Federation of Independent Business v. Sebelius*, aka Obamacare, for the next class.'

The mass of students parted like the Red Sea before Moses. Half rushed for the doors. The other half surged down to the front and around Book, peppering him with questions and pushing copies of his latest book, *Con Law: Why Constitutional Law is the Greatest Hoax Ever Perpetrated on the American People*, for him to sign. It was currently number one on the *New York Times* nonfiction print and digital bestseller lists.

'Professor, would you sign your book for my mom? Her name's Sherry.'

He signed the book with a Sharpie. Another came forward.

'Sign my book, for my dad. Ken.'

He signed. Another hand came forward.

'Sign my Kindle.'

'Your Kindle?'

'I have your e-book on it.'

He signed her Kindle. She then stepped close and held out her cell phone in front of them.

'Can I take a picture of us? For my dad? He said when you're on the Supreme Court—'

Book had made many shortlists of potential candidates.

'—you'll straighten those crazy bastards out.'

She snapped a photo.

'My dad never misses you on those Sunday morning talk shows. He loved that line yesterday on *Face the Nation*—'

Book had participated via a satellite feed from the local Austin studio.

'—when you told that senator that you were neither liberal nor conservative, Republican nor Democrat, but that instead you were the last known practicing Jeffersonian in America.'

'It wasn't a line.'

The students drifted off. Book gathered his casebook and notes and walked out the door and down the narrow corridor crowded and noisy with aspiring lawyers chatting about their

31

lucrative job offers from large law firms. Thirteen years before, he had walked the corridors of Harvard law school, aiming to do something important with his life, perhaps even to change the world. But not to get rich. Money had never motivated him. He had found that he needed few material things in life. He lived in a small house near campus. He had acquired the Harley secondhand and made it his own. He had never owned a car, and he no longer owned a suit. Having things meant nothing to him. Doing things meant everything. And he did everything at a fast pace.

Because he knew he didn't have much time.

Chapter 2

'Get a haircut, Bookman.'

Book took the stairs two steps at a time, so he was quickly past the white-haired man dressed immaculately in a suit and tie walking down the stairs. He was the dean of the law school.

'Right away, Roscoe.'

Tenure had earned Book a fifteen-foot-by-twenty-foot office, a lifetime salary, a secretary, and the right to wear his hair long. He arrived at the fifth floor, turned a corner, ducked between students, and entered the front room of the two-room office suite where a middle-aged woman wearing reading glasses secured to her neck by a glittery strand of beads sat at a desk and held a phone to her ear.

'Here he is,' Myrna said into the phone. She covered the mouthpiece and whispered, 'The police. Again.'

Book put the phone to his ear. 'John Bookman.'

'Yeah, uh, Professor, this is Sergeant Taylor, Austin PD. We found your mother.'

'She wandered off again?'

'Yes, sir. She was at the mall. Victoria's Secret. Walked out with an armful of lingerie, said she had a date tonight. They called us, we took her home. I called your sister. She's on the way. I'll stay till she gets here.'

'Thanks, Sergeant.'

'Don't mention it. I worked with your dad.' He paused. 'Uh, Professor, I don't mean to mind your business, but you should really consider putting your mom in a home. Folks in her condition, they wander off, get lost, end up outside all night. One day we might not find her in time. Your dad wouldn't have wanted that.'

Book thanked the officer and hung up the phone. He could not abide the thought of his mother in a nursing home. Myrna regarded him over her reading glasses.

'You okay?'

He wasn't, but he nodded yes.

'Messages?'

Myrna held up pink call slips. 'Fox wants you on the Sunday morning show, by satellite. To debate the Supreme Court's decision on Obamacare.'

'With whom?'

'McConnell.'

'Again? After our last debate?'

'He's a politician, doesn't know you made him look like a fool.'

'Wasn't exactly hard work.'

'And *Meet the Press* wants you to debate Schumer.'

'Him, too?'

She shrugged. 'They're gluttons for punishment.'

'What else?'

'They're stupid, they're egomaniacs, they're—'

'The messages.'

'The *Wall Street Journal* and the *New York Times* want your comments on the case.'

'When?'

'Today. Front-page articles in tomorrow's editions. And you're late for the faculty meeting.'

Myrna reached down to her oversized purse and came up again with a sealed plastic container. Several years back, she started bringing him leftovers from dinner the night before because he ate protein bars for breakfast, bachelor and all; it was now a daily ritual.

'Chicken quesadillas,' she said.

'With your guacamole?'

'Of course.'

'Thanks.'

'Stu said I should charge you, even if they are just leftovers.'

'Remind Stu that I didn't charge him for his murder case.'

A year before, Myrna's husband had accidentally run over an armadillo in his four-wheel-drive pickup truck. An animal-rights activist, which is to say, a resident of Austin, had witnessed the 'murder' and called the police. The district attorney, up for reelection, charged Stu with animal cruelty. Book defended him and won an acquittal.

'Mail?'

Myrna pointed a thumb at his office door behind her. He walked through the open door and into his office crowded with a leather couch, a bookshelf filled with casebooks and a crash helmet, law review articles stacked along the walls, Southwestern art and framed photographs of himself with Willie Nelson and ZZ Top and other Texas musicians, a cluttered desk with an open laptop, and a work table where a young woman sat reading his mail.

'Who are you?'

'Nadine Honeywell. I'm a two-L. The dean of students sent me over. I'm your new intern.'

Tenure had also earned Book a paid student assistant to help with his research, his law review articles, and his correspondence.

'Where's Renée?'

'She quit.'

'*Why?*'

Nadine shrugged. 'All she said was, "I didn't go to law school to get shot at." She was just joking, right, Professor?'

Book dropped the armload of books and notes and Myrna's plastic container onto the couch then stepped to the solitary window and stared out at the treed campus. He had grown to like Renée. Just as he had grown to like all of his interns. But sooner or later, they all quit.

'Right, Professor?'

He sighed. 'Yes, Ms. Honeywell. She was just joking.'

'I thought so.'

He turned from the window. Nadine squirted hand sanitizer from a small plastic bottle into one palm then rubbed her hands together. The room now reeked of alcohol. She wore a T-shirt, shorts, sandals, and black-framed glasses riding low on her nose. Her black hair was pulled back in a ponytail, and Book could discern no sign of makeup or scent of perfume. She was skinny and looked thirteen. She picked up an envelope and used a pocketknife to slice open the flap.

'Is that my pearl-handled pocketknife?' Book asked.

'Must be. I found it on your desk.'

She gestured with his knife at the pile of mail on the table in front of her.

'Myrna said you get hundreds of these letters every week.'

'Every week.'

'So people all over the country write to you and ask for help? Like you're some kind of superhero or something?'

'Or something.'

'And do you?'

'Do I what?'

'Help them.'

'A few.'

'Why the snail mail? Haven't they heard of email?'

'I don't publish my email address. I figure if they want my help, they should at least be willing to write a real letter. And you can tell a lot more about a person from a letter.'

'I can tell there are a lot of sad people out there. Single mothers not getting their child support—'

'Send those over to the Attorney General's Child Support Office.'

'—inmates claiming innocence and wanting DNA tests—'

'Send those to the Innocence Project.'

'—people wanting to sue somebody—'

'No civil cases.' Book took a step toward his desk. 'Tell me if you find something interesting.'

'I did.'

Nadine held up an envelope.

'You should read this one.'

Book took the envelope, walked over to his desk, and was about to drop down into his chair when he heard Myrna's voice from outside.

'Faculty meeting!'

He pushed the envelope into the back pocket of his jeans, grabbed the plastic container with Myrna's quesadillas, and walked out of his office and down the corridor.

Chapter 3

The University of Texas School of Law opened its doors in 1883 with two professors teaching fifty-two students. White students. State law forbade admission of black students. In 1946, a black man named Heman Sweatt applied for admission to the UT law school; his admission was denied solely because of his race. The infamous 1896 Supreme Court ruling in *Plessy v. Ferguson* had deemed the Equal Protection Clause of the Fourteenth Amendment satisfied if a state provided 'separate but equal' accommodations for the races. So, rather than admit Mr. Sweatt, UT opened a separate law school for blacks only. But while the UT law school then had sixteen professors, eight hundred fifty students, a 65,000-volume library, and alumni in positions of legal power throughout the state, the blacks-only law school had three professors, twenty-three students, a 16,500-volume library, and exactly one graduate who was a member of the Texas bar. Mr. Sweatt sued but lost in the state trial court, state appeals court, and state supreme court. So he took his case to the U.S. Supreme Court. In *Sweatt v. Painter*, the Court ruled in 1950 that the blacks-only law school did not offer a legal education equal to that offered whites and ordered Mr. Sweatt admitted to the UT law school. Sixty-two years later, the University of Texas School of Law had seventy-two full-time professors, 1,178 students, a million-volume library, and sixty-two black students.

Book opened the door and stepped inside the faculty conference room where most of the full-time faculty were already engaged in vigorous debate. He tried to walk unnoticed around the perimeter of the large room, but the discussion abruptly stopped, and all heads turned his way, as if a student had invaded their private sanctum.

'Ah, our very own Indiana Jones is honoring us with his presence this morning. How wonderful. My, the press does love our dashing young professor, don't they?'

Addressing Book from the head of the long conference table was Professor Jonah Goldman (Harvard, 1973, Environmental Law), the faculty president. Book's exploits in East Texas had made the national press.

'And your book is still number one on the *New York Times*, I see. I would think you could afford a suit with all those royalties.'

Professor Goldman had lived the last thirty-five years of his life in this law school, seldom venturing far from campus, preferring instead to live like a nun cloistered inside a convent. Like many of his contemporaries, he had entered law school to avoid the draft during the Vietnam War and had stayed on to enjoy the benefits of lifetime tenure. He was short and portly and sported fluffy white hair and a trimmed white beard; he wore a brown plaid three-piece suit and a brown bowtie; there was still one law professor in America wearing bowties. Book ignored him (and his bowtie) and found a seat in the back corner next to his best friend among the faculty, which is to say, his only friend among the faculty.

'Henry.'

'Book.'

Henry Lawson (UT, 1997, Oil and Gas Law) was an associate professor of law. His face held the expression of a middle-aged man with no job security. Which was what he was. He occupied a rung on the academic career ladder one below that of a tenured professor of law. And his tenure was on the agenda that day.

His chances were not good. First, forty-three of the seventy-two professors in the room held law degrees from Harvard and Yale while Henry held a law degree from this very law school. Only four other professors on the full-time faculty were UT law graduates; no other Texas law school, or Southern law school for that matter, was represented on the faculty. When Harvard- and Yale-educated professors did the hiring, they hired Harvard and Yale graduates, not Texas and Alabama graduates. They demanded diversity in all things academic, except professors' law schools and political ideology.

Second, Henry had spent five years working in the legal department of an international oil company. That experience served him well as a professor teaching oil and gas law, but as far as the Harvard and Yale professors were concerned, he might as well have been in-house counsel to the Grand Order of the Ku Klux Klan. Which at one time would not have disqualified one from teaching at UT. William Stewart Simkins, a Klansman turned law professor, taught at the UT law school from 1899 to 1929; the university even named a dormitory in his honor in 1954, coincidentally the same year the Supreme Court handed down its landmark ruling in *Brown v. Board of Education* overturning *Plessy* and declaring that 'separate but equal' violated the Constitution. The Board of Regents had renamed the dorm just the past year.

And third, the slim chance Henry did have would become no chance at all if the Harvard–Yale cartel discovered that he had voted for George W. Bush. Twice. Henry's expression revealed his despair.

'I'm forty-one, Book,' he said in a low voice. 'There's no other law school out there for me. With this economy and law jobs plummeting, schools are freezing new hires. I've been denied tenure twice. Three strikes, and I'm out.'

He put his elbows on his knees and his face in his hands. After a long moment, he turned to Book.

'Ann's pregnant again.'

Book chucked him on the shoulder.

'Congratulations.'

Henry did not seem thrilled at the prospect of becoming a father for the third time. So Book did the only thing he knew to perk up his friend's spirits: he popped the top on the plastic container and offered Henry a quesadilla.

'Chicken.'

'With Myrna's guacamole?'

'Of course.'

They ate the quesadillas while the other professors renewed their debate in earnest.

'What are they fighting about today?' Book asked.

'What else? Money and tenure. And the vacant assistant deanship.'

The assistant dean had been fired when it came to light that the UT Law School Foundation, a nonprofit run by alumni, had handed out—on the dean's sole recommendation—$4.65 million in 'forgivable loans' to twenty-two professors in amounts ranging from $75,000 to $500,000. Purportedly to attract and retain key faculty by allowing them to purchase homes in the high-dollar Austin residential market, the loans were forgiven if the professor remained on the faculty for a negotiated term of three to ten years. The assistant dean himself had received a $500,000 loan, apparently to ensure his loyalty to UT. The secret faculty compensation numbers had become public when several professors made an open records request; the information ignited a firestorm among the faculty, not because the other professors thought the loans too 'Wall Street' during this Great Recession when the law school was increasing tuition on its middle-class students by double digits, but because they wanted in on the action. The controversy reached the university president, and worse, the Austin newspaper and the legal blogosphere, which proved an embarrassment to the administration; the president then fired the assistant dean. He couldn't fire the dean who doled out the money because the Longhorn football coach and the law school dean—a legendary law professor at UT who had taught most of the senior partners at the major Texas law firms and who was now a legendary accumulator of donations and endowments from those law firms—ran the only two profit centers on the UT campus. But someone had to be fired.

'I want more money!'

Professor Sheila Manfried (Yale, 1990, Feminist Legal Theory and Gender Crimes) was addressing the faculty. She waved a thick document in the air.

'I have the faculty compensation numbers. I knew I was getting screwed, and this proves it. I can't believe how many male professors are making more money than me. I want a salary increase, and I want one of those forgivable loans. I've been on this faculty for eighteen years. I've been tenured for twelve. I publish more articles than the rest of you combined. My law review articles have been published in the *Yale Law Review*, the *Harvard Law Review*, the *Michigan Law Review* . . .'

She pointed at male professors (who referred to her as 'Professor Mankiller' behind her back) in succession as if identifying guilty defendants in court.

'. . . But you're making more than me? And you? And you? You guys haven't published anything in years.'

Professor Herbert Johnson (UT, 1974, Contracts), one of those guys, offered the male rebuttal.

'Well, Sheila, when I did publish something, it was useful, not your feminist crap. What's your latest article? "The Tort of Wrongful Seduction." You want men to be liable for damages if they really didn't mean it when they said, "I love you." How stupid is that?'

Professor Manfried glared at him then jabbed a long finger in the air as if to stab him.

'That's it, Herb. I'm putting you on my witness list.'

Professor Manfried had sued the university for gender discrimination over her compensation. She made $275,000.

'Liberals fighting over money like Republicans,' Henry said.

'The desire for money transcends politics.'

'But tenure doesn't.' Henry shook his head. 'I was ROTC at A&M, served in the army for four years, graduated top of my class at this law school, worked to pay off my student loans . . . but I'm an outcast here because I worked for an oil company.'

'And voted Republican,' Book whispered.

'Shh! They don't know.'

Book could count the number of professors who might have voted Republican on his fingers and toes, and he didn't need to take his boots off. Of course, it was mere speculation; one did not speak publicly about such things inside an American law school, not if one wanted tenure or a salary hike. Law school faculties leaned hard to the left, which was to be expected at Harvard and Yale, but at Texas? That fact—that Ivy League-educated liberals who disdained all things Texan (except their University of Texas paychecks) and whose fondest dream was to be called home to Harvard and Yale were teaching the sons and daughters of conservative UT alumni— had always amused him. If only those conservatives knew that their beloved university had a faculty only slightly to the left of the ruling party in Havana.

'I propose a faculty resolution demanding that the new

assistant dean be a woman,' Professor Manfried said. 'Better yet, a lesbian.'

'They're bringing in an outsider,' Professor Goldman said. 'A heterosexual male.'

'How do you know?'

'He's married with two children.'

'That they hired a man?'

'I have my sources in Admin. I hear that Roscoe will finalize the deal before the semester is out.'

'Then I propose a resolution that Roscoe be fired and replaced with a lesbian.'

Roscoe Chambers was the law school dean. He was seventy-seven years old and a crusty old fart who ran the law school with an iron fist.

'He's untouchable, Sheila,' Professor Goldman said.

'He's a Republican dinosaur. It's embarrassing to go to law school conferences and have professors from other schools laugh at us because we have a Republican dean.'

'He controls too much alumni money to be fired. He can pick up the phone and pull in five million today. He'll hire whomever the alumni want for the next assistant dean.'

'Well, he might control who runs this school, but we control who teaches here.'

Professor Manfried sat, and the collective blood pressure of the faculty receded to normal levels. Which gave Professor Robert Stone (Chicago, 2006, Law and Economics) an opening. He stood to groans. He had a law degree and a Ph.D. in economics and looked like Book's accountant. He was one of the new breed of law professors, a multi-disciplinarian who thought outside the box, normally not considered a positive character trait in a non-tenured professor. Book didn't know him well, but he liked what he did know.

'My fellow colleagues, in one month, accredited law schools across the country will graduate forty-eight thousand new lawyers, the most in history. But only twenty thousand legal jobs await them. The big corporate law firms are hiring fewer graduates, they're firing attorneys, and they're outsourcing their low-level legal work overseas to lawyers in India and the Philippines just like the tech companies do their call centers.'

Professor Goldman: 'Where'd you read that?'

'The *Wall Street Journal*.'

'You read the *Wall Street Journal*?'

'Of course. Don't you?'

'No. I read the *New York Times*. If it's not in the *Times*, I don't need to know it.'

'Jonah, you need to know that our graduates are facing the worst legal job market in two decades. We're dramatically oversupplying the market. But we're immune from market forces because the federal government is now the sole provider of student loans and lends the full sticker price for law school, including cost of living, whatever the cost. Last year's graduating law class nationwide owed a collective three-point-six billion in student loans. The students don't have a prayer of repaying that debt.'

'What's your point, Bob?'

'My point is, Jonah, we can't keep bringing four hundred new students into the law school each year, charge them thirty thousand dollars a year, and put them into a market where there aren't enough jobs to go around. Nationally, one hundred fifty thousand students at two hundred law schools pay five billion a year in tuition. Law schools are cash cows on university campuses, Jonah, but in this job market, a law degree will be worthless for three-fourths of the students. Actually, less than worthless since they'll owe a hundred thousand or more in debt.'

'Why's that our fault?'

'Because we continue to raise the cost of a legal education. Over the last decade, we tripled tuition and doubled our salaries.'

'But they keep paying it.'

'With federal loans, debt that pays our salaries. We're like peanut farmers, Jonah, subsidized by the federal government.'

'How many peanut farmers have advanced degrees from Harvard?'

Professor Goldman let out an exasperated sigh.

'Okay, Bob, so what's your brilliant proposal this time?'

'We need to teach more and be paid less. We need to be honest with our students about their job prospects. We need to reduce the supply of lawyers to the demand for lawyers. I propose a faculty resolution that we reduce next year's incoming class by twenty-five percent.'

Professor Stone's proposal evoked a collective gasp from the faculty. Professor Goldman stared at his younger and untenured colleague as if he were a homeless person urinating at the corner of Eleventh and Congress downtown.

'Have you lost your mind? Twenty-five percent, that's a hundred tuition-payers—'

'*Tuition-payers?* You mean, students?'

'Yes. Them. And that's over three million dollars in lost tuition revenue. You know what that would mean? Pay cuts. No summer stipends. No research funds. Maybe no secretaries or interns. You want that? Besides, these tuition-payers— excuse me, these students—aren't here to save mankind. They're here to get a law degree and hire on with those corporate law firms and get rich. Just this morning, I posed a hypothetical fact situation to my class and asked a student which side he wanted to represent. He said, "Whichever side can pay more." We didn't teach them that. The world did. These kids are capitalists through and through.'

'And we're not? Fifty-one of us in this room make more than two hundred thousand and nineteen more than three hundred thousand, for teaching, what, six hours a week for twenty-eight weeks? We're paid summer stipends of sixty, seventy, even eighty thousand dollars to write on a beach. This

46

public law school paid the seventy-two full-time professors in this room a total of eighteen million dollars in compensation last year—not including those forgivable loans some of you got—for part-time work.'

'*Part-time?* My God, man, we're in class six hours each week. At Harvard, they're in class only three hours. Besides, we're a top-tier law school—we shouldn't have to teach.'

'Someone's got to, Jonah. It's a school, which implies teachers. So the school has to hire twenty lecturers and one hundred thirty-five adjuncts to teach for us. And it's all paid for by increasing tuition on middle-class students who borrow to pay it. Total student debt now exceeds one trillion dollars, more than credit card debt, and it can't be discharged in bankruptcy. It's a huge drag on the economy. Even the employed grads can't qualify for home mortgages.'

'They need forgivable loans,' Professor Manfried said.

'They've got them,' Professor Goldman said. 'I hear Obama's going to forgive all that student debt—it's all owed to the federal government anyway, so we're just passing the cost on to the taxpayers, like the General Motors bailout.'

Henry whispered to Book, 'And the public thinks we spend our time teaching contracts and torts.'

Professor Goldman turned back to Professor Stone. 'Why shouldn't we be well paid? My Harvard classmates sitting atop those corporate law firms in New York are making millions.'

'They're real lawyers, Jonah, working for real clients paying real money. That has value in the marketplace. Most of us don't have a clue what real lawyers do.'

'I don't want a clue. We're not practitioners, Bob. We're not a trade school. It's not our job to teach students how to practice law. We're here to teach the theory of law. And we do have value—we're the only path to the legal profession. If you want to be a real lawyer, you've got to go to law school. That gives us value.'

'A hundred-thousand-dollar value?'

47

Professor Goldman addressed Professor Stone as if he were a 1L who hadn't answered a question correctly.

'Tell you what, Bob, let's take a quick vote. A show of hands from those in favor of Professor Stone's proposal to reduce enrollment, tuition, and our salaries.'

Book raised his hand. Henry couldn't; without tenure, he had no academic freedom. No other professor raised a hand.

'Yes, we know you would be in favor of something like that, Professor Bookman.'

Professor Stone sat and slumped in his chair. His regular economic analyses of law school finances over the last few years of the Great Recession had always proven unpopular with the faculty. Denial was far more popular; in fact, denial defined the Academy, aristocrats blissfully ignorant of the plight of the masses living off-campus. They fought over forgivable loans and summer stipends, they wrote law review articles with four thousand footnotes, they dreamed of being appointed to a federal appeals court; they taught the theory of law and lived theoretical lives, 'what-if' lives as if life were a hypothetical fact situation. They railed against Republicans and Wall Street and the one-ercenters, but they sat happily ensconced in chairs endowed by corporate law firms in Houston and Dallas, by Joe Jamail, the billionaire plaintiff's lawyer famous for winning a $3 billion verdict in *Pennzoil v. Texaco*, and even by Frederick Baron, the now-deceased millionaire asbestos lawyer infamous for funding John Edwards' mistress during his failed presidential campaign.

Such was the Academy.

Book did not live an Academy life. He lived out there, among the people. In the real world. On the road. Less traveled or more traveled, but at least traveled. He didn't want to teach theory; he wanted to live reality. With each passing day, he became more disillusioned with the Academy. It seemed less relevant, less in touch with the real world, less concerned with the problems of real people. More disconnected from life. More unconcerned with life off-campus.

'All right,' Professor Goldman said. 'Let's move on to tenure. Would those professors up for tenure please exit the meeting?'

Henry stood. He looked like a man about to face a firing squad.

'I love teaching the law.'

'You'll still be teaching the law next year, Henry.'

After Henry and Professor Stone and the other tenure candidates had departed, Professor Goldman, as chair of the Tenure Committee, opened the meeting for discussion.

Book stood. 'I propose Henry Lawson for tenure. For the third time. Henry is a gentleman and a scholar. He has published five law review articles—'

Professor Goldman interrupted: 'In what reviews?'

'Texas Tech, Tulsa . . .'

'Texas Tech and Tulsa. Not exactly the "A" list, is it? Any in the Harvard or Yale reviews?'

'Those reviews aren't interested in articles about oil and gas law, Jonah.'

'Then how important can his articles be? How much value can we attach to publications in the *Texas Tech Law Review*?'

'You write about the rights of trees, Jonah—how valuable are your articles, except perhaps to an evergreen? How many people read your articles? How many times have your articles been cited, anywhere? Truth is, no one reads our law review articles, you know that. We write them to get tenure. Most legal scholarship is worthless drivel. But Henry is a nationally recognized expert in oil and gas law—'

'Yippee.'

'—He's served on the White House's Energy Task Force—'

'Promoting oil and gas drilling—including fracking, for God's sake!'

'—He's in demand as a speaker to industry groups—'

49

'Oil company executives.'

'—We all know that Henry is smart enough, dedicated enough, a hell of a teacher, his students love him—'

'Tenure is not a popularity contest.'

'—Henry worked in the real world—'

'For an oil company.'

'—Which means he can teach the students about being real lawyers.'

'So?'

'So he can relate to the very alumni who support this university and this law school. For all of you Harvard and Yale grads who don't know, this university was built on oil money. And I remind you that Henry—'

'Voted for Bush! Twice!'

Another even louder collective gasp went up from the professors.

'How do you know?'

'I have my sources. He can't have voted for Bush and be our next tenured professor.'

'You're right, Jonah. Henry shouldn't be the next tenured professor. He should be the next assistant dean, and then the next dean when Roscoe retires. He could run this school better than any of us.'

'Having a Republican dean like Roscoe is why we dropped in the rankings. If word gets out that one of our tenured faculty members voted for Bush, we'll be a joke in the Academy. Our reputation among our peers—which accounts for twenty-five percent of our *U.S. News* ranking, I remind you—will take a dive. Do you want that?'

UT law school had dropped from fourteenth to sixteenth in the latest *U.S. News and World Report* law school rankings; panic had ensued. Twenty years before, *U.S. News* began the rankings. At first, the rankings were viewed by the Academy as amusing anecdotes; today, the rankings are viewed as critical to a law school's success. Move up in the

50

rankings, and celebrations begin in the faculty lounge; move down, and heads roll. Prospective law students decide which schools to apply to based upon the rankings; thus, rankings drive applications; and applications put butts in seats worth $30,000 to $50,000 each. With so much money riding on the rankings, some schools had gamed their reports to achieve higher rankings, inflating their Law School Admission Test numbers, including among 'graduates known to be employed nine months after graduation' those grads working at Starbucks because they couldn't find legal jobs, and even hiring their own unemployed grads for short-term stints spanning February 15—the effective date for the schools' reports—so those students could be counted as employed. Rankings now drive every decision made in law schools across America.

'If we hope to move up in the rankings, we must hire and grant tenure to star professors,' Professor Goldman said.

'And all the stars come from Harvard and Yale?'

'They're sure as hell not Republicans from UT.'

'But we're top ten in football,' Professor Al Harvey (UT, 1985, Property Law) said. 'Can't be tops in football and law.'

'Tell the alumni that,' Professor Goldman said.

'Did you see the spring game? The team's looking good.'

'Shut up, Al.'

'I'm just saying.'

'Jonah,' Book said, 'this isn't about rankings.'

'Everything's about rankings. If we grant tenure to Henry, we'll be lucky to stay in the top tier. Are we going to be the Harvard of the Southwest or not?'

'Not. Jonah, we're chasing Harvard and Yale in the rankings even though we all know the methodology employed by *U.S. News* is flawed and their results laughable. I've got a better idea: let's drop out of the rankings.'

'You've gone mad! If we take ourselves out of the rankings game, we'll never hire another Harvard or Yale graduate.'

51

'Good.'

Jonah Goldman's pale face turned bright red, which clashed with his brown suit. Book figured, what the hell, might as well go all the way.

'Jonah, you're living in the past. But our students will live in the future, so this school must look to the future. And that future will not be made following in the footsteps of Harvard and Yale. It will be made by cutting our own path right here in Texas. Therefore, I propose that we refuse to participate in the rankings. I propose that we teach our students to be real lawyers. And I propose the best person I know to lead this school into that future: Henry Lawson. I propose Henry for tenure and to be our next assistant dean.'

'Fine,' Professor Goldman said. 'All in favor of Professor Bookman's proposals, raise your hands.'

Book stuck his hand defiantly in the air and waited for reinforcements . . . and waited. Four other hands finally went up, all from the UT professors. But no Harvard or Yale hand. Or Columbia. Or Stanford. Or the others. Professor Goldman turned to Book with the smug look of the rich boy in grade school who always got the best toys money could buy.

'Your propositions fail, Professor Bookman.'

Book dropped down in his chair. Institutional inertia prevailed. Fear of the future. Professors hanging on to the past. Hoping the past lasts until they retire with full benefits. The school would continue to chase Harvard and Yale in the rankings, and the students would lose. Henry Lawson would not be the new assistant dean. He would not be granted tenure. Not that year. Not any year. He was the best teacher on the faculty, but he would soon be teaching at another law school. Or perhaps at a high school.

Other professors stood and championed their protégés. Book slumped down in his chair and felt something in his back pocket. He pulled out the envelope Nadine had given him. It

52

was postmarked 'Marfa, Texas,' on April 5, four days before. He removed the letter, unfolded the single sheet, and read the handwritten note.

Dear Professor Bookman,

Remember me? Nathan Jones? I was your intern for one month four years ago. I'm sorry I quit so abruptly back then, but I didn't want to die before getting my law degree. (Just kidding.) Anyway, I'm married now, my wife's pregnant, and I'm a third-year associate at the Dunn firm in West Texas. I work in our Marfa office which we established to represent our largest client, an oil and gas company. Mostly gas. They're fracking in the Woodford shale field north of town. Professor, our client is contaminating the aquifer with the frack fluids. I have proof. That aquifer is the sole source of drinking water for this part of West Texas. I took the matter to my senior partner in Midland. He told me to keep my mouth shut, that any information I have is confidential under our ethics rules. Which means if I go public, I'll get disbarred. So I'm required to keep this secret while our client contaminates the aquifer with toxic chemicals. That doesn't seem right. But I don't know what to do. Can you help me? Funny. Now I'm writing one of those letters to you.

Regards,

Nathan

PS: I think someone followed me home last night. My wife is scared.

Book walked down the corridor at a fast pace then stopped and stuck his head into Henry's office. Henry looked up.

'I'm sorry, Henry.'

'They know I voted for Bush?'

Book nodded.

'Damn.'

Book continued down the hall. He had secured tenure four years before, at age thirty-one. Clerking for Justice Kennedy, winning two Supreme Court cases, and making the shortlist of potential candidates for the Court does that sort of thing for a law professor. The law school would be embarrassed to have a faculty member nominated for the Supreme Court but denied tenure. Henry Lawson was not a Supreme Court candidate.

Nor was he a celebrity law professor.

Book was. After his Supreme Court clerkship, he could have taught at any law school in America. But he came home to be near his mother after she had been diagnosed with early-onset Alzheimer's. Eight years later, she still lived in the same house where she had raised her children, but she did not know her children and could not find her way home. Book entered the outer office of his suite. Myrna held pink message slips in the air.

'Your sister called. She wants to put your mother in a home.'

'Did you tell her, "Hell no"?'

Myrna knew not to answer. 'And James Welch called.'

'Who's he?'

'Our boss. Chairman of the Board of Regents. Appointed by the governor himself.'

'Another billionaire alumnus wanting to fire me because he didn't like what I said on *Face the Nation*.'

'He doesn't want to fire you. He wants to hire you.'

'For what?'

'Didn't say. Might have something to do with his son.'

'Who's his son?'

'Sophomore. Arrested for drug possession. On Sixth Street. It made the paper.'

Book took the pink slip. 'I'll call him from Marfa.'

'*Marfa?*' She groaned. 'Oh, no, not another letter.'

Book waved Nathan Jones's letter in the air as he walked

into his office where Nadine Honeywell still sat reading his mail. He grabbed the crash helmet off the bookshelf and held it out to her. She frowned at the helmet as if it were a bloody murder weapon.

'What's that for?'

Chapter 4

'I'm hungry, my butt's numb, and I think I swallowed a bug!'

It was just after eleven the next morning. Nadine Honeywell required twenty-four hours' advance notice prior to leaving town. She wore the crash helmet, goggles over her black glasses, and number 100 sunblock on all skin exposed by her short-sleeve shirt and shorts. She sat higher in the second seat. Book wore jeans, boots, a black T-shirt, black doo-rag, and sunglasses. He glanced back at his intern; she was holding her cell phone out. He yelled over the engine noise.

'What are you doing?'

'Trying to text!'

'Why?'

'I always text when I drive!'

'You're not driving. You're riding.'

'Close enough!'

Book had installed the windshield so they didn't eat (all the) bugs for four hundred miles, the leather saddlebags to hold their gear, and the second seat for Nadine. He had picked her up at seven. Four hours and three hundred miles on the back of the big Harley hadn't improved her mood.

'There's a rest stop up ahead. I'll pull over. We can stretch.'

'I've got a better idea. Let's turn back!'

They had ridden west out of Austin on Highway 290 through the Hill Country then picked up Interstate 10, the 'Cowboy Autobahn' where the posted speed limit was eighty but the actual limit pushed one hundred. They were now deep in the parched high plains of West Texas. Other than the four-lane interstate and the wind farms—thousands of three-hundred-foot-tall turbine windmills dotted the land-scape on both sides, their blades rotating as if propellers trying to push Texas eastward—the landscape remained as desolate and untouched as it had been at the beginning of time. Book steered off the highway and into the rest stop. He slowed to a stop, cut the engine, and kicked the stand down. Nadine hopped off as if she had been adrift at sea and now touched land for the first time in a year.

'My God, you never heard of cars? With climate control and CD players?'

She yanked off the helmet and goggles, shook out her shoulder-length hair, and wiped sweat from her face. Book removed his sunglasses and the doo-rag then pulled two bottles of water from a saddlebag. He handed one bottle to his intern; she drank half.

'I could really use a caramel frappuccino right about now, but I haven't seen a Starbucks since we left Austin.'

'I don't think you're going to find one out here, Ms. Honeywell.'

'It's like a desert.'

'It is a desert. The upper reaches of the Chihuahuan Desert.'

'What are those?'

She pointed to the horizon where a low ridgeline with craggy peaks stood silhouetted against the blue sky.

'Mountains.'

'In Texas?'

Mountains in Texas. Book had ridden the Harley through much of Texas, but not this part of Texas. Of course, it took some amount of riding to cover all of Texas; the state encompassed 268,000 square miles.

'How much longer?' Nadine asked.

'Couple of hours.'

'I'm hungry.'

Book reached into a pocket of his jeans and pulled out a package of beef jerky. He handed a strip to Nadine. She took the jerky with her fingertips and held it out as if examining a dead rat.

'You're joking?'

'High in protein.'

She made a face and extended the jerky his way. He took the jerky and clamped the strip between his teeth then reached into another pocket and removed a granola bar. He offered it to her.

'Good carbs.'

She regarded the granola bar a moment then gestured at his clothing.

'You got another pocket with hot dogs?'

'Sorry.'

Her shoulders slumped in surrender. She set the water bottle on the bike and pulled out a bottle of Purell hand sanitizer; she squirted the gel and rubbed her hands together then took the granola bar and bit off a piece. He chewed the jerky.

'I'm missing my Civ Proc class,' she said.

'You can learn rules anytime.' Book spread his arms. 'This is where a real lawyer works, Ms. Honeywell—in the real world. Not in an air-conditioned office on the fiftieth floor.'

'I'm going to write wills.'

'Why? That's boring.'

She shrugged. 'Not a lot of danger in estate planning.'

'You ever meet an heir cut out of his daddy's will?'

They came to law school without a clue what it meant to be

a lawyer. It wasn't sitting in a fancy office poring over discovery for eight hours and billing ten. Being a lawyer was about helping people in need. Real people, not rich people. Book was determined to teach his interns that the law wasn't found in the casebooks but out here in the world beyond the classroom. They came to him as law students; they would leave as lawyers.

'Professor, can I ask you a question?'

He chewed the jerky and nodded.

'Why are you doing this? You read that letter then jump onto this motorcycle and ride to the middle of a desert? And drag me along? Why? Why do you care so much about Nathan Jones?'

'He was my student four years ago.'

'How many students have you taught? A few thousand? What makes him so special?'

'He was also my intern.'

'For how long?'

'One month.'

'You knew him for one month four years ago, and now you're dropping everything to help him?'

Book stared at the distant ridgeline and thought of Nathan Jones.

'He saved my life.'

She frowned. '*How?*'

'Long story. And we've still got a long ride.'

She regarded him for a long moment while she finished off the granola bar. Then she said, 'Next time, get the kind with the chocolate coating.'

Book donned the doo-rag and sunglasses then swung a leg over the Harley.

'You ready?'

'No.'

But she bucked herself up then strapped on the goggles, pulled on the helmet, and climbed on behind him. He started

59

the engine, shifted into gear, and accelerated past roadside signs that read 'Burn Ban in Effect' and 'Water 4 Sale' and onto the long black ribbon of asphalt disappearing into the distant horizon.

One hundred thirty years before, Hanna Maria Strobridge saw the same distant horizon from her seat inside her husband's private railroad car. His name was James Harvey Strobridge, and he built railroad lines for the Galveston, Harrisburg, and San Antonio Railroad. He had built the very line they rode on that day. Hanna had ridden in that private car from California to Texas; she had even been at Promontory Point in the Utah Territory for the driving of the golden spike in 1869 when the first transcontinental railroad was completed. At the time, James was the foreman for Central Pacific Railroad, which built the track eastward from California. After a moment, Hanna dropped her eyes from the horizon to her book, Feodora Dostoyevsky's latest, *The Brothers Karamazov*. She fancied Russian novels and striped skirts.

Two hours later, the train stopped at a water depot bordered by three mountain ranges. Hanna had no idea where they were because the depot had no name. Her husband, as superintendent of railroad construction, possessed the sole and absolute authority to name every water depot and other unnamed locale within the railroad's right-of-way. But he had no imagination for naming persons or places, so he had delegated his authority to his wife.

'Well, Hanna, what are you gonna name this little no-count place?'

She pondered a moment and thought of the servant in her book named Martha Ignatyevna. Of course, 'Martha' was the English translation; in Russian, her name was—

'Marfa.'

And so it was.

'And that's how Marfa got its name,' Book said.

60

From the back seat: 'Fascinating.'

Sitting four hundred miles due west of Austin, two hundred miles southeast of El Paso, sixty miles north of the Rio Grande, and a mile above sea level, the high desert land colloquially known as *el despoblado*—'the unpopulated'—and geologically as the Marfa Plateau is generally unfit for human occupancy. It's not bad for cattle, if it rains. If it doesn't, it's not so hospitable to them either. But man's nature drives him to settle the unsettled frontier; and so men have tried in Marfa, Texas.

From a distance, as you come down off the Chisos Mountains from the east and onto the plateau, you see the Davis Mountains to the north and the Chinati Mountains to the south; between the ranges lies a vast expanse of yellow grassland. And smack in the middle you see a small stand of trees, hunched together as if seeking safety in numbers against the relentless wind whipping across the land. The trees, planted by the first settlers, offer the only shade for a hundred miles in any direction and define the boundaries of the town of Marfa. As you come closer, you see the peach-colored cupola atop the Presidio County Courthouse peeking above the treetops as if on lookout for rampaging Indian war parties. But no savage Comanche galloping across the land on horseback threatened the peace in Marfa that day; only a Con Law professor riding a Harley with his reluctant intern perched behind him.

Book downshifted the Harley as they entered town on San Antonio Street and rode past a Dollar General store on the north side and dilapidated adobe homes on the south; Presidio County ranked as the poorest in Texas and looked it, except for a few renovated buildings housing art galleries. He braked at the only red light in town then pointed to the blue sky where a yellow glider soared overhead in silence. Nadine pointed south at an old gas station on the corner that had been converted into a restaurant called the Pizza Foundation; her face was that of a child who had spotted Santa Claus at the mall.

61

'Pizza!'

'Let's talk to Nathan Jones first. Maybe he'll have lunch with us, tell us his story.'

'What time's your appointment?'

'Didn't make one.'

'Why not?'

'Better to arrive unannounced. Nathan was always given to drama, probably read too many Grisham novels.'

'Just so you know, if he made me ride six hours on this motorcycle for nothing, I'm going to beat him like a redheaded stepchild.'

In the rearview mirror, Book saw a green-and-white Border Patrol SUV pull up behind the Harley and hit its lights. He cut the engine and kicked the stand down; he noticed Hispanics on nearby sidewalks scurrying away. Two agents wearing green uniforms and packing holstered weapons got out of the SUV and sauntered over. Both were young men; one was Anglo and looked like a thug, the other Hispanic and an altar boy. The thug eyed the Harley.

'What's that, an eighty-nine softtail classic?'

'Eighty-eight.'

'You restore it yourself?'

'I did.'

'Turquoise and black, I like that. And the black leather saddlebags with the silver studs. Cool. What engine is that?'

'Evo V-2.'

'Damn, that's a fine ride.'

The thug admired the bike then Nadine perched high in the back seat and finally turned his attention to Book.

'You Mexican?'

Book glared at the agent.

'Do I look Mexican?'

'You look like an Injun, but we don't get Injuns around here no more, just Mexicans.'

The Hispanic agent's expression seemed pained. He took a

step slightly in front of the thug. He was either the good cop in a good cop/bad cop routine or genuinely embarrassed by his partner.

'You look familiar. Where have I seen you?'

'On national TV, you dopes,' Nadine said from behind. 'He's famous.'

'Who you calling dopes?' the thug said. Then he turned to Book and said, 'Were you the bachelor?'

A look of recognition came across the Hispanic agent's face; he smiled broadly.

'No, he's the professor. Bookman. I watch you every Sunday morning. It's an honor to meet you, sir. I'm Agent Angel'— *AHN-hell*—'Acosta.'

'John Bookman.' They shook hands then Book aimed a thumb at the back seat. 'My intern, Nadine Honeywell.'

'And this is my partner, Wesley Crum. Please excuse his bad manners, Professor, he was raised by the scorpions in the desert.'

'Funny,' the thug named Wesley said.

'Did you come to Marfa to see the art?' Agent Acosta said. 'Judd's boxes? Chamberlain's crushed cars? Flavin's fluorescent lights?'

'Uh, yes,' Book said. 'That's why we're here.'

Agent Crum's eyes loitered on Book's back-seat passenger. 'I got fluorescent lights in my trailer,' he said with a grin, 'if you want to see them.'

Nadine sighed. 'Dope.'

Agent Crum's grin turned into a frown.

'Enjoy your stay, Professor,' Agent Acosta said. '*Bienvenidos.*'

Book fired up the engine and gunned the Harley through the light and turned north on Highland Avenue. He saw in the rearview the two agents engaged in an animated conversation.

'Dopes, Ms. Honeywell?'

'I call them as I see them, Professor.'

They cruised slowly up Highland, apparently the main street in town. It dead-ended at the courthouse that loomed large

63

above the low-slung buildings. They rode past the Marfa City Hall on the right and then a row of refurbished storefronts occupied by the Marfa Public Radio station, the Marfa Book Company, and a shop called Tiend M that sold handmade jewelry. On the very visible side exterior wall of one building graffiti had been painted in large strokes like a billboard: *The Real Axis of Evil is the US, UK, and Israel.* A city crew with brushes prepared to paint over the message, no doubt unappreciated in West Texas. They crossed El Paso Street, and Nadine pointed again.

'Food Shark!'

Parked under a large shed with picnic tables was a silver food truck with 'Food Shark' stenciled across the side and a few customers at the service window. A sign read *Marfa Lights Up My Judd.* Bicycles were parked under the shed and foreign-made hybrids at the curb; one had a bumper sticker that read WWDJD? On the north side of the shed ran railroad tracks; Book hit the brakes hard as the crossing arms came down. The red lights flashed, and a train whistle sounded; a cargo train soon roared through downtown Marfa on its way west to El Paso. Hanna's train still came through town, but it was now the Union Pacific.

When the arms rose, Book accelerated over the tracks and across Oak Street and past Quintana's Barber Shop, the state Child Protective Services office, and the Iron Heart Gym. Other than the activity under the shed, downtown Marfa sat silent—no car horns, no sirens, no squealing tires, no sounds of the city. There was no traffic and few pedestrians. No joggers, cabs, pedicabs, or panhandling homeless people that one encountered in downtown Austin. It was as if the town were taking a siesta. Across Texas Street was a building with a replica of an oil rig on the roof; on the far side of Highland sat the two-story, white stucco El Paisano Hotel.

'Back in the fifties, they filmed *Giant* here,' Book said. 'All the stars stayed there.'

'That was a movie?'

'You've never heard of *Giant*?'

'Nope.'

'It's an epic about Texas' transformation from a cattle economy to an oil economy.'

'Sounds exciting.'

'It's a classic. Rock Hudson played a cattle baron.'

'Never heard of him.'

'He's dead. James Dean played a ranch hand turned oil tycoon.'

'Never heard of him either.'

'You've never heard of James Dean?'

'Is he on Twitter?'

'He's dead.'

'Well, there you go.'

'What about Elizabeth Taylor? She played the cattle baron's wife.'

'Is she that blonde movie star who used to date Clinton then committed suicide a long time ago?'

'That'd be Marilyn Monroe. She dated Kennedy. Overdosed on pills.'

'Never heard of her.'

'She's dead, too.'

'How am I supposed to know about dead people?'

'How about Donald Judd?'

'You're making these names up, right?'

'No.'

'Who did he play in *Giant*?'

'No one. He was an artist here in Marfa.'

'Let me guess: he's dead, too?'

'He is.'

'Is there anyone in this town who's not dead?'

Book turned right at the shuttered Palace Theater onto Lincoln Street and parked in front of a one-story building facing the courthouse. A small sign on the stucco façade read:

THE DUNN LAW FIRM with MIDLAND–LUBBOCK–AMARILLO–MARFA in smaller letters below. They got off the Harley. Book removed his sunglasses and doo-rag and knocked the dust off his T-shirt and jeans. Nadine removed the crash helmet and goggles and smoothed back her hair. They entered the law firm offices and stepped into a well-appointed reception area. Hallways extended off both sides. In the center along the back wall sat a receptionist behind a desk. Her head was down. They walked over to her. She wore a black dress. She wiped tears from her red face with a white tissue then blew her nose. She finally looked up at Book.

'You okay?' he asked.

'Funeral.' She wiped tears again. 'This afternoon.'

'I'm sorry for your loss.'

She nodded then forced a professional expression.

'Can I help you?'

'I'm John Bookman, to see Nathan Jones.'

Her professional expression evaporated; she frowned and appeared confused.

'*Nathan?* But . . . it's his funeral.'

Chapter 5

'Rock Hudson, James Dean, Elizabeth Taylor, Donald Judd, Nathan Jones . . . does everyone in Marfa die?' Nadine Honeywell asked.

'Eventually.'

On the western edge of town, out on San Antonio Street past the Thunderbird Motel and the Pueblo Market, across the street from a junkyard and adjacent to a mobile home park, was the Marfa Cemetery. A chain link fence ran down the center of the cemetery. West of the fence were the graves of the deceased of Mexican descent; some of the gravesites would qualify as religious shrines. East of the fence were the graves of Anglos; small American flags fluttering in the wind marked many of the gravesites. A dirt road crisscrossed the cemetery. They had ridden the Harley in and now leaned against the bike a respectful distance from the burial of Nathan Jones.

'A car accident,' Book said. 'Same day he mailed the letter.'

Through tears, the receptionist had provided the basics of Nathan's death.

'Coincidence.' Nadine turned to him. 'Can we go home now?'

'No.'

'Why not?'

'Because I don't believe in coincidences.'

'I was afraid you were going to say that.'

Book hadn't been to a funeral in twenty-one years. Five hundred police officers from around the state of Texas had turned out in full uniform for Ben Bookman's funeral; they do that for a fellow officer killed in the line of duty. Not so much for lawyers. Only a few dozen people were gathered at the gravesite. Some were dressed like lawyers, most like cowboys in jeans and boots and plaid shirts. A young woman wearing jeans and a black T-shirt stood alone off to one side; she looked their way for a moment then looked away. Book spotted the receptionist in her black dress; she dabbed her eyes with a handkerchief. An older couple seemed distraught; probably Nathan's parents. A young, very pregnant woman stood next to them; she stepped forward and placed a red rose on the casket. No doubt Nathan's wife. Next to her stood one of those locals, a large young man with blond curly hair; he put an arm around her shoulders. Family or family friend. A white-haired man snapped photographs from the perimeter. After the service ended and the crowd began to disperse, Book approached the pregnant woman.

'Ms. Jones?'

'Yes.'

'I'm Professor Bookman. From UT. Nathan wrote to me.'

Her eyes darted around then she stepped close and lowered her voice.

'Not here. They're watching. Come to my house. Tonight. I'm in the book.'

'I'm not sleeping in a teepee.'

El Cosmico occupied eighteen acres just south of town and adjacent to the Border Patrol station. Its website touted a 'unique communal outpost in West Texas,' but Nadine wasn't convinced. Accommodations ranged from refurbished Airstream trailers to safari tents and authentic Sioux teepees. A community bathhouse with a tub and toilet came with the price. Dubbed a 'hippie campground' by the locals, El Cosmico was the latest venture of the woman behind the Hotel San José and Jo's Coffee in Austin. Book was a regular at Jo's, so he had decided to give it a try. But his intern was having none of it.

'And I don't share toilets with strangers.'

She sighed and shook her head as if faced with an impossible task.

'I can't even imagine how many sanitizing wipes I'd go through.'

'Ms. Honeywell, you're a mighty picky traveling companion, you do know that?'

'So sue me.'

'Spoken like a true lawyer.'

Ten minutes later, they stood at the front desk of the El Paisano Hotel. The lobby of the Spanish baroque, pueblo-deco style hotel featured leather chairs and ottomans, colorful Mexican tiled floors, exposed wood beams, and—

'OMG,' Nadine said. 'Is that a buffalo head on the wall?'

'And a longhorn.' Book turned to the desk clerk. 'Just one night.'

Nadine dug her cell phone out of her canvas bag and took a photo of the stuffed heads.

'No one back home will believe this.'

'Your name?' the clerk said.

'John Bookman.'

The clerk broke into a big smile. 'Professor Bookman, welcome to the Paisano. We were expecting you.'

'You were?'

'Your secretary—Myrna?—she called ahead and made reservations for you and Miss Honeywell. I have some messages for you.'

The clerk disappeared behind the counter.

'Where's the nearest Starbucks?' Nadine asked. 'I'm dying for caffeine.'

The clerk reappeared and said, 'No Starbucks in Marfa.'

Nadine stared as if the clerk had said, 'No oxygen in Marfa.' 'You're joking?'

The clerk shrugged at her then handed three message slips to Book: Myrna, his sister, and James Welch. Nadine shook off her Starbucks shock and held her phone up as if trying to gauge the wind in the lobby.

'Why can't I get through?'

'Cell phone service,' the clerk said, 'it's a bit sketchy out here.'

Nadine responded with the same look of utter disbelief.

'No Starbucks or texting—are we still in America?'

'You're still in Texas.'

The clerk handed room keys to Book.

'Professor, you're in the Rock Hudson suite, and Miss Honeywell is in the Elizabeth Taylor suite. Rooms two-eleven and two-twelve.'

'Great, now we're sleeping in dead people's beds,' she said.

'They were alive when they slept here. Let's wash up and get some lunch, figure out where we go from here.'

'Home.'

'Enjoy the art,' the desk clerk said.

Book carried their gear up the flight of stairs—there was no elevator—and down the corridor to their rooms.

James Dean practiced rope tricks in the courtyard of the El Paisano Hotel. Rock Hudson and Elizabeth Taylor partied with the cast and crew in the dining room. Director George Stevens reviewed the 'dailies' in the ballroom each evening; locals were welcome. And they came. For six weeks in the summer of 1955, Hollywood lived in the Paisano, and Marfa was Cinderella at the ball.

70

But the ball ended, Hollywood went home, and Marfa was left to its old life. The town and the hotel began a steady slide. By 2001, Marfa was the county seat of the poorest county in Texas, and the Paisano was sold at a tax foreclosure auction on the steps of the Presidio County Courthouse. No one imagined that day that there would be a Hollywood ending for both the town and the hotel. But there was—but not because of Hollywood.

Because of art.

Book deposited Nadine in Elizabeth Taylor's room then went next door to his room. Rock Hudson had been comfortable: living room, full kitchen, bedroom, and private rooftop balcony. Book dropped his bag then looked for the room phone. There wasn't one. So he dialed Myrna on his cell then stepped out onto the balcony. Myrna's voice soon came over, a bit scratchy but audible.

'You made it to Marfa safely?'

The mother in Myrna.

'We did.'

'How's Nadine?'

'Homesick. How'd you know we'd stay at the Paisano?'

'Nadine didn't seem like the camping-out type, not with all that hand sanitizer. When are you coming back?'

'Tomorrow, probably. You remember Nathan Jones? He interned for me four years back?'

'Of course I remember Nathan. He saved my job.' She thought that was funny. 'Why?'

'He wrote me that letter, asking for help.'

'Are you going to help him?'

'No.'

'Why not?'

'He's dead.'

Book called his sister next. Joanie was thirty-one and a new mother. He had given her away at her wedding three years before to a doctor named Dennis. Book's new brother-in-law

71

had advised them to put their mother in a home. But what the hell did he know about Alzheimer's? He was a proctologist.

'Book, we've got to talk about putting Mom in a home.'

'No.'

'I know you don't want to, but—'

'She didn't put us in a home. She went back to work after Dad died.'

Clare Bookman had kept the books and paid the bills for a dozen small businesses in Austin; now she couldn't balance her own checkbook.

'And Dad sure as hell wouldn't have put her in a home.'

Alzheimer's had made his mother a stranger in her own body. In her own house. To her own children. She would not have wanted to live like that. But it was too late for her to make that choice. The disease had made the choice for her. When the time came for Book, he would make the choice before the disease made it for him.

'Book, she doesn't even know who we are anymore.'

'We know who she is.'

'Book—'

'Joanie—that's not going to happen. She can live with me.'

'And all your sleep-over girlfriends?'

'They won't sleep over anymore.'

'And how will you take her anywhere? On the back of that Harley?'

'I'll buy a car.'

'What would you buy that's fast enough and dangerous enough?'

'A minivan.'

She laughed. He liked Joanie's laugh.

'Indiana Jones in a minivan? I don't think so. Besides, Book, you're always gone. Like now.'

'I'll hire around-the-clock caregivers.'

'That's expensive.'

'Can you say "book royalties"?'

'I thought that was going to be your retirement fund?'

From the rooftop balcony two stories up, Book could see all of Marfa and the desert beyond. The prairie grass gleamed yellow in the sun.

'I don't figure on living to retirement age.'

'Oh, Book, don't talk like that. Just because Mom . . . that doesn't mean . . .' She sighed into the phone. 'What are you doing in Marfa?'

'Working.'

'Another adventure?'

'A dead lawyer.'

His last call was to James Welch, chairman of the Board of Regents for the University of Texas System, a nonprofit organization possessing a $21 billion endowment, numerous real-estate developments, two million acres of prime oil land, stakes in a world-class golf club, a radio station and a cable TV sports channel, the most expensive and profitable football team in America, and fifteen universities and medical schools throughout Texas educating over two hundred thousand students. The University of Texas at Austin is the flagship campus. James Welch had earned an MBA from UT thirty-three years before; today, he boasted a $3 billion net worth. He was the most powerful man in higher education in Texas.

'Professor Bookman, thanks for calling me back.'

'Sorry for the delay, Mr. Welch. I had to leave town unexpectedly.'

'Your secretary said you were in Marfa. The wife and I went out there a few years back. She wanted to see the art. Boxes and crushed cars and fluorescent lights—I didn't get it.'

He exhaled.

'Well, as you may have heard, Professor, my son, Robert, was arrested for drug possession with intent to distribute. They took his blood without his consent.'

73

'What was he doing when the police arrested him?'

'Leaning against his car parked on Sixth Street. Cop came along and arrested him.'

'He didn't say or do anything to the police officer?'

'Knowing Bobby, he probably smarted off. Never been one to keep his mouth shut. Like his mother. But how can they do that, take his blood without his consent? Is that constitutional?'

The definition of a liberal: a conservative who had been arrested.

'Good question. No answer as yet. So they arrested your son, searched his car, and found drugs?'

'Cocaine.'

'How much?'

'The police report says a pound.'

'That's more than recreational.'

'Bobby's not a drug dealer, Professor. He's a user. And he's going into rehab at the Betty Ford Clinic, if he gets out of jail. And the case is dismissed. And his record expunged.'

'Mr. Welch, you should hire an experienced criminal defense lawyer.'

'I did. Scotty Raines. He said the search and seizure was illegal, no probable cause to search his Beemer or take a blood sample. He suggested I hire you.'

'Why?'

'Because if Scotty says the search and seizure was illegal, the judge will still hold a trial. But you're a famous constitutional law expert. If you say the search and seizure was illegal, the judge will dismiss the case.'

'You want me to write a brief?'

'And argue the issue in court, if necessary. I'm prepared to pay you handsomely.'

'You don't think your status is enough to'—Book wanted to say, 'Get him off,' but didn't—'remedy this situation?'

'In Dallas, sure. But this is Austin, not exactly a hotbed of Republicans. The D.A. is a Democrat. I'm a big Republican donor in Texas, and I supported the D.A.'s opponent in the last election.'

'Whoops.'

'Whoops is right, Professor.'

Book pondered a moment. Sitting in the Travis County Jail for six months to a year with hardened criminals wouldn't do the young Welch any good. He needed to be in rehab.

'Professor?'

'I'll do it. I'll talk to your lawyer and write your brief.'

'Thank you. What do I owe you?'

'Nothing.'

'You're going to work for free?'

As if Book had said a recount had made Romney the winner.

'No. In return, I want two promises from you. And these are non-negotiable, Mr. Welch.'

'Shoot.'

'First, your son goes into residential rehab, not some one-hour-a-week outpatient therapy. Six months minimum.'

'Six months? He'll fall behind in school.'

'Better than falling behind in life.'

'All right. Six months. I'm taking him out there myself. Professor, I love my son. I will take care of him.' He hesitated a moment then said, 'When I was at UT, we got drunk on Lone Star beer. Now it's cocaine. Why do kids use drugs?'

'I don't know, Mr. Welch.'

The line was silent for a long moment then Welch's voice came across.

'What's the second promise?'

Chapter 6

His intern didn't answer her door when Book rang the bell—the Rock Hudson and Elizabeth Taylor suites had doorbells—so he went downstairs. He checked the phone book at the front desk for Nathan Jones's home address and jotted it down in the small notebook he always carried in his back pocket. He asked the desk clerk for the local paper, but it was a weekly and the last edition had come out the day before Nathan died; the new edition would come out the next day. He asked the clerk for the location of the newspaper office. He then searched for his intern.

He found her in the *Giant* museum.

In a small space off the lobby, *Giant* memorabilia, movie posters, photographs, coffee mugs, T-shirts, caps, and shot glasses were offered for sale, and on a small television the film ran in a loop. Nadine Honeywell sat in a leather chair in front of the screen with her feet kicked up on an ottoman and her eyes focused through her black glasses on the movie. Book had watched *Giant* several times, as had every Texan of age; it was the national movie of Texas. On the screen, Jett Rink, the ranch hand turned oil tycoon played by James Dean, had just struck oil on the small tract of land he had inherited from Luz

Benedict. He drove straight to the Reata ranch house and sucker-punched his former employer, Bick Benedict, the cattle baron played by Rock Hudson.

'He's gorgeous,' Nadine said. 'And gay.'

'Jett Rink?'

'James Dean.'

'He died a few weeks after they finished shooting the movie here. He was driving fast, heading to a road race in southern California in his Porsche, truck pulled out in front of him, he couldn't stop in time. He was only twenty-four. Lived fast and died young. Never saw the movie, but he was nominated for an Oscar. He made only three films: *Giant, East of Eden,* and *Rebel Without a Cause.*'

Nadine's eyes turned up from the screen to Book. 'So, what, you're trying to be another James Dean?'

'I'm not gay.'

'A rebel without a cause . . . except you're a rebel with too many causes.'

Jett's Grill fronts the courtyard just off the hotel lobby. It's a civilized place with cloth tablecloths, a pink-and-green tile floor, and a wait staff dressed in black. Book ordered tilapia tacos and iced tea. Nadine ordered the *Giant* cheeseburger—one-half pound of Black Angus beef—Parmesan fries, a root beer, and coffee and a chocolate brownie for dessert.

'Ms. Honeywell, would you like a stick of butter with that?'

'No.'

She looked up at the waitress, a young woman with a rose tattoo on her ample bosom. She was an artist; waiting tables was her day job.

'I want ice cream. Vanilla.'

'You know what you're putting inside yourself?'

'Better than a man.'

'Amen,' the waitress said. She winked at Nadine then left with their orders.

His intern had cleaned up and pulled her hair back in a ponytail. Her face was innocent and unadorned. She dug in her canvas bag and pulled out a sanitary wipe packet; she tore open the packet, removed the wipe, and proceeded to rub down the salt and pepper shakers, the silverware—she reached for his, but he moved them away—and her water glass.

'You can't be too careful,' she said.

'I don't know. Maybe you can.'

She again reached into her bag and came out with the Purell hand sanitizer. She squirted the gel into her palm and rubbed her hands as if she were a doctor prepping for surgery. Their table now smelled like a hospital.

'You like that stuff?' Book said.

'Purell is pretty good. Sixty-two percent ethyl alcohol content. Germ-X has sixty-five percent. My favorite is Outlast. It has seventy percent ethyl alcohol, it kills ninety-nine-point-ninety-nine percent of germs, and it lasts six hours. But it's kind of hard on my skin.'

'You don't get out much, do you?'

'The world is full of dangerous germs.'

'Life is dangerous.'

'It was for Nathan.'

Nathan Jones was dead at twenty-nine. He had been Book's intern at twenty-five. For one month. Until that first letter had arrived in the mail. And they had gone to South Texas.

'Was it dangerous for Renée?'

'I guess she thought it was. But I always protected her.'

She sat silent for a moment then said, 'You're right.'

'About what?'

'I don't get out much.'

'You will as my intern.'

Nadine contemplated her sanitized hands.

'Professor . . .'

She turned to him; she was that thirteen-year-old kid again.

'. . . can you protect me?'

'Yes, Ms. Honeywell, I can. And I will.'

'Nothing personal, but you're a law professor. And it's a harsh world.'

'I have skills.'

She regarded him a moment then finished rubbing her hands. She offered the sanitizer to Book.

'I washed upstairs.'

The waitress returned. She placed their drinks on the table then handed a card to Nadine.

'Text me.'

She winked again then walked away.

'I attract lesbians,' Nadine said. 'And no, I'm not.'

Book emptied a sweetener into his iced tea, stirred, and took a long drink. Nadine sucked her root beer through a long straw.

'You ever write a brief?' Book asked.

'In law school?'

'Time you learned.'

'What's the issue?'

'Search and seizure. Fourth Amendment.'

'Who's the client?'

'Bobby Welch.'

'That regent's son.'

'You don't know who Elizabeth Taylor was, but you know who Bobby Welch is?'

'Someone tweeted me that he got arrested for drug possession.'

'That's how you get your news? On Twitter?'

'That's how everyone my age gets the news.' She shrugged. 'No commercials.'

'If I owned CBS stock, I'd sell.'

'What's CBS?'

Book sat back and reread Nathan Jones's letter.

'He said his client was contaminating the groundwater, but didn't say who his client was. Said someone followed him

79

home. Said his wife was scared. Said he had proof. Said he needed my help.'

Book blew out a breath.

'How do I help a dead person?'

'So what are we going to do?'

'If you die from unnatural causes in a small town, there'll usually be an article in the local paper. And an obituary. So, Ms. Honeywell, we're going to find the newspaper office, see what we can learn there. Then we'll ask around town, try to learn the identity of Nathan's mystery client. And we'll visit his wife tonight, see if she has his proof.'

'And go home tomorrow?'

'Probably.'

'*Probably?*'

Book folded and replaced the letter inside the envelope then checked the postmark again.

'He mailed this letter on the fifth, died that night.'

'Coincidence.'

Chapter 7

His intern brushed and flossed her teeth after every meal to prevent cavities and gum disease, or so she had advised him. When she returned downstairs, they proceeded through the hotel courtyard, across Texas Street, and south on Highland Avenue past a row of renovated storefronts. The first display window featured a sleek wood desk; stenciled on the window was *Evan Hughes, Furniture Design and Fabrication*, and below that *Marfa, TX – Brooklyn, NY*. The next storefront sat vacant, but after that was a shop called Stuff that sold stuff. Parked at the curb was an old hearse painted in a Wild West motif with horses and cattle and gunslingers; longhorns had been mounted on the grill.

'Odd,' Nadine said.

She abruptly stopped and examined her arm then stuck her hand inside the canvas bag looped over her shoulder and came out with an aerosol can. She sprayed her arms and legs and neck.

'Germs?' Book asked.

She turned the can so he could read the label: OFF*!*

'Mosquitoes. They carry the West Nile virus. It's an epidemic.'

'In April?'

'You can't be too careful.'

She offered the can to him, but he declined. She was now cleared to continue down the sidewalk. A white two-story adobe-style building with inlaid tile, elaborate wrought iron, and *Brite Building 1931* in black print across the front façade occupied the next block. It housed a restaurant called Maiya's behind a red door, the old Marfa National Bank, and the Ayn Foundation gallery. The featured exhibits were by Maria Zerres and Andy Warhol.

'Let's check it out,' Book said.

They entered the gallery. Displayed inside the bare space were three of Andy Warhol's works based on Da Vinci's *The Last Supper*. A large black-and-white sketch on one wall depicted Jesus at the Last Supper. On another wall was a color version of Jesus. Another had Jesus next to a bodybuilder with the caption, 'Be a Somebody with a Body.'

'Also odd,' Nadine said.

'What's odd is an Andy Warhol exhibit in Marfa, Texas,' Book said.

'You're doing it again.'

'What?'

'Making up names.'

'I'm not making it up. Andy Warhol's a famous artist.'

'Is he dead?'

'He is.'

They walked outside just as two young men bounced in as if entering a trendy coffee shop in SoHo; they carried iPhones and wore Keds, skinny jeans, white T-shirts—one had *WWDJD?* stenciled across the front—and porkpie hats like the cop in *The French Connection*.

'They're gay,' Nadine said when they stepped onto the sidewalk.

They continued south and encountered similar young men engaged in their electronic devices and animated conversations. Book said 'howdy' to the next group and got a look in response. He tried 'hidee' on the next ones and got nothing. They wore black-framed glasses, mismatched clothing, fedoras and bowler hats, colorful hair that stuck out like porcupine quills, tattoos, and piercings. Boys walked hand in hand, about as common a sight in West Texas as cattle being herded down Fifth Avenue in New York City. The young men acted with the same aloofness the hipster creative types in the SoCo part of Austin displayed, as if trying too hard to appear endowed by God with genius; which is to say, they acted much the same as law students at UT.

'Also gay,' Nadine said.

'Stop.'

'Just saying.'

'Don't.'

She made a face.

Situated on the north side of the railroad tracks was the old Marfa Wool and Mohair Building. The sandstone-colored building had been converted into an art gallery featuring the works of John Chamberlain. They went inside and were greeted by a young docent wearing a pink T-shirt with *Chinati* printed across the front. He explained the layout of the exhibit then left them to tour on their own.

'Gay,' Nadine whispered.

Book sighed then turned to his intern.

'Why do you do that?'

A perfectly innocent face.

'What?'

'Your gay or straight game.'

She shrugged. 'It's not a game. It's a basic survival skill in San Francisco. For girls. You know, you get all gooey-eyed over this great-looking guy, turns out he likes boys. It can be pretty embarrassing, especially if you've already taken your clothes off.'

'I would think so.'

'You wouldn't believe how many times that's happened to me.'

'Taking your clothes off?'

'Romancing a gay guy. That ever happened to you?'

'Romancing a gay guy? No.'

'Romancing a lesbian and not knowing it?'

'If I didn't know it, how would I know if it happened?'

'Sounds like a law professor's answer. Of course, the odds of finding a straight guy in San Francisco are about the same as finding a gay guy in West Texas.'

She regarded the gay docent.

'Or not.'

John Chamberlain was not gay. He had four wives and three sons and was a renowned sculptor of automotive steel. Bumpers, door panels, fenders—he crushed and twisted the pieces into massive modern art. One of his sculptures had sold for $4.7 million just prior to his demise. Twenty-two of his works were displayed in the building in which Book and Nadine now stood. She stared at a mangled steel sculpture titled *Chili Terlingua*.

'That's art?'

'Well . . .'

'Exactly. Does this Chamberlain guy live here?'

'He's dead.'

'Figures.'

'Marfa sits at the same altitude as Denver,' Book said. 'Hence, the cooler air.'

'But Denver has a Starbucks,' his intern said. 'Hence, I'd rather be in Denver.'

They proceeded along Highland Avenue until they arrived at a storefront with *The Times of Marfa* stenciled across the front plate glass window. Taped to the window was a 'Burn Ban in Effect' notice.

'Small-town publishers, they know everything about

everyone—and they trade in information. You give them a little, they'll give you a lot.'

'Like my aunt.'

'Is she in the newspaper business?'

'The gossip business. If I want my mother to know something, I tell my aunt. Faster that way.'

'Well, if you want to know what's going on in a small town, you read the local paper. And if you want to stir the pot in a small town, you put a story in the paper.'

'And do we?'

'Do we what?'

'Want to stir the pot?'

'Yes, Ms. Honeywell, we do.'

'That sounds dangerous.'

'It can be.'

They opened the screen door—the inside door was propped open with a large rock—and stepped into a small office. An older man sat at a desk behind a waist-high counter with his head cocked back slightly, apparently so he could focus on the computer screen in front of him through his reading glasses. He glanced at them over his glasses then went back to his typing. After a moment, he stood and walked over. He looked like one of the Beach Boys on their fiftieth reunion tour; his hair was white, his eyes blue, and his shirt Hawaiian. He wore a red 'MARFA' cap. A toothpick dangled from his lips like a cigarette. He was the photographer at Nathan Jones's funeral. He stuck a weathered hand across the counter.

'Professor Bookman, I presume.'

They shook hands.

'Sam Walker . . . owner, publisher, reporter, typesetter, printer, and delivery boy. I write the paper up front and print it out back. That's what you're smelling, the ink.'

'John Bookman. And Nadine Honeywell, my intern.'

'Welcome to Marfa.' Sam Walker chuckled. 'Boy, you really

lit into McConnell and Schumer last Sunday. I like that—you don't play favorites.'

'I don't have favorites.'

'I expect not.'

'How'd you know I was in town?'

'Word travels fast from the Paisano. We know who's in town before they get up to their rooms. We get all kinds of celebrities these days. Robert Redford was in town last week, flew in to see the art. And that Quaid boy—not the one that was in *G.I. Joe*—'

'*G.I. Joe?*'

'No, the other one. He and his wife moved here, bought a storefront on Highland next to Evan Hughes's furniture shop, figured on fixin' it up for their home, but then Hollywood hit men came gunning for them so they hightailed it up to Canada.'

'Hollywood hit men?'

'That's what they said. Course, I'm not sure all the lights are on. Anyway, he defaulted on the purchase note, the owner foreclosed, and they had a sheriff's auction on the sidewalk, sold all his stuff.'

'Sounds like you know everything going on in your town.'

'I've lived seventy-two years now, Professor, all but my four college years right here in Marfa and the last fifty right in this spot, observing and reporting. So I keep up with things. Course, it ain't that hard, not when there's only two folks per square mile in all of Presidio County. Only so much news those few folks can create.'

'Is Marfa a better place now than when you started the paper?'

'It's different. Better is a point of view, not a fact.'

'You sound like an old-style newsman.'

'Well, I am old.'

'This the only newspaper in town?'

'In the county. Weekly. Next edition comes out tomorrow.'

86

Sam held up two mock front pages.

'Slow news week, so I'm trying to decide on the lead story. I got one story about the roller derby returning to Marfa and another about a ton of marijuana found by the Border Patrol in a bulldozer blade. What do you think, Professor?'

'Roller derby.'

'That's what I figured.'

'Mr. Walker—'

'Sam. So you folks come out to see Judd's boxes and Flavin's fluorescent lights?'

'And a former student. Nathan Jones.'

Sam grimaced. 'Boy, that was a damn shame. Married, about to be a daddy.'

'Did you know him?'

'Never heard of him till he died last week. Must've been low profile, for me not to know him. Bad accident out on Sixty-seven. Folks out here drive too damn fast. Course, when you drive a hundred miles for lunch, hard to drive the speed limit, even if it is eighty.'

'Did you write an article about the accident or an obituary?'

'Both. They'll be in tomorrow's paper.'

'Mind if I read them today?'

Sam shrugged. 'Sure. Why not?'

He walked over to his desk and returned with two short articles. He placed them on the counter. Book read the first article.

LOCAL LAWYER DIES IN ONE-CAR ACCIDENT

Nathan Jones, 29, a lawyer with The Dunn Law Firm in Marfa, was killed in a one-car accident on the north side of Highway 67 nine miles east of town Thursday night about 11 P.M. Sheriff Brady Munn investigated the accident and reported that Jones apparently fell asleep, ran off the road, lost control of his vehicle, and crashed into a pump jack.

87

The pickup truck's gas tank ruptured and exploded. Jones died at the scene. 'Speed was a contributing factor in the accident,' Sheriff Munn said. Jones was returning to Marfa from Midland where he had business at his law firm's offices. Thomas A. Dunn, senior partner at the firm in Midland, expressed shock at Jones's death. 'He was a fine young lawyer and a fine young man. We will miss Nathan.'

'Good-looking boy,' Sam said.
A photograph of Nathan accompanied the obituary.

JONES, NATHANIEL WILLIAM, 29, went to be with his Lord and Savior on April 5th. Nathan was born on February 12, 1983. He grew up on his family's cattle ranch west of Marfa. He graduated from Marfa High School then Texas Tech University with a degree in English. He attended law school at the University of Texas in Austin and received his law degree in 2009. He was a member of the Texas Bar Association and was employed with The Dunn Law Firm in Marfa. Nathan is survived by his wife, Brenda, who is expecting their first child, and his parents, William and Edna. Funeral services were at the First Baptist Church with burial at the Marfa Cemetery.

'Only problem with a weekly,' Sam said. 'Sometimes the deceased is already in the ground before the obituary comes out. Least he had a nice funeral.'
'We saw you there. You went even though you didn't know him?'
'When there's not but two thousand folks in town, one dies, it means something. Out here, Professor, folks aren't fungible.'
As law students often seemed to be.
Book had lost contact with Nathan after he had graduated from the law school. He viewed his role as similar to a parent's: to teach the students skills for life in the legal world so they

could survive on their own. Consequently, the students leave law school and their professors behind; they get on with their lives and legal careers. They seldom have contact with their professors except to shake hands at continuing legal education seminars. They return to campus for football games, and if they're successful, to make a donation to the school. If they're very successful, their firms might endow a chair. If they become fabulously rich, they might buy the naming rights for a building or space on campus. Hence, the law school had the Susman Godfrey Atrium, the Joseph D. Jamail Pavilion, the Jamail Center for Legal Research, the Kraft Eidman Courtroom, and the Robin C. Gibbs Atrium. His former intern had not become a rich and famous lawyer. He had not made a donation, endowed a chair, or bought a naming right. He had simply returned home to Marfa and gotten on with his life. And now his life was over. Book could not help but feel that he owed an unpaid debt to Nathan Jones.

'And I took some photos of the funeral service,' Sam said.

'Why?'

'A life ended. Deserves to be documented. So folks won't forget.'

'Do you have a photo of the guests at Nathan's funeral?'

Sam again went to his desk and returned with a computer-generated photograph. He placed it on the counter in front of Book.

'Who are these people?' Book asked.

Sam pointed at faces in the photo. 'She's the wife . . . his parents . . . lawyers, I figure, who else would wear suits? . . . the sheriff . . . Sadie, the court clerk . . . other locals.'

'May I have this photo?'

'Sure.' Sam's eyes turned up to Book. 'You looking into his death, figure maybe it wasn't an accident?'

'What makes you say that?'

'Just hoping for a lead story better than the roller derby.'

'Sorry to disappoint you.'

'Then what brings you to Marfa?'

'We came for the art, stopped in to say hello to Nathan, learned he had died.'

'Same day the boy was buried?'

'Coincidence.'

'Myself, I don't believe in coincidences.'

Nadine threw her hands up. 'What does everyone have against coincidences?'

Sam picked up a digital camera from his desk.

'Mind if I take your picture? For my wall.'

He gestured to the side wall on which photos of celebrities were hung. Book shrugged an okay. He figured Sam Walker might be a friend in Marfa—and he might need a friend. Sam snapped a few photos then held the camera out to Nadine.

'Would you take one of me and the professor?'

Sam came around the counter and stood next to Book. Nadine took their photo and handed the camera back to Sam. He went over to his desk, put the camera down, and picked up a book.

'Would you sign my book? I mean, your book?'

Book autographed the title page.

'I read that article about you in the *New York Times*,' Sam said. 'How people write you letters asking for help and you go off on these adventures, crusades they called them . . . photo didn't do you justice.'

Book decided to take Sam Walker into his confidence.

'Sam, can I trust you?'

Sam leaned in a bit.

'Sure, Professor.'

'Nathan Jones wrote me one of those letters.'

Book pulled out Nathan's letter and handed it to Sam. He looked at both sides of the envelope then removed the letter and read it. His expression turned somber. He slowly folded the letter, put it back inside the envelope, and handed it back to Book, almost as if he didn't want it in his possession.

'Noticed the postmark,' Sam said. 'Same day he died. Another coincidence.'

Book nodded.

'So you came to Marfa because he wrote this letter, only to find him dead. Said someone followed him home, said his wife was scared. Might make a man suspicious.'

'It might.'

'You seen his proof?'

'Not yet.'

'That'd be a big story, fracking contaminating the water. Hope it's not true.'

'Because of the water?'

'Because something like that could blow this town apart.'

'Or get someone killed.'

'Might could.'

Sam studied Book a long moment.

'Professor, mind if I ask you something?'

'Shoot.'

'Why do you care so much about Nathan Jones?'

'I owe him.'

Sam nodded slowly. 'Sheriff said his death was an accident.'

'You trust him?'

'Brady Munn? He's as honest as the desert.'

'Know who Nathan's client might be?'

Sam tapped the image of a big bald man in the funeral photo.

'Gotta be Billy Bob Barnett. Why else would he be at a lawyer's funeral? Biggest fracking guy in the Big Bend. Rolled into town five years back from Odessa. Office is just down the street, oil rig on the roof, can't miss it.'

'I didn't. So Mr. Barnett is an important person in town?'

'You could say that. Twice.'

'Why?'

'Because he's got what Marfa's never had and everyone wants: jobs. Before he came to town, we had damn near twenty-five percent unemployment. Now it's damn near zero. We're still a poor county, just not as poor. Which makes you feel rich, after you've been so poor for so long.'

'So tell me about Marfa.'

Book had shared information with Sam Walker, and now Sam wanted to share with Book. Most lawyers view every conversation as an opportunity to practice their interrogation of a hostile witness; but Book had learned a skill most lawyers never learn: to listen to other people. Sam stepped to the wall and pointed at an old black-and-white photo. The courthouse towered over the town.

'That was Marfa back in the late eighteen-hundreds, only about eight hundred residents. Then they built the courthouse, and we became the county seat. Town started to grow. Government stationed the cavalry here during the Mexican Revolution—they called it Camp Marfa until they changed the name to Fort D. A. Russell. By nineteen thirty, we had almost four thousand residents.'

Sam tapped a framed photograph that showed cavalry soldiers in formation on horseback.

'That's the way the fort looked back then. During World War Two, the government built a POW camp out there, brought in a few hundred German prisoners from Rommel's Afrika Korps. Geneva Convention says prisoners are supposed to be detained in the same climate they were captured in, so it was desert to desert for them. Not sure those Germans might not have opted for California or Colorado if given the choice, but they got Marfa. Apparently they were well behaved, didn't try to escape. Grew vegetables in a garden and painted murals on their barracks, old Building Ninety-Eight. You can go look at it. And we had the Marfa Army Air Field east of town, brought pilots in for flight training. Can't see much from the highway, but go on that Google Earth, you can still see the

92

runways. That was our peak time, over five thousand folks lived here.'

'What happened?'

'We won the war. The army closed up shop, and the Germans went home. Shut down the fort, except for the part used by the Border Patrol to stop bootleg coming across the border. Beer and whiskey, seems kind of quaint now, doesn't it, compared to cocaine and heroin?'

He worked the toothpick.

'And then the rain stopped. Seven years it didn't rain, in the fifties. The great drought. Destroyed cattle ranching and the local economy, such as it was. Old-timers had to sell the herds then the land. Only break from the suffering was when *Giant* came to town. I was fifteen back then. Exciting time. They hired locals for extras, money people damn sure needed. My folks were in the barbecue scene, when Rock brought Liz home to Texas. Cast mingled with the locals between shots, nights at the Paisano—I watched the dailies in the ballroom every night, me and the rest of Marfa. I thought Jimmy Dean was about the coolest guy I'd ever seen, started combing my hair like him. Never knew he was gay. Or Rock Hudson till he died of AIDS.'

Nadine gasped. 'OMG—Bick Benedict was gay?'

Sam eyed her, apparently unsure if she was serious.

'She's been watching the movie at the Paisano,' Book said.

'Oh. Well, I'm afraid he was, little lady.'

'Wow. I didn't see that one coming.'

'Anyway, *Giant* allowed us to forget our troubles for a few months. When they packed up and that train pulled out of town, it was like Marfa's funeral procession. Population's been dropping ever since. Kids get out of high school then out of town—last census, we were down to nineteen hundred and eighty-one souls living here full time. This place was damn near a ghost town. Last one to leave, turn out the lights.'

Sam removed the cap and scratched his head.

'That was before Judd.'

Sam pointed at a photo of an older bearded man.

'Donald Judd. Big-time artist up in New York City, decided to move his operation to Marfa in nineteen seventy-three. Wanted his art to be set in place permanently. "Installation art," they call it. Judd bought vacant buildings on Highland—there were many to choose from—the Marfa National Bank Building, the Crews Hotel, the Safeway grocery store, the Wool and Mohair Building . . . renovated them into studios and galleries.'

'We checked out the Chamberlain exhibit in the Wool and Mohair Building.'

Sam gestured with the toothpick. 'I'm an open-minded sort of man. I've actually grown fond of Judd's boxes, and I'm warming up to Flavin's lights. But crushed car parts? That's art?'

'See?' Nadine said to Book. 'I'm not the only non-believer.'

'Then Judd bought the fort. Three hundred forty acres. Turned the artillery sheds and barracks into galleries, put up outside art—sixty big concrete boxes, damnedest thing you've ever seen, right on the field where Patton played polo. He was an interesting man, Judd. Loved bagpipes. I don't know why.'

'You knew him? Personally?'

'I did. Talked to him many times. Said he moved to Marfa because he hated the show business and commerce art had become in New York. Wanted to get away from that world. And if you want to get away from the world, by God, this is your place. From here to Hell Paso—thirty thousand square miles—there's not but thirty thousand people. Judd kept to himself, and locals didn't bother him—hell, no one knew who he was, or cared. He fell in love with this land, bought forty thousand acres south of town, called it Las Casas. He's buried out there, died in ninety-four. Lymphoma. Place was still a ghost town when he died. No jobs, no celebrities, no

94

businesses, the Paisano was shuttered, tourists came for the Marfa Lights not the art, and Highland Avenue was nothing but vacant storefronts except for Judd's galleries.'

'People weren't coming to see his art?'

'Judd shunned publicity like the Amish shun the modern world. He lived like a monk out there on his ranch, no electricity, no hot water, no people. Like I said, he came here to escape the world, not invite it in.'

'What happened? The buildings on Highland aren't vacant now.'

'After Judd died, the mayor and other movers and shakers in town, people in the game—'

'What game?'

'The money game.'

'And you don't play that game?'

Sam Walker spread his arms to the small office.

'My media empire. Professor, I publish this paper because the history of Marfa and the Big Bend needs to be recorded. I think that's important. This isn't a business to me—hell, I barely break even most months. I expect constitutional law means more to you than your paycheck.'

'It does.'

'The mayor asked me to join in, but I declined. I don't make news, I just report it.'

'Maybe I should meet the mayor.'

'Just walk around town, he'll find you. He can sniff out a celebrity like a bird dog on a hunt. Man was born kissing ass.'

'You and the mayor enemies?'

'Enemies? Nah. You want enemies, go to Houston or Dallas. Me and the mayor, we just look at the world from different angles. Anyway, him and those ol' boys got together, decided to market the "Marfa concept," they call it, the art, a way to put Marfa on the map. "Marfa myth" is what it is. But the national media bought it, descended on our little town, told the art world that this is the place to be. We don't have a doctor, a dentist, a drug store, a movie theater, a McDonald's, a Walmart—'

'A Starbucks,' Nadine said.

'—but Marfa's the place to be? I don't get it. But everyone drank the Kool-Aid. Then the Triple As descended on us.'

'The Triple As?'

'Attorneys, artists, and assholes. That's what the locals call them, the Triple As, outsiders who came to town to make Marfa their own. Attorneys came first, double-barreled rich, flying out here from Dallas and Houston in their private jets, acting like they had discovered Judd's art, buying up old adobes and downtown buildings like they were buying lunch. Then the artists came, from New York, gays mostly, bit of a culture shock to cowboys.'

'I told you,' Nadine said.

'We're like L.A. now, except with artists instead of actors. Everyone making coffee, scooping ice cream, or waiting tables is an artist hoping to be discovered.'

'In Marfa?'

'Like an artist version of *American Idol*. They're all young and hip and hate Bush, but bottom line, they're all desperate to be as rich as Republicans and as famous as that Kardashian gal.'

'Khloe?' Nadine said.

'No. The other one.'

'Oh. Kim.'

'They're just passing through, like the trains. But they brought a little variety to town, opened these fancy restaurants serving French food and Italian cuisine, little place called Maiya's—'

'We walked past it. Red door, in the Brite Building.'

'Gal from Rhode Island, she owns it. New Yorker came to town to design costumes for that movie *There Will Be Blood*, decided to stay, started a dry goods store. Others came and opened up more restaurants, galleries, jewelry shops, a book-store, organic grocery store, coffee houses, live music bars, and that Ballroom Marfa, what they call a multimedia art space. Now, with Judd's and Flavin's and Chamberlain's masterpieces installed here, they say Marfa's the new art Mecca, so New York artsy types trek out here like they're making some kind of religious pilgrimage.'

Sam seemed to reflect on his own words a moment.

'Funny how things worked out. We were a ghost town of old ranchers, old-timers, old Mexicans, and old buildings, only two places to eat, but hell, you can't eat but one place at a time. We were here because we belonged here. On this harsh, unforgiving land. Then Judd moved here because he didn't belong in New York anymore. Twenty years, he made his art and his home here, became a bona fide Texan—I told him so the day he bought that ranch, that's every Texan's dream, to own a part of Texas. Now, twenty years after he died, the mayor and the Triple As have taken something real and made it something phony, turned this town into Santa Fe South or Marfa's Vineyard, take your pick, and Judd's art into the commerce and show business he hated. Marfa's a goddamned art theme park, and we're just running the rides for the tourists.'

Sam returned to Donald Judd's photo.

'Don wouldn't want to live here now. All the New Yorkers followed him here—hell, we got more Yankees than cattle. Folks fly in for the weekend, pay two hundred thousand for adobes worth twenty 'cause they think they're cute, then they triple the size and turn the places into walled compounds like they're living in Guadalajara in fear of the cartels. Drove real-estate prices and taxes up and the locals out. What you call ironic, New York liberals who profess to care so much about the poor and Mexicans, but they're buying third and fourth homes as trinkets and driving the poor and Mexicans out of Marfa. I tell them that, and they just smile and shrug their shoulders, as if it's out of their control. Like the weather.'

97

Sam dug at his teeth with the toothpick.

'Before the Triple As, this town was peaceful, hardly any conflict, just the normal stuff between the Anglos and the Mexicans—this *is* Texas—but basically everyone minded their own business and got along.'

'Not now?'

'Not hardly. Now we've got conflict. Hell, it's a goddamned civil war. "New Marfa" versus "old Marfa." Haves versus have-nots. Anglos versus Mexicans. Mexicans versus the Border Patrol. Artists versus cowboys. Homosexuals versus hetero-sexuals. And we're all at odds with Mother Nature, trying to make a life in this desert. Now we've got the fights over fracking.'

Sam waved at a passer-by outside.

'Is Mr. Barnett the only fracker in town?'

'Far as I know. He's the man in Marfa. Employs damn near everyone in town who ain't a Border Patrol agent or an artist. Bought up leases, hired locals to work the rigs, and started punching holes. Pays good wages—some of those boys had been unemployed for years, all of a sudden they're able to buy new pickups. Art made Marfa fashionable. Fracking made us profitable.'

'So where's the fight?'

'Fights. Plural. We got the environmentalists and artists trying to stop the fracking 'cause they think it's the end of the world, and we got the cattle ranchers fighting the pipeline easements. Can't truck gas out like you can oil, so Billy Bob's laying pipelines. If folks won't sell—and they won't—he's condemning their land, which is apparently legal in Texas.'

'It is.'

'Hell of a law.'

'Has Billy Bob filed condemnation suits?'

'Yep.'

'I assumed that didn't make him any friends?'

'Nope.'

'So what's your opinion of Mr. Barnett?'

'My opinion? Fact is, he's one of the assholes.' Sam glanced at Nadine. 'Pardon my French.' Back to Book: 'Out here, you don't mess with a man's land. It can be dangerous.'

Chapter 8

They had seen Marfa from the outside looking in; now they saw Marfa from the inside looking out. Standing in the cupola atop the three-story, Renaissance-revival-style Presidio County Courthouse that offered a 360-degree panorama of the Marfa Plateau, they could see the entirety of the town, all the way to the edges where civilization petered out into desert. The land beyond lay stark and yellow and bare of trees all the way to the brown mountain ridges that framed the plateau.

'I'm scared of heights.'

'Ms. Honeywell, you're only four stories up.'

'I think I'm going to throw up.'

They walked back down the stairs to the district courtroom on the second floor. The courthouse had been built in 1886 for only $60,000, but the solitary courtroom was the grandest Book had ever seen, and he had seen a few. It had a ceiling twenty feet high, elaborate crown molding, and old-style seating with individual chairs secured to the wood floor. They sat and took in the space.

'You let Mr. Walker go on and on about Marfa. Why didn't you question him about fracking?'

'Most folks get defensive when a lawyer interrogates them like a guilty defendant, Ms. Honeywell. They don't open up. They shut down. So I've learned to listen. Everyone has a story to tell, and they want to tell it. We learned a lot from Sam Walker.'

'We did?'

'We did.'

'I thought you wanted him to put a story in the paper?'

'I do. And he will.'

Her eyebrows crunched down. 'You say that as if you've done this before.'

'I have.'

'Why does that make me nervous?'

Book gestured at the grand courtroom that bespoke the history of West Texas.

'So, Ms. Honeywell, what's your career plan? To be a small-town lawyer and probate wills in a courtroom like this? Or a big-city lawyer?'

'I don't want to be a lawyer.'

Book turned to his intern. 'Then why are you in law school?'

'My dad didn't have a son to take into his practice, so he's making do with me.'

'What do you want to be?'

'A chef.'

'A law student who wants to be a chef? That's different.'

'A law professor who rides a Harley? That's different.'

If you want to sue over a contract, a car accident, or condemnation of land for a gas pipeline in Presidio County, you file a lawsuit in that courthouse. With the district clerk. Who smiled at Book.

'Professor Bookman,' she said. 'Sam Walker called, said you were heading my way. I'm Sadie Thomas. I think you should be on the Supreme Court.'

'You should take my Con Law class first.'

She was a middle-aged woman with a sweet face. Which face appeared in the funeral photo.

'So what brings you to our courthouse?'

'I need some information.'

'About what?'

'Whom. Billy Bob Barnett.'

Her smile disappeared.

'I understand he filed lawsuits against landowners?'

'Pipeline condemnation cases, about two dozen so far.'

'Who represents him?'

'The Dunn Law Firm.'

'What lawyer?'

'Nathan Jones. But he died in a car accident last week.'

'He was my intern four years ago. Did he file lawsuits for any other clients?'

'As far as I know, Billy Bob was his only client. He always joked about being a one-client lawyer. Too bad his only client was an asshole.'

'So I've heard.'

'You'll hear it more. Condemning folks' land for a pipeline, it's legal, but it's not right. Landowners got together, hired the same lawyer out of Santa Fe, but they always lose. Billy Bob's got the law on his side. Folks are fighting mad.'

'Mad enough to kill?'

'Him, but not his lawyer.' Sadie exhaled heavily. 'He was a sweet boy, Nathan. Brought me a red rose on my birthday. Every year. He was really excited about becoming a daddy.'

Book thanked her and turned to leave.

'Professor—'

He turned back.

'I wouldn't get in the middle of this fight. Might not be healthy.'

★   ★   ★

'They killed Nathan, Professor.'

At half past seven, Book and Nadine rode over to Nathan Jones's house on Austin Street north of the railroad tracks. It was a neat frame house with a black 4x4 Ford pickup truck parked out front. The large young man with curly blond hair who had stood next to the wife at the funeral met them at the door. His name was Jimmy John Dale. He and Nathan had been best friends since childhood. He smelled like a brewery.

'Why do you say that, Ms. Jones?'

'Brenda. Because they said he was speeding, but Nathan never drives fast.'

Only five days after her husband's death, she still spoke of him in the present tense.

'He was a boy scout?'

'Eagle.'

She was due in three weeks; it was a boy. She sat uncomfortably in an armchair. Book and Nadine sat on the couch; Jimmy John paced the wood floor with a beer in his hand and a frown on his face, as if he had something on his mind and that something had irritated him. A wedding portrait of Nathan and Brenda hung on one wall of the small living room. She wore a white wedding dress, he a black tuxedo.

'Wow,' Nadine said. 'He's James Dean's identical twin.'

'That's what everyone says,' Brenda said.

Several other photos of Brenda and Nathan showed them walking a beach, lying on a picnic blanket, and dancing at a party. They were an odd couple, physically. Brenda was a cute girl with a round face who would struggle with the baby weight after giving birth, the same as Book's sister was now struggling. Nathan Jones looked like a male model in one of those glossy fashion magazines; his features were sharp, his eyes dark, and his body lean. He seemed almost too perfect to be a real man, just as he had seemed too introverted to be a lawyer; next to him, Ms. Roberts seemed like a talk show host. He made an A in Con Law; he often drew in a small sketchbook he carried.

'Check out his crazy photos,' Jimmy John said.

On another wall were framed black-and-white photos, all of the stark West Texas landscape. One showed cowboys on horseback herding cattle across the dusty plains, but in the foreground as if observing the scene was a perfectly clothed Barbie doll, its vivid color a sharp contrast to the black-and-white scene. Another was of the open land and a low mountain range in the distance with a tall red rose stuck in the dirt in the foreground. A third showed a drilling rig standing tall above the land, roughnecks working on the deck, and in the foreground pink lacy lingerie. Nadine stood and examined each photo as if she were an art critic.

'I know,' Brenda said. 'They're weird. I didn't get them either. But Nathan loves to take those photos. It's his passion.'

'He had an eye for the landscape,' Book said. 'Did he ever try to sell his photos?'

'No. It's just a hobby. He's happy being a lawyer. Was. Which was good, because he works . . . worked a lot of late nights.'

'What else did he do? When he wasn't working?'

'Nothing. He works at the firm and spends the rest of his time with me. And Jimmy John.'

'What did you and he do?'

She shrugged. 'Normal stuff. Sundays after church, we'll pack a lunch and drive the desert looking for landscape for him to shoot. We'll put out a blanket, and he'll take hundreds of pictures from different angles. He's got some great photos from up in the Davis Mountains.'

'Did he hang out with anyone else?'

'He doesn't have a lot of friends in Marfa.'

'But he grew up here.'

'He wasn't a cowboy,' Jimmy John said.

'Any siblings?'

'He's an only child,' Brenda said.

104

'So how'd you two meet?'

'We all grew up together, here in Marfa. Nathan and I, we've been sweethearts since grade school. After high school, we went to Tech together. I got a degree in education, he majored in English. I came home, been teaching kindergarten in the public school seven years now. Nathan went to UT for law school. You were his hero, Professor. He talked about you a lot. We always watched you on TV.'

'You really got a black belt in kung fu?' Jimmy John said.

'Taekwondo.'

'When he got his law degree,' Brenda said, 'he came home, we got married, and he hired on with the Dunn firm. That was right when they opened the office here.'

Book addressed Jimmy John. He had a red face and a thick body. His jeans dragged the ground in the fashion of cowboys. Given his obvious state of inebriation and irritation, Book decided not to pepper him with questions but to just let him talk—and he seemed anxious to talk.

'So, Jimmy John, what's your story?'

Jimmy John took a swig of his beer then swiped a sleeve across his mouth.

'My *story*?' He snorted as if amused by the question. 'My story is, Brenda and Nathan went off to college, I stayed here. I only got a high school education, so I was low man on the totem pole for jobs around here, right below the Mexicans 'cause they'll live twenty to a trailer so they can send money back home to Mexico. You know they send thirty billion dollars back home every year? But they ain't taking money from American workers. Yeah, right. So I worked the cattle, dug holes and laid asphalt for the city, whatever work there was. Then this place becomes some kind of hot spot for art and all of a sudden every goddamn homosexual in New York City is moving to Marfa, artists with more money than sense, paying too much for homes, driving up the prices, now locals like me, we can't afford nothing but trailers on the Mexican side of town. Biggest employers in town were the tomato farm and Border Patrol. I applied, but they want agents who can speak Spanish.'

'You could learn.'

'We shouldn't have to speak Spanish to work in America, Professor, especially not for our own government. But we speak English on the rigs.'

'Who do you work for?'

'Billy Bob Barnett. He don't hire wets.'

'You like the work?'

'I like to work. Never had a regular job till fracking came to town. Give people like me a chance.'

'For what?'

'A life.'

The economy had left the Jimmy Johns of America behind. Manufacturing jobs had gone offshore to Mexico and Asia, and the oil and gas business had gone to the Middle East. Twenty-three million Americans were unemployed; most felt betrayed by their country. Bitter. Angry. Most had no hope for a steady job. Ever. Until fracking came along. But it came with a price. Jimmy John pulled out a white handkerchief from his back pocket and blew his nose. Blood stained the white cloth.

'He gets nosebleeds,' Brenda said. 'And headaches. From working the rigs.'

Jimmy John shrugged. 'Lot of chemicals and gases coming up the well hole.'

'You have a doctor check you out?'

'No doctor in Marfa.'

He dug in his shirt pocket and pulled out a small container and swallowed two pills then chased them with the beer.

'He takes Advil like he's eating candy,' Brenda said. 'Nathan begged him to go to Alpine, see a doctor there.'

Jimmy John waved off her concerns with his beer can. 'Ain't like I'm gonna quit my job.'

'You married?' Book asked.

That question amused Jimmy John even more.

'*Me?* Hell, ain't no white girls in town.'

Book turned back to Brenda Jones. 'Did you know that Nathan had written a letter to me?'

'He said he was going to.'

'Did you know why?'

'He said something wasn't right. With the water. Said Billy Bob was cutting corners. Nathan was scared to death of him.'

'His own client?'

'Billy Bob bullied him. He bullied everyone.'

'Aw,' Jimmy John said, 'he's all bark and no bite. Oil men are rough around the edges, is all.'

Book pulled out Nathan's letter and handed it to Brenda. She read it then gave it to Jimmy John.

'He asked for your help, Professor,' Brenda said.

'How do I help him now?'

'Find the truth.'

Jimmy John handed the letter back to Book and said, 'Well, Billy Bob's the only fracker in Marfa.'

'And Nathan's only client,' Brenda said. 'If you work for the Dunn firm in Marfa, you work for Billy Bob Barnett. Nathan worried about it, having only one client. If Billy Bob got mad at him, he'd be out of a job.'

'But he still wrote this letter to me.'

'Professor,' Jimmy John said, 'them environmentalists been claiming that bullshit about groundwater contamination since we fracked the first well out here. Now they got the artists joining in, gives 'em something to do, I guess. They're liberals who hate the oil and gas industry. They want us all to ride bicycles like they do. I've worked those rigs for five years, and I can tell you, there's no contamination. I see the pressure readings on the casing. We've never had a leak.'

'Then why did Nathan say in his letter he had proof of contamination?'

'I don't know. He asked me, I told him we go by the book. He never told me he had any proof.'

Book turned back to Brenda. 'Did he show you any proof?'

'No. Nothing.'

'Did he tell you that he had shown the proof to his senior partner?'

She shook her head.

'Do you know him?'

She nodded. 'Tom Dunn. I met him once before the funeral. He gave me the creeps. He's the type who talks to a woman's breasts instead of her face.'

'If Nathan had proof and went public with it, the government would've shut down the frack wells.'

'Maybe,' Jimmy John said. 'Maybe not. This is Texas, Professor.'

'I told him to keep quiet about it,' Brenda said.

'Why?'

'Because if he went public, he'd either be out of a job or dead. He sent you that letter, and now he's dead. That seem like a coincidence to you, Professor?' She fought back tears. 'They killed him. Billy Bob's men.'

'Why?'

'Money.' She pointed at the floor. 'That gas down there is worth billions.'

Jimmy John put his free hand on Brenda's shoulder.

'It was an accident. Billy Bob, he's already rich.'

'People like him, they never have enough money.'

She could no longer fight the tears.

'They followed me home.'

Jimmy John shook his head. 'Nathan had her so scared she was seeing ghosts. Look, Professor, I loved Nathan like a brother. I miss him every minute. But it was just an accident. He was driving back from Midland late, and he fell asleep at the wheel.'

108

'That's what he said,' Brenda said.

'Who?' Book said.

'The sheriff.'

When they said their goodbyes, Brenda Jones gave Book a hug and whispered, 'Professor, you were his hero. Be his hero now. Give him justice. Find his truth. It wasn't an accident.'

He and Nadine walked outside and climbed on the Harley, but Book did not start the engine. Instead, he stared at the stars above them. He had pursued truth and justice—or as close thereto as the law allows—on enough occasions now to know that justice was more crushed car art than an act certain—in the eye of the beholder rather than an eye for an eye—and truth was found in one's heart rather than one's head. Maybe Justice Kennedy was correct: perhaps we are each entitled to define our own existence, our own meaning, our own truth. So he would not search for the truth, but for Nathan's truth. He owed him that much.

'What did we learn today, Ms. Honeywell?'

'I don't like riding six hours on a Harley.'

'About Nathan Jones's death.'

'A, official cause of death was accidental.'

'And?'

'B, Billy Bob Barnett is the client in his letter who is allegedly contaminating the groundwater.'

'And?'

'C, he didn't show his proof to either his wife or his best friend.'

'Very good.'

'And D, he was gay.'

'*Who?* Jimmy John?'

'Nathan Jones.'

Chapter 9

Border Patrol Agent Wesley Crum yelled back to his partner: 'Angel, you run like a goddamn queer! Hurry, they're getting away!'

It was after midnight, and Wesley and Angel were chasing wets through the desert again. Wesley wore night-vision goggles which allowed him to spot the wets running through the brush—not as good as the Predator's 'eyes in the sky,' but the goggles gave him an on-the-ground advantage over the wets. He was after two males and two females, no doubt a mom-and-pop operation who brought the kids with them for a lifetime in America. A chance at the American Dream: free education, free healthcare, free welfare, free this, free that, free everything, living at the expense of hard-working, tax-paying Americans. What a deal. First thing they do is get pregnant and punch out a baby in America—an American citizen with exactly the same rights as Wesley Crum—which guarantees them an extended stay in the U.S. of A. Consequently, Wesley viewed his job as deficit reduction: every Mexican he caught and deported back across the river equaled four or five Mexican babies the federal government wouldn't have to support.

Hell, if he caught enough wets, he could single-handedly balance the fucking budget.

Wesley Crum was thirty years old and had been on the job twelve years. He had grown up in Marfa and wanted to stay in Marfa, but there were no jobs in Marfa. Most of his high school buddies had moved away to Odessa to work the oil fields. Wesley hired on with the U.S. Customs and Border Protection Agency, now part of the Department of Homeland Security. That was back when agents didn't have to speak Spanish to get hired. Now Border Patrol hired Hispanics like Angel.

His partner was an odd duck. Read books. Listened to Marfa Public Radio. Knew stuff. Liked art and the artists. Three years younger than Wesley, Angel had grown up in Presidio and went to college at Texas A&M. Graduated, but he came back to work the border. They were as different as night and day—or Anglo and Hispanic—but they had forged a partnership that had lasted Angel's entire five years on the job, which was five years longer than any other relationship in Wesley's adult life. Of course, everyone liked Angel Acosta. He was that kind of guy. They worked the Big Bend Sector, which covered 165,000 square miles including seventy-seven counties in Texas and all of Oklahoma and 510 miles of the Rio Grande. Which pretty much guaranteed that they would chase wets every night. But Wesley liked the desert at night. He stopped and waited for his partner to catch up. Angel arrived; he was breathing hard. They addressed each other through the night-vision goggles.

'Let them go, Wesley. They just want to work.'

'Are you having one of them eccentric crises I heard about on TV?'

'Existential. You watching Dr. Phil again?'

'Are you?'

'You've got to do something else during the day when we work the night shift.'

'Like what?'

'Well, you could try reading.'

'*Reading?*'

As if Angel had said 'yoga.'

'I just don't see why we chase these people when they just want to work.'

'So we can keep working. So we keep our jobs, that's why we chase wets. Angel, there ain't no other jobs in Presidio County for guys like us, especially me. We either chase wets or collect unemployment.'

'We could work the frack rigs.'

'Man, chasing wets is a hell of a lot easier than that. And the federal government's benefit plan is much better than anything in the private sector.'

Angel shrugged. 'That's true.'

'Okay. You got your head on straight?'

'Yeah, I guess.'

'Good. They're hunkered down about a hundred yards due north. You circle around east, I'll go west. We'll trap these wets and deport their Mexican butts back to Chihuahua.'

They ran into the dark desert.

Chapter 10

'Saw you out running this morning,' Presidio County Sheriff Brady Munn said from the other side of his man-sized desk. 'Dawn in the desert's nice, ain't it?'

Nadine eyed Book through her black glasses. 'You ran at dawn? What is that, like, eight A.M.?'

'Six. I always run at dawn.'

'I sleep at dawn.'

'You folks want a cup of coffee?'

'No, thanks,' Book said.

'Sure,' his intern said. 'With cream. The real stuff, not the powdered.'

The sheriff cracked a little smile. 'I'll get the jail chef right on it.' Instead, he called out through the open door: 'Rosa, two coffees. With real cream.'

A hearty laugh came back. Then a voice with a Spanish accent.

'Real cream? Are you serious?'

'Run across the street to SqueezeMarfa, they'll have some.'

Now Spanish words came back, which turned the sheriff's smile into a chuckle.

'You folks speak Spanish?'

'No,' Book said.

'Nunh-huh,' Nadine said.

'Good.'

It was nine the next morning, and they sat in the sheriff's office in the county jail across the street from the Presidio County Courthouse. They had arrived without an appointment, but the sheriff had agreed to see them. He greeted them in the lobby then escorted them to his office. When he turned his back, Nadine had whispered to Book, 'Not gay.' Her San Francisco skills were not required to render that verdict in Presidio County. Sheriff Munn stood well over six feet tall and outweighed Book by at least fifty pounds; his body appeared as solid as an oak tree, even in middle age. He had thick hair with gray streaks and wore a Western-style uniform, tan cowboy boots, a massive handgun on his hip, and a droopy mustache. He smelled like leather and looked like Wyatt Earp; he called everyone 'podna.'

'So, podna, you figure you can do my job better than me?' the sheriff said.

'Pardon me?'

The sheriff tossed a newspaper onto the desk in front of Book. It was the latest edition of *The Times of Marfa*, just out that morning. On the front page was the photo of Book that Sam Walker had taken the day before. The sheriff pointed a gnarly finger at the newspaper.

'Says you're a famous law professor, come to Marfa to figure out what happened to the lawyer. Says his death might have something to do with fracking.'

Book had already read the article. The desk clerk at the Paisano had handed the newspaper to Book on his way back up to his room after his morning run, when Book had advised him that they would be staying another night. (He hadn't yet broken the news to his intern.) His hunch had played out; Sam Walker couldn't resist a better front-page story than the roller

114

derby. But he picked up the paper anyway and read the article as if for the first time. He then folded the paper and set it on the desk. He looked at the sheriff.

'Nathan was my student intern four years ago. He wrote me a letter six days ago.'

Book handed Nathan's letter across the desk to the sheriff just as a Hispanic woman entered with two cups of coffee on a little tray with sugars and real cream. She placed the tray on the desk but eyed Book with suspicion. He held his hands up in mock surrender then pointed at Nadine, who practically dove for the coffee.

The sheriff said, '*Gracias*, Rosa,' without diverting his eyes from the envelope. He checked the postmark then removed the letter and stroked his mustache and randomly grunted as he read. The sheriff's office was spacious and manly and filled with weapons. Modern military-style rifles stood in a glass case; vintage Western-style rifles were mounted on the walls next to photos of the sheriff on horseback in calf-roping competitions. A police radio sat on a table behind the sheriff; voices of law enforcement personnel came over sporadically. The sheriff finally looked up from the letter.

'Pretty serious accusation.'

Book nodded.

'I reckon he meant Billy Bob Barnett.'

'Nathan's only client.'

'You talk to him? Billy Bob?'

'I will.'

'You figure what the lawyer says in this letter might be a motive for murder? Someone who didn't want that proof made public?'

'It's a developing theory.'

'You got any facts to back it up?'

'Not yet.'

The sheriff grunted again then eyed the envelope again. 'Postmarked same day he died.'

'How do you feel about coincidences?' Nadine asked.

'Reckon they happen.'

'Good.' She turned to Book. 'Can we go home now?'

She had been packed and ready to roll when he returned from his run.

'Tomorrow.'

'*Tomorrow?* I've got to study for my Crim Law final.'

'You're learning criminal law in the real world, Ms. Honeywell.'

'I feel safer in a classroom.'

The sheriff took his coffee, poured sugar and cream, and sipped. He addressed Nadine.

'Good call on the cream.'

Static then a loud voice came across the radio; the sheriff cocked his head that way.

'Rosa, tell the sheriff we got us a dead Mexican out Ninety past the Aerostat. Looks like he was walking north barefooted, got bit by a rattler. Leg's swollen up like a damn balloon.'

'Rosa doubles as the dispatcher,' the sheriff said.

He reached back and grabbed the mike. He clicked a button.

'Rusty, I'm in an important meeting with a couple of folks from Austin. I can't come running out there for a dead Mexican. Rosa's gonna call Border Patrol, get them to handle it. Their jurisdiction—"Securing America's Borders," like their motto says.'

The sheriff smiled, as if at an inside joke.

'Reporters?' Rusty said over the radio.

'What?' the sheriff said.

'That *Vanity Fair* reporter back in town? She's a cutie.'

'*Vanity Fair* reporter? Rusty, get your head out your butt and get to work. After the Border Patrol takes over there, get over to the Randolph spread, see about their rustling complaint. Probably just lost count and not cows.'

The sheriff clicked the button on the mike and exhaled.

'County pay don't attract Ph.D.s for deputies.'

He replaced the mike on the table and turned back to Book.

'I agree the timing's a mite suspicious, Professor, but we don't do murder in Marfa. We get calls on dead Mexicans, stranded motorists, stoned artists riding bicycles naked, that sort of thing. Our big crimes are drug busts, shipments coming north across the border—Presidio County stretches all the way south to the Rio Grande. But we don't get violent crimes like in the cities.'

'Did you know Nathan Jones?' Book asked.

'Nope.'

'You were at his funeral.'

'He was a Marfan. One of us. That's why I was there. That's why I cared.'

He sipped his coffee.

'What about you, Professor? Why do you care so much about Nathan Jones?'

'I owe him.'

The sheriff grunted. 'Well, I never crossed paths with him. Must not have done criminal defense work.'

'Oil and gas. Mostly gas.'

'Lot of that going around these days.'

He drank his coffee.

'I worked up the accident scene myself, Professor. No signs of foul play. Everything I saw said it was just an accident. So that was my official cause of death: accidental. We get half a dozen of these car crashes every year, main cause of death in Presidio County, right after old age and boredom.'

'Sheriff, have you ever heard anything about fracking contaminating the groundwater?'

'Nope. No brown water, no one's been lighting their tap water on fire like I seen on TV. We still drink the water, don't need to pay extra to have it served in a bottle.'

He held up his cup of coffee.

'Tap water.'

Nadine frowned at her coffee cup. The sheriff noticed and half smiled.

'But environmentalists been crawling all over West Texas, trying to prove up contamination, which would be a pretty serious matter around here.'

'Because of the water?'

'Because of the jobs. Fracking brought jobs to Marfa, Professor, good jobs for good ol' boys. When you got a family to feed, you don't worry about a little arsenic in your drinking water.'

Nadine's eyes got wide; the sheriff chuckled.

'Look, Professor, I don't want to drink frack fluids either, but I've never heard anyone complaining about contamination. And trust me, folks would call us—hell, we're the only thing resembling authority in Presidio County. Damn near four thousand square miles we cover.'

'Nathan said he had proof.'

'Find it.'

He replaced the letter inside the envelope and flipped it across the desk to Book.

'In the meantime, I wouldn't go waving that letter around town, Professor. You're threatening a lot of people's jobs. Folks around here don't abide outsiders stirring up trouble.'

'Not the first time I've heard that.'

'I don't want it to be the last time.'

The two men regarded each other for a long moment.

'May I see the autopsy report?' Book asked.

The sheriff grunted again, which apparently was a basic form of communication for him.

'Well, you see, Professor, there wasn't enough left to autopsy.'

'Fire got real hot, I expect.'

Book, Nadine, and the sheriff stood in the impound lot on the northern edge of town. The prairie stretched in front of

118

them all the way to the Davis Mountains. Nathan Jones's pickup truck—or what was left of it—sat before them on the dirt ground. The vehicle had been cut nearly in half and burned down to the steel frame. With Nathan Jones strapped in his seat. Book could hear his screams.

'Figure he fell asleep.'

'The rumble strip didn't wake him?'

Rumble strips ran along the shoulders of most Texas highways, grooves cut into the asphalt that cause a vehicle to vibrate if the driver veers out of his lane. Intended as a safety feature to alert inattentive drivers, they were dangerous to motorcyclists. Book always took care to avoid rumble strips while on the Harley.

'Apparently not. He must've been running ninety, ninety-five. Got sleepy, lost control, ran off the road, slammed into a pump jack on the passenger's side. Impact split the vehicle, ruptured the gas tank, knocked the pump jack loose. Between the oil and the gas, must've been one hell of a fire. Damn lucky the wind was down, or it might've burned half the county to dirt.'

The sheriff grunted.

'Bad way to go,' he said. 'Course, there ain't no good way. I got photos from that night, if you want to see them.'

'No, thanks.'

Book wanted to remember Nathan Jones as the law student he knew, not as a charred corpse.

'Where'd this happen?'

'East of town, north side of Highway Sixty-seven, just past the Marfa Mystery Lights Viewing Center.'

Every evening the hopeful gather at a man-made rock structure nine miles east of Marfa on the south side of Highway 67. When night falls, they stand at the low rock wall and face south. They stare out beyond the runways of the old Marfa Army Air Field and into the dark desert toward the Chinati

119

Mountains, focused on an area known as Mitchell Flat situated between the Marfa and Paisano passes.

They are hoping to see the lights.

Since 1883 when a young cowboy reported seeing mysterious lights between the passes, the 'Marfa Mystery Lights' have drawn tourists from around the country to that very spot. A few see the lights—red, green, orange, or yellow balls—hovering above the land, darting back and forth, even giving chase—but most do not. But that does not dissuade more tourists from coming. For ninety years, the mystery lights defined Marfa—until Donald Judd moved to town.

The Viewing Center sits on the south side of Highway 67. Nathan Jones died on the north side. Book slowed the Harley and made a U-turn. They rode slowly along the shoulder until they came to a spot where a wide swath of the tall prairie grass had been scorched bare, as if a wildfire had swept across the land. He stopped and cut the engine.

'He ran off the road here.'

They got off the Harley and followed the tire tracks across the burnt earth. Small pieces of debris from the vehicle littered the ground. The wind blew strong from Mexico.

'Veered off at an angle, then the truck slid sideways, hit the pump jack.'

They stood at the pump jack. It had not yet been repaired. Book could play out the scene in his head like a movie, Nathan Jones driving this dark road late at night, getting drowsy, falling asleep then jerking awake when the truck left the smooth asphalt and hit the rough ground, panicking, yanking hard on the wheel, the truck sliding sideways, slamming into the pump jack, exploding into flames . . . screaming.

'Nathan Jones died right here.'

The young man who had saved Book's life had lost his own life at the very spot where Book now stood. They remained quiet for a time. Then Book turned back to the highway. Nathan had come off the road a long way.

'He must've been going really fast.'

'Like James Dean,' Nadine said.

Chapter 11

They rode a hundred miles in silence. Nadine didn't ask to go home or complain that she was hungry. They rode east through Alpine then turned north and descended from the high desert plateau and onto the plains. The mountains disappeared behind them and were soon replaced by pump jacks as they rode above the great Permian Basin oil field where vast Texas fortunes had been made during the boom and lost during the bust. The land lay flat and bare and depressing, inhabited only by cell phone towers and power lines and thousands of black-and-yellow pump jacks, their horse heads bobbing up and down rhythmically, as relentless as the wind but more profitable, ten strokes pumping one barrel of black gold—and at $100 a barrel, it was black gold—up from the depths of the earth. The foul smell of the oil industry clung to the landscape like wet toilet paper. Nadine yelled over the engine noise and the wind.

'What's that smell?'

'Money.'

They came upon Odessa from the south; the view was no better from the north, east, or west. The town was nothing more than a glorified oil camp inhabited by one hundred thousand people. Oil fed them, clothed them, transported them, and sheltered them. Oil was their past, their present, and their future. Oil was their hope and their fear. Oil was their life.

'Yuk.'

'Don't say yuk, Ms. Honeywell. That oil subsidizes your education. A lot of those pump jacks belong to UT. The school has made about five billion dollars so far from this field.'

'Then why do they keep raising my tuition?'

Refineries, low-rent motels, and strip joints occupied both sides of the highway; one sign touted 'Joe's Steakhouse and Fabric Free Entertainment.' Only a few pickup trucks sat in Joe's parking lot. Either Joe's steaks were lousy or his sign too subtle for Odessa; the strip joint next door offered 'Totally Naked Gals,' and its parking lot was packed. Drilling rigs and casing pipes were stacked high on frontage lots, awaiting the next well hole to be punched into the earth. Eighteen-wheelers and pickup trucks crowded the lanes adjacent to the Harley; tattooed arms hung out the windows and hard-looking men gazed down at them. Book had visited inmates at the state penitentiary on several occasions; these men's eyes told the same story: they were doing hard time.

'Why's the land so bare?' Nadine asked after they had cleared the city limits.

Much of the land looked like a moonscape. No trees, no brush, no grass. Just gray dirt.

'Salt water, from the oil wells. Back in the old days, they pumped the salt water into unlined evaporation pits. The salt water seeped into the ground, killed the vegetation. That was thirty or forty years ago. Nothing's ever grown back, probably never will.'

'Place makes me want to throw up,' Nadine said. 'Why do people live here?'

'Jobs. When you don't have a job, you'll live anywhere for a job. Do anything for a job. You hear politicians on TV talking about the working class? This is it, Ms. Honeywell. High

123

school educated workers. Most of their jobs were outsourced overseas for cheap labor, but the oil is here so these jobs are still here.'

'I don't want to live here.'

'You won't have to. You're educated. But never forget what these people's lives are like. Never forget that these people need jobs, too.'

Book accelerated the Harley east on Interstate 20 toward Midland as if trying to keep pace with the train running on the tracks that paralleled the interstate. A vulture circled overhead.

'Most people make an appointment.'

'We were in the neighborhood.'

'You were in Marfa. I get the paper.'

From a distance, the buildings of downtown Midland seemed to pop up out of the prairie like yucca plants. Midland was known for oil and gas and George W. Bush. He had grown up here. When he left the White House for the final time, his first stop back in Texas was Midland; twenty thousand locals turned out to welcome him home. Then George W. retired to Dallas.

Thomas A. Dunn had also grown up in Midland. He left for college and law school at UT then returned home for good. He was now sixty-three years old and the senior partner at The Dunn Law Firm, which employed one hundred thirty lawyers and maintained offices in Midland, Lubbock, Amarillo, and Marfa. From a corner office on the twentieth floor, Tom Dunn oversaw a legal empire that spanned West Texas. He was an oil and gas lawyer, and West Texas was oil and gas country. The Permian Basin covered seventeen counties and seventy-five thousand square miles; an estimated thirty billion barrels remained to be extracted. It was a very good time to be in the oil and gas business. Or a lawyer to the oil and gas business. And Tom Dunn was all business, the kind of lawyer who probably had sex by the billable hour. Book didn't know Mrs. Dunn, but he felt a twinge of sympathy for her nonetheless.

'Saw you at Nathan's funeral,' he said.

'He worked for me. Nathan was a good young lawyer, billed his quota every month without complaint.'

'What's the quota for young lawyers these days, Mr. Dunn, so I can tell my students?'

'Three thousand hours a year.'

Nadine gasped. 'OMG.'

Dunn chuckled. 'A common reaction among our new associates.'

'That's what, two hundred fifty billable hours a month?' Book said. 'Doesn't seem realistic.'

'Reality is, Professor, I start billing when I wake up in the morning and stop when I fall asleep that night. I'm always thinking about my clients. And that's what I'm paid to do: think.'

'It's easier once you can rationalize it, isn't it?'

'Much.'

Book had met many senior partners at many large law firms; when they visited the school, the famous Professor Bookman was always part of the dog-and-pony show, a circus act to attract endowments. Senior partners were more Wall Street than Main Street, more businessmen—every senior partner he had met had been male—than lawyers. Perhaps the law was just a business these days, and lawyers were in the business of buying and selling the law. Some firms boasted thousands of lawyers and billions in revenues. Billable hours were inventory, and young lawyers fungible commodities. Book had never regretted his decision to forgo the private practice of law. He hadn't gone to law school to be a businessman. He had gone to be a hero like his dad, but wielding the law instead of a gun.

'So you rode four hundred miles on that Harley to investigate Nathan's death?'

'With me on the back,' Nadine said.

'That's not why I came.'

'Newspaper said that's why you came.'

'Nathan wrote a letter to me.'

Book handed Nathan's letter to Dunn. He sat down behind his desk, put on reading glasses, removed the letter from the envelope, and read. Book pulled out the funeral photo and circled Dunn's face, as he had circled the faces of all the other locals they had met. He then surveyed Dunn's office. The same interior decorator must design every law office in America, or at least every one he had been in. The furniture, the rugs on the floor and the art on the wall, even the photos scattered about seemed to be from a stock lawyer template. Perhaps lawyers were comforted by conformity, soothed by sameness, as they fought boredom and billed hours. Book could not imagine himself in Tom Dunn's chair. Dunn removed his glasses and exhaled heavily, as if he had just learned that his wife was cheating on him; or worse, that she had embezzled funds from their joint bank account.

'Nathan wrote this?'

'He did. I've learned that Billy Bob Barnett was the client he referenced.'

'Professor, I don't know what Nathan thought he found, but it wasn't evidence of groundwater contamination. Frack well holes are encased in redundant layers of steel and cement. Billy Bob doesn't cut corners with his drilling.' He chuckled. 'Hell, Billy Bob's a walking Aggie joke—he's too dumb to be a crook.'

'But he's rich enough to hire your firm. How much does he pay you each year?'

'That's confidential, Professor.'

But he couldn't restrain a thin smile.

'Eighteen million last fiscal year.'

'That buys a lot of loyalty from a lawyer.'

'Part of the job description.'

'Nathan said in his letter that he brought your client's contamination to your attention.'

'He didn't.'

'Wonder why he said he did?'

'I don't know.'

'May I look in his office?'

'You know better than that, Professor. Client confidentiality.'

Tom Dunn stood and walked to the window. He was a tall, gray-haired man who seemed as hard as the land. He gestured at West Texas beyond the plate glass.

'See all those pump jacks pumping oil out of the ground twenty-four/seven? You know what that means around here, Professor? Jobs. Midland–Odessa, we're booming again. One hundred and fifty thousand producing wells in the Permian Basin. Thirty-six billion a year in revenues. That pays a lot of wages to a lot of workers. But not that long ago those pump jacks were still, the wells shut in, workers sitting idle, oil field equipment rusting on the side of the interstate. Old wells and low prices, couldn't produce enough oil to make economic sense. Billy Bob changed all that.'

'How?'

'Fracking.'

'On oil wells?'

'You bet. See, he grew up in Odessa, his dad was a rough-neck. Billy Bob decided he wanted to own the oil not just work the oil. So he went to A&M, got a degree in petroleum engineering. Learned about hydraulic fracturing. Fracking's been around sixty years, but no one thought about reworking these old oil wells with fracking, going deeper, going horizontal, to open up the reservoir to let more oil out faster. Billy Bob did. Now everyone is. Then he started fracking for natural gas before anyone else. He knows more about fracking than anyone in Texas, which means anyone in the world. Fracking started right out there.'

He turned from the window.

'Point is, Professor, folks around here are real happy to have work again. They need the jobs. They're not going to take

127

kindly to some liberal law professor messing with their livelihoods.'

'Is that a threat?'

'An observation.'

'I'm not liberal.'

'You're sure as hell not conservative.'

'What's Billy Bob?'

'Rich.'

'He's taking people's land for his pipelines.'

'Which is perfectly legal in Texas, as you well know.'

'Legal doesn't mean right.'

'Please, Professor, this isn't first-year law school.'

'I heard the landowners aren't too happy.'

Tom Dunn shrugged. 'Hell, I wouldn't be either.'

'Nathan was handling those lawsuits. Think one of the land-owners might've run him off the road because of that?'

Dunn shook his head. 'Too much trouble. If they wanted to kill Nathan, they would've just shot him. This is West Texas, Professor. Everyone's got a gun. Or ten.'

'Mind if I meet with your client?'

'Yes, I do mind.'

'Well, since we're not opposing lawyers in litigation or a transaction, I guess I can meet with him whether you mind or not.'

'I'll let him know to expect you.'

Book stood. 'Thanks for your time, Mr. Dunn.'

'Professor, why do you care so much about Nathan Jones?'

'I owe him.'

'Must be a big debt, to come way out here. That's why I avoid owing anyone.'

'Even your biggest client?'

Book walked to the door; Nadine followed. But Book stopped and turned back.

'You know, Mr. Dunn, if a lawyer aids and abets a criminal violation of the federal environmental laws, he gets to share a prison cell with his client. Most lawyers aren't willing to go to jail for their clients. I wonder how much money a client would have to pay a lawyer to get him to risk prison time. What do you think, maybe eighteen million a year?'

Dunn fixed Book with a searing glare, as if he were a young associate who had failed to bill his monthly quota—for the second consecutive month.

'First, I'm not in your Con Law class, Professor, so don't lecture me. And second, I hope that's a law professor's hypothetical fact situation and not an accusation because if you're accusing me of a crime, I'd have to pick up that phone and call the UT law school dean and express my displeasure, which might have repercussions for the professor making those false and defamatory accusations.'

'I'm tenured, Mr. Dunn.'

'I'm pissed, Professor.'

'And Nathan's dead.'

'I didn't kill him, and neither did Billy Bob. The sheriff said it was an accident.'

'Then neither you nor your client has anything to fear.'

'From what?'

'Not what. Whom.'

'From whom?'

'Me.'

'I thought that went well,' Nadine said. 'Is that what you call stirring the pot?'

'It is.'

'Do you do that often?'

'I do.'

'Has anyone ever taken offense?'

'Define "taken offense."'

'Attempted injury upon your body.'

'They have.'

'Was there gunfire?'

'On occasion.'

'How many occasions?'

'A few.'

'Define "a few."'

'Seven.'

'People shot at you seven times?'

'Maybe eight.'

His intern sighed heavily. 'So in the newspaper reports, I'll be the "innocent bystander caught in the crossfire."'

'I promised to protect you, Ms. Honeywell.'

Sit on a bench in downtown Austin for five minutes and five panhandlers would've already hit on you. Not so in downtown Midland. Law and order—mostly order—prevailed. They sat on a bench outside the Dunn Building, taking a breather before riding back to Marfa. The West Texas wind funneled between the buildings and threatened to blow them over. Pedestrians leaned into the wind, making it seem as if the earth had tilted on its axis. Young men in suits and women in dresses walked past and into the building, apparently lawyers returning from lunch.

'Thomas A. Dunn,' Nadine said. 'The "A" must be for asshole.'

'Fortunately, it's not a crime in Texas, or we'd have a lot more lawyers in prison.'

'Professor, why didn't you ever practice law? You could've been another Tom Dunn.'

'That's why.'

Book pointed up, as if to the corner office on the twentieth floor.

'I knew that life wasn't for me. Working inside. Wearing suits. Counting my life away by the billable hour.'

'He looks rich.'

'I'm sure he is. Each lawyer chooses the life he or she wants, Ms. Honeywell, just as you will have to choose. I chose a life on a Harley instead of in a Mercedes-Benz.'

'You ever regret that choice?'

'Only when it rains.'

She smiled.

'You could've worked at a nonprofit.'

'It's called teaching law school.'

'Hey, I read about those forgivable loans.'

'They made Twitter?'

'Oh, yeah.'

'Well, I didn't get one.'

'You could've done legal aid for the needy.'

'That's why we're here—to use our legal skills to aid someone in need.'

'But the person in need is dead.'

'So he is.'

'Professor, Tom Dunn is an asshole, but he's right: Nathan's death was an accident.'

'Are you just saying that so I'll take you home?'

'I want to go home, but I believe it was an accident.'

'Why?'

'The sheriff doesn't seem like a fool. He's investigated a lot of car accidents. If Nathan was murdered, he'd know it. And why would Billy Bob murder his own lawyer? For money? He's rich enough to pay eighteen million in legal fees to Dunn. To stay out of prison? How many rich guys go to prison? He'd blame any contamination on his employees, the company would pay a fine, and he'd stay in business. And if Nathan had proof, he would've shown it to his wife or his best friend. Professor, you're emotionally invested in this case. You're not looking at it objectively. Because Nathan saved your life.'

'He saved my life, but I wasn't there to save his. I owe it to him to find out how he died.'

'You did. Nathan Jones died in an accident.'

'He shouldn't have died that way.'

'And my sister shouldn't have died of cancer when she was eight.'

131

'*Eight?*'

His intern's voice cracked. 'It destroyed my parents. Their marriage. Our family.'

She paused.

'After she died, we never had a real Christmas tree. My mother bought an artificial one.'

Book's instinct was to embrace his intern, but he resisted.

'I'm sorry, Ms. Honeywell. That's just not . . .'

'Fair? One thing I've learned, Professor, life is unfair. I couldn't make it fair for my sister, and you can't make it fair for Nathan.'

Or his own mother.

'Professor Bookman?'

Book looked up to a young man smiling down at him. He stood.

'I'm Tim Egan. I took your class five years ago. What brings you to Midland?'

'Nathan Jones.'

The smile left his face. 'Bad deal. He was a good guy.'

'You work at the Dunn firm?'

'We all do.'

'Oil and gas?'

'Yep.'

'Fracking?'

'Fracking *is* the oil and gas business today.'

'You know anything about groundwater contamination caused by fracking?'

'Nope. And I don't want to know. I do what I'm told and keep my mouth shut.'

Book's thoughts of disapproval must have registered on his face.

'Look, Professor, we're not cops. Our clients hire us to do their bidding, not to turn them in to the Feds.'

'I take it you didn't go to law school to make the world a better place?'

'I went to law school to make money.'

Disapproval turned to—

'Don't look so disgusted, Professor. I graduated with a hundred thousand dollars in student loan debt, money I borrowed so UT law professors can make three hundred thousand a year teaching two classes a semester. I couldn't pay my loans off working at a nonprofit. So you guys are as much to blame for the state of the legal profession as we are.'

'What grade did I give you?'

'B.'

'I should've given you a C.'

Nadine had scooted down the bench when the lawyer had engaged the professor. She now smiled. The professor was growing on her.

'*Nadine?*'

She turned to the familiar voice and saw a familiar face.

'*Sylvia?*'

She stood, and they hugged. Sylvia Unger had graduated law school the year before. She was holding a venti Starbucks cup.

'There's a Starbucks here?'

'Right around the corner.'

'Oh, thank God.'

Nadine fought the urge to snatch Sylvia's cup and suck the coffee into her caffeine-depleted body.

'I thought you wanted to work in Dallas?'

Sylvia shrugged. 'No jobs in Dallas, so I came to Midland.'

'You still dating that lawyer in Dallas?'

'He dumped me for an SMU cheerleader.'

Nadine shook her head. 'Guys say they want brains and personality, but what they really want are big tits and a tight ass.'

'He left me for a male cheerleader.'

Nadine groaned. 'I hate it when they do that. Leaving you for another girl is bad enough, but for another boy?'

'Tell me.'

Sylvia was not from San Francisco, so it was probably her first experience with romancing a gay guy. Her expression said she had not gotten over him. Nadine thought it best to change the subject.

'You like it out here?'

'Beggars can't be choosers.'

The wind tried to blow Sylvia's dress over her head. She clamped her arms down both sides of her body like a vise.

'Does the wind ever stop blowing?' Nadine asked.

'No. It doesn't. And the oil smell never goes away.'

'Is the practice of law fun?'

'*Fun?*' Sylvia almost laughed. 'Nadine, "fun" and "the practice of law" do not belong in the same sentence.'

'What kind of work are you doing?'

'Estate planning.'

'Do you like it?'

'It's a living. So what are you doing here?'

Nadine aimed a thumb at the professor. 'Working for Bookman.'

'Wait—you're not his intern?'

'Uh . . . yes, I am.'

'Be careful.'

'He's a nice guy.'

'He's crazy. He's got a death wish or something.'

'We rode out here on his Harley.'

'See?'

'Sylvia, did you know Nathan Jones?'

'We met. I'm up here, he's in Marfa. Was. He seemed like a nice guy. I didn't work with him, but he must've been a good lawyer, working for the firm's biggest client.'

'Billy Bob Barnett?'

'Yeah. What are you and Bookman doing in Midland?'

'We came to see Tom Dunn.'

Sylvia frowned. 'The dark lord. He's so creepy. When he talks to me, he talks to my breasts.'

'I noticed. And I barely have breasts.'

'It's just the thought of it, for guys like Dunn.'

They shared a giggle.

'I didn't see you at Nathan's funeral yesterday,' Nadine said. 'Did you go?'

Sylvia shook her head. 'Dunn said he was going for the firm, told us to stay here and bill hours. He's sentimental like that.'

'Nathan wrote a letter to the professor, said there was some funny business going on with fracking. Is there?'

Sylvia shrugged. 'I don't know. Those guys in the oil and gas department, they're like a fraternity. They don't talk to us girls in estate planning. And the first thing you learn in the practice is to not ask questions and to keep your mouth shut.'

'Nathan must have missed that class. Anyone else who might know if anything odd was going on?'

'Becky.'

'Who's she?'

'Nathan's secretary.'

'Nathan treated all the girls like sisters instead of secretaries,' Becky Oakes said. 'Most lawyers treat us like slaves.'

Becky had been Nathan's secretary for the entirety of his legal career.

'Becky, did you know about the letter Nathan sent to me?'

Nadine had passed on a tour of the Petroleum Museum in Midland, so after a quick stop at the Starbucks—Nadine had drunk a venti frappuccino on the ride back—

'Don't spill that down my saddlebags,' Book had cautioned her.

'Nobody likes a tidy freak,' she had responded.

—they had returned to Marfa and caught Becky as she was leaving for the day. She glanced up and down the sidewalk then lowered her voice.

'He told me about it. What he thought was happening, with the groundwater.'

'Did you tell anyone?'

'No. I swear. No one.' She hesitated. 'Except my husband.'

'What does he do? Your husband.'

'He's a roughneck. For Billy Bob.'

Chapter 12

Padre's Marfa on West El Paso Street across from the Godbold Feed Store had once been the place to die for in Marfa. It used to be a funeral home. It was now a restaurant/bar/live music venue. Outside, the white adobe gave it the appearance of an old Spanish mission; inside, the wood bar and neon signs gave it the appearance of an old Texas honky-tonk. Book fully expected his intern to break out latex gloves, but she apparently satisfied her sanitary concerns by wiping down the entire table and then her glass, utensils, and chair. They sat at a table along the wall opposite the bar; Sean Lennon sang onstage.

'He's John Lennon's son.'

'Who's that?'

'Ms. Honeywell, please tell me you're not serious.'

Her innocent expression.

'What?'

'John Lennon? The Beatles?'

'Wait, don't tell me. He's dead.'

'He is, shot by an insane fan in nineteen eighty.'

'I wasn't born until nineteen eighty-nine.'

137

'Still, you haven't heard of Rock Hudson, James Dean, Elizabeth Taylor, Donald Judd, Andy Warhol, or John Lennon?'

'If it's not on Twitter, I don't need to know it. And, Professor, I can name a dozen people everyone my age knows but you've never heard of.'

'True enough, Ms. Honeywell. But what about the events of the day? What's happening in China, North Korea, the Middle East . . . or the east and west coasts of America?'

'I especially don't want to know that stuff.'

'Why not?'

'Because it's all bad stuff. Last time I watched the news on TV, I had to get a prescription for an antidepressant. A mass murder at an elementary school . . . politicians pushing the country over a fiscal cliff . . . suburban stay-at-home moms reading porn, which really creeped me out, by the way. Who wants to know that stuff? My generation turned off the TV, Professor.'

'Willful ignorance.'

'Willful ignorance' is a legal term, also known as 'conscious indifference,' for intentionally not knowing some fact, typically CEOs intentionally avoiding knowledge that their companies' subcontractors produce their apparel in Asian sweatshops or that nicotine is addictive, thus allowing the CEOs to testify under oath, 'I didn't know,' when in fact the correct response was, 'I didn't want to know.'

'Exactly,' his intern said. 'We live our lives that way. It's safer.'

Book gestured at her hand sanitizer. 'You sanitize your hands and yourself from all the bad things in life.'

'What's wrong with that?'

'You're not experiencing the world you live in.'

'It's your world. Not ours. Your generation screwed it up. Not us.'

'You could change the world. Make it a better place.'

She appeared bemused. 'Please, Professor.'

'You're a law student.'

'I'm in law school because I possess the two attributes required to gain admission to the finest law schools in the country: A, I'm book smart, which allowed me to score high on the LSAT'—the Law School Admissions Test—'and B, my daddy can pay the tuition. Anyone with those two attributes can get into any law school today. You don't have to know what's happening in the world . . . or care.'

She was right. And a typical law student. A few students like Ms. Garza and perhaps Mr. Stanton seemed engaged in the world outside the law school, but only a few. Most were singularly focused on grades: those in the top ten percent of their class would have jobs upon graduation; those who were not would not. So they had no desire or time to keep up with current events. They did not watch the news or read newspapers. They read casebooks. Torts. Contracts. Property. Civil Procedure. Criminal Procedure. Con Law. For three years, the study of law constituted life.

'Well, John Lennon was a musician, singer, and songwriter, one of the best ever.'

'If you say so.'

They had first tried the outdoor patio with Christmas lights strung overhead and gravel underfoot and Willie Nelson on the jukebox, but the tables were taken by artists on iPads and hippies past their prime and a young woman who looked out of place in a glittery red cocktail dress; her black cowboy boots said she was making a fashion statement. A pit bull wearing a red bandanna lounged beneath her long crossed legs; a metal sculpture of a sombrero-clad mariachi stood behind her. The dance floor and adjacent game room with pool tables, shuffleboard, and foosball were crowded with young women in short-shorts and young men in jeans and boots and T-shirts. Of course, Book also wore jeans, boots, and a T-shirt. But he was a skinny law professor; they were thick-bodied roughnecks who worked the fracking rigs. Some wore red jumpsuits with *Barnett Oil and Gas* stenciled across the back. Their waitress was an artist; waiting tables was her night job. Book had ordered the tuna melt on sourdough, a cold pickle, and iced tea. Nadine went for chips and queso, frito pie with cheese and onions, chili cheese fries, a chocolate soda, and a moon pie. Book circled Becky Oakes's face in the funeral photo then consulted his pocket notebook.

'What did we learn today, Ms. Honeywell?'

'Are we going to have a pop quiz every night, Professor?'

'We are indeed.'

She exhaled dramatically.

'A, Tom Dunn is a creep.'

'Agreed. What else?'

'B, either he's a liar or Nathan Jones was a liar.'

'Nathan said he showed his proof to Dunn, but Dunn denied it.'

'My money's on Dunn. He's the liar.'

'Agreed.'

'We talked to the sheriff, Nathan's senior partner, and his secretary, but we uncovered no proof of contamination or evidence of murder. All we have is coincidence.'

'Nathan's wife seemed convinced that he was murdered.'

'She's emotional about his death. Which is to be expected. But we can't be. What did you always say in class? "We're lawyers. We must keep our heads while everyone around us is losing theirs."'

'You took my class?'

'Last year.'

'At least you listened.'

'Can I eat my moon pie now?'

From across the room, Jimmy John Dale watched the professor and the girl named Nadine eating dinner. You don't generally see white girls eating moon pies like that. He sat at a table with five other roughnecks who also worked for Billy Bob Barnett; they had just gotten off their shift and still wore their red

140

jumpsuits. While he was watching Nadine, they were watching another woman across the room.

'I'd love to jump her bones,' Mitch said.

'I'd love to beat the shit out of her,' Sonny said. 'She's trying to shut down fracking, take our jobs.'

'Still, Carla's got a great body.'

Mitch was always practical like that. Jimmy John rubbed his temples. The headache was coming back.

'Can we go home now?'

'No.'

The band took a break. Book was watching his intern devour the moon pie when a young woman walked up and sat down at their table across from Book and next to Nadine and scooted in close. Nadine frowned at her then moved her chair over a bit. Book read her shirt: *Fracking is for Gas Holes*—

'Funny,' he said.

—and she read his Tommy Bahama shirt: *I Plead the Fifth* with a bottle of rum.

'Yours, too.'

She seemed familiar. He had seen her before. He looked at the funeral photo in front of him. She was the young woman standing off to the side during the burial of Nathan Jones.

'Professor Bookman, I'm Carla Kent. I need to talk to you.'

'I'm listening.'

'Nathan came to me.'

'Where?'

'My teepee at El Cosmico.'

'You have your own teepee?'

'Long-term stay.'

'What did he come to you about?'

'Fracking.'

'Why you?'

'Everyone in town knows me. I'm trying to shut down fracking.'

'You're an environmentalist?'

'From Santa Fe. Professor, Nathan was scared. Now he's dead. Because he knew something he wasn't supposed to know.'

'What?'

'Billy Bob's fracking is contaminating the Igneous Aquifer, the sole water source for this whole area—Marfa, Fort Davis, Alpine. Nathan said he had proof. They killed him to prevent that proof from becoming public.'

'It was an accident,' Nadine said.

'It was murder.'

'Billy Bob Barnett is a murderer?' Book asked.

'He is.' She seemed deadly serious. 'Professor, help me put that bastard in prison where he belongs.'

'Do you have any evidence of murder?'

'No.'

'Did you see Nathan's proof of contamination?'

'No.'

'Ms. Kent, I'm not here to shut down fracking. I'm just trying to find out how my student died.'

'And I'm trying to tell you how he died—he was murdered!'

Her emotions resided close to the surface. She took a deep breath to gather herself.

'Professor, I cared about Nathan.'

'You were at his funeral.'

'And Nathan cared about this land. And the people who live on it. The water they drink. He didn't know what to do, but he said he knew someone who would help us—he said *us*—a professor at UT. I thought he meant a petroleum engineering professor. Not a law professor.'

'I have other skills.'

'The paper said you came here for Nathan.'

'I might've come for the art.'

'Can I see it?'

'The art?'

'The letter.'

'Ms. Kent . . .'

'You showed it to everyone else in town.'

'That's true,' Nadine said.

Book gave his intern a sharp look then handed the letter to Carla. She read it.

'See, he said his client is contaminating the aquifer. He meant Billy Bob. And now he's dead.' She checked the postmark on the envelope. 'Died the same day he mailed the letter. That seem odd to you?'

'Oh, God,' Nadine said. 'Don't tell me you don't believe in coincidences?'

'Not that much of a coincidence. Professor, Nathan said he hadn't put all the pieces together yet, said he'd come back to me when he did. Maybe he did. Maybe he put the pieces together. Maybe Billy Bob killed him. Professor, work with me. Please.'

'I'm sorry, Ms. Kent. I work alone.'

'Then why'd you bring me?' Nadine said.

'I mean, alone with an intern. This is Nadine Honeywell.'

'If you didn't come to Marfa to find the truth,' Carla said, 'then why'd you come?'

'To fish.'

'*Fish? Where?* There's no water between here and the Rio Grande, and if you eat fish from that cesspool you'll die.'

Carla now gave him a sharp look; she stood.

'Don't toy with me, Professor.'

She marched over to the bar. Book watched after her. She was an attractive woman, lean with a low body mass index, no older than thirty, with dark hair and eyes. She wore tight jeans, boots, and the T-shirt. She looked tough.

'Don't worry,' Nadine said. 'You won't be romancing a lesbian.'

'I don't plan on romancing her, but how do you know she's not a lesbian?'

'Because I attract lesbians. I don't know why. But she wasn't attracted to me. She was to you. She'll be back.'

Nadine sipped her soda.

'Why'd you play coy with her?'

'Because I don't know her.'

Nadine nodded at the bar.

'Everyone else does.'

The locals at the bar regarded Carla as if she had a communicable disease; she was apparently well known but not welcome. She stood alone.

'Come on,' Sonny said. 'Let's have some fun with Carla.'

'I wouldn't do that if I was you,' Jimmy John said.

'Why not?'

'Looks like she's friends with the professor.'

'What professor?'

'Don't you read the newspaper?'

'Hell, no.'

Jimmy John pointed with his forehead in the professor's direction.

'Him?' Sonny said. 'That skinny-ass guy she was talking to, he's a professor?'

'Yep.'

'That long hair, he looks like one of them queer artists. We're supposed to be scared of him?'

Sonny grabbed his Lone Star longneck and headed over to Carla at the bar. Mitch and the others followed. Jimmy John popped two Advil and chased them with a beer.

'We'll get started on the Welch brief tonight,' Book said to his intern. But his eyes were on the bar where several roughnecks wearing red *Barnett Oil and Gas* jumpsuits and holding longnecks walked up and bookended Carla. They said something to her, and she said something to them. It was obviously not polite conversation. She got in one man's face and said what appeared to be the F-word and not 'fracking.' She turned to leave, but the roughnecks grabbed her arms. She struggled against their holds. Her eyes went to Book. She no longer looked tough.

He groaned then pushed himself up and walked over to Carla and the roughnecks. They were bigger, stronger, younger, and drunker.

'How about a dance, Ms. Kent?'

'I'd love to.'

She again tried to pull away, but the roughnecks maintained their hold.

'The lady wants to dance,' Book said.

The biggest roughneck held up one finger and said, 'A, she ain't no lady.'

A second finger.

'Two, there ain't no music playing.'

A third finger.

'And D, this ain't—'

'No, no, no,' Book said. 'You either say "three" or "C," not "D." D would be four fingers.'

'Oh.'

The roughneck held up four fingers.

'And C, this ain't none of your goddamned business, Pocahontas.'

Book sighed. The Indian thing again. A few more rough-necks holding longnecks joined the party. They had Book pinned to the bar.

'Oh, shit.'

Those big brutes would beat up the professor for sure. He really was crazy. Nadine searched the crowded room and spotted a familiar face. She stuffed the rest of the moon pie into her mouth then jumped up and hurried over to the young man sitting alone at a table. His eyes turned up to her; she pointed at the professor.

145

'He needs help! Do something!'

Her words sounded garbled through the moon pie. She swallowed and tried again.

'He needs help! Do something!'

The Border Patrol agent named Wesley Crum offered only a lame shrug.

'No jurisdiction. He's an Injun, not a Mexican. Call someone at the Bureau of Indian Affairs.'

He thought that was funny.

Book pointed a finger as he counted the men in the red jumpsuits.

'One, two, three, four . . . Are you with them? . . . Five. You know, this really isn't a fair fight.'

'So?'

'So there are only five of you.'

'He's a funny Injun,' the big roughneck to his right said.

Five men, five moves, five seconds max. Right to left down the line. They would go down like dominoes. Book needed the big roughneck to his right to start the action, so he said, 'And you're an asshole.'

The roughneck reached for Book with his non-beer-holding hand and took a step closer. That was a mistake. Book drove his left knee into the man's groin . . . he went down to his knees . . . then a right-hand throat strike to the second man . . . he gagged and fell backwards . . . now a left-hand back fist to the third man's temple . . . he stumbled back and grabbed his head . . . then a reverse punch to the fourth man's face . . . he collapsed to the floor . . . and finally a—but the fifth man stepped back out of range.

Book gestured with his fingers for him to come closer. He shook his head. Book gestured again. The man's eyes turned from Book to behind Book. He spun around just in time to see Nadine slam a beer bottle over the bald head of another roughneck holding a pool cue as if he were about to clock Book in

146

the head. The roughneck's eyes rolled back, and he crumpled to the floor. Nadine held the broken beer bottle in one hand and the chocolate soda in the other. She sucked from the straw.

'Can we go home now?'

Carla's eyes went from Book to the roughnecks groaning and holding various parts of their bodies and then back to Book.

'I thought you're a law professor?'

'I said I had other skills.'

Her eyes twinkled. 'Are those all your physical skills?'

They shared a long gaze, which was not interrupted when a meaty hand clamped down on Book's right arm and a gruff voice said, 'Time for you to leave, buddy.'

Book maintained his gaze with Carla but grabbed the man's hand and turned his wrist counterclockwise and dug his fingers into the man's palm pressure point until his knees buckled and he went down to the floor.

'I'll leave when I damn well please.'

He broke eye contact with Carla, released the man, and then turned to Nadine.

'Let's leave, Ms. Honeywell.'

'Town?'

'This bar.'

They headed to the door, but he heard Carla's voice from behind.

'I'll take a rain check on that dance, Professor.'

From across the bar, Jimmy John shook his head. He hated to be an 'I told you so,' but Sonny and Mitch never listened. The girl named Nadine was kind of cute and good with a beer bottle to boot.

'Is it unconstitutional under the Fourth Amendment's prohibition against unreasonable searches and seizures for the police to draw a suspect's blood without consent?'

Nadine Honeywell typed on the laptop, but she couldn't focus on the Welch brief because her body still tingled with fear and excitement and adrenaline—she had actually smashed a beer bottle over that big brute's bald head! OMG! She had never done anything like that in her entire life! Normally, when faced with such a physical conflict, she would have grabbed the moon pie and chocolate soda and dove under the table and hidden from the danger. But the professor's kung fu butt-kicking had shifted her adrenal glands into high gear, and she had just acted out all her fantasies—well, not the one with that tall guy at the fish shop in San Francisco, where she's at home cooking in her apron and nothing else and he delivers a big salmon and one thing leads to another and soon their bodies are covered in extra virgin olive oil and . . . she blew out a breath . . . God, that's a great fantasy . . . but the one where she wasn't a timid law student afraid of life who cowered before conflict and ran from . . . okay, okay, we've been through that too many times, just let it go . . . Where was she? Oh, yeah, she hadn't even made a conscious decision to do it; she had just done it. She saw him advance on the professor from behind with the pool cue and knew he was going to hit the professor. He could have been killed. Her future flashed before her eyes: the professor is dead; she's stuck in Marfa; no one to call but her father; he flies in from San Francisco; he is not happy with his daughter. That dire prospect gave her the incentive to grab the bottle and swing it as hard as she could at the guy's head. She still couldn't believe she had knocked him unconscious. But she was always strong for her size.

It felt really good. Not to be afraid.

She sat propped up in Elizabeth Taylor's bed. The professor had put her to work on the Welch brief then gone next door to Rock Hudson's room to return phone calls. Cell phone reception was better on the outdoor patio.

★   ★   ★

148

Joanie had left three messages for Book at the Paisano. He called his sister back from the rooftop patio. The sky was dark and the stars bright. And a young lawyer was dead. Did he fall asleep at the wheel or was he run off the road? Was his death an accident or a murder? Was it just a coincidence that he died the same day he mailed the letter? And the most perplexing question of all: how do you find a dead man's truth?

Chapter 13

At dawn, Book exited the courtyard at the Paisano and ran south on Highland Avenue past the Andy Warhol and John Chamberlain exhibits and the railroad tracks just before the crossing arms came down and a train roared through town and the yellow corrugated buildings at the Border Patrol sector headquarters and the sign that read 'Chinati Foundation' and the teepees at El Cosmico—

Carla Kent stood under the shower and let the water wash over her body. The air was cold, but the water was hot. The open-air community bathhouse had a roof and partial wood sides that provided some modesty if one were modest, but it offered a majestic view of the mountain ranges that surrounded the Marfa Plateau and Cathedral Rock to the east, a mountain peak shaped like the Great Sphinx. She loved dawn in the desert. An unspoiled land she would fight to protect from fracking. It was her mission in life. That and to see Billy Bob Barnett in prison or dead. Preferably dead. She rinsed the shampoo from her hair; when she opened her eyes, she saw a lone runner heading south on Highway 67 that fronted El Cosmico.

The professor.

—and a strange configuration of large concrete boxes aligned in an open field parallel to the road; his breath fogged in the morning air. He cleared civilization and ran on the strip of asphalt cutting through the desert; not a single car passed him. He thought of the Comanche when they had roamed this same desert; they accepted it on its own terms with no need to make it something more. Then Hanna's train had come and changed the desert and their lives. He felt the desert changing him—and he knew it would change him more before he rode the Harley home. He ran several more miles then turned back and headed north. But he stopped to observe the shadows cast onto the yellow prairie grass by the rising sun off the concrete boxes.

It was oddly mesmerizing.

When he arrived back at the hotel, he did not enter the lobby. The Paisano did not serve breakfast, so he continued up the sidewalk past the small Chamber of Commerce office and Consuelo's Bookkeeping and Tax Service and then turned west on Lincoln Street. Half a block down, he ducked into the small courtyard of SqueezeMarfa, the sheriff's favorite breakfast spot. He went inside and ordered a Strawberry Banana Cabana smoothie with nonfat vanilla yogurt then sat outside and pondered the life and death of Nathan Jones.

His life was short.

His death was fast.

Was it murder?

Or just an accident?

Book wanted Nathan's death to be something more than an accident—just as he had wanted his father's death to be something more than a drug-addicted homeless man grabbing his

151

service gun and shooting him. Perhaps that was the human ego at work: his father had been important in his life; *ergo*, his life should warrant an important ending. Nathan had saved his life; therefore, his life should warrant a more important ending than a car accident.

But that was not life.

Life seemed to be one continuous accident. Birth—where, when, and to whom—is just an accident of fate, a genetic lottery. Win that lottery, and you're born in a first-world country with opportunities in life and a life expectancy of seventy-eight years or more. Lose, and you're born in a third-world country with no opportunities and a life expectancy of forty-eight years or less. Death—early, late, natural, violent— no matter your station in life, death would come to you. Would it come at age five, thirty-five, or seventy-five? Would it come by crime or disease or old age? Was that destiny or luck? God's will or man's mistake? In the end, it didn't really matter. It is what happens between birth and death that matters. That makes us matter. As Ms. Roberts had said in class, 'Do we matter? Or are we just matter?' And so Book was left to wonder:

Had Nathan Jones's life mattered?

Had Ben Bookman's life mattered?

Would his own life matter?

Book entered the hotel and stopped at the front desk.

'Another night, please.'

'Yes, sir, Professor,' the desk clerk said. 'But Miss Honeywell won't be happy.'

He took breakfast back to Nadine—a large coffee, sandwich baguette (scrambled eggs, Swiss cheese, and ham on a toasted demi-baguette), and a waffle with chocolate syrup and whipped cream. He figured that would hold her until lunch. He had granola and more yogurt.

But she wasn't in her room.

Fear shot through him like a bullet. Perhaps the bald guy she had clocked at Padre's had come looking for her. Book had promised to protect her. He ran back downstairs and checked the *Giant* museum; she wasn't there. Or in Jett's Grill. Or in the small library. Or in the ballroom. Or in the—

She was in the pool.

It had been built just off the ballroom where an outdoor patio had once stood, surrounded by thick adobe walls but open to the sky. The sun was now shut out by a plastic corrugated cover, which created a sauna-like atmosphere at pool level. Steam rose off the water; it was a heated pool. The space smelled of chlorine. Nadine Honeywell was alone in the pool, swimming laps. He breathed a sigh of relief. When she swam back his way, she saw him and stood. Her skin looked like a sheet of white paper against the blue water.

'Ms. Honeywell, has your skin ever seen the sun?'

'I don't think so. I use sunblock with a two hundred SPF rating.'

'They go that high?'

'No. I put on two coats of a hundred.'

'Why?'

She gave him a puzzled look. '*Hel-lo?* Melanoma?'

Book pointed up. 'The pool is covered. And it's still morning. The sun's not overhead yet.'

'Can't be too careful.'

She climbed out of the pool.

'I found this suit in the gift shop.'

The snug one-piece suit revealed a lean body he hadn't noticed before with her baggy clothes. She caught him appraising her.

'I have a swimmer's body. Might be why lesbians are attracted to me.'

She wrapped a green-and-white striped towel around herself. They sat in patio chairs around a small table. She dug her sanitizing materials out of her canvas bag and went through her standard routine. Then they ate breakfast.

'You're a good swimmer.'

'I trained when I was a teenager.'

'Is that why you eat so much, your swim training?'

'You should've seen what I used to eat. Four hours a day in the pool burns some calories. And I have a high metabolism.'

'Did you compete?'

'No.'

'Why not?'

'Afraid.'

'Of drowning?'

'Losing.'

'So you never won?'

'Story of my life.'

She finished the last of the waffle and drank the coffee.

'Thanks for last night,' Book said. 'That pool cue wouldn't have done my head much good.'

'I guess that means if I ever get into trouble, you'll have to help me.'

'Ms. Honeywell, you've earned a lifetime pass.'

She pondered that prospect a moment then smiled.

'Okay,' Book said, 'what have we learned since the last quiz?'

'A, I know you can protect me now, that kung fu fighting.'

'Taekwondo.'

'B, I like to hit bad guys with beer bottles.'

'Do you now?'

'I do. And C, Nathan didn't show his proof to that Carla girl either. Which makes me question if there ever was any actual proof. Maybe Nathan just wanted there to be proof.'

'Very good, Ms. Honeywell. You're questioning every assumption and every supposed fact. You'll make a good lawyer.'

'Chef.'

She sipped her coffee.

'Professor, can I ask you something?'

'Of course.'

'So far you've shown Nathan's letter to everyone we've met in town except the desk clerk. Why?'

'Bait.'

'Bait?'

'See if anyone bites.'

'Fish. You told Carla you were here to fish. Funny. So who do you want to catch?'

'Whoever killed Nathan.'

'What if no one bites?'

'Then it was just an accident.'

She considered that through several sips of coffee. Then she said, 'You're kind of sneaky, aren't you?'

'Comanche.'

Chapter 14

'Professor, I've heard "fracking this" and "fracking that" ever since we rode into town, but I don't even know what fracking is.'

'You're about to find out.'

'From whom?'

Book unfolded the funeral photo and pointed at the big man with the bald head.

'The big fish.'

A four-wheel-drive maroon Cadillac pickup truck with a *Gig 'em, Aggies* decal on the back window sat parked at the curb outside the Barnett Oil and Gas Company Building on Highland Avenue just down from the hotel. They walked inside. On the floor was maroon carpet; on the walls were photos of the Texas A&M University football field, the football team, and the male cheerleaders. The school's colors were maroon and white. Book stepped over to the receptionist—a broad-shouldered young woman who looked a bit manly—and asked to see Billy Bob Barnett.

'And you are?'

'Professor John Bookman, from UT.'

'A professor?'

'Is that a problem?'

'The UT might be. Billy Bob hates the Longhorns.'

'The cattle or the people?'

'Funny. What do you teach?'

'Constitutional law,' a deep male voice behind them said.

Book turned to the same big man in the funeral photo. He had a bald head—not bald with fuzz on the sides but shaved-to-the-bare-skin bald, as if a white bowling ball sat atop his shoulders—and a black goatee streaked with gray. He wore jeans, a maroon cowboy belt with a fancy silver buckle, maroon boots, and a maroon A&M golf shirt. He looked to be in his late forties, stood six-two, and weighed two-fifty or more.

'He's the famous law professor, Earlene. He's on TV damn near every Sunday morning, making those senators look stupid. Course, that ain't exactly man's work.'

He sniffled and swiped the back of his hand across his nose then walked over, stuck out the same hand to Book, and flashed a big smile.

'Billy Bob Barnett.'

Book hesitated then shook hands.

'John Bookman.'

'Professor, it's an honor. Course, you didn't have to dress up for me.'

He hadn't. Book wore jeans, boots, a blue Tommy Bahama T-shirt, sunglasses on a braided cord around his neck, and his black running watch. No rings.

'And my intern, Nadine Honeywell.'

She wore shorts that revealed her swimmer's legs. Billy Bob's eyes roamed her body with lascivious intent.

'Well, honey.'

He had amused himself with his play on her name. Book gestured at the photos on the wall to divert Billy Bob's leer from his intern.

'Did you play football at A&M?'

'Yell leader.'

Unlike the University of Texas, which offers gorgeous coeds in leather chaps, biker shorts, and torso-revealing fringed cowgirl shirts as cheerleaders at football games, Texas A&M offers five male students in white shirts and trousers as 'yell leaders.' The former Aggie yell leader standing before Book abruptly threw his arms out and broke into a yell.

Squads left! Squads right!
Farmers, farmers, we're all right!
Load, ready, aim, fire, BOOM!
Reload!

Nadine had recoiled in fright when Billy Bob began his yell. 'Wow,' she now said. 'That's really scary.'

'It is for Longhorns,' Billy Bob said with a big grin.

A&M boasted a proud agricultural and military tradition, although the A and the M originally stood for 'Agricultural' and 'Mechanical,' and the students were initially called 'Farmers,' but later became 'Aggies,' a common nickname for students at Ag schools. The downside is that the nickname encouraged UT Longhorn students to make up jokes mocking Aggies as dumb farmers, such as:

How do Aggies practice safe sex?
They get rid of all the animals that kick.

'Anyway,' Billy Bob said, 'I got a degree in petroleum engineering, minor in international politics, which is damn near required knowledge to play the oil and gas game today. Not like back in the day, when the Texas Railroad Commission controlled the price of oil in the world, before OPEC came on the scene. Before my time, but old-timers tell me the oil and gas business was really fun back then. How 'bout some coffee and donuts?'

'No, thank—'

'What kind of donuts?' Nadine asked.

'Honeywell, we got chocolate donuts and glazed donuts and sprinkled donuts and crème-filled donuts and just about every kind of donut they make. You like donuts?'

'I love donuts.'

'Me, too. Come on back, we'll get you sugared up . . . sugar.'

Billy Bob abruptly turned away and sneezed—Nadine used the opportunity to make a gagging gesture with her finger at her mouth—then he blew his nose into a white handkerchief.

'Damn head cold.'

They followed him down a hallway; he jabbed a thumb behind them.

'Receptionist, she's more an Earl than an Earlene, but she can double as my bodyguard in a pinch.'

'You need a bodyguard in Marfa?' Book asked.

'Never know, all these artists and environmentalists.'

Nadine pulled out her hand sanitizer and offered Book a squirt; he was about to decline when Billy Bob sniffled and then wiped his hand across his nose again. Book stuck an open palm out to her; she gave him a good squirt. He rubbed the gel into his hands as they followed Billy Bob into a lunchroom. On a table sat a platter of donut paradise. Nadine's eyes sparkled.

'Oh, boy.'

She squirted sanitizer into her hand and rubbed quickly while she studied the donuts. Billy Bob grabbed a massive donut with colorful sprinkles on top; his belly testified to a serious donut habit. He waved a hand at the platter of sugar.

'Take what you want, Honeywell.'

She did. A big chocolate-covered donut.

'Can I have coffee, too?'

'Help yourself.'

She did. A tall Styrofoam cup of caffeine.

'Read in the paper you were in town, Professor,' Billy Bob said. He stuffed half the donut in his mouth. Blue and red and

159

pink sprinkles now dotted his goatee. 'And I heard you roughed up a couple of my boys last night at Padre's. With that kung fu crap.'

'Taekwondo. Only after your boys accosted a lady.'

'Carla's no lady. Cusses like a roughneck and votes like a Commie. She's an environmentalist.' He had amused himself again. 'Course, she fits right in now, all those New York homosexuals moving down here, voting Democrat . . . Hell, Presidio County went for Obama, only county in all of West Texas. That's pretty goddamn embarrassing, if you ask me.'

'I didn't.'

'If you did.' He finished off the donut. 'You know, Carla, her—'

Billy Bob stopped short his sentence as if he had thought better of it. He abruptly pivoted and lumbered out. Nadine crammed the last of her donut into her mouth as if she were in a donut-eating contest then quickly grabbed another chocolate one; they followed Billy Bob farther down the hallway. Book whispered to Nadine.

'You know how much sugar you're putting in your body?'

'Better than a man,' she said through a mouthful of donut.

They entered an expansive office with the courthouse cupola framed in a wall of glass. Billy Bob gestured at two chairs in front of a massive wood desk that looked as if it had been carved out of a redwood tree.

'Take a load off.'

He circled the desk and dropped into a leather chair that resembled a throne. They sat in the visitors' chairs. The office featured wood and leather and the aroma of cigars. A tall bookshelf behind Billy Bob held more Aggie memorabilia, signed footballs and framed photographs of Billy Bob with coaches and the governor of Texas, a former yell leader himself. On the wall opposite the desk hung a huge flat screen television; on the side wall were large maps of Texas, the U.S., and the world. The desktop was clean except for a copy of *The Times of Marfa* with Book's photo on the front page, a remote control, and a Western-style handgun sitting atop a thick stack of papers. Billy Bob swiveled in his chair, reached into a cigar box on the shelf, and removed a long cigar. He held it out to Book, but Book shook his head. Billy Bob clamped his teeth around the cigar.

'I hate Commies, but the Cubans do make good cigars.'

He picked up the handgun, pointed the barrel at Book, and pulled the trigger. A flame shot out the barrel.

'Lighter.'

He moved the flame to the end of the cigar, but Book's intern stopped him cold.

'No!'

Billy Bob looked at her. 'What?'

'I have allergies.'

Billy Bob studied her a moment then released the trigger of the handgun-lighter. The flame disappeared. He replaced the lighter on the stack of papers. His gaze returned to Nadine, as if expecting a show of appreciation for his chivalry. But all he got was, 'Thanks.' Book decided to use the moment to begin his cross-examination of Billy Bob Barnett.

'Mr. Barnett, are your fracking operations contaminating the groundwater?'

Some lawyers believe that aggressive rapid-fire questioning is the most effective form of cross. Perhaps it is in a courtroom where the witness knows he is the target. But outside a courtroom, when you're still stalking the target, when the witness does not yet know he is the target—when you're not even sure he is the target—such questioning is not effective. The witness simply refuses to answer your questions; and there is no judge to force an answer.

Book wanted answers from Billy Bob Barnett.

So he opted for a different technique. One that encouraged the witness to talk—about himself, his work, and his life. That technique required a provocative opening inquiry

161

and a certain amount of patience. Most people want to convince you that they're good, that their work is important, that their lives are relevant. If given the opportunity, they will talk. And if their favorite topic of conversation happens to be the person they see in the mirror—and Billy Bob Barnett seemed that type of man—they will talk a lot. Reveal a lot. Perhaps even incriminate themselves. Book felt certain that the man sitting across the desk had much to offer in the way of self-incrimination.

Billy Bob's eyes slowly came off Nadine and onto Book; he held his expression a moment then broke into a hearty laugh.

'Well, good morning to you, too, Professor. Damn, you sure don't waste any time with small talk, do you? Hell, and I was gonna try and recruit you away from UT for our new A&M law school. Professor of your stature, just what we need to get it off the ground. Five years from now, our law school will be better than yours.'

Only a hundred miles separates the University of Texas at Austin and Texas A&M University at College Station, but the two schools have been bitter archrivals for over a hundred years. Both enroll fifty thousand students, but the student bodies resemble the national political parties: UT is liberal, green, anti-war, and Democrat; A&M is conservative, oil and gas, the corps, and Republican. The Lyndon Baines Johnson Library and Museum stands on the UT campus; the George H. W. Bush Presidential Library stands on the A&M campus. The schools have competed in putting prominent politicians, business leaders, scientists, military officers, academics, artists, actors, and athletes into the world—but never lawyers. Because A&M had no law school. Until now. The A&M alumni had finally gotten their law school, and they were determined to fund it to whatever extent necessary to top UT. Billy Bob jabbed the unlit cigar in the air.

'And we're sure as hell not gonna hire a bunch of goddamn left-wing professors from Harvard and Yale, I guarandamntee you.'

'Not enough jobs for law grads as it is, might not be the best time to start a new law school.'

'Not to worry, Professor. Aggies take care of each other. We're akin to a cult, like Mormons without the extra wives. We'll make damn sure every graduate gets a job. And Mr. Barnett was my daddy. I'm just Billy Bob.'

'Billy Bob. Same question. Are your fracking—'

'Hydraulic fracturing,' he said, carefully pronouncing each syllable as if he were a kindergartner sounding out the words. 'We don't say "fracking." Myself, I prefer "hydraulic stimulation."'

'Why not fracking?'

'Stimulation sounds fun; not so much fracking. And some sci-fi movie used it like the F-word, to mean sex. Environmentalists picked up on it, plastered it on T-shirts, billboards, bumper stickers. "Frack Me" . . . "Frack You" . . . "Frack Off" . . . "Frack This" . . . "Frack That" . . .'

Nadine giggled.

'It ain't funny,' Billy Bob said.

'It's pretty funny.'

Billy Bob bit down on the cigar, leaned back in his throne, crossed his thick arms, and studied Nadine Honeywell a long uncomfortable moment. He removed the cigar.

'You want a job, Honeywell?'

'I want to be a chef.'

'The hell you doing in law school?'

'My dad wants me to be a lawyer.'

Billy Bob nodded. 'My dad wanted me to be a lawyer, too. Respectable. Instead, I'm rich. Course, I wouldn't have been a good lawyer, never was much for book work. So I went to A&M.'

'Was he mad when you didn't go to law school?'

163

Billy Bob grinned. 'Fit to be tied.'

'Did he ever forgive you?'

'He died.'

That thought lingered like cigar smoke until Book broke the silence.

'Billy Bob, is your hydraulic stimulation contaminating the groundwater?'

Billy Bob snapped back to the moment. 'Hell, no. The Energy Institute at your own UT confirmed that, said there's no direct connection between hydraulic stimulation and groundwater contamination.'

'Well, that might be so, but your own lawyer said otherwise.'

'The hell you talking about?'

Book pulled out Nathan's letter and slid it across the desk. Billy Bob examined the envelope then removed and read the letter. He sniffled and breathed through his mouth. He finally looked up with a frown.

'Aren't lawyers supposed to be loyal to their clients?'

'Some lawyers have consciences.'

'Not the ones I hire.'

The frown left, and he sighed.

'Nathan was a good boy and a good lawyer. Smart and dependable. Cute gal for a wife. What's her name?'

'Brenda.'

'Yeah, Brenda.' He shook his head. 'His kid's gonna grow up without a dad.'

'Was Nathan your primary lawyer?'

'Here in Marfa. Tom Dunn—you met him, I heard—he's my main lawyer. Nathan handled my day-to-day matters down here—lawsuits, leases, permits, contracts, that sort of thing. He was a hard-working lawyer. I liked him. Real sorry he died. Terrible accident. I told him to slow down—'

'He drove fast?'

'This is West Texas. Everyone drives fast. But I don't have a clue what he's talking about in this letter, Professor. I'm a

164

fracker'—he grimaced—'a stimulator and damn proud of it. I'm saving America from the Muslims and Europe from the Russians.'

'What do you do on weekends?'

'And contrary to what you hear and read in the left-wing media, fracking'—another grimace—'stimulation is completely safe to humans and the environment.'

He picked up the remote control and pointed it at the TV. The screen flashed on to a YouTube video showing a drilling rig.

'Watch and learn, Professor—the ABCs of hydraulic stimulation.'

The video played on the screen narrated by a friendly male voice, as if Mister Rogers were explaining fracking to the neighborhood kids.

The narrator: '*Geologists have known for years that substantial deposits of oil and natural gas are trapped in deep shale formations. These shale reservoirs were created tens of millions of years ago. Around the world today, with modern horizontal drilling techniques and hydraulic fracturing, the trapped oil and natural gas in these shale reservoirs is being safely and efficiently produced, gathered, and distributed to customers. Let's look at the drilling and completion process of a typical oil and natural gas well.*'

A color animation depicted the drilling of a well through a cross-section of the earth.

'*Shale reservoirs are usually one mile or more below the surface, well below any underground source of drinking water, which is typically no more than three hundred to one thousand feet below the surface.*'

The video showed a drill bit cutting through a blue aquifer at '300–1,000 feet' and then descending down to a gas reservoir at '5,000–13,000 feet.'

'*Additionally, steel pipes, called casing, cemented in place, provide a multi-layered barrier to protect fresh-water aquifers.*'

Book raised his hand, as if he were back in third grade. Billy Bob paused the video and raised his eyebrows.

165

'Yes, Professor?'

'Steel and cement casing,' Book said. 'Isn't that what they had on that offshore rig that blew out, spilled millions of gallons of crude oil in the Gulf of Mexico?'

'What they had were idiots making decisions.'

Billy Bob clicked the remote and resumed the video.

'During the past sixty years, the oil and gas industry has conducted fracture stimulations in over one million wells worldwide. The initial steps are the same as for any conventional well. A hole is drilled straight down using fresh-water-based fluid, which cools the drill bit, carries the rock cuttings back to the surface, and stabilizes the wall of the well bore. Once the hole extends below the deepest fresh-water aquifer, the drill pipe is removed and replaced with steel pipe, called surface casing. Next, cement is pumped down the casing. When it reaches the bottom, it is pumped down and then back up between the casing and the bore hole wall, creating an impermeable additional protective barrier between the well bore and any fresh-water sources.'

Book raised his hand again. Billy Bob paused the video again.

'Impermeable?' Book said. 'Cement sidewalks crack over time, why not cement casings? Can you guarantee no leakage?'

'Industry guidelines only require no *significant* leakage.'

'Significant? What does that mean?'

'More than insignificant.'

Billy Bob restarted the video.

'What makes drilling for hydrocarbons in a shale formation unique is the necessity to drill horizontally. Vertical drilling continues to a depth called the "kickoff point." This is where the well bore begins curving to become horizontal.'

The animation showed the drill bit slowly turning to a ninety-degree course through the earth.

'When the targeted distance is reached, the drill pipe is removed and additional steel casing is inserted through the full length of the well bore. Once again, the casing is cemented in place. Once the

drilling is finished and the final casing has been installed, the drilling rig is removed and preparations are made for the next steps: well completion. The first step in completing a well is the creation of a connection between the final casing and the reservoir rock. This consists of lowering a specialized tool called a perforating gun, which is equipped with shaped explosive charges, down to the rock layer containing oil or natural gas. This perforating gun is then fired, which creates holes through the casing, cement, and into the target rock. These perforating holes connect the reservoir and the well bore. Since these perforations are only a few inches long and are performed more than a mile underground, the entire process is imperceptible on the surface.'

Book held up a hand. Billy Bob exhaled then stopped the video.

'You're setting off explosive charges inside the earth?'

'Same thing they do in mining.'

'I read something about fracking causing earthquakes.'

Billy Bob snorted. '*Minor* earthquakes.'

He resumed the video.

'*The perforation gun is then removed in preparation for the next step: hydraulic fracturing. The process consists of pumping a mixture of mostly water . . .*'

Book raised a finger; he felt almost apologetic. Billy Bob paused the video.

'How much water?'

'Five million gallons.'

'Per well?'

'Yep.'

'What's your source?'

'Aquifer.'

'That's drinking water.'

'Not after I use it to fracture a well.'

'Lot of water.'

'Lot of gas. But actually, Professor, it's not that much water because it's a one-time usage with fracturing. A regulation

167

golf course uses five million gallons of water every month. And we only use two gallons of water per million BTUs. Ethanol production uses twenty-five hundred gallons to produce the same amount of energy.' Another snort of disgust. 'What a joke that is. And Bush gave 'em the ethanol tax break. Now every farmer in America is growing corn for the ethanol plants.'

He restarted the video.

'. . . and sand plus a few chemicals . . .'

Nadine shot her hand into the air and waved it like Ms. Garza wanting attention. Billy Bob paused the video and regarded her.

'You too, Honeywell?'

'What chemicals?'

'Same stuff you find under your kitchen sink.'

'Like Drano?'

'You want your kids drinking frack fluids?' Book said.

'Maybe, but the little bastards live in Houston with their mother. My first ex. Second ex, she lives in Dallas. Third, she got my house in Aspen. Goddamn community property laws. You'd think I'd learn about women.'

'Or they'd learn about you.'

'Hey, they did just fine by me.'

Almost as if he were bragging about how much he had lost in his divorces.

'But not to worry, Professor, we're not contaminating the groundwater. The chemicals we use, they're harmless. Watch.'

He restarted the video. On the screen a list of chemicals came up. Book read the list aloud.

'Chloride.'

'Table salt,' Billy Bob said.

'Polyacrylamide.'

'In contact lenses.'

'Ethylene glycol.'

'Household cleaners.'

'Sodium and potassium carbonate.'

'Laundry detergent.'

'Glutaraldehyde.'

'Disinfectant.'

'Guar gum.'

'Ice cream.'

'Citric acid.'

'Sodas, ice cream, cosmetics.'

'Isopropanol.'

'Deodorant.'

Billy Bob turned his hands up as if innocent of all charges.

'See, Professor, that's just regular stuff. We ain't putting diesel fuel down the hole anymore.'

'You used to?'

'Back in the day. But the Environmental Protection Agency banned diesel in slick water back in oh-five.'

'Slick water? Is that the same as frack fluid?'

'We don't say frack, so we call it slick water.'

'I guess that does sound better than "toxic brew" or "chemical cocktail."'

'Much.'

'. . . under controlled conditions into deep underground reservoir formations. The chemicals are generally for lubrication, to keep bacteria from forming, and help carry the sand. These chemicals typically range in concentration from zero-point-one to zero-point-five percent by volume . . .'

Book raised his hand; Billy Bob sighed and stopped the video.

'Damn, Professor, I wouldn't want to go to a movie show with you.'

'One-half percent of five million gallons is still, what—'

'Twenty-five thousand gallons,' Nadine said

Book and Billy Bob both cut their eyes to her. She shrugged.

'I'm good with numbers.'

Book turned back to Billy Bob. 'Twenty-five thousand gallons of toxic chemicals pumped down into the earth? In each well?'

'Can we watch the video? This is the good part.'

Billy Bob pointed the remote, and the animation went into action.

'. . . *and help to improve the performance of the stimulation. This stimulation fluid is sent to trucks that pump the fluid into the well bore and out through the perforations that were noted earlier. This process creates fractures in the oil and gas reservoir rock. The sand in the frack fluid*—'

Nadine gave a fake gasp. 'OMG—he said frack.'

Billy Bob shook his head as if exasperated with a child.

'—*remains in these fractures in the rock and keeps them open when the pump pressure is relieved. This allows the previously trapped oil or natural gas to flow to the well bore more easily. This initial stimulation segment is then isolated with a specially designed plug and the perforating guns are used to perforate the next stage. This stage is then hydraulically fractured in the same manner. This process is repeated along the entire horizontal section of the well, which can extend several miles. Once the stimulation is complete, the isolation plugs are drilled out and production begins. Initially water, and then natural gas or oil, flows into the horizontal casing and up the well bore. In the course of initial production of the well, approximately fifteen to fifty percent of the fracturing fluid is recovered.*'

Book raised his hand. Billy Bob stopped the video.

'So only fifteen to fifty percent of five million gallons—'

He glanced at Nadine.

'Seven hundred fifty thousand to two-and-a-half million gallons.'

'—is recovered. Which means at least fifty percent of those chemicals—'

'Twelve thousand five hundred gallons.'

'—and maybe as much as eighty-five percent—'

'Twenty-one thousand two hundred fifty gallons.'

170

'—isn't recovered. What happens to all those chemicals?'

Billy Bob shrugged. 'They stay in the reservoir. There's five to ten thousand feet of rock between the gas formation and the aquifer, Professor. Fluids can't migrate through a mile or two of rock. That's why they call it rock. Those chemicals ain't going anywhere.'

'You sure?'

'Pretty sure.'

Billy Bob restarted the video.

'This fluid is either recycled to be used on other fracturing operations or safely disposed of according to government regulations.'

Billy Bob paused the video before Book could raise his hand.

'Do you recycle your frack fluid?' Book asked.

'Slick water. And no. Too damn expensive.'

'What do you do with it?'

'Pump it down disposal wells.'

'What's a disposal well?'

'Deep salt-water wells. We dump everything from sewage to radioactive substances down those holes—'

'Like frack fluids?'

'—stuff the law won't allow to be disposed in rivers and streams. We got fifty-two thousand disposal wells in Texas, more than any other state.'

'Is that something to brag about? That we're putting more toxic chemicals into the earth than any other state?'

'Don't worry, Professor. The Railroad Commission regulates what goes down the hole.'

'Why doesn't that make me feel better?'

Billy Bob resumed the video.

'The whole process of developing a well typically takes from three to five months. A few weeks to prepare the site, four to six weeks to drill the well, and then one to three months of completion activities, which includes one to seven days of stimulation. But this three- to five-month investment can result in a well that will produce oil or natural gas for twenty to forty years or more.'

171

Billy Bob ended the video. He sighed wistfully. 'I love that movie.'

As if he had just watched *Casablanca*.

'I take it that video wasn't put out by the Sierra Club?' Book said.

'Marathon Oil. Put it on YouTube.'

Billy Bob Barnett seemed satisfied with his defense of fracking. But Book wanted him to continue, in the hope that he would over-talk, as guilty witnesses often felt compelled to do. Thus, another provocative question was called for, an inquiry that called into question the validity of his life's work, which is to say, his manhood.

'Billy Bob, is it really worth it?'

'Is what worth what?'

'Fracking. I mean, it's a huge environmental controversy, here and around the world. Is it really worth fighting over?'

Billy Bob's face registered an expression of absolute disbelief. He pointed at the screen on the wall.

'Did you hear what he just said? Twenty to forty years, Professor. Twenty to forty years of turning the lights on, cooking on the stove, heating and cooling your home, watching reality shows on TV . . . twenty to forty years of electricity. Unless you want to live in the dark, it's damn sure worth fighting for.'

His face glowed red.

'Why not solar and wind power?'

Billy Bob rolled his eyes. 'You liberals think the sun and the wind can do it all. They can't. Not yet. I want us to be energy independent, too, Professor, so I'm all for solar, wind, geothermal, hydro, you name it. Anything that'll get us off Muslim oil. And maybe in twenty or thirty years those technologies will be able to power the planet or at least America. But not today. Oil, gas, and coal supply eighty-five percent of our energy today. And we need energy today. Easy to sit in your ivy tower—'

'Ivory. Like the elephant tusk, not ivy like the plant.'

'Oh.' He rebooted his thought. 'Easy to sit in your ivory tower and preach your liberal politics, but what'll happen to America when the Muslims decide to sell their oil to the Chinese instead of us 'cause they'll pay more? When we don't have the energy to power our factories and light our homes? Our cars, trains, and planes? What happens to America then, Professor?'

Billy Bob stood and walked over to the U.S. map on the side wall. They followed.

'Current estimate is that we've got a hundred years' supply of natural gas in North America.' He pointed the cigar at shaded areas on the map. 'The big shale plays are the Horn River and Montney up in Canada, the Barnett—no rela- tion—Eagle Ford, and the Woodford in Texas, Haynesville in Louisiana, Fayetteville in Arkansas, and the big daddy of them all, the Marcellus Shale. That one field covers ninety-five thousand square miles of New York, Pennsylvania, Ohio, and West Virginia, contains two-thirds of U.S. reserves.'

'I thought they put a moratorium on fracking in New York?'

Billy Bob nodded. 'Vermont, too, even though no one's found shale gas in the state. Said it was a show of solidarity. Goofy liberals.'

He now stepped to the world map and again used the cigar as a pointer.

'Shale gas has been found in northern UK and Europe— Poland, Austria, Sweden, Romania, Germany, France . . .'

'Didn't the French ban fracking?'

He shrugged. 'They're French.'

Billy Bob pointed the cigar at other nations.

'China, they've got more recoverable shale gas than us, about thirteen hundred trillion cubic feet. Argentina, they've got almost eight hundred. Mexico, seven hundred. South Africa, five hundred. Australia, four hundred. And all that shale gas

173

requires hydraulic stimulation. That's our technology. We're not outsourcing American jobs, Professor, we're creating American jobs by outsourcing our technology. Our hydraulic stimulation is taking over the world.'

'Like our fast food?'

'Except it's better for you. Gas is good, Professor.'

Billy Bob held up one finger.

'It's cleaner than coal and safer than nuclear. Right now we're using mostly coal-fired plants to generate electricity. We switch over to natural gas, greenhouse gases are cut in half. And we don't risk a Chernobyl or Fukushima.'

A second finger.

'It's cheap and abundant. The same amount of energy from gas costs one-fourth what it takes in oil to produce. And we've identified twenty-five thousand trillion cubic feet of extractable gas in the world—outside the Middle East. That's enough to power the world on natural gas alone for fifty years.'

A third finger.

'It's ours, not the Arabs'. Right now we're sending a trillion dollars a year to Muslims who want to kill us. We get off Muslim oil, we keep one trillion dollars a year, every year, here at home. It's simple: drill at home or get killed at home.'

A fourth finger.

'Jobs. The world is starving for jobs, Professor, and hydraulic stimulation provides jobs. Lots of jobs. But Ivory League-educated environmentalists—'

'No, that one is Ivy.'

'But you just said . . . never mind. Liberal environmentalists drive around in their Priuses and don't give a damn about the unemployed working class. People are desperate for jobs. We got workers living in man camps in shale plays all over the country.'

'Man camps?'

'Trailers, cheap motels and rent houses, ten to twenty men living in each, because there's not enough housing in these boom towns. Men leave their families so they can work in South Texas or out here, send money home to Houston or Chicago, to mama and the kids like Mexicans send money home to Chihuahua. I guess we're all migrants when it comes to jobs.'

He added his thumb.

'And most important of all, Professor, shale gas is single-handedly causing a shift in the world's geopolitical balance of power.'

'How?'

'I'm fixin' to tell you how.' Back to the world map. 'Seventy percent of the world's conventional natural gas—that's everything except shale gas—is located in exactly two countries: Russia and Iran. What's that tell you?'

'God has an odd sense of humor?'

Billy Bob chuckled. 'That He does. What it tells us is that we can't let the bad guys control the world's natural gas supply like they do the oil supply. See, most of Europe is tied to Russian natural gas, the rest to Iran. So Putin carteled up with that loony bastard Ahmadinejad, put European countries in a political and economic vise. Remember back in oh-eight when Russia invaded Georgia—'

'The Russians invaded Georgia?' Nadine said. 'OMG, my aunt lives in Atlanta. Will she be okay?'

Billy Bob regarded Book's intern as one might Paris Hilton giving financial advice.

'She gets her news on Twitter,' Book said.

Billy Bob grunted. 'Anyway, the Euros, they opposed UN sanctions because they couldn't risk Putin cutting off their gas supply. Which is how Putin operates—he ain't selling gas, he's wielding a political sledgehammer. And he vetoes every UN sanction on Iran because they're partnered up, so Iran just goes merrily down the path to a nuclear weapon. And where does that path end? With Israel bombing Tehran back to the fifties. Which ignites the Middle East and puts U.S. troops on the ground again.'

175

'And shale gas can prevent all that?'

'Damn straight it can. Shale gas makes the U.S. energy independent and gives Europe the chance to tell Putin and Ahmadinejad to pump their gas up their—'

He glanced at Nadine.

'—where the sun don't shine. If they'll just go get it. Poland's got almost two hundred trillion cubic feet of shale gas—that's a two-hundred-year supply—and they're damn sure going after that gas. But France, they're not, even though they've got a hundred-year supply. They'd rather depend on nuclear power. How stupid is that? Waiting for another Fukushima? But that's what happens when environmental socialists are making the decisions. They'd rather hand the world over to Putin and Ahmadinejad. They don't get it. This ain't about a frackin' well dirtying a little water—it's about the future of the goddamn free world!'

He caught himself.

'Hydraulic stimulation,' he said carefully. 'What happens then, Professor? What happens when no one in the world needs Russian or Iranian gas? When Putin can't tell the Euros how to vote at the UN? Putin's power drops with the price of gas. The UN pushes Ahmadinejad back under his rock. Which makes the world a safer place. A better place. The good guys win, and the bad guys lose. That's got to sound good even to a liberal.'

'I like it!' Nadine said. 'And I don't even know who Putin and Ack . . . Achjim . . . that guy are. His name probably has too many characters for Twitter.'

Billy Bob smiled at her, as if she were a precocious child.

'You're a pistol, Honeywell. You sure you don't want a job?'

'I'm sure.'

'All the donuts you can eat.'

'On the other hand . . .'

Billy Bob turned back to Book and put the cigar in the air.

'And never forget, Professor—we are the good guys.'

'But we need clean water. And fracking is dangerous.'

Billy Bob shook his head with a bemused expression on his face. 'Liberals. God bless the children. Professor, people texting while driving is dangerous. Riding that Harley is dangerous . . .'

'Amen,' Nadine said.

'. . . Life is dangerous. Hell, yes, drilling is dangerous. Accidents happen. Get over it. Or start riding a bike, and not that Harley. The kind you pedal.'

Billy Bob stepped over to another map that depicted a satellite view of the world at night. Most of North America was brightly lit. As were the UK, Europe, India, Japan, and the perimeter of South America. But much of Russia and China was dark, as was all of Africa except the northern nations and South Africa. It was a telling view of the world.

'You want to live with light or in the dark? You don't get light without electricity. You generate electricity with oil, coal, nuclear, or natural gas. Pick your poison, Professor.'

He turned his hands up.

'Gas is the best choice, and shale gas gives us that choice. The world needs to cut carbon emissions, the world needs a bridge from oil to alternative energy sources, the world needs to get off Middle Eastern oil and Russian and Iranian gas . . . Shale gas does all that and more. Is it perfect? No. But what is? But shale gas makes for a more perfect world. It's a no-brainer, Professor, even for a liberal like yourself.'

He stepped over to the desk, grabbed the thick document under the handgun-lighter, and returned. He handed the document to Book then gestured with the cigar.

'Don't take my word for it, Professor. Take MIT's word. And Harvard's. And the Baker Institute at Rice. Read their reports on shale gas and geopolitics. I'm not making this stuff up.'

Nadine raised her hand.

'You got a question, Honeywell?'

'Where's the girls' restroom? Coffee goes right through me. Sorry, that's an over-share.'

'Down the hall, past the donuts.'

Nadine pivoted and walked to the door; Billy Bob's eyes followed her out.

'Boy, I'd sure like to have her on my payroll.'

'She's my intern.'

'Keep your prick out of the payroll—I learned that lesson the hard way. Several times. You know, it's outrageous what a gal can get for sexual harassment these days.'

He chuckled then walked around his desk and sat in his leather throne. Book took his seat again. Billy Bob chewed on the cigar and regarded him.

'Professor, why do you care so much about Nathan Jones?'

'I owe him.'

'You rode that Harley four hundred miles just because you owed Nathan a favor?'

'Because he wrote me that letter.'

'Well, Professor, I don't know what Nathan thought he knew or what you've heard around town, but I'm a good guy.'

Book had spent the last hour trying to get Billy Bob Barnett to incriminate himself in the death of Nathan Jones; Billy Bob Barnett had spent the last hour trying to convince Book that fracking was good for the world. Neither had succeeded. Nadine returned with another donut.

'I couldn't resist.'

Billy Bob winked at her. 'I like women who don't resist.'

She sat and ate the donut then licked chocolate from her fingers. Billy Bob watched her like a teenage boy with a serious case of puppy love. He finally broke away and tapped the newspaper on the desktop.

'There's no murder mystery in Marfa, Professor. Nathan drove too damn fast, like everyone else in West Texas. He fell asleep at the wheel. He ran off the road and hit a pump jack. He died. It's a damn shame. But it wasn't a crime.'

He tossed Nathan's letter across the desk to Book.

'My operations are run by the book. Hell, I'm an Aggie. We don't cheat. If we did, we'd have a better football team.'

He grinned. Billy Bob Barnett had not taken the bait. Perhaps he was guilty of nothing more criminal than being a boor. Or perhaps he was smarter than he put on; perhaps his good ol' boy routine was just that. Book decided to take one last shot at baiting Billy Bob, to lure him with a big piece of in-your-face red meat. He held up Nathan's letter.

'You know, Billy Bob, what Nathan wrote, some people might consider that a motive for murder. Your own lawyer accuses you of environmental crimes that could destroy your company and put you in prison for the rest of your life and says he has the evidence to prove it, that might make a person take action. Maybe even murder.'

Billy Bob's grin was gone. His jaw muscles clenched so tightly he bit the cigar in two; the end dangled from his mouth. The clenching spread upward until his entire bald head seemed to clench; his skin turned red and his dark eyes stared Book down, like two kids seeing who'd blink first. Book thought, Wait for it . . . like when he went fishing as a kid, watching a big catfish circling the bait, trying to decide . . . but the big fish didn't bite. Instead he took the cigar and tossed it into a trash basket.

'And some people, Professor, might consider it rude to walk into my office uninvited, eat my goddamn donuts, and then accuse me of murdering my own lawyer.'

His expression softened. He blew out a breath.

'Professor, I punch holes in the ground. I don't break laws and I don't kill lawyers, although we'd be a hell of a lot better off if we followed Shakespeare's advice. So why don't you and Honeywell play tourist today, go look at Judd's boxes, eat at Maiya's, maybe take in the Marfa Lights tonight, then get up

179

tomorrow morning and ride that Harley back to Austin and wait with all those other liberals for the sun and the wind to power your world.'

'Are you trying to run me out of town?'

'Is it working?'

'No.'

'Then I'm not.'

'Good. And I'm not a liberal.'

'Professor, if it waddles like a duck and quacks like a duck, it's a duck.'

Billy Bob Barnett, fracking zoologist, escorted them out of his office and down the hallway—Nadine ducked into the lunchroom and grabbed another chocolate donut—past Earlene the receptionist, and out the building. They stood on the sidewalk; Nadine finished the donut and licked her fingers.

'So, Ms. Honeywell, what did we learn in there?' Book said.

'Billy Bob's a creep who breathes through his mouth. I generally don't trust mouth-breathers, but he's got good donuts.'

'What else did we learn in there?'

'Earlene is a lesbian.'

'No. We learned that Billy Bob Barnett didn't take the bait.'

'And Earlene's a lesbian.'

Book exhaled. He was trying to be patient with his intern.

'Okay, so this gay-and-lesbian identification skill you've mastered allows you to assess a person's sexuality simply by looking at them, is that correct, Ms. Honeywell?'

She shrugged a yes. He decided to demonstrate for his intern's benefit how skillful cross-examination can make such assertions seem utterly foolish and the person making such assertions even more foolish. He employed his courtroom voice and questioned her as if she were sitting in the witness chair.

'So what gave Earlene away as a lesbian? Her clothes? Her hair? Her lack of makeup? The way she looked at you and not me? The fact that she's got shoulders like Michael Phelps? Ms. Honeywell, please tell the jury how you can know conclusively that Earlene the receptionist is in fact a lesbian?'

Nadine shrugged again.

'She grabbed my butt in the bathroom.'

Chapter 15

'They're boxes.'

'Works of art, Ms. Honeywell.'

Nadine Honeywell stared.

'Boxes.'

They stood in a renovated artillery shed on an abandoned cavalry outpost just south of town; it was more monastery than museum. Arrayed before them were fifty-two of Donald Judd's *100 Untitled Works in Milled Aluminum*. The other forty-eight were installed in an adjacent shed. The works were rectangular boxes, each with identical exterior dimensions—41 × 51 × 72 inches—but unique interior configurations—a box within a box, a floating box, partitions like cards in a deck or slanted shelves on the wall—that created optical illusions; each was open to the inside, each weighed one ton, each had been factory fabricated to exacting specifications, each cost $5,000. The boxes were perfectly aligned in three north–south rows under a high ceiling topped by a Quonset hut roof; massive east- and west-facing windows allowed the sun to bathe the boxes in light and set the shiny surfaces aglow. A young man sat cross-legged on the floor before one box, his elbows on his knees and his hands cupping his chin, and stared as if in a trance, like a disciple before a religious shrine. Donald Judd was a crusty gray-haired and bearded Midwesterner; he lived on a ranch overlooking Mexico; he was a towering figure in contemporary art in New York; and he created his life's masterpiece in Marfa, Texas.

Which masterpiece was funded by oil money.

Donald Judd began his artistic career as a painter but became renowned as a sculptor of boxes. He was a leader of the Minimalist art movement in New York in the sixties, but he became disenchanted with the New York art scene. He hated museums. 'Art is not commerce or show business,' he said. He believed that art cannot be separated from the space around it and said he put as much thought into 'the placement of the piece as into the piece itself.' He wanted to permanently install his art in big open spaces, inside and outside, where it would exist forever. In 1973, he moved to Marfa to realize his vision.

Which required money. A lot of money.

Philippa de Menil had a lot of money and a love of contemporary art. Her money came from oil; she was the granddaughter of Conrad Schlumberger, the French physicist who founded Schlumberger Ltd., an international oilfield service company. Her love of art came from her mother, Dominique de Menil, who founded the Menil Collection, a contemporary art museum in Houston. In 1974, Philippa founded the Dia Art Foundation in New York with her husband, Heiner Friedrich, and her inheritance, Schlumberger stock. Their vision was 'one artist, one place, forever,' to be achieved by funding permanent installations of major art projects; that is, one-man museums.

Heiner had long been a dealer of Donald Judd's work, both in his native Germany and in New York. Dia's vision matched up perfectly with Judd's. In 1978, Philippa and Heiner agreed to fund Judd's Marfa project, including the one hundred aluminum boxes as well as sixty large concrete boxes to be installed in an adjacent field just to the east of the artillery sheds. Dia purchased the decommissioned Fort D. A. Russell, paid Judd a monthly stipend of $17,500, and poured $5 million into the project. Dia funded other artists as well, including John Chamberlain and Dan Flavin; it acquired hundreds of artworks, many by Andy Warhol. It was a heady time indeed for the Dia Foundation and Philippa's Schlumberger stock, which traded in the $90 range.

But the oil crash of 1982 hit oil stocks hard; Schlumberger's stock price plunged to under $30. Despite putting $35 million of her inheritance into Dia, the foundation faced financial ruin. Philippa and Heiner told Judd that Dia could no longer fund his Marfa project.

Judd was not pleased.

After he threatened a lawsuit, Dominique de Menil stepped in to save Dia and her daughter's fortune. Heiner was removed from the board; Philippa's inheritance was placed in a trust overseen by her brothers. Dia conveyed the entire Marfa project—the buildings, the fort, and the art—and $2 million to Judd's new Chinati Foundation. They parted ways. Judd completed his masterpiece in 1986.

Judd's boxes are now something of a shrine. Art lovers from around the world make the pilgrimage to the old fort. With permanent installations of masterpieces by three giants of contemporary art—Judd's one hundred boxes, Chamberlain's twenty-two crushed cars, and Flavin's 336, eight-foot-long fluorescent lights in four colors (green, pink, blue, and yellow) installed in six U-shaped barracks at the fort, which the *New York Times* dubbed 'the last great work of 20th-century American art'—Marfa itself has been deemed 'Minimalism's masterpiece'; but Marfa will always be about Donald Judd. Marfa is a one-man museum; one artist, one place, forever. The vision of Judd, Heiner, Philippa, and Dia was realized and validated. The vision lives on without them.

Donald Judd fell ill on a trip to Germany in early 1994 and died in a New York hospital at the age of sixty-five. He is buried on his beloved ranch south of Marfa. The Dia Foundation survived but without Heiner or Philippa. Heiner Friedrich, now seventy-four, recently opened a museum in Germany and bought a $2 million home in the Hamptons. Philippa de Menil, now sixty-five, converted to Sufi Islam and is known as Shaykha Fariha Fatima al-Jerrahi; she is on Facebook. And the source of it all—Schlumberger stock—now trades near $80, giving it a market cap of $103 billion. The company is a leading international player in shale gas fracking.

'You reading a book at lunch?'

Border Patrol Agent Wesley Crum stuffed the last of the large pepperoni pizza into his mouth. He and Angel Acosta sat on stools at the counter.

'What are you reading?'

His words came out garbled through the pizza he was chewing. Angel looked up from the book.

'What?'

'What are you reading? That *Shades of Grey* book they was talking about on *The View*?'

'No, I'm reading his book.'

'Whose?'

Angel nodded past Wesley; he turned and saw the professor and his gal walk into the place. Angel waved like a kid to a sports star. Wesley shook his head. This was goddamn embarrassing.

'Professor,' Angel said. He held up the book. 'Would you sign my book?'

The professor stepped over, greeted them, and autographed the title page.

'It's very enlightening,' Angel said.

'Thanks, Agent Acosta,' the professor said.

He and the girl found a table across the room. Angel stared at the professor's signature on his book. Wesley sighed.

'Jesus, Angel—he ain't one of the Kardashian sisters.'

'It smells great in here,' Book's intern said. She inhaled the place. 'Olive oil. I love extra virgin olive oil.'

Her eyes glazed over and her mind seemed to drift off into another world.

'Ms. Honeywell?'

Nothing. He spoke louder.

'Ms. Honeywell.'

She snapped.

'What?'

She had a wistful expression on her young face.

'Oh, sorry, Professor, I was, uh . . . thinking about olive oil.'

'Cooking with it?'

'Something like that.'

She shook it off with a full-body shiver.

'So why'd we go look at the art?'

'You're a student. I'm a professor. I'm trying to educate you.'

'In art?'

'In life.'

She eyed him with suspicion. 'You're not telling me the whole truth.'

'See? You've already learned an important life lesson.'

'Don't trust law professors?'

Book smiled.

'Can we go home now?'

'No.'

'When?'

'Tomorrow.'

She groaned then pulled out her cell phone and began tapping with her thumbs on the little keyboard.

'What are you doing?'

'Tweeting.'

'What?'

She read off her phone: '"Help! I'm being held hostage in West Texas by a deranged law professor."'

'How many followers do you have?'

'Two. Including my mom.'

She replaced the phone and folded her hands on the table.

'Most law professors love to hear their own voices so they lecture the entire class. You didn't.'

'I don't lecture. I'm just a tour guide through Con Law.'

'Problem is, we never knew what you were thinking.'

'Good.'

'But we're not in your classroom, Professor. We're in Marfa. So tell me what you're thinking.'

It was past noon, and Nadine was homesick and hungry. He had not yet found Nathan's truth, so he couldn't take her home, but he could feed her. They had ridden back into town for lunch at the Pizza Foundation, just a few blocks up Highland Avenue from the Border Patrol headquarters. The building had been a gas station in a prior life. A purple Vespa was parked outside.

'I'm thinking there's a connection. Between Nathan, the art, fracking, his death . . . my gut tells me it's all tied together.'

'Maybe your gut's just telling you it's hungry.'

'Could be.'

'Connected by what?'

'Not what. Whom.'

'Hi, I'm Kenni with an "i." I'll be your waiter.'

A skinny young man wearing skinny jeans and a T-shirt that read *Frack Off* stood at their table. He seemed too somber to be a waiter in Marfa. He wore purple with a passion—in his hair, on his back, and on his feet. He was young, pierced, and tattooed. On the fingers of his left hand letters had been inked into his skin, one letter per finger: WWDJD.

'I've seen that WWDJD all over town,' Nadine said. 'What's it stand for?'

'"What would Donald Judd do?"'

Nadine frowned. 'Isn't it supposed to be wwjd? "What would Jesus do?"'

'Not in Marfa.'

Kenni's face was puffy, and his eyes were red, as if he had been crying. Or as if he were stoned. Or both.

'You okay?' Book asked.

Kenni gave a weak nod. 'Just sad.'

He offered no more, so Book ordered the chicken, tomatoes, spinach, and olive oil on thin crust. Nadine went for pepperoni, sausage, Canadian bacon, and extra cheese and her hand sanitizer. When Kenni left, Nadine said, 'He's gay.'

'You're not going to stop, are you?'

She shrugged. 'Just stating the obvious. He walks with his palms to the ground.'

Book turned and observed Kenni. He walked with his arms tight to his body and his wrists angled up so his palms faced the floor.

'Telltale sign,' his intern said.

'All right, Ms. Honeywell, since you're apparently an expert on this sort of thing, why do you think Nathan was gay?'

'His photos.'

'Explain.'

'What did you see?'

Book shrugged. 'Black-and-white photos.'

'You're not gay.'

'I know. But why do you think Nathan was?'

'The brilliant law professor is clueless. I love it.' She smiled and wiped the table down then rubbed sanitizer on her hands. 'All the photos were black and white, manly scenes, cattle and cowboys, the rugged landscape, a drilling rig, but in each photo there was one object in color, one thing that didn't belong in the scene—a Barbie doll, a red rose, pink underwear.'

'Okay.'

'Like Nathan. He was saying he didn't belong here. He was a gay guy in manly West Texas, living a black-and-white life, forced to hide his true colors.'

Book pondered her words a moment.

'Ms. Honeywell, either you're really smart or all that ethyl alcohol is poisoning your brain.'

A gray-haired man wearing a plaid shirt, creased khakis, and cowboy boots walked up and stuck his hand out to Book.

'Ward Weaver, mayor of Marfa.'

They shook.

'John Bookman. And Nadine Honeywell.'

'Read in the paper you were in town, Professor. Mind signing my Nook? Got your e-book on it. Been carrying it everywhere with me the last couple days, hoping to run into you.'

Book used a Sharpie to sign the mayor's Nook.

'Mind if I sit?'

'Pull up a chair.'

The mayor sat then sniffed the air. 'Smells like a hospital.'

He waved at Kenni across the room.

'So how do you folks like our little town? Number eight on the Smithsonian's "twenty best small towns in America" list.'

'The museum?' Nadine said.

'The magazine.'

He reached into his shirt pocket and pulled out a newspaper clipping.

'Got the article right here.'

He unfolded it on the table like a teenage boy with a *Playboy* centerfold. He read.

'"It's just a flyspeck in the flat, hot, dusty cattle country of southwest Texas—closer to Chihuahua than Manhattan. But it's cooking, thanks to an influx of creative types from way downtown."'

The mayor looked up with a grin.

'We beat out Key West.'

189

He carefully folded the article and replaced it in his pocket. He then reached into his other shirt pocket and removed another clipping. He spread it on the table and read.

' "The Art Land. In Marfa, the worlds of beef and art collide, giving the town a unique kick." *New York Times*. Course, you know what that's like, being in the *Times*, don't you, Professor? I read that story, "Indiana Jones Goes to Law School." Was all that true?'

'It was.'

The mayor grunted then folded and replaced that article. He patted his shirt and then the pockets of his khakis. He returned with several more clippings.

' "Marfa makes an art out of quirky." *Chicago Tribune*. "Minimal, marvelous Marfa: avant-garde art, deep in Texas." *Pittsburgh Post-Gazette*. "Marfa, oasis d'artistes." *Le Monde*. You read French?'

Book shook his head.

'Don't know what it says, been hoping someone could translate it.'

Nadine reached over, took the article, and read: ' "This is a charming and strange village, a world apart. In the late afternoon, you can enjoy a Spritz (Champagne, Campari, seltzer water) on the terrace of the only restaurant on the main street . . ."'

The mayor smiled and nodded in approval. 'That's nice.'

Nadine scanned down the article. 'It goes on to tell the history of the town, how Marfa got its name, blah, blah, blah, Judd's story, the boxes, blah, blah, blah . . . Oh, this is interesting.'

'Read it to me,' the mayor said like a kid wanting his mother to read the ending to a Harry Potter book.

Nadine translated. ' "The widening gap between the arts and the Marfa 'from below' also casts a shadow on the picture. At the last census, the population was seventy percent Hispanic, and the median income less than half of

Texas. But there are few artists who are interested in Marfa's poor and Mexicans. Chicanos, for their part, do not mix with the 'chinatis,' as they call the newcomers . . . The next contention could focus on education. Founded by two personalities from the art world, an international private school will open in September for twenty students. Do we want to educate the entire community or a few? Donald Judd enrolled his children in the public schools. This is one of the poorest counties in Texas or in the United States. Our schools are starving for money."'

The mayor's excited child's face had turned into a deeper frown with each word of Nadine's translation. He gestured at the article.

'That's what those French words say? You sure about that?'

'Unh-huh.'

'Well, hell's bells, that ain't a good story at all. And I've been carrying it around all this time. Goddamn French people.'

He snatched the article and wadded it into a ball and threw it at a distant trash basket. Nadine turned to Book; she was trying not to laugh.

'French, Ms. Honeywell?'

'The finest private school education available in San Francisco.'

The mayor spit out the bad taste of French and put his other prized articles away.

'Anyway, we've been written up in *GQ*, *Vogue*, *Vanity Fair*, *Wall Street Journal*, *Texas Monthly*, papers and magazines from California clear to New York City. Before Judd, all we had was the Marfa Mystery Lights. After Judd, we got art. And that's a marketable concept.'

'A concept?'

'You know, a promotional gimmick.'

'Judd's art is a gimmick?'

The mayor shrugged. 'Disneyland has Mickey Mouse.'

Kenni brought a glass of iced tea for the mayor. He grabbed

191

the sugar dispenser and turned it up. And left it there, dispensing a load of sugar into the tea.

'You like a little tea with your sugar?' Book said.

'What? Oh, I've got a bit of a sweet tooth.'

'Lucky you still have teeth.'

'Don't pay him any mind, Mayor,' Nadine said. 'He doesn't know anything about the sweeter things in life. Like sweet tea and chocolate-covered donuts and . . . pizza!'

Kenni had returned with their pizzas, which kept Nadine quiet.

'See,' the mayor said, 'when you think of Dallas, you think of J. R. Ewing and the Cowboys. Austin, you think of music and hippies. Houston, you think of . . . mosquitoes. We want you to think of art when you think of Marfa. And let me tell you, Professor, art is a promotional gimmick that works.'

He drank his sugar with tea then continued.

'I mean, we're an airplane flight and a four-hour drive from anywhere, but ten thousand art tourists make the pilgrimage every year. And that's what it is for those folks, a religious experience, like Judd was a god and Marfa's a shrine. I don't get it myself—hell, they're just boxes—but they come and they see and they spend. We got a bookstore, fourteen art galleries'—the mayor pointed out the window—'right over there, that's the inde/jacobs gallery, two homosexuals from Minnesota moved down here and opened it—and nine restaurants. Got a French place called Cochineal, gay couple owns it, they had a place in New York called États-Unis, cost you a hundred bucks to eat there, place is packed—homosexuals, they can cook. We got Italian, Mediterranean—that's the Food Shark. Serves falafel, hummus, fatoush salad . . . folks like the stuff, but it gives me gas.'

'Good to know.'

'But it gives the town a bit of flavor. And they buy real estate. Home values, they've skyrocketed.'

'Taxes, too, which I've heard is forcing locals to sell and move out of town.'

192

The mayor shrugged away any such concern. 'Price of progress. I've got a house listed for half a million dollars. Ten years ago, you could buy all the houses in town for less than that. That's progress.'

'You're a real-estate broker?'

The mayor nodded. 'I was an accountant, but never much money in Marfa to count, so I got my real-estate license. And business is booming, all the newcomers buying up homes and land. The Ryan Ranch, where they filmed *Giant*, it's up for sale—for twenty-seven million.'

'Is it a big ranch?'

'Nah. Only about thirty-four thousand acres. But I read it's half as big again as Manhattan Island, and only the son lives on it now. Maybe he'll get his price. New Yorkers, they think our prices are cheap. Homosexuals, they've got beaucoup bucks, I guess because they don't got children. Kids are expensive.'

He shook his head as if in wonderment at the world around him.

'Art and homosexuals on the plains of West Texas. Is life funny or what?'

'Or what.'

The mayor looked around, leaned in, and lowered his voice.

'These homosexuals, they're the best thing to ever happen to Marfa, even if they are abominations in the Lord's eyes.'

'Good of you to look past their human faults.'

'I'm a Christian man.'

'And a real-estate broker.'

'That, too.' He leaned back. 'Before the artists, don't believe we had a homosexual in town . . . well, there was the Johnson boy, everyone wondered about him. But he moved over to Alpine. They got a university there.'

As if that explained the Johnson boy's change of venue.

'During the Chinati Open House in October, we'll have more homosexuals per square foot in Marfa than in San Francisco'—Nadine gave Book an 'I told you so' look—'and most of them are Jewish to boot. Got me to thinking about a motto for Marfa, you know, like "Muslims to Mecca."'

'That's Mecca's motto?'

The mayor had the look of a man about to make a big announcement.

'"Jews to Judd." What do you think? Kinda catchy, ain't it?'

The mayor smiled proudly, as if he had just coined another 'What happens in Vegas stays in Vegas.' Nadine eyed the mayor as she had the Border Patrol agents that first day; Book hoped she would not express the same evaluation of the mayor.

'*Jews to Judd?* Are you a dope?'

'I'm the mayor.' He turned his hands up as if innocent. 'I figured we could run an ad in the *New York Times*.'

Book shook his head. 'I wouldn't go there, Mayor.'

The mayor seemed perplexed. But he quickly shook it off and continued with his sales pitch.

'Anyway, we got the largest hydroponic tomato farm in the world, they produce twenty million pounds of tomatoes every year.'

'Lot of tomatoes.'

'Damn straight it is. We got that El Cosmico hippie camp-ground. I heard tell folks smoke dope out there.'

'You're kidding?'

'Nope. And we're fixin' to have an art-house drive-in movie theater, designed by the same architects that designed the Museum of Modern Art in New York.'

'You need a Starbucks,' Nadine said.

'We got a Frama's.'

'Coffee shop?'

'Yep.'

'Fresh ground beans?'

'Yep.'

'Real cream?'

'Yep.'

'Where?'

'Block west of the Paisano.'

'I'm there.'

'How much coffee do you drink?' Book asked his intern.

'As much as I can.'

The mayor pressed on. 'Press calls us "Santa Fe South" and "Marfa's Vineyard."'

'Is that a compliment?'

'Yankees like the sound of it. And it brings the celebrities to town. Robert Redford was just here—'

'We heard.'

'—and Michael Nesmith performed here last year.'

'Who's he?' Nadine asked.

'The Monkees.'

'He's a monkey?'

'*The* Monkees. TV show about a band back in the late sixties.'

'I wasn't born until the late eighties. Is he dead, too?'

'He wasn't when he sang here.'

'We heard there's some conflict between the newcomers and the old-timers?' Book said.

'Sounds like you've been talking to Sam Walker?'

'We have.'

'He tell you about the Triple As?'

'He did.'

'Well, those attorneys, artists, and assholes brought a lot of money to Marfa. See, I want this town to grow. Sam wants to write about the dying West. Sometimes I think he'll only be happy when he's the last person left in town to read his paper.' He shook his head. 'Sam, he's . . . he's just not a big thinker.'

'Like you?'

The mayor turned his palms up and offered a 'What can I say?' expression. 'Marketing the art, that was my idea.'

'And "Jews to Judd,"' Nadine said.

'I'm trying to get folks interested in making a sequel to *Giant*, like they did with *Dallas*.'

'But all the stars are dead,' Nadine said.

195

'That is an obstacle. I was thinking, maybe we could pick up the story after Bick and Jett are dead. Remember at the end they showed Bick's two grandsons, one was Anglo, the other Mexican? Hollywood loves that multicultural angle. We could even make one of them a homosexual. I was hoping the Quaid boy could star in it, but he had to leave town pretty fast, to escape those assassins.'

'We heard.'

'Hell of a deal, Hollywood assassins running around Marfa.'

'So Sam says there's conflict in town . . . other than assassins after old movie stars.'

'Oh, there's a little friction, is all.'

'Friction?'

The mayor nodded. 'Friction. When you've lived your life a certain way among similar people for fifty, sixty years, then new folks come to town who live a different way, they rub each other the wrong way, creates a little friction. Nothing to fret about . . . long as it don't slow down the real-estate market.'

'We wouldn't want that.'

'Nope.'

'Well, glad things are going well in Marfa, Mayor.'

The mayor regarded Book a moment. His civic booster expression turned serious.

'We got a good thing going, Professor. Don't screw it up for us.'

'And how would I do that?'

'Acting like we got a murder mystery in Marfa.'

Book unfolded the funeral photo on the table. He could not find the mayor's face among the funeral guests.

'You didn't go to Nathan Jones's funeral?'

'I didn't know him. When they said Billy Bob's lawyer was killed in a car wreck, I said, "Who?" Which is odd since I make it a point to know every voter in town. Can I see it?'

'What?'

'The letter.'

'You know about the letter?'

'Hell, Professor, everyone in town knows about the letter. You been showing it off like it's a war medal.'

Nadine nodded in agreement. Book handed Nathan's letter to the mayor. He read it and then exhaled.

'You see his proof?'

'Not yet.'

'You've been in town, what, three days, and you haven't seen his proof?'

'No.'

'Maybe there is no proof. You think about that?'

'I have.'

'Heard you met Billy Bob this morning.'

'We did.'

'He do a yell for you?'

'He did.'

'I wish he hadn't,' Nadine said.

'Didn't he tell you fracking was safe?'

'He did.'

'He show you that fracking video?'

'He did.'

'Then what's the problem?'

'In my experience, Mayor, when there's money at stake, people tend to slant their testimony.'

'You saying Billy Bob's a liar?'

'I'm saying there are two sides to every story.'

'And you're getting the other side from Carla?'

'You know Carla?'

'Everyone knows Carla. Heard you had a meeting with her at Padre's last night.'

'We met. We didn't have a meeting.'

'You sure beat up those roughnecks for her.'

'They were rude.'

'They're roughnecks. So what'd you think of their boss?'

'He's a mouth-breathing creep,' Nadine said through her pizza.

'Says he's got sinus problems. And gals tend to think he's a little creepy, but, hell, he's an Aggie.' The mayor chuckled. 'Look, I've known Billy Bob since he moved to town. I've seen him sober and I've seen him drunk—don't invite him to your Christmas party, by the way. He's a skirt-chasing fool, but he ain't a killer.'

He held up the letter.

'This is pretty serious stuff.'

'Enough to get Nathan Jones killed?'

'Sheriff ruled it an accident, boy driving too fast. You met him, Brady. He seem like he knows what he's doing?'

'He did.'

'He does. If Brady Munn says it was an accident, it was an accident. Case closed. Folks don't murder each other in Marfa.'

The mayor downed his iced tea like a drunk downing his last shot of whiskey and stood as if to leave. But he hesitated; he had one more question for Book.

'Why do you care so much about Nathan Jones?'

'He was my student. I owe it to him to learn the truth.'

'The truth?' The mayor seemed amused. 'I've lived sixty years now, Professor, and I've learned there's no such thing as truth. There's just points of view.' He paused a moment, as if contemplating his own words, then said, 'Speaking of students, don't you still have classes to teach in Austin?'

The mayor walked away. They watched him glad-hand a few folks on their lunch break, then exit the establishment. Book turned to his intern.

'You get the feeling people want us to leave town?'

'I know I do.'

Chapter 16

'Henry, thanks for calling me back.'

'Just updating my resumé. How's Marfa?'

'Different.'

Book sat on Rock Hudson's rooftop patio. The sky was blue, and the afternoon warm. He had called Henry Lawson at the law school for legal advice. He often consulted Henry because he had worked in the real world. He had dealt with the reality of the law and not just the theory. He provided an objective view of the world. And he was smart.

'What are you doing in Marfa? You left kind of fast.'

'A former intern named Nathan Jones wrote me a letter—'

'Uh-oh, another letter.'

'—said he was now a lawyer here in Marfa representing an oil and gas client involved in fracking. Said his client was contaminating the groundwater. Said he had proof.'

'So what'd he have to say?'

'Nothing. He's dead. Died in a car accident, same day he mailed the letter to me.'

'Odd timing.'

'I thought so.'

'You suspect foul play?'

'I do.'

'Another quest for justice?'

'I'm afraid so.'

'Why do you care so much about Nathan Jones?'

'He saved my life.'

'He was the one? Down in South Texas?'

'He was. His wife's pregnant, due in a few weeks.'

'Damn. So you're playing detective again?'

'I talked to the sheriff—'

'What did he have to say?'

'Accident.'

'He got a stake in the game?'

'No.'

'Go on.'

'Then we visited the accident scene, talked to Nathan's senior partner in Midland—'

'Who's that?'

'Tom Dunn.'

'He's an important lawyer in West Texas.'

'Nathan said he took his proof to Dunn, but Dunn denied it.'

'That's what lawyers do.'

'Then we met with his client.'

'Who?'

'A fracker named Billy Bob Barnett.'

Henry laughed. 'You met Billy Bob?'

'You know him?'

'Everyone in the business knows Billy Bob. He's like a character out of a movie, a modern-day Jett Rink. Last I heard, he was sitting on a gold mine out there, held oil and gas leases on all the land in the Big Bend. So this dead lawyer had proof that Billy Bob is contaminating the groundwater?'

'Said he did. But I can't find it.'

'That kind of proof wouldn't be good for Billy Bob. You think he killed the lawyer, to shut him up?'

200

'It's a theory.'

'Book, I trust Billy Bob as far as I can throw the fat bastard, but a murderer? People murder for money, and he's already got lots of money.'

'He doesn't have a good reputation in the industry?'

'When he dies, they're going to have to screw him in the ground. He's like a lawyer—you figure he's lying anytime his lips are moving.'

'Not a straight shooter?'

'Only when he's shooting you in the back.'

'So the lesson is . . .?'

'Don't turn your back on Billy Bob Barnett.'

'I'll try to remember that.'

'So how can I help?'

'What do you know about fracking?'

'Everything. Fracking *is* the oil and gas business today. Virtually every gas well in the U.S. is fracked, and sixty percent of oil wells. Fracking accounts for fifty percent of all natural gas production, twenty-five percent of oil.'

'Billy Bob took me through the process. I thought I'd fact-check with you.'

'Shoot.'

'Water usage. Billy Bob said he uses five million gallons of water to frack a well, but says that's really not much water compared to ethanol.'

'He's right. Relative to other energy production, fracking uses very little water. But he didn't tell you the whole story.'

'Which is?'

'Which is, shale gas wells are short-life wells because the gas flows very fast out of the reservoir. The decline curves are steep, production levels drop off fast. So they have to constantly frack more wells to keep their production revenues up to cover expenses—fracking is expensive, about seven million dollars per well—and turn a profit. So even though on a per-well basis water usage is relatively low, the fracking industry uses a massive amount of water in total, something like three to four trillion gallons annually, mostly from lakes and aquifers, the sources for our drinking water.'

'He didn't mention that.'

'They never do.'

'Groundwater contamination.'

'Environmentalists have been trying to connect the dots from a frack well to a contaminated aquifer for the last decade. If they ever do, the Feds might shut down fracking. Which is what they want.'

'Why? Billy Bob said switching from coal to gas cuts carbon emissions in half.'

'And switching to green energy cuts it to zero. That's what the environmentalists want, to shut down the oil and gas industry and go straight to renewables—without a bridge. Just a big leap from eighty-five percent carbon energy to one hundred percent renewable. We're three, maybe four decades from that.'

'Billy Bob said the Energy Institute at UT found no direct connection between groundwater contamination and fracking.'

Henry laughed again.

'He didn't read the entire report. They also said that contamination is not unique to fracking, that casing failures and improper cement jobs occur in conventional drilling as well. But so far, no one's found direct evidence of contamination, not even the EPA. There's some anecdotal evidence—tap water turning brown and smelling foul, folks in Pennsylvania lighting their water on fire because of methane, the so-called "flammable faucets"—but hard to know if it's caused by fracking. So that's the first potential for contamination, failure of the well hole casing, which would allow frack fluids to flow directly into the aquifer. And we don't want those chemicals in our drinking water.'

'He said it's all under-the-kitchen-sink-type stuff.'

'But you don't want to drink any of that stuff. And some

202

frackers have used known carcinogens like benzene and formaldehyde in their frack fluids. We don't know who or when or where because they're not required to disclose their chemicals.'

'Federal water and pollution laws don't regulate this stuff?'

'If you want to inject any chemical into the earth for any reason, you're subject to the EPA rules and regulations under the Safe Drinking Water Act . . . unless you're fracking. Then you're free to pump any chemical you want down that hole.'

'Why?'

'Back in oh-five, Congress exempted fracking from the Water Act at the behest of Halliburton's ex-CEO, Vice President Cheney. Since Halliburton invented fracking, the exemption became known as the "Halliburton Loophole." So they can put anything except diesel fuel down the well hole without a permit or disclosure.'

'Doesn't sound smart.'

'What about politics is?'

'You said first potential for contamination. What's the second?'

'Migration. Even if the frack fluid goes down the hole without leakage, most of it stays in the reservoir. Over time it might migrate up through the rock and contaminate the aquifers from below.'

'What's the likelihood?'

'Shale gas formations are two or three miles below the aquifers, so migration through the rock is highly unlikely, at least that's what the geologists say. But they've been wrong before. And now they're "super fracking," using more powerful explosives to make even deeper cracks in the shale rock, which offers more migration paths. Problem is, migration contamination would be worse because the fracking process releases arsenic, underground shale gases like radon, radium two-two-six, methane, benzene, and what they call "NORM," naturally occurring radioactive material—'

'I see why they use an acronym.'

'—all of which is picked up by the fluid and transported up. That stuff gets into the drinking water, we're in a world of hurt.'

'Is there a third potential?'

'Flow-back. That portion of the frack fluid that's pushed up the hole by the gas. It's highly toxic after the fracking process, so you can't just dump the stuff into surface waters, rivers and lakes. You can recycle and reuse the flow-back, which is the best solution because we'd also cut down on the total water usage in fracking. But recycling is expensive. A few of the majors are recycling some of their frack fluid, but the independents like Billy Bob, they can't afford to. So they inject it down Class Two disposal wells. Should be Class One wells for hazardous wastes, but the industry got oil and gas waste exempted under the Resource Conservation and Recovery Act, so flow-back is deemed nonhazardous no matter what's in it.'

'Why'd they want flow-back exempted?'

'Cheaper to dispose in Class Two wells. We've got a hundred forty thousand of those wells, only five hundred Class Ones. We're putting every waste imaginable down those wells.'

'Why?'

'We've got to put it somewhere. Problem is, the industry disposes of a trillion gallons of flow-back every year, so Class Two disposal is getting more expensive. Supply and demand. Some operators push too much down the hole under too much pressure, and that's caused the reservoir walls to crack and the flow-back to migrate and contaminate nearby water wells. The Railroad Commission is supposed to regulate that sort of thing, but they've always been puppets of the industry. When you're in the industry, you like that. When you're out, you wish to hell they'd do their job.'

'Jobs.'

'Lots of jobs. Fracking employs fifty thousand workers in the Eagle Ford in South Texas, a hundred thousand in the Barnett, maybe three hundred thousand if the Marcellus is developed. And those jobs pay well—roughnecks can make a hundred thousand— and that's money to buy homes and cars, food and clothes, pay taxes. And gas powers factories, so cheaper gas makes the U.S. more competitive in the global economy. Which means more manufacturing jobs, more income, more prosperity. Which in turn creates more jobs in the service and retail industries. The economy grows. Cheap energy is good for America. Good for the world. And shale gas is cheap energy. For a long time.'

'Last thing: tell me about the geopolitics of shale gas.'

'It's a game-changer. If shale wins, the West wins and Russia and Iran lose big-time. If shale loses, they win and we lose. Energy equals political and economic power. It's that simple.'

'That's what Billy Bob said.'

'He's right about that.'

'So Billy Bob Barnett's not just a dumb-ass Aggie?'

'That "I'm just a dumb ol' Aggie" routine is a role he plays. Figures it's better to have people underestimate him. But don't you make that mistake. He's not stupid. He knows the business. He knows how to find oil and gas and how to make money. He's rich, and he's made a lot of important Aggies in Texas rich. Not me, but other Aggies.'

Henry paused.

'I'm applying to the new Aggie law school. Next time you see Billy Bob, ask him to put a good word in for me.' He laughed. 'Just kidding. Look, Billy Bob Barnett's a driller. He knows how to punch holes in the earth. He's fracked maybe a thousand wells over the last decade—he was fracking before fracking was fashionable. He knows the environmentalists are gunning for fracking, praying a fracker contaminates an aquifer so they can shut it all down. He's not dumb enough to kill his golden goose. Fracking is a money machine for him. He's not going to blow it all by intentionally contaminating ground-water. You don't get rich in the oil business by being a dumb-ass.'

'So what's your advice, counselor?'

'Get the lawyer's proof.'

'I've shown his letter all over town, trying to get a bite. No takers. I've talked to everyone who might know anything about that proof, but no one does. Nathan didn't show his proof to his wife, his best friend, or the environmentalist he was working with.'

'Okay, Book, let's take an objective look at the facts: first, the lawyer said he had proof, but no one's seen it and you can't find it. Second, the sheriff said there was no evidence of foul play. All facts point to an accidental death. Third, Billy Bob's too rich and too smart to shoot himself in the foot. He doesn't need to cheat to make money. And fourth, you're suffering a serious sense of guilt about this intern, so you're searching for something that's not there. All of which leads me to conclude that there is no proof. And no murder. It was just an accident.'

Henry paused.

'Sometimes, Book, there is no mystery. Sometimes things are exactly what they seem to be.'

Chapter 17

'Nothing in this movie is what it seems to be.'

Book had again found his intern in the *Giant* museum watching the movie. She held a large coffee cup with one hand—'I found that Frama's'—and pointed at the screen with the other.

'The big Reata ranch house, it was just a façade. There was no inside or back to it. They only built the front, made it look like a mansion.'

'The magic of movies.'

'Bick Benedict's this macho cattleman and Jett Rink's a surly ranch hand turned ruthless oil tycoon, but in real life Rock Hudson and James Dean were both gay.'

'Back then, if the world knew they were gay, their acting careers would've been over. So the studios kept up their heterosexual images, had them appear with starlets around Hollywood. They had to keep their true lives secret. They lived façade lives, like the ranch house.'

'Like Nathan Jones.'

Book watched the movie, Rock Hudson and James Dean in the big fight scene on the front porch of the ranch house, all pretending to be something they weren't. All just acting out roles in Marfa, Texas. Had Nathan Jones pretended to be someone he wasn't? Had he just acted a role in Marfa, Texas? If Nadine were right, Nathan had lived a hard life out here, hiding himself from his wife and his friends. That thought made Book sad for his intern. But it didn't make Nathan's death anything more than just a tragic accident.

He had found Nathan Jones's truth.

His truth—the truth—was that he had died in a horrible accident. The sheriff was right: there was no evidence of foul play. No evidence of murder. No proof of contamination. Nadine was right: Book was emotionally invested in Nathan's death. He had not remained objective. He had searched for a murder instead of the truth. For something that wasn't there. There was no murder. It was time to close this case and return to the law school. Henry was right: sometimes things are exactly what they seem to be.

'I'm just like Rock and James and Nathan,' Nadine said.

'Gay?'

'A pretender. They were gays pretending to be straight. I'm a chef pretending to be a law student.'

'Perhaps you are, Ms. Honeywell. So I suggest we see what chefs do here in Marfa, try out one of those fancy restaurants tonight. Before we leave town tomorrow morning.'

Nadine's mouth gaped, and her eyes got big.

'Well, shut the front door.'

The red front door of Maiya's contrasted with the white adobe of the Brite Building where the restaurant occupied a ground-floor space. Marfa gathered at Maiya's for drinks and dinner each night Wednesday through Saturday. They walked in and saw the mayor at a table, apparently selling the Marfa concept to his dining companions. He waved at Book, and Book waved back. At one end of the bar was Border Patrol Agent Angel Acosta with a young woman; he was not dressed in a green uniform but in all black. He waved, and Book waved back. At the other end of the bar was a group of young males in hipster attire, no doubt artists. Talking to them as if lecturing a class were Carla Kent and a young man dressed in a suit without a tie. She saw Book and came over with the man in the suit.

'Professor,' Carla said, 'this is Fred Phillips. He's an environmental lawyer from Santa Fe.'

Book shook hands with Fred and introduced him to Nadine.

'Professor, it's an honor. I've read all your books and watched you on TV. I really appreciate your point of view.'

'So what brings you to Marfa?'

'Carla got me down here, to represent landowners in condemnation suits brought by Barnett Oil and Gas.'

'Tough cases given the law in Texas.'

'We can't win, but we can drag it out, slow him down, make it very expensive.'

'Well, good luck.'

'Thank you, Professor.'

Fred returned to the bar. Carla took a step closer to Book.

'Saw you out running this morning,' she said. 'While I was showering. At the El Cosmico.'

'Must've been cold.'

'Water was hot.'

'Ms. Kent, we're leaving in the morning.'

She took a step back.

'Nathan Jones was murdered,' she said.

Book showed her the funeral photo with the circled faces.

'Ms. Kent, I've interviewed everyone in Marfa who had a connection with Nathan—his wife and best friend, his senior partner, his secretary, his co-workers, his client, the sheriff, the mayor . . . no one took the bait.'

'What bait?'

'His letter. I found no evidence of murder and no proof of contamination. His death was an accident.'

'Same day he mailed the letter to you?'

'Just a coincidence.'

She pointed a finger in his face. 'You're wrong, Professor.'

She returned to her place at the bar but gave him a long stern look. She seemed a very intense woman. His prior experience with such women proved to be too intense to last; the relationships burned hot, then quickly burned out. But he had to confess, such relationships were exciting while they lasted—which could explain his attraction to such women. That or the fact that he would never marry, and such women never entertained marriage.

'Told you,' his intern said.

'What?'

'There would be romance.'

'No time for romance. We're leaving in the morning.'

'What about Nathan's wife?'

'We'll talk to Brenda on our way out of town.'

They were led to a table by their waiter; he was an artist. Maiya's was elegant and expensive with white tablecloths and a $150 price tag for two, but that did not dissuade Nadine from wiping down the silverware and table accessories and then her hands.

'What did Professor Lawson say about fracking?'

'That Billy Bob didn't tell the whole truth—'

'Like law professors.'

'—but that what he said was basically true.'

'So what's the truth about fracking?'

'The truth? That's a hard thing to know, Ms. Honeywell. What do the words of the Constitution mean? Which politician is correct about fixing the economy? Is global warming real? Was Oswald the lone gunman? Should Roger Clemens be in the Hall of Fame? Is fracking good or bad? I don't have any answers. Maybe there's no such thing as the truth. Maybe it's all just a point of view, like the mayor and Ms. Garza said.'

'Irma?'

Book nodded.

'She scares me sometimes, she's so committed. Like that Carla girl.'

Maiya's smelled of food and sounded of life. Patrons talked and laughed. Judd's boxes and Maiya's food; Marfa was growing on Book. He had the spinach lasagna; Nadine had the grilled rib eye steak with Gorgonzola butter, red-skinned mashed potatoes, and pistachio ice cream with dark Belgian chocolate. She finished off the last bite then sat back and sighed as if utterly satisfied.

'That was an incredible dinner.'

It was.

'This is my dream.'

'To eat pistachio ice cream?'

'To own a restaurant like this. To create dishes like these.'

'A law student who wants to be a chef.'

'And a law professor who wants to be a hero.' She regarded him. 'Who *needs* to be a hero.'

His intern was getting too close to the truth for his comfort.

'How old are you?'

She smiled and sipped her coffee. She seemed at home, as Book was on the Harley.

'I want to cook all day and make people happy,' she said.

'You want to make people happy so you went to law school?'

'I went to law school to make my dad happy.'

'That's his dream, Ms. Honeywell. Chase your own dream. Live your own life.'

'I'm too afraid.'

'Of what?'

'Everything. Germs. Heights. Mosquitoes. Melanoma. Cavities. Gum disease. Failure. My dad.'

'You want to live life with a net.'

'What net?'

'Like acrobats in a circus. They have a net beneath them, so they don't get hurt if they fall.'

'What's wrong with that?'

'Nothing . . . if you're in a circus. In life, it's fatal.'

'But I won't get hurt.'

'You won't live. Life hurts, Ms. Honeywell. That's the price of admission.'

'You're not afraid of getting hurt?'

'I'm living without a net.'

'That's dangerous.'

'I don't live with fear—of failing, getting hurt, dying. I live every day as if it's my last, because it might be.'

'You're not afraid of dying?'

'I'm afraid of not living.'

'What's the difference?'

'Not living is worse than dying. Death is inevitable. So I'm going out on my own terms, while I can still make the choice. But I can't accept not doing something with my life. With the time I have. I'm going to matter. Not just be matter.'

'My therapist says I'm afraid of life because my sister died, and I don't want to die.' She studied her coffee. 'Do you know why?'

'Why you don't want to die?'

'Why you need to be a hero.'

'I don't have a therapist.'

'What do you have?'

'Regrets.'

John Bookman had always wanted to be a cop like his dad. Wear the uniform. Carry a gun. Ben Bookman had left home that morning in his blue uniform with his holster on his waist and his gun on his hip. He wore a bulletproof vest that protected him against a gunshot to the chest.

But not to his head.

Book rode his bike to school that day, as he did every day. And he rode it home, past Mary Elizabeth's house; she was practicing her cheers in her front yard, so he stopped and flirted a bit. She was cute and perky and acted interested in him. He felt manly when he pedaled away. He didn't know that he was about to become a man in the worst way possible. He turned the corner onto his street and saw the police cars out front of his house. He saw the officers at the front door talking to his mother. He saw her hands go to her face. He saw her collapse on the porch.

He was fourteen years old, and life as he knew it ended that day.

'Professor?'

Book returned to the moment.

'My dad was a cop. He died in the line of duty. Shot in the head by the man he was trying to help.'

'OMG. How old were you?'

'Fourteen.'

'Not fair.'

'No. Not fair at all. As you well know.'

They pondered their losses—his father, her sister—for a quiet moment in the elegant restaurant in Marfa, Texas. Book knew from her expression that she was wondering what her life would have been like if her sister had survived the cancer, just as he always wondered what his life would have been like if his father had survived the bullet. The moment ended, and their eyes met.

'So you're helping people because he can't?'

'He made me proud, being a cop. I want to make him proud, being a lawyer.'

'Professor, your dad would be proud of you.'

Book fought back his emotions and stuck a finger in the air to attract their waiter's attention. When he arrived, Book asked for the bill.

'Your bill's already been paid, sir.'

'By whom?'

'Him.'

The waiter nodded toward the back of the restaurant. Book turned in his chair and saw Billy Bob smiling and holding up a beer bottle as if saluting Book. A young woman kept him company. Book gave Billy Bob Barnett a gesture of thanks; as he turned back, he noticed Carla at the bar. She had observed his interplay with Billy Bob; she shook her head with utter disgust, as if Book had betrayed her.

He turned back to his intern. Nadine Honeywell's eyes drifted down to her dessert plate. She ran her index finger through the remains of the Belgian chocolate then licked her finger as if she would never again taste chocolate. She spoke softly, as if to herself.

'Living without a net.'

Chapter 18

'The Fourth Amendment to the Constitution states that, quote, "The right of the people to be secure in their persons, houses, papers, and effects, against unreasonable searches and seizures, shall not be violated, and no Warrants shall issue, but upon probable cause, supported by Oath or affirmation, and particularly describing the place to be searched, and the persons or things to be seized."'

It was ten that night, and they were sitting on the sofa in Elizabeth Taylor's room on the second floor of the Paisano Hotel. Book was dictating the Welch brief to Nadine; she was a faster typist than Book. They were trying to get the brief finished before returning to Austin the next morning. His cell phone rang. He checked the caller ID.

'Shit.'

'Is shit capitalized?'

'No.'

'It's lower case?'

'No. I forgot I had a date with Carmen tonight.'

'I think you're going to be late.'

He answered the phone. Carmen's voice came over.

215

'I'm waiting.'

'I'm in Marfa.'

'So I bought a new thong for nothing.'

Carmen Castro worked as a fitness instructor at Book's gym in Austin.

'I'll be home tomorrow.'

Nadine sneezed.

'Are you alone?'

'No, Ms. Honeywell is here.'

'Who's Ms. Honeywell?'

'My intern.'

'Isn't there a law about that sort of thing, a professor and a student?'

'Not in college. It's considered a perk.'

'Still, she is a bit young for you.'

'You're young for me.'

'Not that young.'

'We're working on a brief.'

'Just keep your briefs on.'

'Boxers.'

'Whatever.'

'Sorry to ruin your night.'

'That's okay. I'll just go to the gun range instead.'

He ended the call.

'Is she your girlfriend?' Nadine asked.

'Carmen's a girl and a friend. What about you? You got a boyfriend? Or a girlfriend?'

'I'm straight. I'd know if I weren't. And no.'

'Why not?'

'Guys today, their idea of a date is to go to a sports bar, drink beer, watch a football game, and text their buddies about their fantasy football teams, whatever those are. Sometimes I think it might be good to be a lesbian, I'd have someone to talk to.'

'There's always Billy Bob.'

'Gross. Besides, he's an Aggie.'

'Good point.'

'So your reputation, it's true?'

'What reputation?'

'All your women.'

'Just rumors.'

'I don't think so.'

'Okay, where were we on the brief? Oh, read the search-and-seizure cases—'

'I did. Last year, for your class.'

'I still can't place you.'

'I hid out in the back, behind my laptop. I was too afraid to speak up.'

'I don't know why you guys are so afraid of the other students—'

'We're afraid of you.'

'*Me?*'

'You're, like, a god at the law school.'

'I'm just a teacher. Teaching old cases that don't make a heck of a lot of difference in people's lives. But out here, I can make a difference. Sometimes.'

'But not this time?'

'Apparently not.'

'You ready to tell me the story?'

'What story?'

'How Nathan saved your life?'

Chapter 19

'You got me fired, you sorry son of a bitch.'

'Mr. Koontz, my father was a cop. An honest cop. You're a disgrace to the badge. Hell, you're a disgrace to the human race. But you shouldn't worry about losing your job. You should worry about going to prison. You know what the inmates do to dirty cops in prison?'

Book turned away from Buster Koontz. Turning his back on a dirty cop was a mistake, even in a courthouse. He did not see Buster reach to his leg and draw his backup weapon from a concealed ankle holster.

He pointed the gun at Book and fired.

The first letter had arrived four weeks before, on a Monday, the same day Nathan Jones started his tenure as Book's intern. His first assignment was to read and write responses to incoming mail, typically letters seeking speaking appearances, blurbs for books, recommendations for employment, and comments on important appellate cases—not letters seeking justice.

'Professor,' Nathan had said when Book returned from class, 'you should read this letter.'

Back in the eighties, the bureaucrats running the war on drugs in Washington dreamed up 'regional drug task forces.' The idea was to coordinate law enforcement efforts across jurisdictional boundaries to better combat drug distribution in the U.S. Funded by the Feds, managed by the states, and manned by the locals, the task forces were granted authority to fight the war on drugs across wide swaths of America. But federal funding was 'incentivized': the more arrests you made, the more funds you got, similar to farm subsidies. If you subsidize corn, you'll get more corn; if you subsidize drug arrests, you'll get more drug arrests. The one thousand drug task forces now make two million drug arrests each year in the U.S. And the key to 'making the numbers,' as the arrest game is called, is hiring experienced undercover narcotics agents from outside the locality to come in under fake identities and make the 'buy-bust' arrests. These agents move from task force to task force. They are not the Eliot Nesses of law enforcement; they are 'gypsy cops,' as they've come to be known in the business.

Buster Koontz was one such cop. He saw himself as a Dirty Harry type even though he was short and squat instead of tall and lean like Clint Eastwood. But he was dirty. The badge gave him power, and the power fed his ego. Buster rolled into the small South Texas town in the summer of 2007. In less than a year, he had conducted undercover operations that resulted in the arrest and conviction of fifty-three Hispanics, mostly young Mexican nationals with limited English language skills, all for 'delivery of a controlled substance,' i.e., drug dealing. Fifty-three drug dealers in a town of three thousand. His testimony was the only evidence presented at trial. The prosecution offered no corroborating evidence—no surveillance video-tapes, no audiotapes, no wiretaps, no photos—nothing except Agent Koontz's word that he had purchased illegal drugs from the defendants. But his word was enough to secure convictions from juries determined to fight crime in their town and a judge seeking reelection. The mother of one defendant saw

Book on television and wrote him the letter. Book turned to his new intern.

'Mr. Jones, we're going to South Texas.'

'Uh, Professor, I'd rather not.'

'Why?'

'Well, I read it's kind of dangerous down there, with the drug cartels.'

'So?'

'So . . . I'm afraid.'

'Nothing to be ashamed of, Mr. Jones.'

'You're not afraid. Of anything. Even dying.'

'I'm afraid of not living.'

'Me, too.'

'No, you're afraid of dying, Mr. Jones.'

A week later, Book and Nathan Jones rode the Harley to South Texas. Nathan had conducted an Internet search on Buster Koontz and discovered that his past was checkered, to put it mildly. He was a drug task force hired gun, moving from small town to small town, putting up high conviction rates and then moving on. But scandal lingered behind: allegations that he had committed perjury—one convicted defendant was released from prison when his family produced time-stamped videotapes that proved he was at work when the alleged buy went down; another was released because he had been in jail in another county for drunk driving when Buster testified he had made the buy. Their first encounter with Buster Koontz was less than cordial.

'I want to commend Agent Koontz for his courage in wiping out the drug trade in our town. His remarkable work has resulted in twenty-two more arrests . . .'

The local district attorney (up for reelection) was holding a press conference on the steps of the county courthouse to announce the latest victories in the war on drugs. Agent Koontz stood next to him and basked in the glory. Three print reporters and a camera crew from the Laredo TV station captured the moment. When the D.A. paused, Book jumped in.

'Mr. District Attorney, are you aware that Agent Koontz produced the same remarkable results with drug task forces in seven other states over the last eleven years, but that many of the convictions based on his testimony are now being over-turned because Agent Koontz committed perjury and fabricated evidence. That many of his colleagues on those task forces regarded him as a racist, a liar, a bully, a rogue cop, and even mentally unstable. That—'

'Who the hell are you?'

'Professor John Bookman, University of Texas School of Law.'

'And what brings you to our county?'

'Injustice.'

The D.A. cut short the press conference and retreated to his office in the courthouse. Agent Koontz did not retreat. He fought past the reporters asking if Book's claims were true and grabbed Book's arm. Book eyed Buster's hand and then Buster.

'You don't want to do that.'

'What?'

'Grab my arm.'

'Why not?'

'Because I'm going to break yours.'

'You threatening a police officer?'

'I'm threatening a dirty cop.'

Buster released Book's arm and escaped the reporters and camera by driving off in his black pickup truck. Book gave his information to the media. Once the story broke, the D.A. had no choice but to fire Agent Koontz and announce a grand jury to investigate his actions. Buster Koontz would never again carry a badge.

But in Texas, he could still carry a gun.

Book jumped when the gun discharged. He wheeled around and saw Buster running from the courthouse and Nathan Jones slumped to the floor.

221

'Call an ambulance!'

He dropped down and cradled Nathan's head in his lap then felt his intern's body for the wound. His hand came back bloody.

'Nathan, what the hell were you thinking?'

His intern's eyes blinked open.

'Professor . . . you called me Nathan. Not Mr. Jones.'

He passed out.

Nathan Jones had stepped between Buster's gun and Book's back. The bullet struck his shoulder; surgery saved his life, as he had saved Book's. Buster Koontz was found later that day in his truck, dead of a self-inflicted gunshot to the head. His days as a cop were over, as were Nathan Jones's days as Professor Bookman's intern.

Chapter 20

'Wow,' Nadine said. 'And all I had to do was hit that guy with a beer bottle. What happened to all those people they sent to prison?'

'The governor pardoned them. They're back home with their families. Once that story hit the media, the letters started coming, never stopped.'

'Those drug task forces are scary.'

'They are. Bush tried to defund the task forces, but members of Congress don't get reelected by being soft on crime, so they funded them anyway. After this case and several other scandals, the governor disbanded the task forces in Texas.'

'Professor, I understand now, why we came. Why you had to come. Why you care so much about Nathan Jones.'

'Nathan saved my life, so I wanted his death to be something more than an accident, to have a greater meaning. To make sense. But it was just a senseless accident. Just a coincidence that he died the same day he mailed the letter. No one took the bait. There was no proof of contamination. No evidence of a crime. No murder mystery. That's what we learned today, Ms. Honeywell.'

Book's cell phone rang again. It was Joanie. She again pleaded for him to put their mother in a home. After a moment, he checked out of the conversation.

'Book—don't do that.'

'What?'

'Check out.' She sighed. 'Book, you've been my big brother for thirty-one years. You took Dad's place when I was ten. You rode me to school on your bike, you protected me from bullies—'

His dad had taught Book the basics of self-defense in the backyard. After he died, the anger that consumed Book had given him strength. The school bullies were big and mean; Book was mad at the world. They didn't stand a chance. But the anger threatened to destroy the boy, so his mother had put him in a taekwondo class, her version of anger management for her teenage son. It worked. Taekwondo taught him to control his emotions and to channel his anger into martial arts. He came to each class filled with anger and left with a sense of peace. He now taught the class to other angry young boys.

'—but I'm married now. You need to consider what I think. And what Dennis thinks.'

'I don't care what Dennis thinks.'

'He's a doctor.'

'He's not her son. Or her daughter.'

She again sighed into the phone. 'When are you coming home?'

'Tomorrow morning.'

'What about the dead lawyer?'

'It was just an accident.'

'Good. Because I worry when—'

Book heard the distinctive discharge of a shotgun below their window fronting Texas Street and dove for Nadine just as the glass exploded and buckshot peppered the opposite wall. She screamed. He covered her on the floor and heard a roaring

224

engine and screeching tires outside and Joanie's voice on the phone.

'Book! Book!'

He stayed low and reached for the phone.

'Joanie.'

'Book, what was that?'

'Gunfire.'

'Are you okay?'

'We're okay.'

'We who?'

'Me and Ms. Honeywell.'

'Who's Ms. Honeywell?'

'My new intern.'

'What happened to Renée?'

'She quit.'

'Why?'

'Gunfire.'

He disconnected his sister. Nadine had curled into the fetal position on the floor; her body was shaking uncontrollably. He brushed glass shards off her. She cried.

'You're okay, Ms. Honeywell. They weren't trying to hurt us, not with a shotgun. They're just trying to scare us off.'

'I'm not crying about that.'

'Then what are you crying about?'

'Because we can't go home now. A fish just took the bait.'

Chapter 21

Book opened his eyes, but lay still. It was morning, but something wasn't right. Someone was in the room. Someone was in the bed. Someone's arm was stretched across his bare chest. Someone's face was plastered against his shoulder, covered by a mane of black hair. Someone's drool wet his skin. He turned to the someone.

Nadine Honeywell.

He remembered now. Her window had been blown out by the shotgun blast. So she had slept in his room. He had offered her the bed, but she opted for the couch. She stirred awake and realized her position. She didn't move.

'I got scared on the couch.'

'I said you could sleep in the bed.'

'I did.'

She removed her arm, peeled her face from his shoulder, wiped her drool from his skin—

'Sorry.'

—and rolled over onto her back. They both stared at the ceiling. She finally spoke in a soft voice.

'I've never slept with a man before.'

226

'We only slept, Ms. Honeywell.'

'I've had sex, once, but it wasn't an overnight thing. It was a back-seat-in-high-school-with-a-jerk thing. I tried a few more times, but like I said, after I got my clothes off, turned out they were gay. Awkward moment.'

'I bet it was.'

'No. This moment.'

She lay silent, which made the moment even more awkward.

'Sorry, Professor. In awkward moments, I tend to over-share.'

He decided to change the subject. 'You want to run with me?'

She groaned. 'Don't tell me it's only dawn?'

'I'm afraid so. So how about it?'

'Please, Professor. My generation does not run at dawn. We stay up late and sleep late.'

'I'll bring you breakfast.'

'That egg, cheese, and ham baguette, waffle with chocolate syrup and whipped cream, Strawberry Banana Cabana smoothie, and a large coffee with real cream.'

'Fear doesn't dampen your appetite.'

'A girl's got to eat.'

'I'll be back in an hour.'

'I'll be here.'

Book got out of bed; he wore long boxers. Nadine pulled the comforter over her head and said, 'Lock the door.'

An hour later, Book had run five miles around town and then stopped off at SqueezeMarfa. He bought breakfast and headed back to the hotel. He turned the corner off Lincoln Street and onto Highland Avenue and saw a Presidio County Sheriff's Department cruiser parked out front of the Paisano one block down. He broke into a run and sprinted past the front desk—

'Another night, Professor?' the desk clerk asked.

'Every night until further notice.'

—and up the stairs and down the corridor to his room. He found Nadine in the shower. Steam filled the bathroom.

'You okay?'

'Professor!'

'Sorry.'

He placed the breakfast on the kitchen counter then went next door to Nadine's room. He found Sheriff Munn standing at the blown-out window and a young female deputy digging with a pocketknife into the sheetrock on the opposite wall. Her blonde hair was pulled back but strands fell into her face; she wore a snug-fitting uniform that emphasized her curves and carried a big gun in a leather holster. She looked like Marilyn Monroe in a deputy's uniform. She smiled.

'Well, hidee there.'

She put a hand on her holstered gun and jutted her hip out. She gave him a once-over and a coy look; he wore only running shorts and shoes. He caught a faint whiff of perfume, not standard equipment on most of the law enforcement personnel he had encountered. She blew hair from her face.

'And who might you be, cowboy?'

'He's the professor,' the sheriff said from the window. 'Dig, Shirley.'

Book walked over to the sheriff, who jabbed his head in Deputy Shirley's direction.

'Niece.'

He had a jaw full of chewing tobacco. He turned back to the window, leaned into the open space, and spit a brown stream outside. Book peeked down to see if the sidewalk below was clear of pedestrians.

'Well, they're damn sure gonna have to replace this window,' the sheriff said.

'That qualify as foul play?'

'Reckon it does. Where's the gal? She okay?'

'She is. She's next door in my room.'

The sheriff's eyebrows rose; he grunted.

'No,' Book said. 'It's not like that. She was too afraid to sleep alone, so she slept with . . . Never mind.'

'Overnight maid downstairs, she heard the gunshot, saw a dark pickup speed away,' the sheriff said.

'Maroon?'

'I asked. She couldn't say. I take it you talked to Billy Bob, know the color of his truck.'

'We talked.'

'You learn anything?'

'I don't like him.'

'That ain't exactly breaking news.'

'Sheriff, Nathan Jones was murdered.'

The sheriff launched another stream of tobacco juice through the broken glass.

'Maybe. Or maybe those boys at Padre's don't appreciate getting their butts kicked by a professor, decided to let you know. And by the way, I figure those boys got what they deserved, but don't you figure you can run around my county playing Rambo—*comprende*, podna?'

'Birdshot, Sheriff,' Deputy Shirley said. She examined a small pellet. 'Number eight, probably from a twelve-gauge shotgun.'

The sheriff grunted then spat again.

'If they wanted to kill you, Professor, they wouldn't have used birdshot. They just wanted to encourage you to go home.'

'When can we go home?'

'When we find out who murdered Nathan Jones.'

They were eating breakfast on Rock's rooftop patio. Nadine finished off the baguette, waffle, and smoothie and then sipped her coffee.

'And how are we going to do that?'

'Someone took the bait last night. I think I know who. Now we've got to reel that big Aggie fish in.'

She sighed.

'I don't like the sound of that.'

Chapter 22

Sam Walker sat behind his desk wearing the same cap but a different Hawaiian shirt when Book and Nadine walked into *The Times of Marfa* office. He looked up and smiled as if an old friend had reentered his life.

'Well, hello, Professor. You've certainly made an impression around town.'

'Not a good one, apparently.'

'Sold out this week's edition, first time ever. Don't reckon the roller derby would've sold out.'

'Sam, you said I could trust you.'

'You can.'

'You ran the story.'

Sam stood and came over to the counter.

'Professor, I figure you're a pretty smart fella, knew what you were doing when you showed me that letter. Figured you wanted me to run the story, stir the pot in Marfa.'

Book fought a smile but failed.

'We talk slow out here in West Texas, Professor, but that doesn't mean we think slow.'

'I expect not.'

'You've been busy, waving that letter all over town, getting shot at. You folks okay?'

'Just a warning shot.'

'Figure you got a murder case?'

'I do.'

'Figure the killer shot your window out?'

'I do.'

'What're you gonna do about it?'

'Send the killer a message.'

Sam removed his cap and scratched his head, a sure sign he was thinking.

'Well, next edition doesn't come out till next week. You want to send a message today, best to use the radio.'

The Marfa Public Radio station operates out of a small studio in a small storefront befitting the smallest public radio station in America. Its audience totals less than fifteen thousand in the sparsely populated Trans-Pecos. The station's 100,000-watt signal spans an area of 20,000 square miles extending north of the Davis Mountains and south to the Rio Grande, west to the Blue Origin spaceport and east to Marathon. Hence the station's tagline: 'Radio for a Wide Range.' Nadine Honeywell sanitized the armrests of a chair with wipes then sat in the small reception area and listened to the professor on the radio.

'A reminder, folks,' the host said. 'It's April, and we don't want a repeat of last April's wildfires, so don't toss those cigarettes out the window. And the burn ban remains in effect. The land is dry, and the wind is up. If you see smoke, there's fire, so call it in. Okay, our *Talk at Ten* interview today was scheduled to be Werner von Stueber discussing existentialism and crushed cars in our continuing series on the works of John Chamberlain, but we're rescheduling Werner for tomorrow morning to make room for a surprise guest, the renowned constitutional law professor from the University of Texas at Austin, John Bookman. We've all seen Professor Bookman on national TV discussing the constitutionality of abortion or Obamacare, but he isn't here to talk about those subjects. He's here to talk about murder. A murder in Marfa. Professor Bookman, welcome to Marfa.'

'Thanks for having me on your show on such short notice.'

'We all know about the terrible death of a local lawyer, Nathan Jones, last week. We thought he died in a tragic automobile accident. But you think otherwise.'

'He was murdered.'

'Why do you believe that?'

'Nathan wrote me a letter and mailed it on April fifth. He died the same day.'

'Coincidence?'

'I don't believe in coincidences.'

'And what did he say in that letter, Professor?'

'Nathan said that his client was committing environmental crimes. That his client was contaminating the groundwater out here with his fracking operations.'

'That's a pretty serious charge.'

'It is.'

'And who is his client?'

'Billy Bob Barnett.'

Across Highland Avenue, Sam Walker howled in his office.

'Hot-damn! That'll sell some papers next week!'

'So, Professor, you received this letter in Austin before you knew Nathan Jones had died. Why'd you come to Marfa?'

'Nathan was a former student and my intern four years ago. He asked for my help.'

'But upon your arrival in Marfa, you learned of his death?'

'Yes.'

'Professor, how do you help a dead person?'

'You find his truth. You give him justice.'

'And how do you do that?'

233

'You learn about his life, who he was. So I spoke with his wife—'

Brenda Jones sat in her house listening to the professor on the radio. She placed her hands on her belly that held Nathan's child. She cried.

'—and his best friend—'

Jimmy John Dale blew blood from his nose onto the handkerchief. He sat among empty beer cans, empty pizza boxes, and loaded guns. Bushmaster AR-15 assault rifle with a thirty-round clip . . . Winchester twelve-gauge pump shotgun . . . Smith & Wesson .357 Magnum handgun with a heavy load—you couldn't own too many weapons in his neighborhood on the Mexican side of town just south of the railroad tracks. He adjusted his position in his ratty recliner in the living room of his mobile home. He was saving for the down payment on a small adobe house on the same side of the railroad tracks; no way could he ever afford a home north of the tracks. The voices of the kids playing outside and chattering in Spanish—he often felt as if he were living in the state of Chihuahua instead of the state of Texas—came through the thin exterior wall as clearly as if they were standing next to him and made the hammer in his head pound even harder. They always left their toys and bikes and skateboards scattered about the open space between their trailers. He finished off the Lone Star beer and tossed the can at the trash basket in the adjoining kitchen but missed and thought, Their mama ought to teach those kids how to pick up after themselves.

Never figured he'd live with the Mexicans, but it was all he could afford; and besides, the Mexicans couldn't even afford to live on the Mexican side of town now, so they were selling out to Anglos who couldn't afford to live on the Anglo side of town, which was now just a suburb of New York City. Goddamn queer artists. But hell, unless he wanted to live the rest of his life alone, he'd probably have to marry a Mexican girl. All the white girls, they get the hell out of town after high school, most for college, the others for a job in the city or a man with a job in the city. They don't come back. That'd be a hell of a thing, having a Mexican mother-in-law.

The mother next door started yelling at the kids in Spanish, so Jimmy John turned up the radio and searched for his Advil.

'—and learned that she had been followed around town—'
'By whom?'
'She didn't know. So I talked to the sheriff—'

Presidio County Sheriff Brady Munn sat in his office with his cowboy boots kicked up on his desk and Deputy Shirley practicing her fast draw against an imaginary gunslinger. He sighed and shook his head. A niece pretending to be a deputy and a professor pretending to be a detective.

'Should've been a cattle rancher,' he said to himself.

'—and went out to the accident scene. I visited Nathan's senior partner in Midland. And I met Billy Bob Barnett.'
'You showed them Nathan's letter?'
'Yes. They all denied any knowledge of Nathan's allegations. I had concluded that his death was just a tragic accident, as you said, until last night.'
'What happened last night?'
'Someone shot out our window at the Paisano.'
'The killer?'
'Who else?'
'Was anyone hurt?'
'No. My intern was scared.'

'But not you?'

'I've been through this sort of thing before.'

'I bet you have. So, Professor, why did you want to come on the radio today?'

'Because I have a message for Nathan's killer.'

'Which is?'

'I'm coming for you. I will find you. And I will bring you to justice. For Nathan.'

In the Marfa City Hall, Mayor Ward Weaver sighed as if he had lost a real-estate commission. He might have; he just didn't know it yet.

'Hell's bells, a murder in Marfa. Talk like that, he's gonna scare off all the homosexuals.'

Carla Kent drove her old '96 Ford pickup truck south on Highway 17 from Fort Davis. The windows were down, and the radio was on. The professor, he didn't understand West Texas anymore than those New York artists did. Difference was, they were just insulting the locals with their art and public displays of their sexual preferences; they weren't calling them murderers. Locals out here don't take kindly to such remarks. And they carry guns.

'There's a murderer in Marfa,' the professor said on the radio. 'And I'm going to find him.'

In his office two blocks north on Highland, Billy Bob Barnett grabbed the radio and hurled it against the far wall. He hadn't been that pissed-off since his third ex-wife got the ski lodge in Aspen. His pulled out his little pill box and swallowed a blood pressure pill. He blew his nose into a handkerchief then pointed a finger at the two football-players-turned-body-guards sitting across the desk from him.

'Follow him. Don't let him out of your sight.'

★　　★　　★

236

'Goddamnit, Roscoe, Bookman's on the radio out here calling my biggest client a murderer!'

Like most successful lawyers who gave lots of money to judges and their alma maters, Tom Dunn demanded preferential treatment at the courthouse and the law school. So, upon hearing the professor on Marfa Public Radio, he picked up the phone and hit the speed dial for the dean of the UT law school.

'You represent a murderer?' Dean Roscoe Chambers said.

'*What?* No. He's in the oil and gas business. But your professor's calling him a murderer.'

'Oh. What do you want me to do about it?'

'Call him back to Austin. Get him off our fuckin' backs out here.'

'He's tenured, Tom. Which means unless he engages in sexual relations with a freshman, there's nothing I can do to him.'

'College freshman?'

'High school. And he's a celebrity. The press loves him. He makes for a good story, that Indiana Jones stuff. What I'm saying is, he's untouchable.'

'Maybe.'

Chapter 23

'I'm thinking you didn't make any friends in Marfa,' Nadine said.

'Wasn't trying to.'

'What were you trying to do?'

'Ratchet up the pressure on the killer.'

'That sounds dangerous.'

'It can be.'

He held the door to The Get Go open for his intern then followed her inside. The Get Go is an organic grocery store started by the woman behind Maiya's restaurant. It's located on the southeast side of Marfa, catty-cornered from a group of crumbling adobes that appear more like a rundown motel. The structures seemed unfit for human occupancy, but Latinos still occupied the homes.

It was past noon, and Nadine hadn't eaten in four hours, so they had stopped at The Get Go on their way to Brenda Jones's house. They didn't have time for a sit-down lunch, and Book refused to eat fast food. The small store's shelves were stocked like the Whole Foods in Austin.

'I'll meet you at the checkout,' Book said.

They split up aisles. There were vegan and ethnic selections, gourmet dog food, and the *New York Times*. Book walked down the wine and beer aisle. There was a wide selection of international wines and beers, and in a cooler, cheeses—Gouda and goat and brie. He ran into Agent Angel Acosta holding cheese in one hand and a bottle of wine in the other.

'Hello, Professor. I enjoyed your radio interview.'

'You're probably the only person in town who did.'

Agent Acosta shook his head. 'A murder in Marfa. You working with the sheriff?'

'Trying to.'

'He's a good man. An honest cop.'

'Good to know.'

'Professor—be careful.'

Book met his intern at the checkout counter. Book had chosen protein bars, granola bars, and bottled water; Nadine had chosen potato chips, an ice cream bar, and a bottle of root beer. At least they were organic.

'Do you have Twinkies or moon pies?' she asked the clerk.

The clerk laughed. 'A Twinkie? No. They stopped making them.'

'*What? When?*'

'Hostess went under a year ago.'

'It wasn't on Twitter. OMG. What about Sno Balls?'

The clerk shook her head. 'Sorry.'

'I thought this is a grocery store.'

'It's an organic grocery store. Means natural foods. There's nothing natural in a Twinkie or a Sno Ball.'

The clerk turned to the cash register; Nadine made a face at her. Book paid, and they stepped outside and to the Harley. Agent Acosta drove off in a late-model convertible. He waved, and Book waved back. Nadine dug into the potato chips; he ate a protein bar.

'I know what the connection is,' his intern said, 'between Nathan, his death, the art, fracking, and Billy Bob.'

239

'What?'

'Not what. Who.'

'Okay. Who?'

'That Carla girl.'

'Why?'

'She's in the middle of every conflict in Marfa.'

'She's an environmentalist. That's what they do.'

'There's something more.'

'What?'

'I don't know that. But we didn't have this much conflict in San Francisco, and people there fight over everything. Difference is, people there like homosexuals.'

Nadine pointed at the old adobes across the intersection. On one wall graffiti had been painted: *Fuck U ChiNazis*.

'That's what we call the homosexuals,' Jimmy John said. 'The artists. 'Cause of that Chinati deal out there.'

Book and Nadine had ridden over to Nathan Jones's house to meet Brenda. Jimmy John Dale was already there and drinking a beer. Or finishing off a six-pack.

'The Chinati Foundation at the fort? Where Judd's boxes are exhibited?'

'Yeah. At first we called the whole bunch of 'em "Chinatis." Then they took over Marfa, started running the place like they owned it, trying to turn it into another New York City, so we started calling them "ChiNazis." Hell, even the Mexicans hate 'em. First time in the history of Marfa, Anglos and Mexicans are on the same side fighting the same enemy. The homosexuals, they brought us together.'

'Why?'

'They've run up the real-estate prices, locals can't afford homes no more, they got their high-dollar restaurants we can't afford, they got their organic grocery store we can't afford, and now they're starting their own private school we can't afford. They look down their noses at us locals, figure we're all dumb-asses lucky to find our way home at night—hell, least we're not a buncha goddamn queers!'

'Jimmy John!'

Brenda Jones gave him a stern look. His expression eased. 'Sorry.'

'That the friction the mayor mentioned?' Book asked.

Jimmy John laughed. 'Friction? That's funny. More like open warfare, Professor.'

'Over gays in town who pay too much to eat out?'

Jimmy John drank his beer.

'Aw, hell, that stuff just graveled us. But when they started protesting the fracking, they crossed the line with the locals. They're spending a couple hundred bucks to eat French food, but they're happy for us to starve. They come down here and take over our town, now they want to take our jobs. They don't understand, Professor—fracking gave us jobs, and we ain't giving 'em up just 'cause they're worried about a little pollution.'

'Has there been any violence?'

Jimmy John snorted. 'We ain't worried about a buncha queers beating us up, Professor.'

'*Against* the artists?'

'Oh. Not yet. But they keep it up, they're gonna understand why not many folks live in this desert. It can be a hard life.'

'Do you know Carla Kent?'

'Everyone knows Carla. She come down here from Santa Fe, organized the artists to protest the fracking, then they got stories in the New York papers about fracking—they hate it up there. She's a good-looking gal, so the boys are what you call conflicted about her.'

'How?'

'They don't know what they want to do most, screw her or beat the hell outta her.'

Jimmy John grinned. Book didn't.

'Reminds me. Thanks for the help at Padre's the other night.'

'Didn't figure you needed any, not with Babe Ruth watching your back.'

'I hit him hard, didn't I?' Nadine said.

'Real hard. You're pretty good with a beer bottle.'

Jimmy John abruptly grimaced as if a bullet had just bored through his brain.

'Are the headaches getting worse?' Book asked.

'Yeah.'

'How are the nosebleeds?'

'Regular.'

'Better see a doctor.'

He turned to Brenda Jones. She sat in her chair; her belly looked as if it might explode. Her expression said it felt that way.

'Nathan was murdered,' he said.

Brenda Jones regarded Book from across the coffee table.

'What are you going to do about it, Professor?'

Book saw in her eyes the desperation of a young woman, pregnant with her first child, whose husband had been taken from her.

'I'm going to find Nathan's truth. Give him justice.'

Brenda pushed herself out of the chair; Jimmy John helped her up. She came to Book; he stood. She hugged him.

'Thank you, Professor. But be careful. They follow us. They know everything. Where we go. What we do. Who we see. Who we talk to. They're always watching.'

Book blew out a breath. This sad young woman needed more help than a law professor could provide. But finding the truth, bringing her husband's killer to justice, that he could do. That he would do. He took her by the shoulders.

'Brenda, listen, I'm going to find out who killed Nathan, I promise you. But you need to stay strong. Mentally strong. Getting paranoid about things, thinking people are following you, watching you, that won't help you. Or your health. Or your baby. Okay?'

The phone rang. Brenda put one hand on the side of her belly as if to hold it in place then walked over to the landline hung on the kitchen wall. She answered. After a moment, she held the phone out to Book.

'It's for you.'

Chapter 24

There was no traffic on Highway 67 north, the road to Midland. Tom Dunn had called Book at Nathan's house and said he had important information that could not wait until tomorrow. So Book and Nadine were riding the Harley to Midland late in the day.

But how did Tom Dunn know that Book was at Nathan's house?

Book glanced in the rearview. A black pickup truck followed behind them a distance. As it had since they had left Marfa. As it still did when they hit Interstate 20 an hour later. The truck exited the highway behind them when they arrived in Midland. Book beat them through a red light and cut around the west side of downtown. He found a spot a block down from the Dunn Building and waited.

'What are we doing?' Nadine asked.

'Waiting.'

'For what?'

'For them.'

The black pickup truck parked in front of the Dunn Building. The two men inside did not get out.

'Stay here.'

Book got off the Harley and walked up to the pickup. He stayed out of their mirror angle—there was an Aggie sticker on the rear bumper—then he went around to the driver's side. The window was down.

'Are you following us?'

The man jumped—'Shit!'—then quickly gathered himself when he saw Book. 'It's a free country.'

Both of the men were shaved bald in the fashion of pro athletes, and both were large enough to have played pro football.

'A week in the hospital isn't. Free.'

'You threatening us?'

'Yes. Don't follow us anymore. And tell Billy Bob I know he killed Nathan Jones. Tell him I'm coming for him.'

'You'll have to come through us.'

'I'd enjoy that.'

The man snorted. 'Fuckin' kung fu Injun . . . that shit don't scare me, Professor.'

'Taekwondo. And I'm part Comanche. You know, the Comanche once roamed this land on horseback—'

'What, and you roam it on a Harley?'

He laughed and shared a fist-bump with his buddy.

'Where's your bow and arrow, Sacagawea?' the buddy said.

'Sack a shit,' the driver said.

They again laughed. They clearly weren't history buffs, so Book stuck his hand into his pants pocket and pulled out his pearl-handled pocketknife.

'I don't have a bow and arrow. All I've got is this little knife.'

He opened the blade and stepped to the rear of the truck. He leaned down and jammed the blade into the tire.

'And you've got a flat tire.'

Book turned away and saw Nadine standing there.

'I was too scared to stay over there by myself,' she said.

'It's broad daylight in downtown Midland.'

The men jumped out of the truck. Book grabbed her arm and pulled her across the street and into the Dunn Building.

'Do you?' she asked.

'Do I what?'

'Know Billy Bob did it?'

'No. But he had the most to lose.'

Once inside, he looked back at the men. They were not happy. The driver held a cell phone to his ear.

Book's cell phone rang. He checked the number. The dean.

'Hello, Roscoe.'

'Book, you're pissing off important people in West Texas.'

'Well, I've pissed off important people in South Texas and East Texas, why not West Texas?'

'True. But Tom Dunn's a donor.'

'He may be an aider and abettor in a criminal conspiracy.'

'Why do you say stuff like that? He pledged five million to the school. Called me up, said he was going to revoke his pledge if you didn't get off his back. And his client's back.'

'Roscoe, I haven't even gotten *on* their backs yet.'

'Book, come home. Teach your Con Law class. Stop calling people murderers on the radio.'

'Dunn's murderer–client is an Aggie.'

'Really?' The dean got a kick out of that. 'He's also Tom's biggest client.'

'I'm in the lobby of his building in Midland right now. I'm heading up to see him.'

'Book, try to have a cordial conversation.'

'I don't think that's going to happen.'

Roscoe exhaled into the phone.

'Well . . . then get a haircut.'

'Hell of a radio interview, Professor,' Tom Dunn said. 'But you might be jumping the gun.'

'How'd you know I was at Nathan's house?'

Dunn responded with a wry smile. 'My country club's got more members than Marfa's got people. Small town. Everyone knows everything.'

Book and Nadine sat in Tom Dunn's corner office in Midland again. The sun was setting in the western sky. He held out a small baggie containing a green leafy substance.

'We were cleaning out Nathan's office and found this.'

'Marijuana?'

'It ain't lettuce.'

'You're saying Nathan Jones smoked dope?'

'I'm saying we found this in his office. Maybe he smoked it, maybe he was holding it for a friend. Maybe he was high driving home that night. Maybe he passed out and ran off the road.'

'That's a convenient theory, Mr. Dunn, since the sheriff couldn't have an autopsy performed because his body was so badly burned.'

'I'm just giving you information, Professor.' He tossed the baggie to Book. 'You can take it.'

Perhaps it was because the Koontz case was fresh on his mind, but Book couldn't help but wonder if he were being set up to be pulled over by a county sheriff on a dark road between Midland and Marfa, searched, and found to be carrying marijuana. A drug bust might constitute cause to revoke his tenure; of course, many professors were children of the sixties, so perhaps not. But Book saw no reason to take the chance.

'You keep it.'

'Suit yourself.'

'Where would he get marijuana?'

Dunn laughed. 'Where not? Marfa is only sixty miles from the border, Professor. Marijuana shipments come north as regular as the U.S. mail.'

It was after ten, and the highway was dark and deserted. Book recalled Billy Bob's words: 'You want to live in the light or in the dark?' Driving a country road at night makes you

247

appreciate electricity. When the sun goes down in the city, there's still light. Streetlights and neon lights and store lights and building lights. But night in the country defines dark. They were in a black hole, only the moon offering any light, and the moon that night was only a sliver of white in the black sky. Both sides of the highway lay in pitch black. Book could see only the fifty feet of asphalt illuminated by the Harley's headlight.

So he throttled back.

There was no other traffic to contend with, but a collision with a deer crossing the road could be dangerous. When driving a country road in a three-ton pickup truck or SUV at night and suddenly encountering a deer in your headlights, the rule was simple: hit the deer. Most people veer to miss the deer, lose control of their vehicle, run off the road, and roll over. The deer survives, but the humans often do not. So hit the deer and live to feel bad about it.

But the rule didn't apply to motorcycles.

The night air had turned cool, so Nadine wore Book's leather jacket as well as the goggles and crash helmet. They were about thirty miles outside Marfa when he saw headlights in the side mirrors. The lights came closer, fast. No doubt a local running with his pedal to the metal. Book slowed and steered to the edge of the highway to allow the vehicle clear passage, just in case the driver was working on his second six-pack of the night. The lights were soon on them. And stayed on them, high enough above the road that it had to be a pickup truck. He waved for the truck to pass, but it stayed behind them. Close behind them.

Then it got closer.

'Professor!'

The truck was too close. Book turned the throttle hard, and the Harley shot ahead. They got a distance ahead of the lights. He thought he had outrun the truck, but the lights appeared in the mirrors again. Book gunned the Harley, but the lights came closer. And got brighter; the driver had hit his bright lights. Book didn't know the road well enough to put the Harley wide open, but he was about to take the chance when the lights finally came around to pass. Book steered far to the right, onto the rumble strip. He fought to hold the Harley steady. Then the truck steered to the right— and into them.

Nadine screamed.

Chapter 25

'Someone sure don't like you, Professor.'

Sheriff Brady Munn stood by the door of the hospital room at the Big Bend Regional Medical Center in Alpine just north of the U.S. Courthouse and Detention Center. Alpine is the county seat of Brewster County and twenty-one miles east of Marfa, but there is no hospital in Marfa. They had been run off the road in Presidio County, so Sheriff Munn had jurisdiction over the investigation.

'Billy Bob Barnett.'

'Well, hell, podna, I wouldn't like you either, if you all but called me a murderer on the only radio station in town. That tends to piss people off.'

'Sheriff, Nathan Jones was murdered. By Billy Bob.'

The sheriff grunted. 'I reckon you're right—about the murder. Billy Bob's still an open question.'

'Two of his goons followed us to Midland in a black pickup truck. I confronted them.'

'I take it that didn't go well.'

'It was less than cordial.'

The sheriff chuckled. 'I bet it was. Less than cordial.'

'And a dark pickup truck ran us off the road three hours later. It had to be them.'

The truck had forced Book off the road. He managed to keep the Harley upright through the prairie grass, until they hit a railroad track embankment. The bike stopped; they didn't. They both went flying. Book landed in a barbed-wire fence; he required only a tetanus shot, bandages, and a dozen stitches in his forehead. Nadine flew over the fence, crashed through a mesquite bush, and landed hard in the desert; she broke her left arm and right leg and suffered lacerations on her legs and possibly a concussion. The crash helmet protected her head, the goggles her glasses and eyes, and the leather jacket her arms and torso from further cuts; but Book had not protected her as he had promised. It was just after eight the next morning, and she lay in the bed, medicated and asleep, with casts on her arm and leg and a white bandage wrapped around her head; she looked like a child. A monitor beeped with each beat of her heart. Book sat next to the bed, close enough to touch her face. The Harley now sat in the back of a Presidio County Sheriff's Department four-wheel-drive pickup truck in the parking lot at the sheriff's office.

'Mexican name of Pedro, got a shop south of the tracks, fixes cars,' the sheriff said. 'Knows motorbikes, too. You want Shirley to drop your Harley over there?'

'I'll go with her. Before I leave my Harley with a stranger, I want to check him out.'

The sheriff grunted. 'Way my wife used to be with baby-sitters. So you got nothing on the truck? No make or model?'

'The bright lights blinded me. But it was them.'

'Well, that ain't exactly a positive ID, Professor. I need evidence. I can't go around kung-fu-ing everyone I meet. I'm the law. I gotta play by the rules.'

'It's tae— . . . Never mind.'

Nadine stirred and tried to move. Her eyes blinked open . . . and focused on the white casts covering her arm and leg . . . then moved around the hospital room . . . the IV connected to her good arm . . . the beeping monitors . . . the sheriff . . . and finally settled on Book. The realization came over her face. Tears welled up in her eyes and rolled down her cheeks.

'Oh, Professor.'

Book wiped the tears from her face.

'Where am I?'

'The hospital in Alpine.'

A nurse stuck her head in and said, 'Sheriff, there's a call for you.'

The sheriff stepped outside. Nadine's eyes followed him out then returned to Book.

'You know what we learned last night, Professor?'

'What?'

'A, taekwondo doesn't work against a big truck. And B, they're not trying to scare us off anymore. Now they're trying to kill us.'

'That's not going to happen.'

He wiped her tears again.

'I'm afraid of life, so I'm hiding out in law school. Then you bring me out here on that Harley and now I'm in the hospital with a broken arm, a broken leg, bruises, contusions, assorted scratches, possible brain damage . . . by the way, mesquite hurts.'

'I'm sorry.'

'Professor, has this kind of thing happened before?'

'It has.'

'Is that why Renée quit?'

'It is.'

'Why do you do it?'

'Alzheimer's.'

'You've got Alzheimer's?'

'My mother. Early-onset. She doesn't know who I am.'

She studied him a long moment.

'And you're afraid you'll get it early, too? So you take all those supplements and vitamins I saw in your bathroom, you eat organic and run at dawn and hope you don't win that genetic lottery.'

'My mother has one of the mutant genes that guaranteed she'd have Alzheimer's before age sixty-five. She was sixty-two when the symptoms started.'

'I didn't know there was such a gene.'

'There is. Three, actually. All it takes is one.'

Nadine dropped her eyes and did not look up when she asked, 'Professor . . . do you have that mutant gene, too?'

'I do.'

He had been tested. He had never told anyone, not even Joanie. His intern looked up; her eyes were wet.

'I've already lost that genetic lottery, Ms. Honeywell.'

'Maybe they'll find a cure before you . . .'

'Maybe.'

He blew out a breath.

'It's like knowing the day you're going to die. I'm on the clock. So I'm going to make every minute count. I'm going to make my life matter.'

'You're a famous Con Law professor, a best-selling writer, a sure bet for the Supreme Court . . .'

'None of that matters to me.'

'What does?'

'Not what. Who.'

'Who matters? To you.'

'My mother, my sister . . . friends . . . students . . . Nathan . . . Renée . . .' He took her hand. '. . . And you, Nadine. You matter to me.'

'You called me Nadine. Not Ms. Honeywell.'

'I did.'

'I do? Matter to you?'

'You do.'

She pondered that a moment.

'So you live life in the fast lane, no fear of the future because you don't think you'll have a future, not afraid of dying but of not living. I understand now.'

'I try to live every day of my life as if it's my last.'

'Well, Professor, yesterday was almost your last. Mine, too. Only my mom doesn't have Alzheimer's.'

'What does she have?'

'A new husband.'

The sheriff walked back in. 'Miss Honeywell, did you see anything last night?'

'Stars.' She turned her eyes back to Book. 'Professor, I want to go home. I want to sit in a Starbucks and drink a latte and text in relative safety.'

'You can't leave the hospital for a few days. They've got to make sure you don't have a serious head injury. I'll leave the laptop with you. You can work on the Welch brief.'

She blinked back tears. Book felt his blood pressure ratchet up a notch.

'And I've got some unfinished business with Billy Bob Barnett.'

'Hold on there, podna,' the sheriff said. 'If Billy Bob's behind this, I'll find out and then I'll arrest him. But you take the law into your own hands in my county, even if you are a law professor, I'll throw your butt in jail, I don't care how famous you are.'

The professor and the sheriff had left, and Nadine Honeywell lay alone in the hospital room. She started to cry. But just as she was entering the full-scale slobbering and self-pity stage, she thought of Leslie Benedict in *Giant*, the barbecue scene where she passes out from the heat and the sight of the cooked calf's brain, and everyone thinks she's too weak to survive in Texas. She could have run home to her dad in Virginia—just as Nadine now wanted desperately to call her daddy in San Francisco to come and take her home. She didn't. Leslie. Instead, she got up the next morning, determined to be a tough Texan, to work the cattle alongside Bick.

Elizabeth Taylor had been only twenty-three when she came to Marfa to play Leslie Benedict in *Giant*. Nadine was only twenty-three, and she was now in Marfa playing intern to the professor. They had both come from California to Texas. They had both stayed in the same room at the Paisano Hotel. They had both been knocked down to the dirt of this same desert.

Leslie Benedict had gotten up.

Nadine adjusted the bed until she came to a sitting position, wiped the tears from her face, and buzzed the nurse. When she entered, Nadine said, 'Please hand me my glasses and that laptop and take this needle out of my arm.'

The nurse smiled. 'My, we seem to be feeling better now. Are we ready for breakfast?'

'We are. A double order. And a large coffee. With real cream. And we want our own bottle of Purell. We've got work to do.'

'Little tough on your gal back there,' the sheriff said. 'Making her work with a broken arm and leg.'

'That's my job—to make my students tough enough to survive as lawyers.'

'Guess it didn't take with Nathan Jones.'

The sheriff gave Book a ride back to Marfa. He chewed tobacco and spat the juice into a Styrofoam cup; with the wind, spitting out the window could get messy.

'Nathan's senior partner in Midland said they found marijuana in his office.'

The sheriff grunted.

'Of course,' Book said, 'he might've lied.'

'Why would he do that?'

'To get me to go home.'

'I reckon he ain't alone in wanting you to go home.'

'Just about everyone we've met wants us to go home . . . except you.'

'I'm a slow learner.' The sheriff spat into the cup. 'Fact is, I like a change of pace. And we're both in the truth business.'

'You ever find it? The truth.'

'Not as often as I'd prefer. So you figure maybe Nathan Jones got into drugs?'

'Maybe.'

'Wouldn't be the first time. It can take down the best of men. It's the devil, just waiting for a weak soul seeking refuge from this world or a greedy heart wanting to strike it rich. Too much temptation and money for some folks to stay on the good side of the law. Even the law. Sheriff before me, ex-Marine, six-four, wore black boots and a white Stetson, looked like John Wayne on a bad day. Law-and-order sort of guy, worked the West Texas Drug Task Force hard, made a lot of drug busts . . . you ever heard of those task forces?'

'As a matter of fact, I have.'

'Law and order got out of hand there. Anyway, he was a real hard-ass, figured he was twice as smart as anyone else in the county. Half the county loved him, the other half feared him. Which is the way he wanted it. Figured Presidio County was his personal sandbox. Being sheriff for twenty years will do that to a man.'

'How long have you been sheriff?'

'Sixteen years.'

'Take care you don't suffer the same fate.'

'Every day, Professor.'

He slowed the cruiser and drove along the shoulder, eyeing the bare land and grunting now and then. Book had learned that a grunt was a part of speech for the sheriff, but also that it was more rhetorical in nature, so Book did not respond to his grunts.

'Turned out, he was living a double life. Him and a cowboy from Alpine teamed up to run drugs across the border for

256

fifteen years, driving pickup loads of cocaine right across the river—north of Presidio, the Rio Conchos empties into the Rio Grande. Above that, it's usually dry, especially in a drought like this. Stashed the dope in horse trailers at the county fairgrounds. Made a million bucks off each load. Apparently he didn't want to depend on the county pension fund for his retirement. DEA nabbed him bringing a load up one night with twenty armed guards. Now he's retired to the federal prison. Life sentence.'

'Hard way to end your life.'

'I reckon. He's never gonna see another West Texas sunset, eat another steak at Reata, drink another cold Lone Star beer on a hot summer day. Man can live without a lot of things, those would be tough.'

'What about sex?'

The sheriff grunted. 'Hate to break the news to you at such a tender age, Professor, but you're already on the downside of sex.'

'This day just keeps getting worse.'

Which evoked another grunt.

'Anyway, since the artists came to town, recreational use has shot up. Dope's always come through town, just sixty miles from the border. Not much I can do about that, figure that's a job for the Border Patrol and DEA. But now a lot is staying in town. And that is my job.'

He spat.

'We call ourselves Marfans.' He jabbed a thumb behind them. 'Folks in Alpine and Fort Davis, they call us Marfadites. They're jealous of our notoriety. They shouldn't be. 'Cause, damn, we're stocked full up on attorneys, artists, and assholes.'

'Triple As.'

'You been talking to Sam Walker?'

'I have.'

'He's a good man.'

'What about the mayor?'

'He's a real-estate broker.'

'He seems happy to have the artists in Marfa.'

The sheriff spat.

'Reckon he is, making money hand over fist. See, some folks think a town is a place to live. Other folks think it's a place to make money. Mayor, he figures those homosexuals are gonna be struck down by God's wrath one day, but in the meantime he's willing to pocket some real-estate commissions off of them. Me, I don't care what two consenting adults do, long as they do it indoors. They want to get married, I say, Why shouldn't homosexuals have the same right to be miserable like the rest of us?'

The sheriff had amused himself.

'You get along with the artists?'

'I try to get along with everyone. Liking people comes easy for me, just my nature. Guess that's why I'm in the people business. But, those people, I have to confess, they're a hard bunch to like. They segregate themselves, don't want to live in Marfa as much as above Marfa. They don't want to eat with us, live with us, or shop for groceries with us. They don't want their kids sitting next to cowboys and Mexicans in the public schools, so they start their own private school charging more than most folks around here make in a year. They wear those "What Would Donald Judd Do?" caps and shirts, but Judd didn't do that. He put his kids in the public schools like everyone else.'

He spat.

'We've been hoping for a Walmart, but they don't want one here, too working class for their tastes. That's how they view us, a lower class, the little people who don't know modern art from old art. It's like 'cause they're from New York and know art, they got nothing but disdain for us.'

'It's not just you.'

'You try to be friendly, say "howdy" when you walk past them on the sidewalk, even two boys holding hands, but they don't say "hello" or "go to hell," just give you a look like they're telling an inside joke and you're the punch line, got their iPhones and their iPads and their iMentalities.' He exhaled. 'My wife's got one of them.'

'A homosexual?'

'iPad. She reads books on it in bed, you believe that?'

He spat.

'Judd gave us boxes. These young artists, they gave us the finger. They put up that "Hello Meth Lab in the Sun" exhibit and call it art. They paint that "Axis of Evil" sign downtown and call it freedom of speech. I mean, what's the point of getting in people's faces like that? You know, I don't much care for intolerant right-wing Republicans, but these folks taught me I don't much care for intolerant left-wing Democrats either. And these folks are as intolerant as the wind.'

The sheriff pointed.

'Eagle.' He watched the bird soar on the currents a moment then said, 'Sometimes I wish to hell Judd had moved to New Mexico instead of Marfa. I mean, you can't get a goddamn Viagra prescription filled in Marfa, but you sure as hell can buy cheese called Gouda at The Get Go.' He paused. 'You know, if you needed Viagra.'

He spat.

'American cheese ain't good enough for those folks. They got to have cheese from France, so that gal opens an organic store, got all kinds of cheese. Hell, it's just cheese, for Pete's sake. City folks think living out here in this desert's kind of neat at first, then they want what they left behind.'

'Human nature.'

'Reckon so. Course, wanting to eat a special kind of cheese, that's harmless. Trying to take folks' jobs, that can be dangerous.'

'The artists protesting fracking?'

'Put a flame to that gas, someone's gonna get hurt. They don't seem to understand what having a job means to a man.

259

It ain't just the money or a place to be. It's who he is. It gives value to his life. It means he's worth something in this world. What would I be if they took my badge? Or you, if they took your professorship? Folks would look at me and figure I'm just a dumb cowboy. They'd look at you and figure you're just a hippie biker. But our jobs give us our identity. Tell us who we are. You take that away, and a man's got nothing left. And that's what those artists are trying to do to the locals.'

'What do you know about Carla Kent?'

'Why do you ask?'

'Seems like there's a connection between Nathan's death, the art, the artists, fracking . . . and Ms. Kent's right in the middle of it all.'

The sheriff grunted. 'Hell, she just showed up a year or so ago, comes and goes, stays a few months at a time . . . heard she stays in one of those teepees. I wonder what that's like, sleeping in a teepee? She's a nice-looking gal, but she's always stirring up trouble.'

'And you're in the middle of that conflict.'

'Yep. I'm just refereeing this intramural match between the old Marfa and the new Marfa.'

'What do you figure will happen to Marfa?'

'Sooner or later—hopefully sooner—the artists, they'll get bored and move on . . . to the next Marfa.'

The sheriff braked to a stop. They had returned to the scene of the crime. Where Book and Nadine had been run off the road. They got out and walked to the railroad tracks that paralleled the highway. Book had seen nothing the night before, just the bouncing light from the Harley's headlight until they went airborne. Now he saw everything. Where they had gone off the road, the short distance to the embankment, the barbed-wire fence where he had landed, and the mesquite bush that had broken Nadine's fall—and her arm and leg.

'EMTs, they had a hell of a time cutting you out of that barbed wire,' the sheriff said. 'Said that gash on your forehead was bleeding like a stuck pig.'

Blood stained Book's white T-shirt.

'Lucky your gal was unconscious, or she would've been hurting something bad.'

The heat rose inside Book. He took a deep breath to calm himself.

'Damn,' the sheriff said, 'this land is brittle dry. Nothing but kindling. We get a desert storm, one lightning strike could set the plateau on fire, might not stop till the flames get to Fort Worth. Could be biblical.'

The sheriff knelt and grabbed a handful of prairie grass; it broke off in his hand like twigs instead of grass.

'Year ago this time, the Rock House fire ignited two miles west of town, raced across the grassland. If the wind was blowing east instead of north, it would've taken out most of Marfa—downtown, homes, the art. Instead, it went north and burned a lot of Fort Davis. Burned for a month, scorched three hundred thousand acres, killed a lot of livestock. Horses couldn't outrun the flames.'

He shook his head.

'To see those horses burned to a crisp, make a man cry. We put up the "Burn Ban" notices, but folks from out of town, they flick cigarettes out the window 'cause they never witnessed a wildfire, so they can't imagine what it's like, to see that wall of fire coming your way fast. When the wind's blowing fifty miles an hour, neither man nor horse can outrun the flames.'

'Anything you can do, to prevent a fire?'

'Pray for rain.'

Book walked around the scene. The desert lay silent, and the morning air smelled fresh. The grass crunched under his boots. He spotted something near a yucca plant. He squatted and picked it up: a small plastic bottle of Purell hand

261

sanitizer. He squeezed his hand tight around the bottle as if making a fist.

'I need to see Billy Bob Barnett.'

'Now, Professor, I'm conducting a homicide investigation. I'm compiling a list of suspects—'

'Including Billy Bob?'

'He's at the top of my list.'

'Then arrest him, throw him in jail.'

The sheriff smiled. 'See, you're talking like a man whose gal got hurt, not like a law professor teaching all those constitutional rules we gotta follow—Miranda warning, probable cause, plain sight, incident to an arrest—all those fine points of the law just waiting to trip us up out here in the real world. All that sounds real good in a classroom, but out here when there's a victim in the hospital and a bad guy on the loose laughing at you, it don't feel so good, does it? The rules are meant to slow us down, make sure we get the right bad guy, but now it's personal for you so you want to go fast. 'Cause you *think* he did it.'

'So what are you going to do?'

'I'm gonna investigate, not kick someone's ass—and you are not gonna kick any more ass in my county. I'm gonna build a case, prove he did it. I'm going to go back to my office, call Mr. Barnett, and set up an appointment. Then I'm going to interview him and take a look at the black pickup truck his boys were driving, see if there's any evidence they ran you off the road. Now, we can work together, Professor, or you can go home. *Comprende?*'

'I'll take care of Billy Bob Barnett myself.'

The sheriff spat.

'Oh, I see how it is. The famous law professor, he likes to work alone. Running all over the country, saving folks, righting wrongs, just him and his Harley. He helps everyone, but he don't need help from anyone, is that it? 'Cause he's just so damn smart and tough. Well, first of all, Professor, you playing the Lone Ranger got your little gal back there put in that hospital bed, that's a fact. And you got to live with that fact. And second of all, even the Lone Ranger had Tonto.'

'What's that supposed to mean?'

'Means it's okay for a man to need help. And, podna, you need help.'

Chapter 26

The sheriff dropped Book at the Paisano so he could change
before meeting the deputy about the Harley. But as soon as the
sheriff's cruiser turned out of sight, Book ran down Highland
Avenue to Billy Bob Barnett's office. He thought, I don't need
an appointment. I don't need to play by the rules I teach. I
don't need help. And he thought of his intern; he had promised to protect her. He had not. The sheriff was right about
that: his actions had put Nadine in the hospital. His anger built
with each step. His years of taekwondo training to control his
emotions failed him. He was mad.

Billy Bob Barnett had hurt his intern.

He arrived at the Barnett Oil and Gas Company office—the
black pickup truck was nowhere in sight—and barged through
the front door and hurried past Earlene without asking
permission—

'Hey! Professor! He's in a meeting!'

—and down the hall past the lunchroom where donuts were
piled high on the table—

'Wait!' Earlene yelled from behind.

—and opened the closed door and marched into the office.

Billy Bob sat at the conference table with three other men. They wore maroon shirts and were watching the fracking video.

'Mr. Barnett,' Earlene said, 'he rushed right past me.'

Billy Bob held up a hand. 'It's okay.' To Book: 'You just have something against appointments, don't you?'

He looked Book up and down—the bloodstained shirt and the bandage on his forehead—then stood.

'The hell happened to you?'

'You happened to me. And to Nadine. She's hurt.'

'Honeywell? She's hurt?'

'She's in the hospital. Broken arm and leg. She could've been killed.'

'What the hell are you talking about?'

The same two bald goons who had followed them to Midland entered the office and advanced on him. Book closed the distance and got in the driver's face again. He was a side of beef.

'You ran us off the road, didn't you?'

The man's muscles tensed as if to strike Book.

'Do it.'

Taekwondo is not about kicking someone's ass. It's about self-defense, self-control, physical and mental discipline, about knowing you can but deciding you won't . . . But Book wanted to kick this big Aggie's ass so bad it hurt. And he could.

'Please do it.'

'Don't do it, Jimbo,' Billy Bob said from behind. 'I don't want your blood staining my brand-new Aggie gray carpet.'

He didn't do it. He backed down.

'Where's the black truck you were driving yesterday?' Book asked the goon.

The goon shrugged. 'Butch took it to Hell Paso.'

'Convenient.'

'Beats walking.'

Book turned and pointed a finger at Billy Bob Barnett.

265

'Nathan Jones's son is going to grow up without a father because of you. I'm going to prove that you killed him . . . that these two goons ran us off the road and hurt Nadine . . . and that your fracking is contaminating the groundwater. I'm going to put you out of business, Billy Bob. When you hurt Nadine, you made it personal.'

Book now turned to the men in maroon shirts.

'Don't invest with him. He's going to prison.'

Billy Bob smiled. 'Have a nice day, Professor.'

Carla Kent sat at a table in the courtyard at the Paisano Hotel. She had checked with the front desk; the professor and his intern hadn't returned. The clerk said he'd heard there had been an accident the night before out on the highway. A motorcycle wreck. A man and a woman had been taken to the Alpine hospital. She had called the hospital; the professor was not a registered patient. But Nadine Honeywell was. There was no word on her condition.

God, what had she done?

Book stepped out onto the sidewalk fronting Billy Bob's office and took a deep breath to gather himself. His body teemed with anger and adrenaline. He walked back to the Paisano and cut through the courtyard. He stopped. Carla Kent sat on the other side of the fountain, as if she had been waiting for him. He walked over to her. She stood. Her T-shirt read: *Don't Frack with Mother Nature.*

'Is she okay? Your intern?'

'Word travels fast out here. She'll be okay. Broken arm and leg.'

'I'm so sorry, Professor.'

'Not your fault, Ms. Kent.'

Her eyes went to the blood on his shirt and bandage on his head. 'You okay?'

He nodded. 'Got tangled up in a barbed-wire fence.' He blew out a breath to ease his blood pressure. 'I wanted to ratchet up the pressure on the killer, almost got my intern killed.'

'You taking her home?'

'After I prove that Billy Bob hurt her. And killed Nathan. I'm going to get that son of a bitch.'

Her eyes sparkled. 'Wow, the cool law professor gets mad. I like that side of you.'

'Good. Because you're going to see more of it.'

She was the connection between Nathan's death and everything else. She knew something. So he needed to know her.

'Ms. Kent, I'm ready to work together.'

'Carla. We can start now.'

'I've got to clean up first, and then see a deputy about a Harley.'

A frown.

'Not Deputy Shirley?'

Deputy Shirley blew strands of blond hair from her face then wiped sweat from her brow. She was driving Book in the Sheriff's Department pickup truck with the Harley in the back to the repair shop. He had cleaned up and changed his shirt.

'Pedro,' she said, 'he used to have a gas station and garage in town, but the artists drove him out.'

'How?'

'They ran up rents in downtown, drove the local businesses out. Artists converted Pedro's old garage into a studio. So now he works out of his own garage, on the Mexican side of town.'

'There's a Mexican side of town?'

'This is Marfa, Professor, but it's still Texas. North side of the railroad tracks, that's always been the Anglo side. Now it's the Yankee side, big homes behind walled compounds. South side, that's the Mexican side. Trailers mostly, little homes, crumbling adobes.'

The hot wind blew through the cab. Deputy Shirley blew hair from her face again.

'You know what I like to do on hot days like this?' she said.
'No. What?'

'Get a big ol' snow cone—I like root beer, with cream—and drive up into the mountains where it's cooler, find a nice little spot and spread out a soft blanket . . .'

'Sounds nice.'

'. . . and screw.'

She turned to Book and arched her eyebrows.

'What do you say, Professor?'

She offered a country girl's natural beauty and unabashed sexuality, an excellent combination in Book's experience. But now was neither the time nor the place.

'Well, Deputy—'

'Shirley.'

'Deputy Shirley, I appreciate the offer, but—'

'I've got handcuffs.'

Pedro's Repair Shop was a garage to the side of his house on East Galveston Street past the crumbling adobes with the *Fuck U ChiNazis* graffiti. Latino music played on a small radio and Pedro Martinez sat on a stool on the dirt ground in front of the garage, wearing reading glasses and pondering an engine part. They got out and walked over. Brown-skinned children played barefooted in the street. The voice of a woman singing a Mexican ballad and the smell of Mexican food drifted over from the house.

'Pedro's wife, she makes the best tamales in Marfa,' Deputy Shirley said. 'You can get your car fixed and pick up dinner in one stop.'

Pedro watched them over his glasses as they came toward him.

'Deputy Shirley,' he said.

'Pedro, this is Professor Bookman. He needs his Harley fixed.'

Pedro smiled. 'Ah, the karate professor. I have heard of you.'

'On the public radio?'

268

'No. We do not listen to that. It is not for us. It is for the rich Anglos from the north. I have heard of you from word of mouth.' He stood. 'Let us look at the bike.'

'I'm gonna get some tamales,' Deputy Shirley said. 'Have a little girl talk with Juanita.'

She headed to the house. Book and Pedro walked to the truck, leaned on the sideboard, and studied the twisted motorcycle. Pedro pondered for a time then nodded.

'I can fix that.'

'You repair Harleys?'

'*Sí.*'

'Have you ever repaired a Harley?'

'No.'

'I don't know. I restored this Harley by hand.'

His father had taught Book how to restore Harleys. It was his dad's hobby. He restored them and then sold them— 'Adopted them out,' as he said—to worthy Harleyites.

'And I will repair it by hand,' Pedro said. He was a white-haired man in his sixties, perhaps seventies. He removed his reading glasses. '*Señor*, I am Pedro Martinez. I am known all over Presidio County as the *hombre* who repairs the vehicles. I can do this.'

Pedro returned to his stool and sat. He replaced the glasses on his face, turned up the radio, and picked up a wrench.

'So, *Señor*, do you want that I fix your Harley?'

Book pulled out his pocket notebook and began jotting down the terms of this repair contract. First, the price.

'How much?'

'Oh, *mucho dinero.*'

Book sighed. *Mucho dinero* was a bit vague. He put the notebook back in his pocket. Perhaps he would rely on an oral contract.

'I need it soon.'

'Okay. I will do that.'

Deputy Shirley returned with a brown bag. She reached inside and came out with a tamale. She handed it to Book. He hadn't eaten that morning, so he was hungry. He ate the tamale.

'That's good.'

'*Sí*.'

They rolled the Harley down from the truck bed and into Pedro's garage. Book felt as if he were leaving his only child at college. Of course, he didn't have a child and would never have a child; he would not pass the mutant gene on to another generation of Bookmans. He hoped Joanie had not.

'Pedro, you sure you can do this?'

'*Señor*, I can repair motorcycles of all makes and models.'

'What kind of bikes have you repaired?'

'Why, just two weeks ago, I repaired a Vespa.'

'A *Vespa*? That's not exactly the same as a vintage Harley softtail classic.'

Pedro shrugged. 'It had only the two wheels, just as your Harley.'

'*Two wheels?*'

Book knew he was leaving his child at the wrong college.

'Vespas, they're for—'

'*La mariposa*,' Pedro said.

'Means homosexual,' Deputy Shirley said.

Pedro smiled. 'The boy, he was the *artista*. And the Vespa, it was purple, and it had the Chinati sticker. And he had the purple hair and that tattoo, on his fingers: wwdjd.'

'Kenni with an "i." We met him at the pizza joint.'

'Yes, that was him. Kenni. He wrote his check in the purple ink.'

Book took one last look at the Harley.

'Take care of my Harley, Pedro.'

'His friend sent him to me,' Pedro said. 'Nice boy. He was the—'

Book took a step away.

'—lawyer.'

Book stopped. 'Lawyer? What lawyer?'

'The lawyer who died, in the accident. His picture was in the paper. He brought the *mariposa* over to pick up the Vespa.'

'Wait. Nathan Jones was here? With Kenni?'

'*Sí*. That was his name. Nathan. I thought he was also the *mariposa*, but the paper said he had a wife and she is pregnant.'

They got back into the pickup truck. Book tried to process the information about Nathan and Kenni, but his thoughts were interrupted when Deputy Shirley leaned his way and revealed a significant portion of her soft breasts.

'How 'bout that snow cone, Professor?'

Chapter 27

Book took a rain check on the snow cone, so Deputy Shirley dropped him at the Pizza Foundation. The purple Vespa was parked outside; inside, Kenni with an 'i' was serving pizzas to a table of roughnecks wearing red *Barnett Oil and Gas* jumpsuits. Kenni waved at Book; the roughnecks gave him hard looks. Book took a table and waited for him. He pulled out the funeral photo and searched the faces. He found Kenni's face near the back.

'The famous professor.' Kenni had arrived wearing a *Don't Frack the Planet* T-shirt. 'I heard you on the radio. You sure got the town talking. What would you like today?'

'Information.'

'About what?'

'Not what. Whom. Nathan Jones.'

'Oh.'

Book gestured at the other chair. 'Sit down, Kenni.'

The waiter looked around as if to escape, then he accepted his fate. He sat.

'Talk.'

Kenni picked purple paint from his fingernails. He shrugged.

'Nathan wanted to be an artist. He had talent. Did you see his photos?'

Book nodded. 'At his house.'

'He loved the art scene. He wanted to move to New York, but his wife didn't. Her folks are ranchers, so she had the locals' attitude toward us.'

'How did you meet?'

'At the bookstore. That's like our clubhouse. The artists. We all congregate there. He started coming to the art events. He loved art . . . even Chamberlain's car wrecks . . . Then he died in a car wreck.'

'Was he gay?'

Kenni picked paint; he finally nodded.

'He had a wife,' Book said.

'He had a double life.'

'Lot of that going on out here.'

'Nathan the lawyer, husband, and father-to-be . . . and Nathan the gay artist. He said he hoped his son didn't turn out gay, too.'

'Were you two in a relationship?'

'We were friends . . . with benefits. God, he was gorgeous. He loved that movie, *Giant*, I don't know why, combed his hair like James Dean . . . See?'

Kenni held up his iPhone to show Book a photo of Nathan Jones with his hair standing tall.

'I guess he was trying to figure out who he was, you know, like when I went through my Madonna stage.'

'Did his wife know?'

'I don't think so . . . Maybe. Not about me, but about him.'

'Does she need to be tested?'

Kenni shook his head. 'Nathan protected her. He loved her. I'm HIV negative, so was he.'

'Did Jimmy John know?'

'Oh, God, no. They were friends, but Nathan would never have told him about us. He calls us queers, Jimmy John. He hates us.'

'Maybe he'd be more tolerant if the artists weren't threatening his job. Trying to stop fracking.'

Kenni shrugged. 'Fracking's ruining our environment.'

'How long have you been here?'

'Eight months.'

'How'd you keep it a secret? Marfa's a small town.'

'We don't talk to the locals, and they don't talk to us.'

'Why not?'

'We're gay, and they're not.'

'Have you ever talked to a local?'

'About what?'

'Anything.'

'No.'

'Why not?'

'Why? What would they have to say that would interest me? They're a bunch of homophobic, anti-Semitic, unintellectual racists. They have no appreciation of art. They know nothing about wine. My God, they'd rather eat barbecue than crepes. They get their news from Fox. They have zero sophistication. They should be thanking us for bringing culture to this awful place, but instead they call us "ChiNazis" and act disgusted because of our sexual orientation. I hate everything about Texas.'

'What about the weather?'

'Especially the weather.'

'Anything you like?'

'All the interesting people in town.'

'I take it you don't mean the locals?'

Kenni snorted. 'I mean other artists from New York.'

'Why do you want to live in Marfa?'

'I don't.'

'Then why are you living here?'

'Fame and fortune.'

'You're working at a pizza joint.'

'This is a temp gig.'

'Pizza?'

'Marfa. See, we're not Marfans or Texans, we're temps. We're all just temping here. We come down here, get discovered, then move back to New York rich and famous artists.'

'Like a reality show.'

'Exactly.'

'That ever work?'

'Not yet. But the buzz here is incredible. I've got a better chance of being discovered in Marfa than in New York. There's maybe a million artists on the make in New York. Here, maybe a hundred. And with the national media all over Marfa, this place is great for networking—it's like Facebook with French food.'

'So what kind of art do you do?'

'What else? Installation.'

'What are you going to install?'

'A plane. Half buried in the ground, as if it flew right into the prairie but stayed intact.'

'What kind of plane?'

'Triple-seven.'

'A jumbo jet? Won't that be expensive?'

'I'm taking donations.'

'How far along are you?'

'Three hundred and sixty-seven dollars.'

'Only forty million to go.'

'I'm not buying a new one.'

'Did Nathan use drugs?'

'No. Never. Just weed at Big Rick's studio. Part of the creative process.'

'Getting stoned and eating Cheetos?'

'I love Cheetos.'

'Who's Big Rick?'

'Rick Fusini. He's rich and famous.'

'I've never heard of him.'

'Because you live in Texas.'

'Marfa's in Texas.'

'No, it's not. It's a suburb of New York City now.'

'Tell me about Big Rick.'

'Oh, he's outrageous. At a gallery opening week before last, he painted "The Real Axis of Evil is the US, UK, and Israel" on the outside wall of the building next door, so everyone would see it.'

'We saw it.'

'The locals went absolutely apeshit! It was fabulous!'

'Did Nathan have any trouble with any of the artists?'

'Trouble? Like what?'

'Anything.'

'You mean, that would make someone kill him?'

'Like that.'

Kenni went back to picking paint. 'Big Rick kicked him out one night.'

'Why?'

'Because Nathan had sued him. For a pipeline.'

'A condemnation suit?'

Kenni nodded. 'Big Rick bought land outside town, for his installation. He's going to stack automobiles to spell out "Bush Sucks" so people flying overhead on their way to L.A. can see it.'

'There's a masterpiece.'

'Big Rick hates that bastard Billy Bob Barnett. We all do.'

'Why?'

'He's an oil man. Artists hate oil companies. They care only about money while they destroy the planet.'

As if reading from a script.

'You do know that oil money funded Judd's art?'

'*What?* No way.'

'Way.'

He pondered that a moment. 'I wonder if an oil company would fund my art?'

'Maybe Billy Bob.'

Kenni shook his head. 'He hates us. But we hate him because he's a fracker.'

'So you're fighting him?'

'With Carla.'

'You know Carla?'

'Everyone knows Carla. She recruited us to fight the fracking. She hates Billy Bob, too. Gave us these T-shirts. I introduced her to Nathan.'

'Why?'

'Because he said Billy Bob was contaminating the groundwater. She got really excited.'

'About what?'

'Said she finally had an inside man.'

'What did Nathan say?'

'That he almost had the puzzle solved.'

'What puzzle?'

'That would prove the contamination.'

'Did he show any proof to you?'

Kenni shook his head. 'Said he'd be breaking the lawyer code of conduct. But I pushed him to go public, to take his proof to the media, change the world. That's what artists do.'

'Really?'

'But Brenda told him to keep quiet about it. That's what wives do. She was scared. So was he.'

'Of losing his law license?'

'Of Billy Bob. And his beasts. We talked about what he could do. That's when he decided to write that letter to you.'

'Did he show it to you? The letter?'

'Sure.'

'But not to his wife.'

Kenni shrugged.

'So Nathan sued this Big Rick on behalf of Billy Bob.'

'Billy Bob wants to put a pipeline under the land, but Big Rick says that would mess up his art. So he said no. Billy Bob is condemning part of it for a pipeline.'

'And Nathan represents Billy Bob. Did he and Big Rick have words?'

'Big Rick has words with everyone—most begin with an "f." He's not gay. Mostly, he's a drunken bully—he's big and he's mean . . . rumor is, he killed someone back East, that's why he moved here. He has guns.'

'What kind of guns?'

'All kinds. He scares me when he gets drunk and starts playing with them. One night he shot his TV with a shotgun.'

'A shotgun?'

Kenni offered a lame shrug. 'But he pays for everything, so we all hang out there.'

'Did he threaten Nathan?'

'You mean, to shoot him?'

'To out him.'

Kenni picked his fingernails for a time. Then he nodded.

Book stood. 'Where's his studio?'

'West El Paso Street, just past Judd's Block. You can't miss it.'

Book tried to imagine his quiet, studious intern living a secret double life in Marfa, Texas, with Brenda at home and Kenni away from home.

'Was Nathan happy?'

'I think so. With both of his lives. But each life had conflict. He loved her, but he didn't belong here. He loved me, but he couldn't leave her. Maybe that was the way he was supposed to go, a bonfire in the sky.'

'Kenni, he didn't die a romantic death. He burned to death.'

Chapter 28

Book walked down West El Paso past 'The Block,' Donald Judd's one-square-block compound that housed his personal residence, two airplane hangars he converted into a studio and a library, and a swimming pool and chicken coop designed by Judd himself, all enclosed behind a tall adobe wall. West of the wall was a steel structure that looked like a warehouse. Outside sat six cars . . . stacked on top of each other. A big black 4x4 pickup truck was parked by the entrance door. Book walked around the truck and examined the glossy black paint for any damage or scratches; he found none. He rang the bell and was soon greeted by a big man in his mid-fifties wearing shorts, flip-flops, and no shirt; his hair was uncombed and his beard a week old. He looked like Nick Nolte in that infamous mug shot, only worse. His entire upper body was one big multi-colored tattoo that seemed as if someone had thrown a palette of paint on him. He took a swig from a half-empty whiskey bottle.

'Big Rick?'

'You the reporter from *Vanity Fair*?'

'I'm the law professor from UT. John Bookman.'

'What do you want?'

'I want to know why Nathan Jones died.'

'What's that got to do with me?'

'I understand he was suing you on behalf of Billy Bob Barnett and you kicked him out of here one night, threatened to out him.'

Big Rick snorted. 'You been talking to that fucking queer, Kenni with an "i"?'

'Queer? That's a little dated, don't you think?'

'I'm a little dated.'

'Being sued, some folks might consider that a motive for murder.'

'Murder? What, you think Nathan's death wasn't an accident?'

'I think someone ran him off the road.'

'What makes you say that?'

'Someone ran us off the road last night.'

'Professor, I stack cars. I don't run cars off the highway. Saw you checking out my truck—you find any evidence of a hit and run?'

'No.'

''Cause I don't murder people.'

'What about the rumor that you killed someone back East?'

Big Rick howled.

'Hell, I started that rumor myself. Image sells, Professor.' He finally took a moment to size Book up. 'You get in a fight?'

'I got in a barbed-wire fence.'

'Ouch.'

Big Rick belched and pushed the screen door open.

'Come on in.'

Book stepped inside to rock music blaring on surround sound. The interior space was a big barnlike structure, a combination home and studio with a kitchen area, a big bed in the far corner, and a living area with a big screen television on the wall with a cable cooking show playing. Big Rick placed the whiskey bottle on a counter, picked up a remote, and pointed it at the stereo; rock was replaced by country, Hank Williams Jr. singing 'Country Boy Can Survive.' He went to the refrigerator, opened it, and retrieved a carton of chocolate milk.

'You want some?'

'No, thanks.'

He poured a glass. He noticed Book eyeing the whiskey bottle.

'Thought you were a reporter.' He shrugged. 'Like I said, I have an image to maintain.'

'You got that hard-drinking artist thing down.'

'It's a living.'

At that moment, a young girl burst out of the bathroom and hurried out the front door with only a finger wave and, 'Later, Big Rick.' She looked like a high school sophomore.

'She part of the image, too?'

'She's Lorraine.'

'She looks a little young for you.'

'At my age, Professor, all the girls are a little young for me.'

'Be careful, Big Rick. I don't imagine the locals would look favorably on a New York artist violating their young girls.'

He laughed. 'Lorraine? Hell, she's laid more cowboys than a Mexican whore in Boys' Town. It's legal down there, prostitution. Man, I've burned up the highway between here and Ojinaga. They got some cute girls down there, young ones. But, hell, fourteen is middle-aged for a Mexican girl.'

'You do know you're a disgusting individual.'

Big Rick shrugged, as if he had heard it before. 'What can I say? I like young girls. We can't all be perfect, Professor.'

'You could try.'

Big Rick downed the chocolate milk then pulled out a joint, lit it, and took a long drag. He held it for a long moment then exhaled. Book tried to stay upwind.

'Medicinal,' Big Rick said.

'Illegal,' Book said.

281

'You're a law professor, not a cop.'

'So you threatened to out Nathan?'

'Aw, hell, I tend to be a mean drunk. I'm nicer when I'm stoned, like now. Nathan was a nice boy, married with a pregnant wife. His life was fucked up enough, gay and married, no need for me to add to his troubles. I wouldn't ruin his life over a lawsuit. I was mad at Billy Bob, but I took it out on Nathan.' He shook his head. 'Billy Bob Barnett, I'd ruin that bastard's life in a New York minute, trying to fuck up my land.'

'How much do you own?'

'Just a little. Twenty thousand acres.'

'You sound like a real Texan.'

'I wasn't born here, but I got here as soon as I could. I love Texas. Been here twenty years. Started buying land as soon as I got in town. I'm like Judd—I don't want all the land in the county, just what I have, what adjoins me, and what I can see from my land. And I don't want a goddamn gas pipeline under it. God, I'd love to kick Billy Bob's ass. Might could, too. I boxed in college.'

'Where?'

'Princeton.' He waved a hand at his studio. 'Trust fund pays for all this. And my land.'

'Your art doesn't support you?'

'Shit, when I first moved here, early nineties, right before Judd died, I couldn't give my art away. Then this art dealer from Dallas, good-looking woman, she comes down here to check out Judd's boxes. She ended up in my bed. So we made a deal: fifty–fifty on anything she sold. Well, she shipped everything I had back to Dallas and talked it up in Highland Park as the next big thing, and damned if she doesn't sell it all to rich folks like her husband. He made a fortune in asbestos.'

'Mining it?'

'Suing over it. Plaintiffs' lawyer. They've got a fifth or sixth home here, fly down in their Gulfstream. He's sixty, she's forty now. Apparently Viagra didn't do the trick for him. Anyway, they brought other rich lawyers to town—'

'Attorneys, artists, and assholes.'

Big Rick grinned. 'I'm an artist and an asshole. Anyway, most of these lawyers wouldn't know art if it dropped on their fucking heads, but they buy my stuff, so I make nice at dinner parties.'

'Must be hard.'

'Very.'

Big Rick finished off the chocolate milk and went back to the refrigerator for a refill. This time he offered Spam. Book again declined.

'I love this stuff. I don't know why.'

'I don't either.'

Big Rick opened the can and took a big bite of Spam.

'You know what you're putting into your body?'

'Do I look like I care?'

He did not.

'Comes in all kinds of flavors: black pepper, hickory smoked, jalapeño, with cheese, with bacon, hot and spicy . . . this is classic, my favorite.'

He let out a loud fart.

'Whoa. Sorry. Stuff does give me gas.'

Book eased back a step.

'I understand there's quite a bit of drug use among the artists?'

'True enough. Part of the culture. Cutting-edge art. Drugs just seem to be a natural part of all that.'

He laughed.

'A *Vanity Fair* article, I've got it somewhere'—he shuffled through a stack of magazines on the table—'reporter wrote that Marfa's an "art cruise ship where you just hope the last stop is a Betty Ford Center." Boy, they got that right.'

He paused.

'Course, we're not the only Marfans partaking in recreational narcotics.'

'What's that mean?'

Big Rick's expression said he was holding aces. He made Book wait for it.

'Billy Bob Barnett is a cokehead.'

Big Rick seemed pleased with himself. That or he really loved Spam.

'How do you know?'

'Let's just say I have it from a reliable source. That head cold, he's had it for two years now.' He took another big bite of the Spam. 'Public company, his board might not be so keen on having a cokehead for a CEO.'

'Even if you got him fired, that wouldn't stop the fracking or the condemnation lawsuits.'

'True. But at least I wouldn't have to see his fat ass at Maiya's every time I go there to drink and eat.'

'Kenni says you have guns.'

Big Rick shrugged, as if feigning modesty.

'Just a few.'

He stepped over and opened a walk-in closet that housed not clothes but weapons. A lot of weapons mounted on both walls. And military gear—flak jackets, meals-ready-to-eat, night-vision goggles . . .

'I like to shoot shit at night.' He pointed out his collection as if he were pointing out fine art in a museum. 'Forty-four Magnum, nine-millimeter Glock, AK-Forty-Seven, sniper's rifle, shotgun . . .'

'What gauge?'

'Twelve.'

'That's a coincidence.'

'What's that?'

'Someone shot out my window at the Paisano Thursday night with a twelve-gauge shotgun.'

'I never heard of you until five minutes ago when you rang my bell.'

'There was an article in the newspaper.'

'Which I don't read.'

'I was on Marfa Public Radio.'

'Which I don't listen to.'

'So why all the guns?'

'An avant-garde artist with an arsenal makes for good copy back East. And I love to go out to my land and shoot the shit out of everything.'

'Why do you hate Bush?'

'What? Oh, the "Bush Sucks" installation. Just part of the image. You want a New York art dealer to sell your stuff, you gotta loathe Bush and vote Obama. Hating Bush is always a big part of any art crowd conversation. But I voted for him. Both times.'

'Kenni said you painted an "Axis of Evil" sign on a building in town.'

'Nah. Everyone blamed it on me, but that was an asshole from Iceland.'

'Big Rick . . . is there any part of you that's real?'

'Everything you see is real, Professor. Everything you read is myth. About me, about the other artists, about Marfa . . . it's all just a myth. A myth that sells.'

'Is everyone in Marfa on the make?'

'Everyone except the cowboys.'

'Get in, podna.'

Book was walking back to the Paisano when the sheriff pulled alongside in his cruiser. He spat brown tobacco juice out his window. Book got in.

'You kinda stubborn, ain't you?'

'I'm kind of mad.'

'Often the last words before someone ends up in my jail.'

'I went to see Billy Bob.'

'I take it that was a less than cordial meeting, too?'

'It was.'

'He didn't confess?'

285

'He did not.'

'I hate it when that happens.'

'Nathan Jones was gay.'

The sheriff hit the brakes. He slowly turned to Book. He grunted.

'You want to get a cup of coffee?'

Tumbleweeds on Austin Street one block west of Highland Avenue offers washers and dryers by the load and a walk-through to Frama's, which offers home-brewed coffee and Blue Bell ice cream. They walked in just as the mayor of Marfa walked out with a big ice cream cone.

'Heard about your gal, Professor. She gonna be okay?'

'Yes. Thanks for ask—'

'Good. Won't slow you folks getting back to Austin.'

The mayor nodded at the sheriff—'Brady'—and walked away.

The sheriff chuckled. 'The mayor, he's . . .'

'A real-estate broker.'

'Yep.'

Book ordered a small cup of coffee; the sheriff ordered a medium and one scoop of cookies-and-cream ice cream. They went outside and leaned on the hood of the sheriff's cruiser.

'Gay,' Sheriff Munn said. 'And married. Living a double life.' The sheriff grunted then spooned the ice cream past his mustache. 'Seems like that'd be a complicated life.'

'His . . . friend . . . pushed him to go public with his proof.'

'That Billy Bob's contaminating the groundwater, with his fracking?'

Book nodded.

'Who's his friend?'

'Confidential, Sheriff. Nathan had a wife.'

The sheriff grunted; Book took that for a yes.

'Kenni.'

'With an "i"? Over at the pizza joint?'

Book nodded again.

'He's a doper. Damn, sorry the boy got in with that artist crowd.'

'He was an artist.'

'And a doper?'

'Apparently.'

'So the weed they found in his office might've been his?'

'Possibly.'

'Well, that sheds some light on the subject, don't it?'

'An artist named Big Rick threatened to out Nathan because he sued to condemn his land for a pipeline easement.'

'You talk to Big Rick?'

'You know him?'

'Of him.'

'He's a piece of work.'

'He's a pervert. I know about his underage girls. That's stat rape in the state of Texas. Once I get those girls' affidavits, he's gonna be stacking Coke cans in my jail instead of cars.'

'Big Rick said Billy Bob's a cokehead.'

'You getting your information from a pervert?'

'Anywhere I can.'

'Fracking and doping don't add up to murder.'

The sheriff finished off the ice cream then sipped the coffee, which was as good as any coffee in Austin at half the price.

'You figure out the connection between the boy's death and art?'

'I've learned that Nathan was Billy Bob's lawyer and a gay artist living a double life. That art is part of the story.'

The sheriff grunted. 'Art. Why folks would take a plane trip to Hell Paso then drive four hours to look at a bunch of fluorescent lights, I don't figure that. Now, Judd's boxes, I like them. Particularly the concrete ones outside. I go out there and study them from time to time. You know, if you sit on the side of Sixty-seven just south of the boxes, right when the sun's rising, those boxes create some interesting shadows. I reckon that's what Judd was up to.'

'Could be.'

'Or I don't have a clue.'

'Do you have a clue who killed Nathan Jones?'

'Well, the boy was Billy Bob's lawyer, so I figure he had access to incriminating evidence, if there was any. And he talked about it with his . . . friend . . . who pressured him to go public with it, that tells me there's evidence out there, waiting to be found. Which makes Billy Bob Barnett the prime suspect in a murder case. But I got no evidence of murder. Except a dead lawyer.'

'What do you need to arrest him?'

'I need that proof, podna.'

Chapter 29

'Kenni introduced Nathan to you.'

Carla glanced over at Book from behind the wheel of her truck. 'Yes. He did.'

'A man inside Billy Bob's operations.'

'A lawyer. The best possible inside man. Privy to his client's secrets.'

'Did you know you were putting his life in danger?'

'Fracking is a dangerous business, Professor.'

'Fighting fracking can be dangerous as well. How'd you get into that business?'

'My dad was a roughneck. I followed him into the industry. Got an environmental engineering degree at Rice, worked at a major in Houston, thought I'd make the industry greener. But the only green they care about is the kind that folds nicely in a wallet. So I quit and went to the other side, joined an environmental group in Santa Fe. Been fighting the industry ever since. When fracking came on line, I knew it had to be stopped.'

'Did you know Nathan was gay?'

The sudden change of subjects didn't throw her.

'I figured.'

'Why?'

'He was friends with Kenni. Gays and straights don't pal around together in West Texas.'

'Did you know Billy Bob is a cokehead?'

'Heard rumors to that effect. Who'd you hear it from?'

'Big Rick.'

'He's a disgusting prick, all those young girls. But he hates Billy Bob almost as much as I do, and he donates to the cause.' Her eyes went to the rearview mirror. 'Aw, fuck.'

Carla had picked Book up at six in an old dark blue Ford pickup with bumper stickers that read *No Fracking Way* and *We Can't Drink Natural Gas*. A shotgun was mounted in a window rack. Book looked in the side mirror. A Border Patrol SUV had pulled them over. Carla braked and steered the pickup truck to the shoulder of the highway.

'Billy Bob said you had a roughneck's vocabulary.'

'Hang around squirrels long enough, you'll start hiding nuts. Hell, I've been around roughnecks since I was a kid.'

She glanced in the rearview again and gestured back.

'They harass me every time, make me get out while they search the entire truck. I think Billy Bob puts them up to it.'

'Maybe that shotgun got their attention.'

'In West Texas?'

Two agents walked up to their windows, one on either side.

'What do you assholes want?' Carla said.

'Nice to see you too, Carla,' the agent said.

Book looked up to a familiar face.

'Whoops,' the agent named Wesley Crum said.

'We meet again,' Book said.

'Hey, Professor.' Agent Angel Acosta leaned down and rested his arms on the driver's side window frame. 'I finished your book. It was brilliant.'

'Thanks.'

Agent Crum was examining the short radio antenna on Book's side.

'Carla, why do you have this big ol' potato stuck on your antenna?'

'Antenna broke off,' she said. 'Potato gives the radio better reception. Don't ask me why.'

'I won't.'

'Well, you folks have a nice day,' Agent Acosta said.

They returned to their SUV and drove off. Carla watched them away then turned to Book.

'You must be really famous.'

Nadine Honeywell sat in her hospital bed running high on caffeine and working on the Welch brief on the laptop when the door opened and the professor and the woman named Carla entered the room. She tried not to look surprised. The professor held an open hand out to her. In his palm was her Purell bottle.

'Where'd you find it?'

'In the desert. You must've dropped it when you went flying off the Harley last night.'

'I was trying to block out that memory.'

She took the Purell. Ooh, there was still some gel left. She squirted it into her palm and rubbed. She loved the smell of ethyl alcohol.

'So, Professor—what did we learn today?'

'A, Nathan Jones was gay.'

'Told you.'

'B, he had a relationship with Kenni.'

'With an "i"?'

The professor nodded. 'C, Nathan told Kenni about the contamination but never showed him any proof.'

'The lost proof.'

'And D, Billy Bob Barnett is a cokehead. Allegedly.'

Nadine felt her mouth fall open.

'Shut the frack up.'

It took her a moment to recover. She looked from the professor to Carla and back.

291

'So, what, you two are working together now?'

'Looks that way.'

'You think what you're both looking for will lead you to Billy Bob Barnett?'

'I think so.'

'So what are you going to do?'

'Get some proof.'

'Can you get me some food first? I'm starving.'

'Let's get some grub, Jimmy John, before we frack this hole.'

Sonny slapped him on the back. It was after midnight but lunchtime on the well site on the graveyard shift. They both wore red insulated jumpsuits, red *Barnett Oil and Gas* caps, and boots. They walked across the dirt pad toward the mess hall, stepping over pipes and hoses running from the tanker trucks. The pay on the rigs was good; the food not so much. It was like eating at McDonald's three times a day, every day. Jimmy John had had a blood test a few years back, when they had to run him up to the hospital in Alpine after a length of casing had got loose and hit him in the head. Knocked him out cold. Nurse said his cholesterol was high enough to cause two heart attacks. That's what eating rig food would do, hamburgers and hot dogs and sausage and eggs. Roughnecks didn't eat salads.

'Shit,' Jimmy John said. 'I forgot to write down my last pressure reading. I'll catch up. Save some food for me.'

He turned back and headed to the control center. But not to write down readings. He felt the nosebleed coming on, and he didn't want Sonny seeing him bleeding like a stuck pig. Word got back to the boss, Jimmy John Dale might find himself unemployed. And that was a place he didn't want to go. A man without a job ain't no better than a Mexican. He pulled out the handkerchief and ducked behind a tanker truck carrying the frack fluid.

★   ★   ★

292

'They're fixin' to frack.'

After taking a cheeseburger and fries back to Nadine, they had driven out to a Barnett Oil and Gas Company well site that she had been staking out. Book and Carla sat above a low valley in the foothills northeast of Alpine. The five-acre pad down below where the prairie grass had been taken down to the dirt was lit up like Main Street. They were waiting for the crew to take a meal break.

'In the middle of the night?'

'Twenty-four/seven operation.'

'All I see is a lot of trucks and pipes and hoses.'

'The rig's down, and the tanker trucks are here. They're carrying the frack fluid.' She pointed. 'The green tanks surrounding the site, those are the storage tanks. The hoses run to the blender where the proppant is added—those dump trucks carry the sand—then over to the treator manifold and into the pumper trucks—see the red ones?—backed up to the well hole. That equipment next to the trucks, those are compressors to create the pressure they need to crack the rock.'

'What's in those tanks?'

'Diesel fuel to power the equipment. During the day, you can see the black exhaust fumes from the engines, creates ground-level ozone.' She pointed to the sky. 'Way up there, ozone is good. Down here, it's very bad for humans and animals.'

'Smog in West Texas.'

'That trailer, that's the control center.'

'What are those trailers?'

'The man camp. The out-of-town workers live onsite, work twelve hours a day, two-week shifts. They rotate off for a week then back on. It's a hard life.'

'What's that shack over there? Where all the men are heading.'

'Mess hall. They're going to eat first then frack. Odd. Most men like to frack first then eat.'

Carla smiled then dug in her knapsack and came out with beef jerky. She handed him a strip.

'High in protein.'

'You do this often?' Book asked her.

'Actually, I do.'

'Are you afraid?'

'My dad taught me not to be afraid . . . or at least not to show my fear.'

'Good advice. Where is he now?'

'Dead. Well blowout. He went to work one day and didn't come home.'

'When?'

'Six years ago.'

She dug in her knapsack again, but almost as if she were angry this time, and came out with rubber gloves.

'Put these on. This shit is toxic.'

They ran down the rise and to the drill site. They ducked behind the tanker trucks and dodged roughnecks walking past. Male voices came from all around them; the foul smell of the well site was suffocating.

'Well hole gases,' Carla said.

They worked their way to the control center and went inside. She went directly to a large notebook on the desk. She ran her finger down the open page.

'Yep, they're fracking tonight.'

They exited and again ducked behind the tanker trucks, but Carla stopped at one. She pulled out a small plastic container and placed the mouth under a valve at the back of the tank. She turned a knob and filled the container with brown fluid.

'I'm gonna find out what's in Billy Bob's recipe. They claim the recipes are proprietary information, trade secrets, like the formula for Coca-Cola, so they can keep them secret from the Feds. Difference is, you can drink Coca-Cola and not die.'

'You think Billy Bob's using something bad?'

'It's all bad. But legal. Frackers use carcinogens like naphthalene, formaldehyde, sulfuric acid, thiourea, benzyl chloride, benzene, ethylene oxide, even lead. But they don't have to tell us what they're using.'

'The Halliburton Loophole.'

'Yep.'

'Professor!'

They jumped at the voice behind them. They turned and saw Jimmy John Dale holding a handkerchief that was as red as his jumpsuit. He glanced around and came closer. He gestured at Carla.

'You working with her now? She got you trespassing on private property?'

Carla hid the container behind her back.

'Jimmy John—'

He pointed toward the desert. 'Goddamnit, get the hell outta here before someone else sees you, calls the sheriff.'

They ran back up the rise to Carla's truck.

'That was a close call,' Book said.

'I've had closer. But we got a sample.' She held up the container. 'People will soon be drinking this toxic brew in their tap water.'

'I thought the EPA hadn't found any confirmed incidents of groundwater contamination, here or anywhere else?'

'Define "confirmed." Frackers don't have to disclose the chemicals they put down the hole, so how can those chemicals be traced to their wells if they show up in the tap water? They say there's no proof that the benzene or methane was from fracking. Fact is, there's been over a thousand confirmed incidents. The Bureau of Land Management found water wells in Wyoming's shale fields that contained fifteen hundred times the safe level of benzene. And the EPA's now supplying drinking water to people living in the frack fields in Pennsylvania. They found arsenic in their tap water. How'd you like to drink a carcinogen with your morning coffee?'

'Not so much.'

She pointed down at the well site.

'Eighty tons of toxic chemicals are going down that hole tonight—and most of it's going to be left down there to migrate to the aquifer or it's going to come back up and then be injected down disposal wells and allowed to migrate to aquifers. Does that make any sense? But the industry says, "Don't worry, we know what we're doing. It's all safe."'

She blew out a breath.

'They'll start collecting the flow-back in the morning, if the gas flows. I need a sample of what comes up the hole. It's usually worse than what goes down the hole. No sense in heading back to town, we'd have to turn right back to get here in time. I've got camping gear in the truck. A sleeping bag, gets cold out at night.'

'Only one sleeping bag?'

'It's a double.'

Chapter 30

Book woke at dawn wrapped in a double sleeping bag, but he was a single. Carla was already up and at work, perched below the rise and peering through binoculars down at the well site.

'Coffee's made,' she said.

He unzipped the bag and got up then went behind the truck for his restroom duties. He came back and poured coffee into a tin cup. Carla was an experienced camper. He went over and squatted next to her.

'See the open pit? It's filling up with the brown water. That's the flow-back. Frack fluid that comes back up the hole. The frack fluid picks up riders down in the earth, stuff released by the fracking process, like radium, radon, methane. They'll pump it into those tankers and then haul it to the disposal wells, inject it into the earth like an addict injecting heroin. Nearest disposal wells are north of here, in Pecos County. I need a sample.'

'How?'

'I'm thinking.'

★ ★ ★

She thought most of the morning. When the last tanker truck left, Carla jumped up.

'Come on. I've got an idea.'

She went to the truck and rummaged through her belongings then pulled out a pair of shorts. She took off her jeans and put on the shorts. They drove the pickup back to the highway and pulled over. Carla got out and lifted the hood. She then rolled the legs of her shorts up until they were short-shorts. She reached inside the pickup and retrieved a jar with a lid.

'That last tanker truck will be along in a minute. Hide in the brush. When he stops, get a sample from the back of the tank. And wear the gloves.'

'What if other cars come by?'

She held her arms out to the vacant highway. 'We got rush hour, Professor.'

'How do you know he'll stop?'

'He'll stop.'

Book hid in the brush next to the highway and wondered if Carla knew what she was doing. He soon learned that she did. He heard the truck and ducked down. Carla stuck her head under the hood and her butt out toward the highway, her long lean legs serving as a stop sign.

The truck stopped.

The Hispanic driver climbed out and walked over to Carla. Book heard him say, '*Señorita.*' When the driver ducked his head under the hood, Book came out of the brush and ran to the rear of the tanker. He found a drain valve and filled the jar with foul-smelling brown water. He screwed the top on, peeked around the tanker, and ran back into the brush. Carla got into the driver's seat of the pickup and started the engine. She squealed like a teenage girl and thanked the driver profusely in Spanish.

'*Gracias, gracias, hombre.*'

The driver returned to the truck packing more than a set of

keys in his pocket. He fired up the big tanker and drove off. Book came out of the brush with the sample.

'You're good.'

A black-and-white videotape played on the big screen in Billy Bob's office. Security cameras had caught Carla and the professor the night before, sneaking onto well site number 356 and collecting a sample of the frack fluid. Billy Bob stuffed a donut into his mouth then said, 'How many times is this with Carla?'

'Ten, twelve,' Willie said.

Willie Freeman was ex-military police turned security director for Barnett Oil and Gas.

'Now she's got a partner in crime.'

'That's the professor,' Billy Bob said. 'He's from Austin, came out here 'cause Nathan Jones wrote him a letter, said I was contaminating the groundwater.'

'We ain't contaminating the groundwater.'

'Nope.' He pointed at the screen. 'Who's that?'

One of his workers had caught the professor and Carla on the well site behind a tanker truck. The video showed him pointing toward the desert. The professor and Carla ran off the site.

'Jimmy John Dale,' Willie said.

'He working with Carla?'

'No.'

'Why'd he let them go?'

'The professor's been to Nathan's house, talking to his wife, couple times. Jimmy John was there each time. He and Nathan grew up here together. Best friends.'

'Boyfriends?'

'No. Jimmy John's a cowboy, straighter than an iron rebar.'

'Good. 'Cause I don't want queers on my rigs. Or wets. Or Longhorns. Or Democrats. Or—'

'I know the list, boss. You want me to do anything with this tape? Take it to the sheriff? Call Tom Dunn, tell him to get another restraining order against her?'

Billy Bob shook his head. 'We got nothing to worry about with Carla. She's chasing shadows. She ain't gonna find nothing in my slick water.'

'Standard slick water, Carla,' the lab tech named Randy said. 'No arsenic, no diesel fuel, just typical ingredients. It's all legal.'
'Shit.'

They had driven to Sul Ross State University on the east side of Alpine. Sul Ross was known for its ranch horse competition team, but the university had a quality chemistry department as well. Randy was an assistant professor and a friend of Carla; he didn't hesitate when she called and asked him to come in on a Sunday afternoon.

'What about the flow-back?'

'Contains methane and benzene, but that's injected down disposal wells, also legal. Shouldn't be, but the EPA signed off on it. Heck, the government puts radioactive waste down disposal wells, why not frack fluid?' Randy shrugged his shoulders as if apologizing. 'Billy Bob's going by the book, Carla. I know you hate him, but he's no worse than any other fracker.'

'William Robert Barnett Jr., aka Billy Bob Barnett, was accused of tax fraud in two thousand one—he settled that case—securities fraud in two thousand four—he agreed to a cease-and-desist order—and got arrested in college for smoking dope.'

Book and Carla had stopped at the Alpine hospital to check on Nadine and found her propped up in bed, her left arm and right leg in slings, Book's laptop on her tray, and a long bendable straw in her mouth leading to a large soda water. She'd been investigating Billy Bob Barnett on the Internet.

'Hospital's got WiFi,' Nadine said.

'What else?'

'Food's okay, not so much the coffee.'

'About Billy Bob.'

'He's worth a hundred million dollars.'

'Lot of money.'

'He was worth five. His entire net worth is in company stock. Took the company public in oh-four, he got ten million shares. Stock opened at twenty, peaked at fifty in oh-eight, now it's down to ten.'

'What happened?'

'Gas prices plunged, from a high of eleven dollars per thousand cubic feet in oh-eight to under two dollars today.'

'Quite a drop.'

'Glut of gas on the market. His company's all in on shale gas, so the stock price rises and falls with the natural gas futures market.'

'So if the government shut the company down because its fracking was contaminating the groundwater—'

'Billy Bob Barnett wouldn't have a pot to piss in, to use the West Texas vernacular,' Carla said.

'Might be a motive for murder.'

'Actually, it's worse,' Nadine said. 'Billy Bob pledged his stock for a one-hundred-million-dollar personal loan when the stock price was worth twenty. If it drops below ten, the bank can foreclose on its collateral—his stock. He'll lose everything.'

'Big loan.'

'He likes the good life—private jet out at the Marfa airport, homes in River Oaks and Santa Barbara, three ex-wives and five kids to support. So he's heavily in debt personally and his company's revenues are down and fracking expenses are up. He's being squeezed from both ends. And his board deferred his bonus—ten million dollars.'

'That would put a dent in my cash flow,' Carla said.

'He can't raise the price of gas, the market sets that. So his only course of action would be to cut expenses.'

'By cutting corners,' Carla said.

'And his shareholders are putting a lot of pressure on him to boost the stock price.'

'He's a desperate man.'

'That's good work, Nadine. How'd you find all that information on the Internet?'

'Professor, I'm twenty-three. My generation might not know current events, but we know our way around the Internet.'

'Call Henry. Professor Lawson. Explain the situation to him, ask him what Billy Bob might do to cut corners.'

'Other than murder Nathan Jones?'

Book nodded. 'Other than that.'

Book's phone rang. He checked the caller ID. Joanie. He answered.

'Book, Mom wandered off again. The police found her at a strip joint.'

'They're open on Sundays?'

'Book, she walked all morning.'

He blew out a breath. 'We'll talk when I get back.'

'When?'

'Soon as we find the killer.'

'Be careful, Book.'

He hung up. Carla averted her eyes. It was an awkward moment until Nadine looked past him and said, '*Daddy?*'

Nadine closed her eyes and shook her head to clear her vision. She thought she had seen her father standing in the doorway. Perhaps she had in fact suffered a closed-head injury causing blood to seep into her brain and resulting in hallucinations—oh, God. But when she opened her eyes, he was still there.

'OMG—Daddy, what are you doing here?'

'Well, young lady, I was about to ask you the same question. I'm here because my health insurance company called me, said a hospital in Alpine, Texas, submitted big bills for a patient named Nadine Honeywell. MRIs, X-rays, ER, OR . . . They wanted to make sure someone wasn't engaged in fraud. Obviously, they weren't. What the hell is going on?'

'I'm fine, Daddy. Thanks for asking.'

'Oh. Are you okay, honey?'

'Just a broken arm and leg. Bruises. Minor contusions. Possible brain damage. I'm fine.'

Her father wore his standard Sunday attire: a suit and tie. He was a lawyer from birth, destined to a life lived in suits and ties with a briefcase attached to his hand. Mother had left him because he loved the law more than he loved her. Harsh, but true. After her sister died, he found solace in his work; her mother never found any solace. Her father now turned his attention to the professor.

'Who are you?'

'Professor John Bookman.'

'He's famous, Daddy.'

'Never heard of him.'

'And this is Carla Kent.'

'Are you famous?'

'Infamous.'

'I'm the professor's intern,' Nadine said.

'His intern?' He turned on the professor. 'So, Professor, why is my daughter, who was in law school in Austin, Texas, the last time I talked to her, now lying in a hospital bed in Alpine, Texas, with a broken arm and leg?'

'Well, Mr. Honeywell, that's a really interesting story.'

'I'm all ears.'

'We're solving a murder case, Daddy.'

'A murder case?' Back to the professor. 'You got her involved in a murder case?'

'Well, I—'

'I sent her to UT to get a law degree, not to get herself killed. All right, let's go. I'm going to check you out, get you back to Austin where you belong.'

'No, Daddy.'

'What?'

'I said, no. I'm not leaving. We're trying to find a murderer. The professor needs my help.'

Her father frowned. He gave her that familiar suspicious squint then turned it on the professor. He gestured back and forth between her and the professor with his hand.

'You two got one of those professor–student romances going on?'

She laughed. 'Me and the professor? He's trying to get me killed, Daddy, not get in my thong.'

Daddy rolled his eyes. 'Why do you say stuff like that? Now listen, young lady—'

'No, Daddy, you listen. For once, listen to me. What I want to do. I want to stay here and finish this. For once in my life, I am not going to run home scared of life.'

Her father stared hard at her; then he exhaled and all the fight went out of him.

'Have you talked to your mother recently?'

Nadine's father had kissed her on the forehead, secured a commitment from Book to ensure that his daughter got home to Austin safely, and then left to drive to El Paso and catch a flight back to San Francisco.

'Nadine,' Book said, 'I'm sorry I—'

'Don't be. That was a breakthrough moment for Daddy and me. And I don't really wear thongs, I just say that kind of stuff to get him worked up.'

'You know he cares about you?'

'I know. Oh, I finished the Welch brief and emailed it to the D.A., like you said.'

'Reminds me, Scotty Raines called and left a message. Said the D.A. called him this morning, wasn't real happy after he read the brief. Wanted me to call him. On Sunday.'

Book stepped out into the hall and called the number Scotty Raines had left; it was the Travis County D.A.'s cell phone. He answered on the second ring.

'Professor.'

'Mr. Anderson.'

'Don.'

'Book.'

'The hell you doing in Marfa?'

'Murder.'

'You're killing people in Marfa?'

'Trying to find a murderer.'

'Lot more fun than teaching Con Law, isn't it?'

'It has its moments.'

'Your secretary's husband murder any more armadillos? I'm still not happy with that verdict.'

'It's been a year, Don.'

'So, Professor, why are you working for a guy like Welch? He's one of the Republicans ruining Texas.'

'It's not political for me.'

'So what, you're doing it for the money?'

'He's not paying me.'

'Then why? Because he's the chairman of the Board of Regents? What, you want to be president of the university?'

'He promised to put the boy in rehab, for six months.'

'That's it?'

'There's more. But not money.'

The D.A. exhaled. 'You gonna file this brief?'

'If I have to.'

'I can beat you.'

'It isn't about me.'

'Then why isn't Scotty Raines arguing the con law issues? Why'd Welch hire you?'

'He loves his son.'

'Who's a smart-ass punk.'

'Maybe. But just because a college kid gets drunk—'

'And stoned on coke.'

'—and mouths off to a cop doesn't give the police probable cause to search his vehicle, which he was not driving at the time, and to seize his blood without his consent. Thus, that evidence is inadmissible in court, which means you have no case.'

'So you say.'

'So the court will rule. And, Don, the Supreme Court will likely rule this term that the taking of blood without a warrant is an unconstitutional search and seizure under the Fourth Amendment. So even if you go forward with this case and obtain a conviction, it'll be overturned once the Court rules.'

'We'll see. File your fucking brief, Professor. I'll see you in court.'

The D.A. hung up. Book sighed. Another less than cordial conversation. Perhaps it was him. He returned to the room and found Nadine and Carla giggling like girls on a sleepover.

'Daddy wants me to be a lawyer,' Nadine said.

'My dad wanted me to be a boy,' Carla said.

'Okay, you're right. That is worse.'

They laughed again.

'Female bonding?' Book asked.

'We're BFFs,' Nadine said.

'You want some dinner, Carla?'

'I'm game.'

'Where are you guys going?' Nadine asked.

Book looked to Carla for an answer.

'Reata,' she said.

Nadine typed on the laptop keyboard with one finger then stared at the screen.

'OMG, what a menu. Okay, bring me back'—she looked up at Book—'write this down in that little notebook.'

He did.

'The tenderloin tamales with pecan mash for an appetizer, the carne asada topped with cheese enchiladas for an entrée, a side of jalapeño and bacon macaroni and cheese, and for dessert a chocolate chunk bread pudding tamale served with dulce de leche. God, that sounds good.'

'You know how to order,' Carla said.

'She knows how to eat,' Book said.

Nadine squirted Purell into her palms and began rubbing as if preparing to eat.

'Oh, Professor, I need some new underwear.'

'Underwear?'

'The ones I had on, they're gone. My others back at the hotel are dirty. And I wore my spare pair I carry in my bag.'

'You carry a change of underwear in your purse?'

'Doesn't everyone?'

Carla shook her head. Nadine grunted as if surprised.

'Well, someone forgot to tell me to pack for a week. And I don't like this commando thing.'

'Over-share.'

'I'll take care of it,' Carla said. 'I know a store open on Sundays. What kind? Thongs?'

'God, no. I don't like a string up my . . . bikinis. All cotton. No lace. Any color.'

'What size?'

'Four.'

'*Four?* You eat like that and wear a four? That's not fair.'

Nadine waved them away. 'Hurry. I'm hungry, and I need those underwear. And before you leave, Professor, would you empty my bedpan? I really gotta pee.'

Book eyed the bedpan. 'Uh . . .'

'I'll get the nurse,' Carla said.

She went outside to find a nurse.

'I like her,' Nadine said.

'I need you to research her dad. He was killed in an oil rig blowout six years ago. Find out what you can—on him and on her.'

'Why?'

'I don't know.'

'That ain't evidence of a murder,' Sheriff Munn said.

Book had called the sheriff with the information about Billy Bob's shady past and his current financial problems.

'Professor, before I can arrest the second-biggest employer in Presidio County after the Border Patrol and charge him with murder, I need a smoking gun.'

Book did not tell the sheriff about his and Carla's unauthorized entry upon Barnett Oil and Gas Company's well site the night before.

'That's good work by your gal, but it's not enough.'

'I'll talk to Carla at dinner, see what we can do.'

'Carla? You working with her?'

'We teamed up.'

'I asked you to team up with me.'

The sheriff grunted.

'Now, don't take it that way, Sheriff, it wasn't personal—'

Damn. Now he was answering the sheriff's grunts.

'Course, she is a mite better looking than me.'

'Just a little.'

'You figure her out yet?'

'I'm working on her.'

'I bet you are. Taking her to dinner, huh?'

'I am.'

'Where?'

'Reata.'

'Good place.'

'A smoking gun? Any advice, Sheriff?'

'First, the most desperate creature on earth is a cornered bear or a man about to lose everything. Be careful, Professor. And second, order the pecan pie for dessert.'

With six thousand residents, Alpine is like a major metropolitan area compared to Marfa. It has a doctor, a pharmacy, a hospital, a country club, and Reata on Fifth Street in downtown.

'My favorite restaurant in the whole world,' Carla said.

They ate on the back patio, which featured a *Giant* mural painted on the exterior wall of the adjacent building and country-western music playing on the sound system. The clientele was not a hipster artist crowd; it was a cowboy crowd. Deputy Shirley sat at one table wearing her uniform and gun across from a strapping young cowboy. She gave Book a smile and a wink as they walked past. When they sat down, Carla glanced over at Deputy Shirley then back at Book.

'You didn't go for the snow cone, did you?'

'Not yet.'

She sighed. 'Men.'

Their waitress was an authentic cowgirl attending Sul Ross on a ranch horse team scholarship. She wore a belt buckle the size of Montana.

'I won that at a cutting horse competition,' she said.

Carla ordered the jalapeño and cilantro soup and fried poblano chile rellenos stuffed with cream cheese, corn, and pepper served with a corn chowder; Book went for the tortilla soup and grilled salmon with Boursin cream sauce. Book took the sheriff's advice and ordered the West Texas pecan pie for dessert; Carla had the Dutch Oven apple crisp with cajeta. And he placed Nadine's to go order. They had already stopped and picked up her underwear.

'So what brought you to Marfa?' Book asked.

'Fracking. That's my mission in life, to stop fracking.'

'Well, good to have something to do each day.'

'Are you mocking me?'

'No.'

'Aren't you passionate about your work?'

'I am.'

'Me, too. I'm a very passionate person.' She gave him a coy look. 'Who knows, if you play your cards right, you might find out how passionate.'

'You want a beer? Or six?'

She smiled. 'It'll take more than that, cowboy.'

'Beers?'

'Charm.'

The waitress brought glasses of water and buttermilk biscuits with pecans and soft butter. Carla held up the water glass.

'That water,' she said, 'it's from the Igneous Aquifer. That's the aquifer Billy Bob's punching through to frack.'

'The aquifer Nathan thought he was contaminating?'

'Yep.'

'How do we prove it? The samples came back clean.'

'They came back legal. The shocking thing about fracking isn't what the industry does—shit, they thought it was brilliant to put diesel fuel down a well hole—but what's legal. Between the trillions of gallons of drinking water used to frack the wells and the billions of gallons of toxic chemicals put down into the earth, ten years from now we'll end up with lots of natural gas but no drinking water. Lots of jobs, but more people with cancer. Lots of energy, but more global warming . . .'

The waitress brought their dinners, but Carla was on a fracking roll.

'Which is so stupid when the answer is staring at us: green energy. Solar, wind, hydro. Over time, green energy would create a lot of jobs, too, and no cancer, no carbon footprint, no global warming, no groundwater contamination, no earthquakes. If the people knew the truth about fracking, they'd rise up against it. But the industry hires New York PR firms to run disinformation campaigns to confuse the public, same thing they did with cigarettes. They say steel-and-cement casing prevents groundwater contamination, but they don't mention that the failure rate for casing is six percent immediately upon construction and fifty percent over thirty years. They say gases released into the air like benzene are safe, but they don't mention that breast cancer rates spike among women living above frack fields. They say fracking's been around for sixty years, but they don't mention that the amount of chemicals and pressure down hole for horizontal fracking is way more than for those vertical wells drilled back then. They learned from the tobacco companies: lying works. And the media says,

310

"Well, there's a big debate about fracking." And the people hear that and believe it. And as long as there's a debate, the fracking continues . . .'

Which continued into dessert.

'. . . And the industry touts the jobs. That's the big sales pitch. Jobs. Jobs to keep the masses pacified. Politicians need to create jobs to get reelected, so they take the billion dollars a year the industry spends to lobby them and give the industry free rein to destroy the environment. Because politicians are inherently corrupt and evil. Like the goddamn oil and gas industry.'

Book listened attentively and ate the pecan pie then sipped his coffee throughout her impassioned plea. He had sat through many such pleas from environmental groups in Austin trying to save the springs, the river, the wilderness . . . but no one had brought more passion to the table than Carla Kent. She finally paused to take a breath; he waited to see if the lull were temporary or permanent. Her eyes danced with passion, which made her even more attractive. She drank her beer and smiled.

'I'm done ranting.'

'Good.'

'I feel better now.'

'Good.'

'So, Professor, how do you feel about sex after dinner?'

'Good.'

Chapter 31

'Being gay in West Texas, that wasn't an easy thing for Nathan. It's a hard land with hard people.'

Brenda Jones knew about her husband's double life. It was the next morning, and Book and Carla had stopped off at Brenda's house to bring her up to date. They had called ahead; she had called Jimmy John. He wore his red jumpsuit; he had just gotten off the night shift. He recoiled when he saw Carla on the front porch.

'We were more like brother and sister. Best friends. But I loved him, and he loved me, I know that. And we had been together since grade school, I couldn't imagine living without him. He was a sweet man, Professor. He took good care of me. He would've been a great dad. He saw on TV that babies in the womb could hear voices, so every night at bedtime he'd put his head close to my belly and read children's books to our baby.'

She looked down at her belly; when she looked up, her eyes were wet. She seemed to have aged ten years since Book had last seen her.

'Brenda, are you taking care of yourself?'

'I can't sleep without Nathan next to me.'

She wiped her eyes and blew her nose.

'After law school, he wanted to live in Austin, but I knew he'd have to face it every day, fighting his demons with so many gays there. Out here, there was no temptation. Until the artists came to town. I saw him weakening, and I knew he had given in to his demons.'

She paused.

'Why would he choose them over me, Professor?'

'Nathan didn't choose to be gay any more than you chose not to be. That's who he was. It's hardwired, like your blue eyes. Brenda, he tried not to be himself for you. But he didn't choose to be gay over you.'

She jerked and grabbed her belly.

'Whoa, he kicked me hard. He must want out.'

She blew out a breath and pondered her belly a moment then looked up at him.

'Professor, you don't think he'll be gay, too, do you?'

'Brenda, he's your son. You'll love him no matter what he is.'

Book turned to Jimmy John.

'Did you know?'

Jimmy John drank his beer then nodded. 'I figured. He never said nothing, but he was different. I mean, he tried to be a regular guy, even played six-man football. But he wasn't big, strong or fast.'

'Not a good combination for football.'

'Nope. And he was so damn pretty . . . not that I was attracted to him that way, I'm just saying. And those pictures he drew, never going to Boys' Town down in Mexico with us, never went for the sheep—'

'*Sheep?*'

'Cowboy joke, Professor.'

'It didn't matter to you?'

Jimmy John shrugged his broad shoulders. 'He was the

brother I never had. And he was the only person I could talk to.'

He paused, and his expression said his thoughts had gone to the past.

'Back in high school, my mom cheated on my dad. With a Mexican. Everyone in town knew except my dad. All the other boys laughed at me. Except Nathan. He cried with me.'

'He must've been a good friend.'

'My best friend.'

Jimmy John Dale referred to gays as 'queers,' but his best friend was gay, and he knew it. Human beings were complicated creatures. And his former intern had led a complicated life. A complicated, short, double life. Book gazed at the wedding portrait on the wall and wondered about Nathan Jones's life.

'Heard about your intern,' Jimmy John said. 'She okay?'

'A few broken bones, but she'll mend. Jimmy John, you ever heard any rumors that Billy Bob uses cocaine?'

He thought a moment then nodded. 'But no one on the rigs talks about it. We're too scared.'

'Of Billy Bob?'

'That it might be true. It's like you're on a pro football team and the star quarterback's a cokehead. He could take the whole team down with him. Is it true?'

'I don't know.' Book turned to Brenda. 'Did you find anything in the house that might be the proof Nathan said he had?'

'Nothing.'

'Anywhere else he might have put it?'

She turned her palms up. Book turned to Jimmy John.

'Any idea?'

'Sorry, Professor.'

'I always gave my important stuff to my dad,' Carla said.

'His obituary said his parents survived him. Where do they live?'

314

'On a ranch west of Valentine.'

'How far out?'

'Forty-five miles.'

'Thirty minutes by pickup,' Jimmy John said. 'Just past Prada Marfa.'

'Back in oh-five,' Carla said, 'these two German artists named'— she read their names on the plaque—'Elmgreen and Dragset, they thought this would be just about the funniest thing in the whole world, a Prada boutique in a ghost town. Locals never got the joke. Hence, the bullet holes.'

Valentine, Texas, qualifies as a ghost town. Only two hundred and seventeen lives play out there; the only thing the town has going for it is its name: every February, thousands of envelopes holding Valentine's cards arrive at the tiny post office to be postmarked 'Valentine, Texas.' One mile west of town on Highway 90, sitting on the south side against a backdrop of cattle grazing on the yellow prairie grass, yucca plants, mesquite bushes, and a distant ridgeline silhouetted against the blue sky was a small white stucco building with plate glass windows (sporting several small bullet holes) under awnings and *Prada Marfa* printed across the front façade. Arranged on shelves and display stands inside were high heels and purses from the Prada Milano 2005 collection.

'A fake Prada store,' Book said. 'In the middle of nowhere.'

'The Jones ranch is a ways out,' Book said.

'Everything in West Texas is a ways out. You think we'll learn anything from them? Nathan's parents.'

'Doubtful. But we've run down every other rabbit trail.'

A rocket suddenly rose into the sky in front of them.

'Look at that,' Book said.

'Bezos, the Amazon guy, he bought a couple hundred thousand acres over there, built a spaceport. Calls it "Blue Origin." They're testing rockets.'

'You're kidding?'

'Hey, we're high-tech out here, Professor. We've got the Air Force's Tethered Aerostat Radar site on Ninety—it's a blimp-type craft, they put it up to detect drug planes and ground transports in the desert. We've got the Predator drones flying the river—they operate those out of the Corpus Christi Naval Air Station. And we've got Bezos's rockets.'

'And modern art masterpieces.'

'Is West Texas one crazy-ass place or what?'

'In *Giant*, Bick Benedict puts his boy on a pony when he's four, maybe five, kid starts wailing. That was Nathan. Hated horses and cows and manure. But I still loved him.'

Bill Jones blinked back tears.

'He was your son.'

'I wanted him to be a rancher, take over the spread. He wanted to be an artist. At least he became a lawyer. Reckon I'll sell out to some rich Yankee like everyone else, move over to Fort Davis with all the other old folks. Play bingo.'

'Maybe your grandson will want to be a rancher.'

'You think?'

Nathan's parents, Bill and Edna, had welcomed Book and Carla into their home on a cattle ranch outside Valentine. Their land comprised twenty sections—12,800 acres—of prairie grassland. The Joneses had ranched that land since after the Mexican–American War. On the wall of their living room were framed photos of Nathan as a boy, a young man, a new lawyer, and a new husband. Book wondered if they knew Nathan's truth: his double life, his secrets, his art, his dreams. His unfulfilled life.

'Professor, why do you care so much about my son?'

'He saved my life, Mr. Jones.'

'Nathan? He saved your life?'

'Yes, sir. He stepped between me and a bullet intended for me.'

'His shoulder?'

Book nodded.

'He told us that scar was because he tore his rotator cuff playing basketball.'

'No, sir. That was because of a bullet.'

Mr. Jones seemed to stand a bit taller.

'Mr. and Mrs. Jones, Nathan interned for me at UT law school four years ago. A week ago, he sent me this letter.'

Book handed the letter to Nathan's parents and gave them time to read it. Edna cried; Bill handed the letter back to Book.

'So you're the professor?'

'Yes, sir.'

'He said you'd come.'

'Nathan told you I'd come to see him?'

'No. To see us.'

'You? Why?'

'Because you'd want this.'

Bill Jones held out a key.

Chapter 32

Fort Davis is the county seat of Jeff Davis County, twenty-one miles north of Marfa. It's a cute little mountain town filled with senior citizens, as if the American Association of Retired People had invaded the community. The key opened a safe deposit box in the First National Bank of Fort Davis. Inside was a clasp folder with a stack of papers six inches thick. Carla flipped through the papers.

'Well logs,' Carla said. 'And Barnett Oil and Gas tax returns. This is it. Nathan's proof.'

'Of what?'

She shrugged. 'It's just numbers. I never was good with numbers.'

'I know someone who is.'

Book and Carla walked into his intern's hospital room and found her sitting up in bed and Jimmy John Dale in his red jumpsuit standing next to the bed. He had rolled up the right sleeve as if showing off his biceps.

'Jimmy John?' Book said. 'What are you doing here?'

'He's showing me where the horse bit him,' Nadine said.

'You drove to Alpine to show my intern a horse bite?'

'Oh, uh, no, Professor. I drove Brenda over here. Her water broke right after you left this morning. She had the baby.'

'Are they both okay?'

'Yep.'

Book dropped the papers from the safe deposit box on Nadine's bed tray.

'What's this?'

'Nathan's proof.'

'Proof of what?' Jimmy John said.

'We don't know.'

Nadine thumbed the pages like a card sharp. 'Numbers. Looks like a job for the geeky intern. All right, Professor, I'm on it. And thanks for the underwear. I love the feel of cotton.'

'Over-share.'

'Where's the nursery?' Carla said. 'I want to see the baby.'

'I'll show you,' Jimmy John said.

He led Carla outside. Nadine turned to Book.

'Carla's dad, Wayne Kent, fifty-four, died in an oil rig blow-out outside Odessa six years ago.'

'I know that.'

'He worked for Billy Bob Barnett.'

'I didn't know that.'

'Carla and her mother sued Billy Bob and his company for negligence. They lost. Carla's been after Billy Bob ever since. He's gotten restraining orders against her in four Texas counties. She apparently snuck onto his well sites trying to get incriminating evidence. Tom Dunn represented Billy Bob and the company in court, said she had a vendetta. Said she was mentally unstable.'

'You're a handsome little boy, aren't you? Yes, you are.'

Carla Kent made faces and baby talk to Nathan Jones Jr. wrapped up like a papoose in the crib on the other side of the glass. Book stood next to her.

'So, Professor, you want to make a baby?'

'Right now?'

'One day.'

He had always thought that he would be a father one day. Until he got the test results back. There would never be a John Bookman Jr. It didn't seem fair. But life was not fair. Not for Nathan Jones Jr. who would never know his father, or for Nathan Jones who would never know his son. Not for Nadine's sister. Or Book's father. Or his mother. Not for anyone.

'Wave to Aunt Carla.'

They stopped by Brenda Jones's room and told her what they had found and that as soon as they knew what it meant, she would know. She cried.

'I wish Nathan was here,' she said.

'I know you do,' Book said.

They then drove back to Marfa and had a late lunch at the Food Shark under the shed in downtown. They sat at a long picnic table where artists had gathered like moths to a flame, fitting since the Food Shark proprietor was himself an artist; his medium was old television sets, which he arranged in various patterns with an image on each screen.

'Kids need a dad,' Carla said. 'Especially boys.'

They did.

'At least he'll have his grandpa.'

At least.

'You still here?'

Book looked up to the mayor of Marfa. He wasn't smiling.

'I'm afraid so.'

'Well, I hope you're happy.'

'About what?'

'I lost a sale today. A New York couple—two boys—they backed out 'cause they heard about the murder, that we got a murderer running the streets of Marfa, killing homosexuals. Said other artists are worried they might be next, figure the locals are targeting them.'

320

'Well, look at the bright side, Mayor. If we find the killer, the *New York Times* might write another story about Marfa.'

His expression brightened.

'You really think so?'

Carla sat inside one of Donald Judd's concrete boxes at the old fort and dangled her legs.

'I love these things,' she said. 'My teepee is right over there'—El Cosmico occupied the adjacent tract—'so I come over here and contemplate life on concrete. You know they're big enough to see on Google Earth? Like God looking down on us. What was he thinking?'

'God?'

'Judd.'

They had driven out to the Chinati Foundation then walked over to the field where Judd had aligned sixty concrete boxes—each exactly 2.5 × 2.5 × 5 meters—into fifteen groupings. Carla climbed through the boxes like a kid on a playscape. A tomboy.

'If I was a boy, my dad was going to name me Clark. He always called me his Supergirl.'

'You miss him?'

'Every day. Hard on my mom. She lives with me.'

'You take care of her?'

'More like she takes care of me. She gave me my passion. He made me tough. Taught me to fight boys—not as good as you—and to never back down. And to use guns. He said men respect a woman who carries a gun.'

She pondered her words a moment then pointed past Book.

'There's a tough man who carries a gun.'

Book turned and saw the sheriff standing in the parking lot between his cruiser and Carla's truck. He waved Book over.

'I'll wait here,' Carla said.

Book walked through the prairie grass and over to the sheriff. A Hispanic woman sat in the back seat of the cruiser.

He shook hands with the sheriff who nodded toward Carla and the concrete boxes.

'You figure her out?'

'I did.'

'Anything I need to know?'

'No.'

The sheriff grunted. 'Well, podna, there's something you need to know about her.' He opened the back door of the cruiser. 'This here's Lupe. She's the overnight maid at the Paisano. Lupe, this is the professor.'

Book said hello. She just smiled in response.

'She's a little shy around Anglos,' the sheriff said. 'Anyway, she remembered something about the truck that sped off the night your window got shot out.'

'It was maroon?'

'Uh, no.'

The sheriff turned to the woman.

'Lupe, tell the professor what you saw.'

'The truck, it had the bumper sticker with that funny word.'

'What funny word?'

'The F-word.'

'The uh, f-u-c-k word?'

Lupe giggled. 'No, not that F-word. The other one.'

'The other F-word . . . *Fracking?*'

'*Sí*. That F-word.'

Lupe pointed at the bumper sticker on Carla's truck that read *No Fracking Way*.

'That is the bumper sticker. And that is the truck I saw.'

'And that's a twelve-gauge shotgun in her window rack,' the sheriff said.

Book took a moment to process that information. He turned to Carla. She lay stretched out on top of a concrete box, as if sunning herself on a beach.

'Sorry to have to break that news to you, Professor. You want to press charges?'

322

Book slowly shook his head. 'No. I want to know why.'

The sheriff nodded at Carla in the field. 'Answer's right out there.'

The sheriff and Lupe left. Book walked back to Carla.

'What'd the sheriff have to say?'

'That you shot out our window at the Paisano.'

Her expression served as a confession.

'Why, Carla?'

'I had to keep you in town. So we could learn the truth about Nathan.'

'So you could have your revenge against Billy Bob.'

'Professor, you've been checking up on me.'

'I have.'

'What's wrong with revenge?'

'It's the wrong motive. I'm here for justice.'

'Billy Bob murdered my dad.'

'You lost your civil trial. The jury said he didn't.'

'In Odessa. Billy Bob cut corners on that rig—on safety, on the environment, on everything and everyone. He doesn't give a damn about the planet or the people. Only his profits.'

'So you're devoting your life to putting him in prison?'

'Or in a grave.' She paused. 'I hate him.'

'Hate's a hard thing to hold onto.'

He knew. He had held onto his hate for a decade.

'It's all I have left to hold.'

'You used me, Carla.'

'No, I didn't. I helped you. You were wrong, Professor. Nathan's death wasn't an accident. It wasn't a coincidence. If you had left town, you would never have learned the truth. And his killer would have gone free. You wouldn't have had your justice. You should thank me, for keeping you in town.'

'For shooting out our window? You could've hurt someone.'

'With number-eight birdshot? Please. Nobody likes a whiner, Professor.'

'You lied to me.'

'Not guilty. I didn't lie. I just didn't tell you the whole truth. That doesn't constitute perjury, they said so on *Law and Order*.'

Book sighed. 'Everyone's a lawyer.'

He stared at Cathedral Rock to the east. That was Carla's connection: she blamed Billy Bob Barnett for her father's death, and she wanted revenge. Book felt no anger toward her; he had had his revenge. The man who had killed his father had been sentenced to death; Book rode the Harley to Huntsville to witness his execution in the death chamber at the state penitentiary. He had looked into the man's eyes from the other side of the glass partition and had seen nothing. Only emptiness. Watching that man die, the man who had stuck a gun to his father's head and pulled the trigger, all desire for revenge had drained from his body. All his hate had dissipated. He found no satisfaction in another human's death. An eye for an eye could not bring his father back. But he felt for Carla; she did not yet know that revenge would not fill the void.

'You mad?'

'I should be.'

'That means you're not. Good.'

'Why?'

She pointed at the teepees on the adjacent El Cosmico tract.

'Because I've never fucked in a teepee.'

Chapter 33

Book woke in a teepee to a ringing phone. He reached down and grabbed his jeans then dug the cell phone out of a pocket.

'Professor.'

Nadine.

'Why aren't you out running?'

She giggled.

'I was up late.'

'I bet. Well, wake up Carla and come over.'

'Why?'

'I figured it out.'

'I did the math. The numbers don't add up.'

An hour later, they all sat in Nadine's hospital room in Alpine. Stacks of paper surrounded her in the bed.

'I talked to Professor Lawson. He said the fastest way to cut expenses is on disposal costs, said they've skyrocketed to about nine dollars per barrel of flow-back. So, if five million barrels of frack fluid go down the hole and fifty percent comes back up, that's two and a half million gallons of flow-back that's got to be injected down disposal wells. A barrel—that's how they measure everything in the business—is forty-two gallons, so two and a half million gallons is roughly sixty thousand barrels. Times nine dollars per barrel, that's half a million dollars in disposal costs per well. That's a lot of money, so I started looking at the disposal numbers.'

She held up a piece of paper from her left side.

'Well number three-twenty-four. Fracked last November seventeenth. The well log says they injected right at three million gallons of frack fluid down the hole.'

She held up another paper, this one from her right side.

'But the expense worksheets—these are the work papers the accountants generate from the actual receipts, bank statements, that sort of thing—for last year's tax return shows Barnett paid for six hundred twenty-five tanker trucks to deliver frack fluid to well number three-twenty-four on November seventeenth.'

'And?'

'And each tanker carries eight thousand gallons. Do the math, that comes to five million gallons.'

'So he's either cheating on his taxes or he's cheating on the amount of fluid used to frack that well. I understand the taxes, but why the frack fluid?'

'I'm getting there.'

She held up another piece of paper.

'After fracking, fifteen to fifty percent of the fluid comes back up the hole—remember, Billy Bob told us that?'

Book nodded.

'That's the flow-back. It's collected in an open pit then pumped into the tanker trucks to haul off to the disposal wells.'

'Okay.'

Back to the second piece of paper.

'The expense worksheet says Barnett paid for three hundred tanker loads to the disposal wells. Do the math, that's two-point-four million gallons. Which is eighty percent of three million—that's too much flow-back—but only forty-eight percent of five million. Which fits.'

'Which leads us to conclude that—'

'They used five million gallons to frack that well and recovered two-point-four million gallons of flow-back.'

'I agree.'

Another paper.

'But, this expense sheet lists all the disposal costs, but by date, not well. On November nineteenth, Barnett paid one hundred seventy thousand dollars to dispose of nineteen thousand barrels of flow-back in the Pecos County disposal well.'

'Which means?'

'He's short.'

'How?'

'Like I said, one barrel equals forty-two gallons. So they disposed of only eight hundred thousand gallons of flow-back from that well.'

'So two-point-four million gallons came back up the hole, but only eight hundred thousand gallons were trucked to the disposal wells?'

'Looks that way.'

'What happened to the other one-point-six million gallons?'

'Never made it to the disposal wells.'

'Where'd it go?'

'He dumped it,' Carla said.

'Why?'

'To save money.'

'About three hundred and forty thousand dollars,' Nadine said.

'On one well,' Carla said. 'Times a hundred wells a year, that's—'

'Thirty-four million dollars,' Nadine said.

'That's real money,' Carla said, 'even in Texas.'

'And especially if you've got three ex-wives to support,' Book said.

'And five children,' Nadine said.

'And a cocaine habit,' Carla said.

'So Nathan was wrong. Billy Bob isn't contaminating the groundwater; he's contaminating the land and surface water.'

'I've gone through the numbers on twenty wells so far,' Nadine said. 'Same deal.'

'But for him to dump that much frack fluid,' Book said, 'the trucking company would have to be a co-conspirator in a criminal enterprise.'

'Wouldn't be the first time,' Carla said. 'The trade treaty with Mexico allowed cross-border trucking, so the cartels bought up a bunch of Mexican trucking companies. They know a little something about criminal enterprises.'

'That's another piece of the puzzle, Professor,' Nadine said.

'What?'

'Apparently someone at the trucking company had a conscience. Wade Chandler, shipping supervisor. Nathan had several manifests signed by Chandler.'

'How?'

She shrugged. 'Who knows? Maybe Nathan figured it out, asked Chandler for the records.'

'Where's this Wade Chandler?'

'Dead. Died in a car accident, two days before Nathan.'

'Why didn't the sheriff mention that?'

'Probably didn't know. Happened in Pecos County. That's two counties north of Marfa.'

'Looks like Billy Bob partnered up with some bad guys, Professor, maybe a cartel,' Carla said.

'Where would he meet cartel people?'

'Cokehead needs a supplier. Maybe he's killing two birds with one stone—buying his cocaine and dumping his flow-back.'

'We need proof.'

'These papers,' Nadine said.

'Too complicated. We need a smoking gun.'

'Don't guns smoke *after* they've been fired?'
'So where would he dump the fluid?'
Carla spread her arms.
'It's a big desert.'

Chapter 34

At three the next morning, Book and Carla sat in her pickup truck parked out of sight off Highway 67 northeast of Alpine, just outside Barnett Oil and Gas Company Well Site 356. They had the high ground; down below, more flow-back fluid in the open pit was being pumped into a long line of tanker trucks. Book was in the driver's seat; Carla was in the passenger's. They ate beef jerky. The evening air had now turned cool, and the breeze brought the smell of distant rain. That night Book would learn Nathan Jones's truth.

'Boo!'

Carla screamed; Book jumped then recovered and saw a face behind night-vision goggles peering in through Carla's window. A hand yanked the goggles off to reveal a familiar face.

'*Big Rick?* What the hell are you doing out here?'

'Scaring the shit out of you two.' He laughed. 'My reliable source said something big is going down at this well site tonight. Thought I'd check it out myself. You know what it is?'

'We think they're dumping frack fluid out in the desert.'

Big Rick opened Carla's door. 'Scoot over.'

She did, and he climbed in with a backpack and an AR-15 assault rifle.

'Is that loaded?' Book asked.

'Why would I carry an unloaded weapon?'

'Point it out the window.'

He did.

'So what's the plan, Professor?'

'We wait. See where those trucks go.'

Carla held up her camcorder. 'We're going to follow them and videotape the dumping. A smoking gun.'

'Well, I've got my gun and I've got my smokes.'

Big Rick pulled out a joint and lit it. He inhaled deeply then offered the joint to Book and Carla; they declined.

'Don't exhale in here,' Book said.

Big Rick stuck his head out the window and exhaled smoke. 'Aah.'

He pulled his head back inside and a big bag of Cheetos from his backpack. He stuffed Cheetos into his mouth then held the bag out; Book declined, but Carla shrugged and took a handful.

'I do like Cheetos.'

Book shook his head. 'Heck of a team. A law professor, an environmentalist with a grudge, and a stoned artist with a loaded weapon and a bag of Cheetos.'

'And ready to kick some ass,' Big Rick said.

Carla pointed. 'Look.'

The tanker trucks carrying the flow-back fluid began exiting the site. They counted fifty trucks that turned north on 67, the road to the disposal wells in Pecos County. But fifty turned south on 67, the road to—

'Mexico,' Big Rick said.

After the final truck had passed, Book started the engine and shifted into gear but did not turn on the lights. He turned south and followed the red taillights. Carla videotaped and narrated. Big Rick smoked pot. Highway 67 turned east and led them through Alpine and toward Marfa. In the distant sky to the south lightning strikes flashed above the mountains. The faint sound of thunder broke the silence of the night.

'Desert storm over Mexico,' Carla said. 'It'll lightning and thunder, but it never rains.'

They passed through Alpine; the streets sat vacant.

'Can we stop and get some potato chips?' Big Rick asked.

'No.'

They cleared the town and wound through the Chisos Mountains then descended onto the Marfa Plateau. Eight miles further, just before the Marfa Mystery Lights Viewing Center, the trucks abruptly turned south on an unmarked dirt road that cut through the desert.

Deputy Shirley liked to come out to the viewing center late at night when she worked the midnight shift. The center was an open rock structure with a cement floor and a low rock wall; people gathered at night in hopes of seeing the mystery lights. But not at three-thirty in the morning. That's when she liked to come out; not to watch the mystery lights, but to screw on the low rock wall under the stars. And tonight the distant lightning made the moment even more romantic. She wore her uniform shirt with the Presidio County Sheriff's Department badge and her leather holster, but her uniform trousers lay on the cement floor. She sat bare-bottomed on the wall with her legs up high and spread for the cowboy named Cody; he was working hard and doing a very good job. The night was cool, but her thick white boot socks and Cowboy Cody's body heat kept her toasty. Shirley felt the heat building down below, and her body began rumbling—

—but not with the throes of an orgasm. The rumbling came from the line of tanker trucks barreling past not a hundred feet away down the Old Army Air Field Road. Cowboy Cody continued his hard work as she watched the tankers—ten, twenty, thirty . . . must be fifty trucks—heading deep into the dark desert. Odd. But then, sculptures made out of crushed cars were pretty odd, too. She turned back to Cody and tried to get her mind and body refocused on the moment before he ran out of gas when another vehicle turned off Highway 67 and headed down the dirt road into the desert. It was a pickup truck, a familiar-looking one, with a driver she recognized in the flash of the next lightning strike: the professor. He was driving with no headlights.

'What the hell?'

Cowboy Cody panted hard.

'Sorry. I held it as long as I could.'

'Not you. The trucks.'

Cowboy Cody backed away to police himself—Shirley insisted her beaus practice safe sex—and she drew the cell phone from her holster.

Presidio County Sheriff Brady Munn slept peacefully in his bed next to his wife of twenty-seven years. With the kids grown and gone, there were no more sleeps interrupted for bottle duty or diaper duty or chaperone duty; and Presidio County was not exactly a hotbed of criminal activity. Consequently, he was startled awake by the ringing phone. He reached out, found the phone, and put the receiver to his ear.

'This better be good.'

'It is.'

Shirley.

'What time is it?'

'Three-thirty.'

His niece told him what she had just witnessed out by the viewing center.

'Goddamn amateurs. They're gonna get themselves killed playing detective. He can't kung fu the cartels. What the hell are you doing out there, anyway?'

'Keeping Presidio County safe.'

'Well, put your pants on and get the hell back to town.'

She giggled and disconnected. He replaced the receiver and rubbed his face. Relatives. If it was just the tankers, he'd call Border Patrol and let them handle the situation. But Carla and the professor made him sit up and say to his wife, 'Honey, I'm gonna run down to the border,' like many a husband might say he was running to the neighborhood convenience store. She grunted and rolled over.

They drove over old runways.

'They're taking a shortcut through the old Marfa Army Air Field,' Carla said. 'Skirting town, to avoid a curious Border Patrol agent wondering what all these trucks are doing heading toward Mexico in the middle of the night. They'll pick up the highway again south of town.'

Rumbles of thunder rolled over the Marfa Plateau. Book's cell phone rang. He answered.

'Hi. I couldn't sleep. Alone.'

Carmen Castro.

'Uh, Carmen, I'm going to have to call you back. I'm right in the middle of something.'

'Does it involve a woman?'

'It's not quite that dangerous.'

Carmen sighed. 'You said you were coming back.'

'I've been delayed.'

'I've gone to the gun range every night, to get over my sexual frustrations.'

'Well, uh, whatever works.'

'It's getting expensive. I've gone through two thousand rounds of ammo. You want to have phone sex?'

'Uh, not a good time.'

A groan from Carmen. 'Call me.'

Book disconnected.

'Carmen?' Carla said.

'How old is she?' Big Rick said.

'Can we focus here?'

Big Rick took a long drag on his joint then hung his head out the window.

Border Patrol Agent Wesley Crum chased the wets into the desert just off Highway 67 about forty miles south of Marfa and twenty miles north of the border. Through the night-vision goggles, he counted five males and five females. No doubt a family reunion. An odd sound broke the silence of the night and caused him to stop and turn back to the highway. He observed an equally odd sight: a long line of tanker trucks heading south like ducks migrating for the winter. Only it was late spring, so they should be migrating north. The ducks, not the tanker trucks.

'Where the hell are they going?'

'Come on,' Angel said, 'let's get these folks.'

'You're always wanting to let them go. Tonight you want to chase them? Look.'

Wesley pointed, and Angel turned and looked. A ways behind the last tanker truck, a pickup truck followed with its lights off. But with the goggles, Wesley recognized the big potato embedded on the antenna.

'I know that potato. That's Carla's truck. And the professor. Maybe he ain't a good guy after all. Let's find out.'

'Come on, Wesley, let's take care of these people.'

Just then another pickup truck with its lights off passed. It was following Carla's truck.

'Who the hell is that? Come on, Angel, they're up to something, and at four in the morning, it ain't no good.'

'They're just tanker trucks, Wesley. Going south, not north. They're not smuggling dope *into* Mexico. Let's do our job.'

'I am.'

Wesley took off running toward the highway and their Border Patrol SUV parked off the road. Angel shook his head then dropped the jug of water he was carrying and yelled to the Mexicans in the desert.

'*¡Agua! ¡Agua!*'

Angel Acosta ran after Wesley Crum.

Twenty minutes later, just outside the town of Presidio, the tankers turned west on Farm-to-Market 170, the river road. Book steered the pickup after them. The Rio Grande was visible to their left in the illumination of the lightning strikes, which came more often now.

'I'm hungry,' Big Rick said. 'You kids hungry?'

'They're going to cross the river,' Carla said.

'How?' Book said. 'The river's full.'

'The Rio Conchos from Mexico joins up just a few miles upriver. Beyond that, the riverbed is dry because of all the dams upstream of El Paso. If not for Mexican water in the Conchos, the Rio Grande would be dry all the way to the Gulf of Mexico.'

'I know an all-night café in Presidio,' Big Rick said. 'We could stop off and—'

Book looked over at Big Rick and put a finger to his lips. 'Shh.'

Border Patrol Agent Wesley Crum drove the SUV. The tanker trucks were leading this caravan south. Carla and the professor were following the tankers with their lights out. The second pickup truck was following Carla and the professor with its lights out. Wesley and Angel were following the whole goddamned bunch of them with their lights out. And Wesley was thinking, Who are the good guys and who are the bad guys? On the border, it was often difficult to tell.

'Am I right, Angel?'

'Yeah, you're right.'

'I figure they're gonna head west on One-seventy, cross the river above the Conchos.'

'Looks that way.'

336

'We could hit the lights and siren, speed to the front of the line, and try to stop the tankers.'

'That would be one option. How many guns we got?'

'Not enough.'

'Exactly.'

'So we follow?'

'We follow.'

Chapter 35

Six hundred miles southeast of Presidio in the Predator Ops command center on the second floor of an airplane hangar at the Corpus Christi Naval Air Station, U.S. Customs and Border Protection Air Interdiction Agent Dwight Ford watched the live video feed from the infrared camera aboard the Predator B drone as the unmanned aircraft banked left and right with the course of the Rio Grande. The drone's camera gave them 'eyes in the sky' above the 1,254-mile Mexico–Texas border. The images on the flat screen were sharp; from twenty thousand feet up, the camera could identify vehicles and humans, but not faces. But all it was identifying at the moment was the bare desert on either side of the river.

Dwight 'liaised'—a word he had never even heard before he was assigned to the drone—between the drone pilots and the Border Patrol agents on the ground. They had gotten a call-in tip that a big drug shipment was coming across the river below Nuevo Laredo, so the Predator had flown over that location most of the night; but it turned out to be another bullshit call. Dwight figured it might be a decoy, so he had the pilot fly the drone west of Nuevo Laredo. They found no activity, so they flew further west. They were now over Presidio.

Dwight wore his military-style tan jumpsuit and brown cap. He was leaned back in his captain's chair, and his feet were kicked up on the desk where the computers and keyboards and phones were situated; his hands were clasped behind his head. He glanced up at the black digital strip on the wall showing military times in red numerals: *Pacific, 02:31 . . . Costa Rica, 03:31 . . . Panama, 04:31 . . . Eastern, 05:31 . . . Zulu, 09:31 . . . Local, 04:31.* He was having a hell of a time keeping his eyes open.

'Dwight—wake up!'

Dwight snapped forward in his chair. The drone pilot was on the radio. Dwight clicked on his radio headset that connected him to the flight trailer parked outside where Lance and Grady, the pilot and co-pilot, flew the drone with a joystick like the kind his sons used to play their video games.

'What?'

'Look.'

On the screen were images of tanker trucks, a long line of tanker trucks. He checked the other flat screen displaying a Google Earth map that tracked the drone's path.

'They're driving west on FM One-seventy,' Lance the drone pilot said.

The drone had cleared Presidio and now flew west over the river road past the point where the big Rio Conchos flowed into the Rio Grande. The trucks seemed to be slowing—yes, they were definitely slowing—and turning south. The line of trucks drove across the dry riverbed and crossed into Mexico as if they were UPS trucks making deliveries in the neighborhood. But what were those tanker trucks delivering to Mexico?

'Follow those tankers,' Dwight said.

'They're in Mexico,' Lance said.

'So?'

'So we're supposed to respect Mexico's sovereign immunity.'

They all enjoyed a good laugh.

'Who the hell is that?'

On the screen, a pickup truck followed the last tanker across the riverbed, far enough back that it was obviously following with the intent of not being spotted.

'Someone with a death wish,' Grady the co-pilot said, 'following a cartel shipment into Mexico.'

Book hit the speed dial on his cell phone. After a few rings, a groggy voice came over.

'Book?'

'Henry, it's me.'

'This is early even for you, Book.'

'Sorry. I'm about to lose cell service.'

'Why? Low battery?'

'Because I'm crossing into Mexico.'

'That doesn't sound good.'

'Henry, listen. Nadine Honeywell, my intern, is in the Alpine hospital.'

'Why?'

'Long story. If you don't hear from me by eight, I need you to drive to Alpine and take her home to Austin. Will you do that for me?'

'Sure, Book. But where will you be?'

'Dead.'

Nadine Honeywell woke with a fright. Sweat matted her body; her heart beat rapidly. Fortunately, she was no longer hooked up to the machines, or the entire nursing staff would be on top of her by now and putting those paddles on her chest and screaming, 'Clear!' She gathered herself. It was just a nightmare. She checked the clock: 4:33.

'It was just a dream,' she said to the empty room.

The professor and Carla were running from a wall of fire—she had been running with them in spirit, hence the sweat—but they weren't fast enough. The fire had taken them. She shook her head. A wall of fire. How silly. Right now the professor and Carla were probably doing the dirty in that El Cosmico teepee. That's where they were. She felt better now. She breathed out all the tension she had awakened with. But still—

It had seemed so real.

Dwight Ford stared at the screen as if watching an action-thriller movie. His pulse had ratcheted up a notch and not because of the cold coffee he was drinking; because something bad was fixing to go down in the desert. People would die. Real people, not actors playing dead. South of the Rio Grande was a killing field. The drone banked south and the camera followed the tankers. They drove on a dirt road along the Rio Conchos deep into the Chihuahuan Desert.

Book steered the pickup carefully due to the dust kicked up by the tanker trucks. Through the dust cloud he saw the trucks' brake lights come on just as they crested a low rise in the desert. Book pulled over on the north side of the rise. They got out. The wind had picked up and carried the scent of smoke; the distant sky now glowed orange.

'Wildfire,' Carla said. 'Ignited by the lightning.'

'Wind's blowing our way.'

'Yep.'

'Let's get this on tape and get out of here.'

Carla took her camera; Big Rick donned his night-vision goggles and grabbed the AR-15. They snuck through the brush and crawled up the low rise. They lay flat on their bellies and observed the scene below. The trucks had backed up to a wide gulch. A group of armed men—'Cartel soldiers,' Carla said—had apparently been waiting for the trucks. They greeted the drivers as if they were *compadres*. The men opened the drain valves on the tankers and dumped the flow-back fluid into the gulch. The men then drank and laughed as if they were at a party.

'Lot of bad guys down there,' Big Rick said.

Carla captured the event on tape. The scene was lit up by the lightning strikes, which were almost nonstop, and the glowing sky from the wildfire. It was closer now.

'Arroyos,' Carla said. 'They lead to the Conchos and then to the Rio Grande. And down to the Gulf of Mexico.'

'I do believe that's an environmental crime.'

'Yep.'

'You got it on tape?'

'Yep.'

'Let's get out of here.'

Big Rick aimed his rifle at the Mexicans.

'What are you doing?' Book said.

'I'm going to take out a few Mexicans before we leave.'

'Don't.'

'Why not?'

'They have a lot more guns than we do.'

'True. But, damn, this sure is fun.'

A shot rang out. Big Rick fell back to the ground with a bullet hole in his forehead. They turned and came face to face with two Mexican men wielding AK-47s.

'*¡No se mueven!*'

'They shot him.'

Air Interdiction Agent Dwight Ford stood in front of the flat screen. He talked to the pilots.

'Zoom in on those figures.'

On the infrared camera, the figures appeared white against the dark background. Three individuals had exited the pickup and run to a spot in the desert and lain down. One held a rifle; another appeared to be aiming a camera at the scene below where the drivers crowded around the tankers. Fluid was flowing from the back of the tankers.

'They're dumping something,' Dwight said.

'Something they're not supposed to dump,' Lance said.

The individual holding the rifle had been shot; the other two had been captured by two men holding weapons.

'Got to be a cartel deal going down,' Dwight said. 'Damn, I wish that Predator had some missiles. We could light up the sky.'

'Something else is,' Lance said. 'Another wildfire.'

The screen was now noticeably brighter. The camera panned south and picked up what appeared to be flames in the distance. Then it panned back as the two individuals were brought into the crowd of men around the trucks.

'*Mis amigos*, look what we have found in the desert,' one of the men yelled.

The other men were grouped together by the trucks with handguns in their waistbands and rifles slung over their shoulders. One man stepped forward; he carried an assault weapon. From the respect he was given by the other men, he was obviously the leader. The men spoke in Spanish, but Book did make out 'kung fu.'

'Ah,' the leader said. 'Then we must have a fight.'

The men whooped and hollered as if they were at a bullfight. And Book soon realized that he was the bull. The drivers went to their trucks and turned on the headlights, illuminating an open area, although the sky glowed bright all around them; the men then formed a wide circle. They pushed Book and Carla into the center. The leader stepped over to them.

'So you are the kung fu professor. Word has spread how you beat up the *gringos*. I would very much like to see you fight.'

'How about Padre's tomorrow night?'

The leader laughed. 'No, I think tonight will be better.'

'And whom will I fight?'

'Ramon.'

The leader called out, and a man stepped into the ring. He removed his shirt; he was thicker and more muscular than

Book, but that did not concern him. What did concern him were the two nunchucks he unbuckled from his belt; he swung them around in the fashion of an experienced martial artist. The scene reminded Book of the first Indiana Jones movie when the crowd parts to reveal a bad guy swinging a sword, but instead of fighting him, Indiana pulls a gun and shoots him. But Book had no gun. He had only his hands and his feet and a certain skill set.

'What happens if I lose?' Book said.

The leader shrugged. 'You die.'

'What if I win?'

'You still die.'

'Then why should I fight?'

'So the *señorita* does not die.'

'If I win, you'll let her go? You promise?'

'Oh, sure, I promise.'

Book did not gain much comfort with his promise. But fighting would gain him time and perhaps provide a distraction that might allow Carla to escape. He stuck up his index finger.

'*Un momento.*'

Book stepped close to Carla and lowered his voice.

'I'm going to fight this guy, create a distraction. When I do, you get to the truck and get back to Texas.'

'Book—'

'Do it, Carla. Or we'll both die. And Nathan will have died for nothing.'

He turned away from Carla. The wind blew strong in his face, and the orange sky seemed much closer now. He breathed smoke. He stepped to the center of the ring and took a fighting stance. He extended his left arm and gestured with the fingers of his hand to Ramon to come closer. Ramon grinned; his *compadres* shouted as if they were at a sporting event. Perhaps they were.

Ramon stepped forward swinging the nunchucks.

★   ★   ★

344

'Shit,' Dwight Ford said, 'they're staging some kind of fucking fight, in the middle of the fucking night in the middle of the fucking desert.'

'Well,' Lance said, 'it's not like they have fucking jobs to go to tomorrow morning.'

Dwight watched the fight on the screen. Unlike a movie, in Mexico the bad guys always win.

The *nunchaku* is an ancient Chinese martial arts weapon, but the Westernized name for the weapon is nunchucks. The weapon consists of two short wood or metal sticks connected by a cord or chain. The martial artist holds one stick and swings the other; when wielded by an expert martial artist, the force generated by swinging the stick can inflict serious and often fatal injuries. Consequently, possession of nunchucks is a crime in a number of countries and in some states in the United States. Book wasn't sure about Mexican law; but then, there was no applicable law in the Chihuahuan Desert at five in the morning when surrounded by armed cartel soldiers. There was only life and death.

Ramon swung the nunchucks—side-to-side wrist spins and around his body with L-strikes and then around his neck and underarm switch-ups and helicopter spins—either to demonstrate his skill level or to intimidate Book. Ramon was experienced with nunchucks. Disarming him would not be easy. He advanced on Book; his *compadres* shouted in Spanish.

Book had two options: waiting for Ramon or attacking Ramon.

He decided on door number two. He abruptly broke and ran at Ramon . . . Ramon's face registered his surprise but he quickly recovered and took his fighting stance . . . Book closed the fifty feet between them . . . but ten feet before he reached Ramon, he dove to the ground as if a swimmer diving into a pool . . . he tucked his body and rolled and then

345

launched himself up into Ramon, too close for the nunchucks to be useful . . . he tucked his right fist and executed an upper elbow strike, driving his right elbow into Ramon's jaw, knocking him unconscious. Ramon's hands dropped, and he fell over backwards. Book grabbed the nunchucks then spun around into a fighting stance. The men turned to the leader for instructions.

The leader's face showed his shock at the unexpected turn of events. He stared at the inert body of Ramon then at Book. His face turned angry. He yelled in Spanish and five men advanced on Book. He maneuvered into striking position and swung the nunchucks. Five swings, five seconds, five more men on the ground.

'Wow, he's good,' Dwight Ford said.

'Not good enough,' Lance the pilot said.

The leader yelled again, and all the men came after Book. He dispatched a few more with the nunchucks, but they over-whelmed him and beat him until several shots were fired into the air. Book lay on the ground bleeding from his nose and mouth; he hoped Carla had made her escape. The men parted for their leader; he straddled Book and pointed his weapon down at him.

'You are a good fighter, Professor. It is too bad you must die.'

From atop the low rise fifty yards out, he saw the Mexican pointing the AK-47 at the professor lying on the ground. He aimed the rifle fitted with the silencer and sighted in through the optic. He pulled the trigger.

The fire was near enough that Book could see the Mexican's eyes; and in his eyes he saw only hardness. He had killed many men. He would pull that trigger and kill Book and then have a beer with his *compadres*. That was the life he knew. The life he was born into. And now their lives had intersected in the Chihuahuan Desert.

Book's last thought was of his mother: who would take care of her?

Lightning illuminated the sky, and a crack of thunder followed quickly—and the Mexican's body jerked and his face registered shock, as if the thunder had frightened him. His hand that held the gun dropped. He looked down at his chest. His shirt turned red. With his blood. He fell to the ground, dead. Bullets sprayed the men; more went down. The others fired their guns wildly into the desert and then disappeared into the darkness. Book looked for Carla; she was gone.

'Holy shit,' Dwight said, 'the bad guys are going down. Someone's shooting them. Pan north.'

The Predator's sixty-six-foot wingspan allowed it to fly slowly above a location. Its camera moved north of the fight scene until it showed a shooter pointing a rifle at the cartel men.

'He's hammering them,' Lance said.

'He's rescuing the two hostages,' Dwight said.

'Hell of a firefight.'

'Literally,' Lance said. 'Look.'

He panned the camera south, but not very far. Flames from the wildfire were coming closer.

'Fixin' to be some fried Mexican food for the coyotes.'

'Oh, man,' Grady the co-pilot said. 'I love flautas.'

'Shut up, Grady.'

Carla crawled up the rise; the truck was parked on the other side. She did not want to leave Book, but she knew he was right. They would both die.

★   ★   ★

347

'That's a female,' Dwight said.

She was trying to escape. She ran hard through the desert brush, stumbled several times, got up and ran again . . .

Carla ran hard until a hand came out of the darkness and grabbed her arm.

Chapter 36

Book crawled through the chaos then got to his feet and ran low to the ground and into the desert. He scrambled up the rise; on the other side, he stopped and called out to Carla. A voice answered, but not her voice. A male voice.

'Hey, Professor.'

Two figures walked out of the darkness and into the light provided by the wildfire. One was Carla; the other was—

'*Jimmy John?*'

He wore a red jumpsuit and carried an assault rifle over his shoulder.

'What the hell are you doing out here?'

'Shooting a few Mexicans.' He chuckled. 'I spotted your truck outside the well site, figured you two were gonna get yourself in a mess of trouble, so I followed you. But why'd you follow the tankers?'

'To get it on tape,' Carla said. 'So we can shut Billy Bob down.'

'Let's get out of here,' Book said. 'Before that fire reaches us.'

'So Billy Bob's contaminating the groundwater with the frack fluid?' Jimmy John asked. 'That's what those papers proved?'

'No.'

'Then what?'

'He's dumping the flow-back out here in the desert,' Carla said. 'To cut costs. That's illegal. It'll flow into the Conchos, then the Rio Grande. We can put Billy Bob in prison and shut down his frack wells.'

'She right, Professor?'

'Yes.'

Jimmy John sighed then pulled the rifle off his shoulder and pointed it at Book.

'I'm sorry, Professor, but I can't let that happen.'

'Is he pointing the weapon at them?' Dwight said.

'Looks that way,' Lance said.

'For Christ's sake. He rescued them, now he's taken them hostage? What the fuck is going on?'

'Welcome to Mexico.'

'You ran Nathan off the road,' Book said.

'I wasn't trying to kill him. I was trying to get him to pull over, so I could talk some sense into him. He was gonna take his proof to the media, like that queer Kenni with an "i" wanted him to. Kenni got him into that queer stuff, thinking he could be an artist, live in New York, smoking dope. Got him thinking like the ChiNazis. Turned him against fracking. Against us. Against me. Like he didn't care about us no more. Like he found better friends. He knew going public would've cost me my job. I begged him, Professor. But he didn't care.'

'Nathan died for your job?'

'You ever not had a job, Professor? You ever go to the store and have to count your pennies to see if you can buy food? You ever live in a dump trailer on the Mexican side of town? You ever look in the mirror every morning and see a loser? Well, I have. Most of my life. But not since I got a job. You shut down fracking, I lose my job. I can't go back to that life, Professor. A life without a job.'

Jimmy John swiped a sleeve across his nose. It was bleeding.

'You drive a big black pickup. You ran us off the road.'

'You wouldn't go home and mind your own goddamn business.'

'You hurt Nadine.'

'Well, what the hell were you doing, putting her on the back of that Harley? That ain't responsible.' He paused. 'Did she ask about me?'

Carla pointed south. 'The wildfire, it's closer.'

'What are you going to do, Jimmy John? Kill us, then go back and ask Nadine out?'

'Well . . . not right away.'

'You figure the sheriff will blame it on the Mexicans?'

Jimmy John pulled a baggie out of his back pocket and tossed it on the ground.

'Mexican black tar heroin. Drug deal gone bad. It happens. I'm sorry, Professor. I like you. Not so much Carla, but you're a good guy, came out here for Nathan just 'cause he was your student back then. I wish it didn't have to end this way.'

'Jimmy John, the sheriff will figure this out.'

'We're in Mexico, Professor. Two more dead bodies don't mean nothin' this side of the river.'

An explosion south of their location sent a fireball into the sky. Jimmy John flinched and glanced that way. Book grabbed Carla, and they ran a few steps into the dark desert then dove into the brush. Bullets zipped through the air over their heads.

'Nowhere to go, Professor. Only coyotes and wolves out there, and they'll eat you both for breakfast.'

Book picked up a rock and threw it at Jimmy John. He twirled and fired but missed.

'Give it up, Jimmy John.'

Book peppered Jimmy John with more rocks.

'I pitched in high school.'

He hit him in his back, his leg, and his face. Jimmy John clamped a hand against his head.

'You got a headache? You want an Advil?'

'You're pissing me off, Professor.'

Screams sounded from the other side of the rise where the sky burned bright orange.

'The wildfire!' Carla said.

More explosions sent more fireballs into the sky.

'The fire's reached the tanker trucks,' Book said.

'We've got to get out of here, make a run for the truck,' Carla said. 'The wind's pushing that fire our way, fast.'

Book threw another rock to the east of Jimmy John—he spun that way—then ran to the west; Book attacked Jimmy John from his rear. Jimmy John heard his footsteps and swung the rifle around, but Book launched himself feet first and struck Jimmy John before he could fire. The rifle went flying, and they went sprawling into the dirt. Book jumped to his feet; Jimmy John did not. He lay in a heap. Then he started crying. Sobbing uncontrollably. After a moment, he pushed himself up; his nose was bleeding. He grabbed his head with both hands.

'Come on, Jimmy John! We've got to outrun the fire!'

'I can't go back to that life. No job and nobody.'

'You want to burn to death?'

Book helped Jimmy John to his feet.

'Come on!' Book yelled.

'I'm sorry, Professor.'

Jimmy John Dale turned and ran up the rise toward the fire. Just as he crested the rise, the flames came over and engulfed him. He fell down the other side.

'Jesus!' Dwight Ford yelled at the video screen. 'He ran into the fire!'

'They better get out of there!' Lance said.

The Predator's camera caught the flames of the wildfire as it engulfed the tanker trucks and set them afire, causing several to explode in fireballs. Cartel men tried to outrun the flames but failed.

'Wind's blowing at forty-three knots,' Lance said. 'I'm having a hell of a time controlling this bird.'

The flames ran across the desert toward the two figures.

'Run!'

Book grabbed Carla's arm; they sprinted to the truck. He jumped into the driver's seat and she into the passenger's. He fired up the engine, shifted into gear, and floored the accelerator. They sped down the dirt road. He saw the flames in the outside rearview; the fire was chasing them to the border.

'Follow them,' Dwight said.

The Predator's camera followed the pickup racing north to the river, fishtailing around curves but staying on the road. The camera panned north to the river.

'Look,' Lance said. 'That's a Border Patrol SUV.'

On the north side of the river was a large vehicle. Two men stood facing south.

'Thank God,' Dwight said. 'Those are the good guys. My guys.'

Border Patrol Agent Wesley Crum peered through the night-vision binoculars into Mexico.

'Man, look at that fucking wildfire. And explosions. I'm telling you, Angel, something big is going down in the desert. Let's call in the Predator.'

'Can't. It's over Nuevo Laredo.'

'How do you know?'

'Daily ops bulletin.'

'Then let's call in the cavalry, set a trap for those tanker trucks when they come back to this side.'

353

Wesley spotted something.

'Look! One of the pickup trucks is coming back. I think it's Carla and the professor.'

Angel sighed. 'I'm sorry, Wesley.'

His partner still had the binoculars pressed against his eyes.

'For what?'

'This.'

Angel reached down to his ankle, pulled up his trouser leg, and retrieved his backup weapon. He stuck the barrel to his partner's head and pulled the trigger.

'Fuck!' Dwight yelled. 'He just shot him! One of the good guys shot the other good guy! What the hell is going on?'

The shooter flung the weapon far downriver then took the dead agent's binoculars and put them to his face. Then he put something to his ear. A phone.

Billy Bob Barnett inhaled the line of white powder then leaned back in his leather chair and waited for the drug to take effect. To take his mind off the pressures that threatened to push him over the edge.

He had always lived life on the edge.

And if a man lived in Texas and wanted to live life on the edge, he played the oil and gas game. He wildcatted. He punched holes in the earth. He hoped he hit oil or gas or both. When that drill bit is digging deep and nearing the producing zone—what you *prayed* would be the producing zone—man, your heart is pounding and your adrenaline is pumping and your nerves are firing and you've never been so alive. If your geology and your hunch play out, life is good. And you are rich. If not . . .

The thrill of victory or the agony of defeat.

He had enjoyed many thrills and a few defeats. But no defeat like this one. His frack wells had hit gas, a mother lode of gas; but so had everyone else's. Consequently, the market had glutted and natural gas prices had plummeted. As had Billy Bob's emotions. He now wallowed in the depths of depression. And as each time before, he had turned to drugs for respite and relief. Marijuana in college, cocaine in business. It was a daily dose now.

First, the glut of gas. Then, the plunge in prices. Followed by the collapse of the stock value. And the pressure—the constant, pounding pressure—from the analysts, the board, the shareholders . . . and then his own lawyer. Nathan Jones had learned the truth and had threatened to go public with company documents. That would have been the end of Billy Bob Barnett.

The cartel had taken care of Wade Chandler. He would take care of Nathan Jones. But a car wreck did it for him. A stroke of luck. A sign that his luck was changing. He would hold out for the futures market to move back up, as it surely would. Drill more, frack more, stockpile more gas for the inevitable rise in prices. He was saved. Until a law professor rode into town on a Harley.

His cell phone rang.

Angel waited for Billy Bob Barnett to answer. When he did, Angel said, 'They're coming, the professor and Carla. What do you want me to do?'

'Don't let them back on this side of the river. It's like Vegas, Angel. What happens in Mexico stays in Mexico.'

'You're the boss.'

Angel disconnected, replaced his cell phone, and returned to the vehicle. He got the AR-15, snapped in a full clip, and grabbed the night-vision goggles. He walked across the dry Rio Grande and waited for the professor and Carla to arrive. And arrive they would. There was no place for them to go but north to the river. The wall of fire would chase them right into his kill zone. All he had to do was wait.

★   ★   ★

355

Dwight could see the pickup truck speeding directly at the Border Patrol agent.

'He's gonna kill those two people in the pickup truck,' Lance said.

'I know.'

A Border Patrol agent had gone over to the dark side. It wasn't the first time, or even the thousandth time. There was just too much easy money to be made. Look the other way and collect a million bucks. That was bad enough. But killing a fellow agent, that crossed a law enforcement line that no officer can cross. Ever.

The agent Dwight was now staring at on the video screen had to die.

He had to die that night.

On that river.

Before he killed those two people.

While there was still time to control the story.

But who could he call? Other Border Patrol agents would be in Presidio County, maybe near enough to arrive in time, but what if they had been corrupted, too? He needed a law enforcer in Presidio County who was incapable of being corrupted.

He grabbed a phone and dialed.

Chapter 37

Sheriff Brady Munn had the Presidio County SUV running eighty miles an hour with the lights flashing but no siren on Highway 67 just north of Presidio when his cell phone rang. Better not be Shirley telling him she was seeing the Marfa Mystery Lights. He answered.

'Sheriff Munn?'

'Yep.'

'This is Air Interdiction Agent Dwight Ford, at the Predator Ops center in Corpus Christi.'

The Predator boys must've spotted some Mexicans coming across the river.

'Agent, I don't have time to chase wets for you—'

'Sheriff, I'm sorry to wake you up but—'

'I'm already awake. I'm hauling ass to the border. We got something strange going on—'

'With tanker trucks?'

'How'd you know?'

'We've been tracking them with the Predator. They drove into Mexico and dumped some kind of liquid.'

'Frack fluid.'

'Frack? Like from gas wells?'

'Yeah. Like from gas wells.'

'Anyway, there was a shootout. We're following two individuals, a male and a female—'

'The professor and Carla.'

'You know them?'

'If that's them, I know them.'

'Well, they're heading north now.'

'Good.'

'Not so good. We got a man on this side of the river, Border Patrol agent.'

'And?'

'He's rogue. Just killed his partner. Gotta be on the cartel payroll.'

'Who?'

'Can't tell.'

'Where?'

'West on FM One-seventy, just past where the Conchos joins up. A Border Patrol SUV is parked on the river road. Can't miss it.'

Dwight paused.

'He's gonna kill those two people, unless you stop him. Sheriff, they need your help.'

Angel Acosta stepped onto Mexican soil. For the last two years, he had been on the cartel's payroll; all he had to do was turn a blind eye to drug shipments coming north. But while profitable, the job carried significant personal risk. So he had approached Billy Bob Barnett about employment in the oil and gas business; Aggies helped Aggies. Billy Bob had a job for him, but it required that he continue his employment with the Border Patrol. Billy Bob had made an arrangement with his trucking company, which had close ties to the cartel, to dump his frack fluid in the desert; but, there was always the risk of a Border Patrol agent spotting the caravan and getting curious. So Angel's job was to make sure no one was watching Highway 67 when the tanker trucks made their run into the desert. To evade the Predator's 'eyes in the sky,' he called in bogus tips of drug deals going down, way downriver, as he had that night. So he would collect two paychecks for that night's work, one from the cartel and one from Billy Bob. What federal employees call 'double dipping.'

A hundred trips, and all had worked just fine. He had remained partners with Wesley Crum because he was the dumbest Anglo Angel had ever met. But Wesley chose that night to become smart.

What had brought Angel Acosta, son of Carlos and Consuelo Acosta, devout Catholics both, to where he now stood in life, on the bank above the great Rio Conchos waiting to kill two more innocents? He had grown up in Marfa and lived as all Latinos lived in Marfa: out of sight and out of trouble. The old sheriff, he had put the fear into every Mexican's heart with his harsh law and order; but it turned out he was a drug runner, in the law for the money. Angel wanted to believe that he did what he did for some noble cause, but in the end, it was just about the money for him, too. He wanted to have something in life. A life. With things. Everything. He wanted the finer things in life, just as the Anglos from New York enjoyed. Good wine and Gouda cheese. A sports car. A fine home behind tall walls on the north side of the railroad tracks. On the Anglo side of town.

And why should he not have what they had, the Triple As? Were they smarter, better, worthier than he? Every attorney he had met was a borderline criminal, out of jail just because his form of criminal activity had been deemed legal by lawyers who write the laws. Every artist he had met was a queer stoner trying to win the Marfa art lottery and become rich and famous. And every asshole he had met was . . . an asshole. Why were the attorneys, artists, and assholes entitled to more than he? He did not feel that what he did was morally wrong . . . well, perhaps killing his partner was wrong. He would say a rosary for Wesley's soul, such as it was. But his other illegal activities were no worse than rich people's legal activities. How many rich people earned their fortunes through shady dealings on Wall Street and political favors? Through favorable laws gained by legal bribes called campaign contributions? Through legalized corruption? Joe Blow goes to prison for trading stock on insider information, but senators and congressmen go to the bank for doing exactly the same thing. How can that be constitutional, for members of Congress to exempt themselves from the very laws they impose on the people? Perhaps he would ask the professor before he killed him.

He fixed the night-vision goggles to his face. He could now see into the night. He could see the pickup truck driving fast toward him, the wall of fire behind it. Smoke filled the air. He aimed the AR-15 and fired.

The windshield blew out.

'Get down!' Book yelled.

Bullets peppered the truck. The shooter had a perfect line on them. There was only one place to go.

'Hold on.'

'They're between a rock and a hard place,' Lance the pilot said. 'Wildfire's chasing them straight at the shooter. No place for them to go.'

Or so Lance thought. Dwight Ford watched the screen as the pickup truck drove straight off the road and flew into the Rio Conchos.

'Shit, they drove into the Conchos!' Lance yelled. 'They're fuckin' crazy!'

'They're fucking alive!' Dwight said.

Two figures were visible on the screen emerging from the

pickup truck as it sank into the river. Above on the bank, the Border Patrol agent fired more shots at them.

'Not for long,' Lance said.

Angel had them dead in his sights. He would not be able to get an answer to his constitutional law question from the professor. Oh, well.

'*Adiós*, Professor.'

But he could not pull the trigger. He could not move his body. He could not hold the rifle. It fell from his hands. His eyes turned down to his chest. A large hole now gaped in his uniform shirt and his insides hung out. Blood gushed forth. He turned and saw the big sheriff standing there, smoke from the barrel of his handgun hanging in the air.

'*Adiós* yourself, podna,' the sheriff said.

Angel Acosta fell over dead.

Sheriff Brady Munn holstered his .44 Magnum and searched the Conchos for the professor and Carla in the moonlight and the light from the fires. He spotted them; they were being swept downriver toward the point a mile east where the Conchos joined the Rio Grande. Which was just as well since the wildfire was coming Brady's way fast. He turned and ran north and crossed over the dry Rio Grande riverbed. The Conchos turned hard east so he lost sight of the professor and Carla.

He jumped into his SUV, fired up the engine, and stomped on the accelerator. He drove east on the river road a mile past where the Conchos merged in, then slammed on the brakes. He cut the engine and got out. He opened the back liftgate and retrieved his rope. He ran down to the river.

The current was strong with the Conchos's water. He searched the river for the professor and Carla, but he couldn't find them. He yelled for them, but got no response. Just when he was about to run back to the SUV and drive farther down-river, he spotted them.

361

'There!'

He yelled to them, and they saw him. He fashioned a loop with the rope then twirled the loop above his head as if he were about to rope a calf in a rodeo competition and flung the loop at the professor. He missed. He reeled in the rope and flung the loop again. The professor grabbed the rope this time. He hung onto the rope with one hand and Carla with the other. Brady dug the heels of his cowboy boots into the earth, leaned his two hundred twenty pounds back, and pulled with all his strength against the current that tried to take them downriver. The rope burned his bare hands, but Brady felt no pain. His hands bled by the time he pulled them to dry land.

Dwight Ford threw his fists in the air. 'Yes!'

The professor and Carla lay there coughing and spitting water, but alive and unhurt. Finally, the professor knelt up and stuck a hand out to Brady. He grabbed the professor's hand and yanked him to his feet. The professor then helped Carla up. They stood there on the bank of the Rio Grande and gathered themselves as one does after having barely escaped death. To the southeast, the sky brightened with the breaking dawn; to the southwest, the sky burned bright with fire. The wildfire came to the river, but did not cross. No doubt it had scorched everything and everyone in its path. Just as well. What happens in Mexico stays in Mexico. After a moment, the professor turned back to Brady.

'Sheriff—thanks for the help.'

'Now that wasn't so hard, was it, Professor?'

Sheriff Brady Munn stretched his big body and gazed upon Presidio County and Mexico beyond. The border carried a harsh beauty and a harsher justice. He shook his head and exhaled at the grandeur of it all. Damn, but he loved the desert at dawn. He grunted.

'You folks want to get a cup of coffee?'

362

Chapter 38

The desert had changed John Bookman. He had come to this harsh land and paid off an overdue debt. And while he would never be a father, he would now be a godfather. To Nathan Jones Jr. Brenda had asked Book when they had said their goodbyes.

'Final exam, Nadine. What did you learn in Marfa, Texas?'

'A, I like to hit bad guys in the head with beer bottles. B, I'm a lot tougher than I thought. And C, I matter. To you. To my dad. To myself.'

'Very good. You made an A on this field trip.'

'Can we go home now?'

'Yes. We can go home now.'

It was Friday morning. Book had brought Nadine back to the Paisano the day before. He and Carla had given written statements to the sheriff and the FBI, DEA, and Border Patrol and an exclusive interview to Sam Walker for his next edition. Nathan Jones had not been killed by an evil oil company or a greedy fracker, but by his best friend who needed a job. But Billy Bob Barnett sat in the Presidio County Jail pending transfer to federal court in El Paso on criminal environmental charges. And his lawyer, Tom Dunn, was under investigation for aiding and abetting his client. But the videotape had been lost, and the tankers burned, and there were jurisdictional issues since the dumping occurred in Mexico. Hence, conviction of either man was doubtful. They were innocent until proven guilty beyond a reasonable doubt. That was constitutional law in America.

Book sat astride the repaired Harley outside the courtyard of the Paisano Hotel; Pedro had done a good job. Nadine sat behind him with her right leg in the cast secured to one side and her left arm in the cast secured to the other. Sheriff Brady Munn and Carla Kent stood next to them.

'Official line is, those two Border Patrol agents died in the line of duty,' the sheriff said. 'Drug bust gone bad.'

'Figures. Thanks again, Sheriff. For your help.'

'It's what we do out here in this desert, Professor.'

Carla bent down and kissed Book on the cheek.

'What are you going to do now?' he asked.

'Make sure Billy Bob's convicted. And fight fracking.'

'It's good to be busy.'

'You ever get up to Santa Fe, look me up, cowboy.'

'Comanche.'

Book, Carla, and Nadine had eaten take-out from Maiya's on Rock's outdoor patio the night before. They drank too much wine and beer. Nadine had fallen asleep, so he had carried her to Liz's bed and tucked her in. Then Carla had collected on her rain check. They had danced under the stars to music drifting over from Padre's Marfa. And they had spent one last night together. Book fired up the Harley and pulled on the doo-rag.

'You know,' Carla said, 'you really should wear a helmet. You're lucky you didn't get brain damage in that crash.'

'It's already damaged.'

'Well, you are a half-crazy Comanche, but you can still find your way home.'

'So far.'

She stared at him then abruptly took his face and kissed him full on the lips. A long kiss.

'There would be romance,' his intern said.

Carla finally released Book and stepped back. The sheriff stepped forward and stuck a hand out.

'I ain't kissing you.'

They shook.

'You take care, podna. You too, little lady.'

Book turned his head to his back-seat passenger. 'You ready to roll?'

Nadine strapped the goggles on over her black glasses. 'Yep. Got on my last pair of new underwear. I'm good.'

'Over-share.'

Book slid on the sunglasses. The sheriff touched his finger to his cowboy hat.

'*Adiós*, podna.'

Book shifted into gear and gunned the Harley south on Highland Avenue. Nadine raised her good arm into the air. Sheriff Munn and Carla Kent smiled at the bumper sticker on the back of Nadine's seat that read: *I ■ JUDD*.

ONE MONTH LATER

Epilogue

'Mr. Stanton, if the federal government can force an American citizen to buy health insurance, can it also force you to buy a Chevrolet vehicle since the government now owns twenty-seven percent of General Motors?'

'Of course not.'

'Why not?'

'That would be unconstitutional.'

'Why?'

'Because I drive a Beemer.'

The class laughed. But not Ms. Garza. Her T-shirt read *I* ♥ OBAMACARE in honor of that day's Con Law topic.

'Let's turn to the majority opinion of Chief Justice Roberts in *National Federation of Independent Business v. Sebelius, Secretary of Health and Human Services*. It was a five-to-four decision—actually, it was two five-to-four decisions—with Roberts being the deciding vote both times. The law under the Court's review was the Patient Protection and Affordable Care Act, also known as Obamacare, the key provision of which is the so-called "individual mandate." Essentially, that provision requires all citizens not covered by a government or employer plan to buy private health insurance. If they fail to do so, they must pay a penalty to the government. What was the idea behind the law?'

Ms. Garza's hand shot into the air.

'Ms. Garza.'

'The individual mandate requires everyone to pay into the health insurance system in order to prevent cost-shifting. If you go uninsured, my insurance premiums will increase to subsidize your care. You will be shifting the cost of your medical care to me. We must force everyone into the system. That's the only way Obamacare works. That's the only way to make the healthcare system fair.'

'Ms. Garza, is fairness the issue before the Supreme Court?'

'It should be.'

'Not my question.'

'No.'

'What is the issue before the Supreme Court, in this or any other case, when the Court reviews a Congressional act?'

'Whether Congress acted within its constitutional authority.'

'Correct. Mr. Stanton, what was the plaintiffs' main argument in that regard?'

Mr. Stanton's head was down. He was texting on the back row.

'Mr. Stanton, if you please.'

'Sorry, Professor, I'm selling my Whole Foods stock. Bought it at seven after the crash, selling it at ninety-four.'

'The appellant's main argument, please.'

'That the individual mandate exceeded Congress's power under the Commerce Clause.'

'And the Commerce Clause authorizes Congress to do what?'

'Regulate foreign and interstate commerce.'

'But the business of health insurance is clearly interstate commerce—commerce that crosses state lines. Why did the plaintiffs think the individual mandate exceeded Congress's authority?'

'Because the Commerce Clause authorizes Congress to *regulate* commerce, not to *create* commerce. Congress can't compel citizens to engage in commerce in order to then regulate that commerce.'

'Congress can regulate what we do, but they can't regulate what we don't do.'

'Exactly. As Scalia wrote, saying the Commerce Clause allows the government to regulate the failure to act "is to make mere breathing in and out the basis for federal prescription and to extend federal power to virtually all human activities."'

'And the individual mandate orders citizens to act, to engage in commerce, to buy a product, in this case health insurance.'

'Yes. Congress said, we've decided it's a good thing for all Americans to have health insurance, so we order all Americans to buy health insurance, and any American who refuses to buy health insurance will suffer a monetary penalty. We are forced to act at the direction of the government.'

'And what did Chief Justice Roberts have to say about that?'

'He said that was a bit much, even under the Commerce Clause. A government order to purchase insurance, enforced with a monetary penalty, is unconstitutional.'

'Who agreed with him?'

'The other four conservative justices. The four liberals thought that was an okay thing for Congress to do. They said Congress was just regulating our future commercial activity today, what they called "regulating in advance." But no one ever accused them of higher intelligence.'

Mr. Stanton shared a fist-bump with his buddies on the back row.

'So, on a five-to-four vote—five conservative justices to four liberal justices—the Court invalidated the individual mandate?'

'Yes.'

'And thus Obamacare?'

'Uh . . . no.'

371

'But you just said the Court invalidated the individual mandate as an unconstitutional exercise of Congress's power under the Commerce Clause.'

'That's correct, but the Court then validated the individual mandate under the Taxing Clause.'

'Please explain, Mr. Stanton.'

'The government made a backup argument, that the individual mandate could instead be upheld as a tax, and there's almost nothing or no one Congress can't tax.'

'What tax? The nine-hundred-page Obamacare law never once mentions the word "tax." It provides for a penalty for refusal to buy insurance, not a tax.'

'The government lawyers made it up after the fact. They realized that they might lose on the Commerce Clause argument, so they said, "Oh, that 'penalty' is really a 'tax,'" because the Taxing Clause gives Congress essentially unlimited power to lay and collect taxes for just about any purpose—why not to finance healthcare?'

'But Roberts and the four conservative justices saw through that ploy, didn't they, and disagreed with that contention?'

'They did. He didn't. Roberts joined with the four liberal justices to uphold the individual mandate as a tax and not a penalty.'

'Even though the law says it's a penalty and not a tax? Even though the Court had never before held that a penalty under a law was also a tax?'

'I'm afraid so, Professor.'

'So Chief Justice Roberts was the deciding vote to hold the individual mandate unconstitutional under the Commerce Clause and also to hold the individual mandate constitutional under the Taxing Clause?'

'Yep.'

'So the individual mandate is the law in America?'

'Yep.'

'And Obamacare?'

'Yep.'

Mr. Stanton leaned down then held up a T-shirt that read: OBAMACARE: YOU CAN'T CURE STUPID.

The class shared a laugh.

'Thank you for the levity, Mr. Stanton.'

'My pleasure, Professor.'

'But, Mr. Stanton, what's the difference between A, Congress ordering a citizen to buy health insurance and enforcing that with a monetary penalty, which the Court said is unconstitutional, and B, Congress taxing a citizen for refusing to buy health insurance, which the Court said was constitutional?'

'Nothing. It's exactly the same result. Congress is using its power to force citizens to do something they don't want to do and taking your money if you refuse to do it. Roberts engaged in constitutional sophistry.'

'Why would he do that?'

'Because Roberts wants the *New York Times* to like him. The liberal media destroyed the legal reputations of conservative justices like Rehnquist and Scalia, and Roberts doesn't want to suffer the same fate. Problem is, he doesn't understand that the liberals might like him now since he upheld the biggest government takeover of American life in history, but the first time he goes against them, they'll crucify him. That's what they do. So he cratered. He betrayed the Constitution.'

Ms. Garza stood and faced Mr. Stanton. The debate was on.

'Roberts grew a conscience, that's why he voted with the liberals.'

'Funny how it's always a conservative justice who crosses over to vote with the liberals, but no liberal justice ever crosses over to vote with the conservatives. Why is that?'

'Because we're always right.'

'And therein lies the problem: self-righteous liberals in America who want the government to make an unfair life fair, unsuccessful people successful, stupid people smart, and everyone ride a bike.'

'Ride this.'

Ms. Garza stuck her middle finger in the air at Mr. Stanton. He turned his eyes to Book and his hands up.

'Holster that finger, Ms. Garza. And please sit down. We're here to discuss con law, not social policy.'

'Con law is social policy.'

'Yeah,' Mr. Stanton said, 'because liberal justices believe government should control our economic lives.'

'And conservative white male justices believe government should control our personal lives,' Ms. Garza said.

'I don't want some uneducated minimum-wage government bureaucrat who wasn't smart enough to get a job in the private sector deciding whether my children get life-saving treatments.'

'You'd rather have a greedy profit-driven insurance company deciding?'

'Yes. You know why, Ms. Garza?'

'Because your daddy owns stock in those insurance companies?'

'Besides that?'

'No.'

'Sovereign immunity.'

'What?'

'If the insurance company denies treatment and my son dies, I can sue them for a billion dollars. That keeps them honest. If a government bureaucrat denies treatment and my son dies, I can't sue the federal government for a penny. It's called sovereign immunity.'

Ms. Garza shrugged. 'That's the price we pay to solve social problems.'

'Name one social problem the federal government has ever solved, Ms. Garza. Education? Drugs? Energy? Poverty? Now they're going to *solve* our healthcare.'

'The forty million poor people who can't afford health insurance deserve medical care, too.'

'They've got free healthcare. It's called the public hospital. And how many of those so-called "poor" people have tricked-out trucks with thousand-dollar wheels and iPhones and tickets to every pro football game, but they just can't afford healthcare? Those "poor" people know they can still get free medical care, so why pay for it? Why not suck off everyone else? We don't have forty million people who can't afford healthcare insurance. We have ten million who can't and thirty million who won't. Who'd rather let the rest of us pay their way.'

Mr. Stanton leaned down again and held up another T-shirt that read: OBAMA-MART: *WHEN EVERYTHING IS FREE BECAUSE THE GUY BEHIND YOU PAYS.*

The class enjoyed the T-shirt.

'Mr. Stanton, did you go shopping this weekend?'

'Yep. In honor of our last class with Ms. Garza and her T-shirts.'

'Ah.'

Ms. Garza was not yet ready to surrender.

'We do too have forty million people who can't afford health insurance—they said so on the evening news.'

Mr. Stanton laughed. 'You shouldn't be so gullible, Ms. Garza. The poverty industry puts out that misinformation so the government will keep sending trillions their way. And the liberal media repeats it without investigation because it fits their political bias.'

'Let's get back to Obamacare,' Book said. 'Under the rationale of this case, is there any human activity or non-activity that Congress may not regulate under the Constitution?'

'Nope,' Mr. Stanton said. 'They've got it all now. In fact, in oral arguments, the justices asked the government lawyer that exact question, and he couldn't think of a single human act that would be free from government control. So now five justices—five lawyers—have given Congress the absolute authority to tell us to do something, to tell us how to do it, and to fine us—I'm sorry, tax us—if we refuse to do it. I think that's what they call communism.'

'It's called social justice,' Ms. Garza said.

'Only if you're a communist.'

'All right,' Book said, 'today's Supreme Court decisions are precedents for tomorrow's decisions. When the Court decided Obamacare, the justices searched for precedents to support their positions. Now that Obamacare has been ruled constitutional—now that the Supreme Court has given its stamp of approval to Congress passing laws that tax citizens if they refuse to engage in a specified commercial activity—what might be the next law that climbs on top of this precedent?'

'Taxing us if we refuse to buy that Chevy to protect the domestic auto industry?'

'Yes. But I'm thinking of something bigger.'

'Taxing us if we refuse to eat vegetables?'

'Come on, people. This requires thought. Think about the Court's prior cases, big precedents that made law, like this case. Put those precedents together and what do you have? If the government can force the citizens to do something they don't want to do by taxing them if they refuse to do it, where might that precedent lead us?'

'To Russia and Comrade Putin,' Mr. Stanton said.

He held up another T-shirt: OBAMACARE: HEALTHCARE YOU CAN'T REFUSE. Which evoked more laughter.

Book scanned the class. Mr. Brennan was dutifully transcribing his every word, other students were texting or tweeting or zoning out. His eyes landed on a head hiding behind her laptop.

'Ms. Roberts.'

She peeked above the laptop.

'You know, don't you?'

She nodded as if confessing to a crime.

'Please, tell the class.'

376

She pushed hair from her face and spoke in her soft voice. The class seemed to lean toward her as one.

'Well, under the Obamacare ruling, the government can't order a woman to have an abortion even though medical care is commerce because that would exceed Congress's authority under the Commerce Clause; but, under the same Obamacare ruling, the government can tax a woman if she refuses to have an abortion.'

'But the Bill of Rights would prohibit the government from doing that.'

'No, it wouldn't. The Court in *Roe v. Wade* ruled that the, quote, "developing organism" inside the woman has no constitutional rights or protections whatsoever under the Bill of Rights because it is not a, quote, "person" prior to birth. Under the precedents of *Roe* and Obamacare, the Court would uphold such a law. And the circle would be complete: we are nothing more than rocks.'

'But why would our government ever do such a thing?'

'Perhaps the sonogram shows the baby has a genetic defect that would require expensive medical care for life. Or the woman is unmarried with no means of support for the child, and public support would add to the deficit. They would do it to save money.'

'But that's just wild speculation, isn't it? I mean, we don't have anything to really worry about, do we? We're an advanced civilization. What civilized nation on earth would ever pass such a law?'

'China.'

'Thank you, Ms. Roberts.'

Mr. Stanton held up another T-shirt: OBAMACARE: BEND OVER, THIS IS GONNA HURT.

'Mr. Stanton, how many of those do you have?'

'Just one more.'

'But, Professor,' Ms. Garza said, 'if the government can't force people to do the right thing, how can the government solve big problems like healthcare?'

377

'Ms. Garza, the Framers did not create a federal government that possesses all powers except those denied in the Constitution, but rather a government that possesses only those powers granted in the Constitution. Perhaps the federal government isn't supposed to solve—or try to solve—every social problem in America. To solve the problem of obesity, the federal government is now telling every school district in America what to feed their students for lunch. Is that what Madison, Hamilton, Jefferson, and Washington intended the national government to do when they created this country? Perhaps that responsibility resides in the fifty states.'

'But we have an obesity problem in America,' Ms. Garza said.

Ms. Roberts raised her hand. Book nodded at her.

'The dissent wrote, "The Constitution enumerates not federally soluble *problems*, but federally available *powers* . . . Article One contains no whatever-it-takes-to-solve-a-problem power." I like that.'

Ms. Garza glared at her. 'Like this, Liz.'

Another middle finger. Book couldn't help but hope that Ms. Garza was put in another professor's Con Law II class next year. Mr. Stanton stood on the back row.

'Professor, in honor of our last class with Ms. Garza and her T-shirts, I offer this final rebuttal.'

Mr. Stanton yanked open his button-down shirt to reveal a white T-shirt underneath that read: F#CK OBAMACARE, I'M MOVING TO CANADA.

The class laughed.

'And with that, ladies and gentlemen, Con Law One is adjourned for the year.'

The students applauded. The males slapped backs and exchanged fist-bumps; the females embraced. Classes were finished; final exams awaited. Some students left, others gathered around Book. He signed books; they took photos.

The Marfa story had hit the national media.

★   ★   ★

Book returned to his office to find Myrna on the phone.

'Here he is.' She held the phone out to him. 'The police.'

'Hello.'

'Professor, it's Sergeant Taylor again. Your mother wandered off, we found her at the Condoms to Go store. Took her back home, I'm waiting for your sister.'

'Thank you, Sergeant.'

'Professor . . .'

'Yes?'

'It's time.'

He handed the phone to Myrna then rubbed his forehead. The stitches had come out, but the scar itched.

Myrna smiled. 'All the girls think that scar makes you look sexy.'

'Oh, good. What time is the Welch hearing?'

'Canceled.'

'Why?'

'Scotty Raines called, said the D.A. dropped all charges against Bobby Welch. And his dad called from the Betty Ford Clinic in Palm Springs. Said he checked the boy in for six months. Said thank you and that he had fulfilled both promises.' She looked up from her notes. 'Promises?'

'Personal.'

She leaned down and came back up with a plastic container. She held it out to Book.

'Fried chicken. And don't worry, I fried it in peanut oil. You won't die if you eat it.'

'Thanks.'

She went back to her notes. 'TV shows want you on next Sunday.'

'I can't.'

She regarded him. 'You okay?'

'No. Mail?'

She aimed a thumb at his office. He turned to his office, but—

'You don't have time. You're late for the big faculty meeting. The new assistant dean.'

Book entered the faculty meeting and found an open seat between Henry Lawson and Professors Sheila Manfried and Jonah Goldman. Professor Manfried whispered to Jonah, 'I wonder if we can make more money at the new Texas A&M law school?'

The school had settled her sex discrimination claim by paying her $25,000 more in salary, giving her a $250,000 forgivable loan, and granting her a contractual right to see every other professor's compensation numbers.

'Admin admitted a hundred fewer tuition-payers for next year's one-L class,' Professor Goldman said. 'That's three million in lost tuition. They've got to cut our salaries.'

'I'll go to A&M for more money,' Professor Manfried said.

Professor Goldman grimaced. 'And be an Aggie? Just the thought of it makes me shudder.'

Book popped the top on the plastic container and offered fried chicken to Henry. He grabbed a drumstick and bit into it. Dean Roscoe Chambers stepped to the head of the conference table. The faculty fell silent. Roscoe looked like a senior U.S. senator. And he had the voice to match.

'I have a big announcement to make. Professor Lawson, would you please step to the front?'

Henry turned to Book with a puzzled look; Book shrugged. Henry stood and walked over to the dean, who put an arm around Henry's shoulders. Henry continued his assault on the drumstick.

'Oh, my God,' Professor Goldman said, 'Roscoe's appointing Henry our new assistant dean.'

'But he's not a lesbian,' Professor Manfried said.

'He's married with two children.'

'I want to be the first to welcome Henry Lawson to the club,' Roscoe said.

'Tenure?' Henry said.

Roscoe laughed. 'Tenure? No, the dean's club.'

'I'm the new assistant dean?'

'No. The new dean.'

Book thought Professor Manfried might faint.

'You're retiring?'

'What? Hell, no, I'm not retiring. You're not the new dean here at UT, Henry. You're the new dean at the new Texas A&M law school.'

Henry almost choked on the chicken. 'I am?'

Roscoe laughed again. 'Listen to him playing coy with us. Now, Henry, you're going to be sitting on a pile of money with the two hundred million James Welch donated to the A&M law school—'

James Welch had earned his MBA from UT, but he had earned his B.S. from A&M. He supported both of his alma maters generously. And he kept his promises.

'—so promise you won't steal all my professors.'

Henry gazed upon the assembled faculty, at the Harvard– Yale cartel.

'Oh, don't worry, Roscoe. I would never do that.'

Dean Roscoe Chambers applauded Henry, and the faculty joined in.

Book waited for Henry to accept congratulations from the other faculty members. Then Henry came over to Book; he arrived with the drumstick in his hand and a suspicious look on his face.

'I think I owe you big time,' he said.

'For what?'

'This.'

'Congratulations, Henry. That's where you belong. Just make your law school the best in Texas, or at least as good as the football team.'

'The football team's got more money.'

'It is Texas.'

Professor Manfried walked past and said, 'Henry, I'll email you my CV.'

After she was out of earshot, Henry said, 'I've got to remember to block her email address.'

They shared a chuckle. Roscoe called to Henry, so they shook hands. Henry took a step away but stopped.

'Book, anytime you want to move to College Station, there's a tenured job waiting for you.'

'Thanks, Henry. But this is where I belong.'

Henry walked over to the dean, and Book walked out. Before he got to the door, Dean Roscoe Chambers yelled to him.

'Bookman . . . get a haircut.'

Book returned to his office and found Myrna on the phone again. She held the receiver out to him and whispered, 'Your sister.'

He took the phone and put it to his ear. 'Joanie.'

'Book—'

'I'm going to move Mom in this weekend.'

'Good. You want to say hi to her?'

'Sure.'

'Hold on. I'll put her on.'

A small voice came over. 'Hello.'

'Mom, it's Book.'

'What book?'

'No . . . it's John. Your son.'

'My son?'

'You want to live with me?'

'Who?'

Joanie came back on. 'Sorry, Book, it's a cloudy day for her.'

'I'll take care of her.'

He would take care of her, but who would take care of him?

★   ★   ★

He walked into his office where he found a young woman sitting at his work table and reading his mail. She had a sucker in her mouth.

'Who are you?'

She removed the sucker. It was a red Tootsie Roll Pop.

'Veronica Cross. I'm your new intern. But I don't work nights or weekends, I don't do—'

'Where's Nadine?'

'She quit.'

'*Why?*'

Veronica shrugged her shoulders. 'All she said was she didn't go to law school to get shot at and run off the road and put into the hospital and drink lousy coffee in West Texas. She was just joking, right, Professor?'

Book walked over and stared out the window at the campus. Sooner or later they all quit.

'Right, Professor?'

He sighed. 'Yes, Ms. Cross. She was just joking.'

'I thought so.'

'The coffee wasn't that bad.'

He turned to his new intern. She was not dressed like a student, but like a lawyer in a high-collared white blouse, long black skirt, and shiny black heels. Her short black hair was neatly done, and her makeup perfect. She sat with erect posture.

'Oh, she did say one more thing.'

'What's that?'

'Something about living without a net, whatever that means. I heard she quit law school and is moving to France to become a chef. Is that crazy or what?'

Book smiled. 'Or what.'

'And she said to tell you that you're her hero.'

'She said that?'

'Uh, yeah.'

Veronica gestured with the Tootsie Roll Pop at the stack of mail on the table in front of her.

'So let me get this straight: pathetic people from all over the country write these letters to you and expect you to drop everything and run off and help them? Like you've got nothing better to do? I mean, seriously?'

'Seriously.'

'So I've got to read about all their pitiful lives every week?'

'Every week.'

She exhaled. 'These people should stop whining about injustice and go out and get a job and make something of themselves.'

'A little compassion–challenged, are we, Ms. Cross?'

Veronica Cross groaned. 'Oh, God. My dad was right. He watches you on TV, said you were a liberal Democrat.'

Book smiled again. Perhaps the internship would prove helpful to Ms. Cross.

'Let me know if you find any letters I should read.'

Veronica held out an envelope, almost reluctantly.

'Well . . . this one is sort of interesting.'

About the author

Born and educated in Texas, Mark Gimenez attended law school at Notre Dame, Indiana, and practiced with a large Dallas law firm. He lives in Texas. He has written six previous novels: *The Colour of Law*, *The Abduction*, *The Perk*, *The Common Lawyer*, *Accused*, and *The Governor's Wife*.